A NIGHT FOR SCREAMING

Mitch Walker is on the run. Just a case of being in the wrong place at the wrong time, but his pursuer, Fred Palmer, has some very effective ways of getting a murder confession. So Walker hops a train and ends up in a small town in Kansas, where he hires on at a huge farm owned by Barton M. Cassel. It looks like a good place to hide out from Palmer and the local cops, but Walker soon finds himself torn between the scheming arrogance of his new employer, and the unsubtle advances of Cassel's willing wife, Eve. Caught between their jealous battle, Walker quickly discovers that he was better off when he was on the run— because one way or the other, nobody leaves the farm.

ANY WOMAN HE WANTED

Mike Ballard works homicide, busted down from lieutenant four years ago for accepting bribes. He had ripped things wide open then, turning on the fat cats whom he had been protecting. But nothing had really changed. Guys were still working the rackets, and shop owners were still getting killed if they didn't pay. DA Tom Flynn tries to enlist Ballard in his own fight against corruption—and dies mysteriously in a car accident the next day. And then there's Lupe, pregnant by the son of one of the most influential men in town, who wants Ballard's help and isn't shy about how she goes about asking. And Naomi, who knows *just* what she wants. There's only so much a man can take. But when they push him too far, Ballard only has one recourse—cop or not, he comes out swinging.

A NIGHT FOR SCREAMING

- - - - -

ANY WOMAN HE WANTED

By Harry Whittington

INTRODUCTION BY DAVID LAURENCE WILSON

Stark House Press • Eureka California

A NIGHT FOR SCREAMING / ANY WOMAN HE WANTED

Published by Stark House Press
1315 H Street
Eureka, CA 95501, USA
griffinskye3@sbcglobal.net
www.starkhousepress.com

ISBN: 1-933586-08-7
ISBN-13: 9781-933586-08-3

Book design by Mark Shepard, www.SHEPGRAPHICS.COM
Proofreading by Rick Ollerman

*The publisher would like to thank David L. Wilson
for his invaluable aid on this project.*

First Stark House Press Edition: July 2006

TABLE OF CONTENTS

HARRY WHITTINGTON BIBLIOGRAPHY

Vengeance Valley (1946)
Her Sin (1946)
Slay Ride for a Lady (1950)
The Brass Monkey (1951)
Call Me Killer (1951)
Fires That Destroy (1951)
The Lady Was a Tramp (1951)
Satan's Widow (1951)
Forever Evil (1952)
Married to Murder (1951;
  reprinted 1959)
Murder is My Mistress (1951)
Drawn to Evil (1952)
Mourn the Hangman (1952)
Prime Sucker (1952)
Cracker Girl (1953)
So Dead My Love! (1953)
Vengeful Sinner (1953;
  reprinted as Nightclub Sinner, 1954;
  abridged as Die, Lover, 1960)
Saddle the Storm (1954)
Wild Oats (1954)
The Woman is Mine (1954)
You'll Die Next! (1954)
The Naked Jungle (1955)
One Got Away (1955)
Across That River (1956)
Desire in the Dust (1956)
Brute in Brass (1956; reprinted as
  Forgive Me, Killer, 1987)
The Humming Box (1956)
Saturday Night Town (1956)
Sinner's Club (1956; reprinted as
  Teenage Jungle, 1958)
A Woman on the Place (1956)
Man in the Shadow (1957)
  [screenplay novelization]
Mink (1957, France)
One Deadly Dawn (1957)
Play for Keeps (1957)
Temptations of Valerie (1957)
  [screenplay novelization]
Trouble Rides Tall (1958)
Web of Murder (1958)
Backwoods Tramp (1959; reprinted
  as A Moment to Prey, 1987)
Halfway to Hell (1959)

Lust for Love (1959)
Strictly for the Boys (1959)
Strange Bargain (1959)
Strangers on Friday (1959)
A Ticket to Hell (1959)
Connolly's Woman (1960)
The Devil Wears Wings (1960)
Heat of Night (1960)
Hell Can Wait (1960)
A Night for Screaming (1960)
Nita's Place (1960)
Rebel Woman (1960)
Trouble Rides Tall (1960)
Vengeance is the Spur (1960)
Desert Stake-Out (1961)
God's Back Was Turned (1961)
Guerilla Girls (1961)
Journey Into Violence (1961)
The Searching Rider (1961)
A Trap for Sam Dodge (1961)
The Young Nurses (1961)
A Haven for the Damned (1962)
Hot as Fire Cold as Ice (1962)
69 Babylon Park (1962)
Wild Sky (1962)
Cora is a Nympho (1963)
Don't Speak to Strange Girls (1963)
Drygulch Town (1963)
Prairie Raiders (1963; reprinted as by
  Hondo Wells, 1977)
Cross the Red Creek (1964)
Fall of the Roman Empire (1964)
  [screenplay novelization]
High Fury (1964)
Hangrope Town (1964)
The Man from U.N.C.L.E #2:
  The Doomsday Affair (1965)
Valley of Savage Men (1965)
Wild Lonesome (1965)
Doomsday Mission (1967)
Bonanza: Treachery Trail (1968;
  pub in Germany as
  Ponderosa in Gefahr)
Burden's Mission (1968)
Charro! (1969)
Rampage (1978)
Sicilian Woman (1979)

As Ashley Carter

Master of Blackoaks (1976)
Sword of the Golden Stud (1977)
Panama (1978)
Secret of Blackoaks (1978)
Taproots of Falconhurst (1978)
Scandal of Falconhurst (1980)
Heritage of Blackoaks (1981)
Rogue of Falconhurst (1983)
Against All Gods (1983, UK)
A Darkling Moon (1985, UK)
Embrace the Wind (1985, UK;
    pub in the US as by Blaine Stevens)
A Farewell to Blackoaks (1986, UK)
Miz Lucretia of Falconhurst (1986)
Mandingo Mansa (1986, UK;
    pub in the US as Mandingo Master)
Strange Harvest (1986, UK)
Falconhurst Fugitive (1988)

As Tabor Evans

Longarm on the Humboldt (1981)
Longarm and the Golden Lady (1981)
Longarm and the Blue Norther
    (1981)
Longarm in Silver City (1982)
Longarm in Boulder Canyon (1982)
Longarm in the Big Thicket (1982)

As Whit Harrison

Body and Passion (1952)
Girl on Parole (1952; reprinted as
    Man Crazy, 1960)
Sailor's Weekend (1952)
Savage Love (1952; reprinted as by
    Harry Whittington as Native Girl,
    1959)
Swamp Kill (1952)
Violent Night (1952)
Army Girl (1953)
Rapture Alley (1953)
Strip the Town Naked (1960)
Any Woman He Wanted (1961)
A Woman Possessed (1961)

As Kel Holland

Strange Young Wife (1963)
The Tempted (1964)

As Lance Horner

Golden Stud (1975)

As Harriet Kathryn Meyers

Small Town Nurse (1962)
Prodigal Nurse (1963)

As Blaine Stevens

The Outlanders (1979)
Embrace the Wind (1982)
Island of Kings (1989)

As Clay Stuart

His Brother's Wife (1964)

As Harry White

Shadow at Noon (1955;
    reprinted as by Hondo Wells, 1977)

As Hallam Whitney

Backwoods Hussy (1952;
    reprinted as Lisa, 1965)
Shack Road (1953)
Backwoods Shack (1954)
City Girl (1954)
Shanty Road (1954; reprinted as
    by Whit Harrison, 1956)
The Wild Seed (1956)

**As Henry Whittier/
Henri Whittier**

Nightmare Alibi (1972)
Another Man's Claim (1973)

As Howard Winslow

The Mexican Connection (1972)

TOUGH LUCK
The Life and Art of Harry Whittington
BY DAVID LAURENCE WILSON

We've all been there, a warm afternoon or early evening. Sometimes it's when you first wake up, or during your last moments of consciousness. It's a sudden knock or an angry phone call. Maybe you're selling cookies, door to door, or passing out American flags. You walk into a bar or a party and there's something wrong, an emotional pressure that you didn't carry in with you. It could be a quarrel, suddenly silenced, or a fight. There's an edge. You're the thirteenth guest. Everyone's dressed in red and you're wearing blue. Maybe there's a mountain lion or an alligator in the closet. You don't know what it is, you just know that you're backing out, walking on. The air is so thick that you've got to use a swimming stroke to get to the door.

Then there's the sound of a slap or a gunshot on the other side of the wall.

This is Harry Whittington's world, an uncomfortable one at best. His characters are the ones who don't back out. They stay. Maybe they've just blown into town and they're looking to hang around until they get into trouble. It's like they're walking vacuums, these characters, and they pull in new and dangerous acquaintances. Sometimes they just need a job, or a place to stay. Sometimes it's lust. Maybe they believed an unreasonable explanation. Or it's honesty that gets them in trouble. For whatever reasons, they stay.

So what do you do? Like... you're moving the neighbor's furniture, you're going up the stairs and wow! — now there's a hand, dangling from that rolled-up carpet. What do you do now?

Raymond Chandler wrote about grabbing crime and murder from the wealthy, from their butlers and tea parties, and giving it to those who truly deserved it. Those deserving few, working class hustlers and heroes.... these are Harry Whittington's characters.

Known as "King of the Paperbacks," Whittington was the author of taut, intense crime paperbacks and a prolific stream of novels in categories including western, nurse, spy, war, swamp and historical fiction, over 170 novels. He wasn't trying for one great book, he was trying for production and steady sales. He wrote under at least twenty different pseudonyms and published over one hundred novelettes, short stories, true confession and true-crime stories. All this was accomplished despite a seven-year break from fiction writing, an interruption which neatly divided a career spanning five decades.

Whittington's novels read like one long roll of paper. This book, that book, they're all just stops along the same highway. The pain and disorientation of the beatings and knockdowns could apply to anyone, in any era. Most of his characters were on the run. Sometimes he wrote with more emotion than plausibility, but he kept it going, topping himself over and over again, like a comedy chase with bullets instead of pies.

Whittington lays out the conflicts right away and if you stay on, if you pick up one of his books and keep reading, you're trapped like one of his characters, start to finish, a quick, one-way ride, maybe a one-sitting read.

He wrote like an angel, sometimes like a tough, flamboyant angel. He could pull at your heartstrings, sometimes literally.

You've got to be strong to resist a title like *A Night for Screaming* ("I turned and the word café struck the rods and cones inside my retina and there was instant reaction in my brain. My mouth began to water.")... or *Any Woman He Wanted* ("He sucked at his bloodied lip for a moment. I let him suck. It was his blood.")

Harry Benjamin Whittington was born February 4, 1915, in Ocala, Florida. In later years he would proudly announce that it was also the release date of BIRTH OF A NATION. On his mother's side he could trace his Southern lineage back nine generations, to 1693. His great-great-uncle was one of Robert E. Lee's generals.

After years of running a successful grocery store, Whittington's parents declared bankruptcy in 1923. By 1930 his family had fallen into deep poverty. A series of events, beginning with the failure of a bank, left Whittington's father without hope of finding work in Ocala. Consequently, the Whittingtons moved to a farm about six miles outside town, where they possessed none of the skills needed to become successful farmers. Nor was there a market for their crops.

"We went steadily down," Whittington wrote. "My last two years in high school became a nightmare of impossible things becoming steadily more impossible.

"In my senior year at high school our family had absolutely no money for anything. My shoes were three years old, and looked it. I was wearing patched castoffs from other branches of the family. There was no money for lunches at school."

Whittington survived his sense of isolation by escapism: by reading F. Scott Fitzgerald and sneaking into movie theaters. "I couldn't afford to buy *The Great Gatsby* so I borrowed it over and over from the public library," he wrote, in 1987. "I haunted used bookstores looking for old magazines in which Fitzgerald might appear."

All along he wrote, beginning as a teenager, producing five novels and hundreds of short stories between 1932 and 1942. None of these were sold and most of them weren't even typed. Whittington wrote longhand, in notebooks, in the styles of Fitzgerald and John Dos Passos. Titles included: "Forget You Saw Me," "Hungry with a Stomach Full," "All the Girls I Kissed" and "Hell's Love Song."

After graduating from high school Whittington moved to St. Petersburg, where he worked at the Griffith Advertising Agency. In 1934 he began working as a letter carrier for the St. Petersburg post office, a job he would continue for 14 years. He played catcher for the post office's softball team until he was involved in a fight on the field.

"I was in two fights," he wrote. "In one, I got my front teeth smashed loose. In the other, overmatched, I was struck sharply in each temple by fists with a third knuckle raised like a knot. When I wrote about pain, I knew what I was talking about."

In 1935 and 1936 Whittington also worked as the Assistant Manager and Advertising Manager of the city's Capitol Theater, where he booked films and handled publicity. Harry was twenty years old and he began to nurture fantasies about making his own motion pictures. Between his advertising layouts for movies like THE PUBLIC ENEMY and BACK-STREET he began sketching posters for a lineup of films produced by "Harry Whittington Productions."

His lineup included DANCING SINNERS and BULLETS AND BAL-LADS, with a new singing-cowboy star, "Cliff Edwards." Lee Tracy would star in MIDNIGHT MELODRAMA. SIN DEEP would star Mae Clarke, Neil Hamilton and David Manners. Harry Beaumont would direct THIS WOMAN DESERTED, A STARVED SOUL and LOVERS NO MORE. "WON'T YOU JOIN US IN OUR 'SAFE HIT AND (LONG) RUN' CAM-PAIGN. Here are no empty promises, but box office pictures with a world of possibilities! Play them now, play them right, plug 'em as they deserve and the Whittington line-up will mean a line up at your box office! ... Play them right now... Four good pics are ready to hop to work for you... in your theater now ... WHITTINGTON PICTURES."

Whittington also roughed-out ads for never-written genre novels, *Swamp Fire, Unholy Night, Candle in a Hurricane* and *Escape into Death* ("He had to break out of an escape-proof prison to get a woman out of his blood.... He could not die until he was free of the woman who made him liar, thief, fugitive and killer!").

In 1935 he met Kathyrn Odom on a blind date with friends in St. Petersburg. She was the girl who had been arranged for his friend. She considered Harry shy but quick-witted and charming, and she liked the sound of his name and his voice. That night the teenagers rearranged the match-ups. Harry loaned her the manuscript of his sad love story, *The World Before Us*, and she read it eagerly. The blind date began a lifelong union. They were married in 1936. Kathyrn was a good companion, a reader and movie fan who was equal to her husband's enthusiasms.

During the Christmas season Kathyrn worked at a St. Petersburg department store. Somehow, for their first Christmas, she saved enough from her $2 a day salary to purchase Harry a set of F. Scott Fitzgerald first editions. A daughter, Harriet, was born in 1937. Their son Howard was born in 1942.

"He always loved films," Kathyrn said in 2000, eleven years after her husband's death. "He liked everything, all categories, just so long as it was a movie."

In 1942 Whittington began writing and editing the *St. Petersburg Advocate*, also editing the *Florida Letter Carrier*, a monthly magazine for mailmen. In 1943 he sold nine short fiction pieces to the United Features Syndicate. One day Kathryn was reading Max Brand in a western pulp magazine. She suggested Harry try a western novel and he wrote *A Gun in One Hand*. In 1944 he entered his manuscript *The World Before Us* in a "New Writer's Contest" sponsored by Doubleday and 20th Century Fox.

The Whittingtons were still working their way out of the depression. Buying a typewriter and a sump pump for the yard were both big events. Paychecks and royalties were cashed immediately and used for everything from groceries to piano lessons. In the early years the neighborhood's butcher would stake the couple two dollars, the price for a night of dancing. Whittington would pay the butcher back when he made a sale.

In 1945 Whittington was drafted and he served two years in the Navy as a Petty Officer in San Francisco and at the submarine base at Pearl Harbor, Hawaii. He had hoped to see action, to become a writer in the mold of Hemingway. Instead he found himself working with the mail. Once again he'd be carrying other people's promises, their dreams and stories. He also produced ten more versions of *The World Before Us* during his stay in Hawaii.

In 1946 Whittington's western sold to Phoenix Press and was published as *Vengeance Valley*. He completed a romance for Phoenix, *Her Sin* (1946), and used his G.I. Bill to fund a correspondence course produced by Thomas H. Uzzell, of Stillwater, Oklahoma ("Low Cost Authoritative Instructions for Writers on the Make"). The Uzzel team found that Whittington had a flair for irony.

By 1948 the Whittingtons had saved enough money to have their house painted. Kathyrn urged Harry to use it instead for a trip to a writer's conference in Chicago. At the conference he met W. T. Brannon, a crime writer and agent who told him that he had a market for mystery and crime stories.

Brannon sold Whittington's first crime novelette to King Features. It became the first of thirty Whittington serials for the syndicate, including western and weird menace stories and a series of novelettes featuring private eye Pat Raffigan. Whittington sold crime stories to "Dime Detective" and "Detective Tales." "Extensions" magazine bought "My Mother Had a Lover", a story about a boy who tries to break up a romance between his widowed mother and a mailman. He sold six stories to "Mammoth Western": "Find This Man—With Bullets," "Dark Duel," "Wyoming Wild Catter," "Last Wagon for Hell," "Vengeance in the Sun," "Mayor Steps In" and "Let Gallows Wait." The magazine folded before the last two sales were printed. "Give a Man Rope" was sold to "15 Western Tales."

Soon Whittington was making more money writing fiction than carrying letters. In 1948 he quit his job with the post office. His first paperback sale, *Slay Ride for a Lady*, (1950, originally titled *Sleigh Ride in July*) sold to Handi-Books, beginning what Whittington called "The Cadillac Years," 1951-1963, when the growing marketplace for original paperback stories soaked up all the short novels he could produce. After all the years of practice his style came together quickly. He became a writer of intense, compulsively paced crime novels. A Whittington story offered a simple, compelling premise and new, unsettling forms of jeopardy for its heroes.

As he wrote, Whittington carried a working-class, small-town sized chip on his shoulder and a general mistrust of the powers that be, whether civil or criminal. He didn't like red tape, hypocrites, bureaucrats or religious con men. His heroes were guys with a grudge who were just out of prison, just out of the army or just out of luck.

Fires That Destroy (1950) was the first of Whittington's sales to Fawcett's Gold Medal series, the classiest, best-paying publisher of original paperbacks. *Saddle the Storm* (Fawcett, 1954) received the Western Writers of America's Golden Spur Award for the best paperback of the year. The company would continue to publish his originals, 12 of them by the year 1963.

Consequently, the books poured out of him, wildly delirious crime novels like *Backwoods Tramp* (Gold Medal, 1956), *A Ticket to Hell* (Gold Medal,

1958), *Strange Bargain* (Avon, 1959) and *A Haven for the Damned* (Gold Medal, 1961). In 1951 he sold twelve novels. In 1952 he sold nine books and another nine in 1953. He received between $1000 and $2000 for each novel and more if it went into additional printings. The second choices, the publishers that didn't pay as well or as quickly as Fawcett, didn't get "Whittington," they got "Whit Harrison," or "Hallam Whitney," the author in a relatively transparent disguise. He wrote short stories for the digest-sized magazines "Manhunt," "Trapped," and "Murder."

Despite a furious pace Whittington found the time to coach Little League. In 1955 he wrote YOUNG AT HEART for the South Side P.T.A. Revue and scripted a "Teenage Fashion Show" which included his son Howard. He wrote PANTS, a one act comedy presented by The Little Theater in St. Petersburg. The Whittingtons visited New York, where they went to Broadway shows and Harry conferred with his agent and editors.

Fortunately, Whittington was not living the same dangerous, action-filled life that his characters suffered. He was a synthetic writer with dreams and melodramas spun from forties film noir. Harry wasn't one of those guys who delivered bootleg or who knew Al Capone. He had lived cheaply and nearly desperately but he'd also seen a lot of movies, and that kept him going.

He was a diligent, three-fingered typist who worked almost every day from nine in the morning until five at night. Writing was the largest part of his life. He'd prepare an outline, a chapter breakdown, and then he'd begin writing the first page of each new novel. Under pressure he could finish thirty pages of manuscript in one day. He didn't like to rewrite. He didn't smoke or drink but he spent at least eight hours a day in a dream state, at his typewriter. "It was his opium," his son would say, many years later.

Whittington worked at home until his children were teenagers. After producing some of the most delirious situations in popular fiction, for novels with working titles like *Feed on My Flesh* and *Naked in Babylon*, he would knock off at 4 pm, walk downstairs and watch "I Love Lucy" with Katherine. He'd read his pages aloud while she listened from a couch. If her legs were crossed she was listening, intent. If her legs started swinging he knew that he had to pick up the pace, to keep things moving. Kathryn handled the family's finances but thought her greatest contribution was just getting Harry the time and opportunity to write. Often she would take the children to visit his sister in Ocala.

He liked to read and go to the movies and discuss plots. He played tennis but was not a particularly physical man: he wasn't very good at repairs around the house but was generous and intellectually exciting. His closest friends included the Tampa pulp writers Day Keene and Gil Brewer. They'd socialize with their wives and talk shop during evenings at the Whittingtons' home.

Despite his success on the newsstands Whittington remained committed to his dream of motion picture production. He subscribed to The Hollywood Reporter and collected books on film making and directors. Ultimately he sold the film rights to fifteen of his novels, including DESIRE IN THE DUST (Twentieth Century Fox, 1960), adapted from a 1955 Gold Medal novel.

In 1957 Whittington's western novel *Trouble Rides Tall* sold to Warner Brothers and Whittington was flown to California, where he spent three months working with the uninterested producer Roy Del Ruth. The result was "Trouble Marshall," a never filmed screenplay intended for Gary Cooper. Later the television series "Lawman" was based upon the novel. The studio paid $600 for his Mammoth Western novelette, "Wyoming Wildcatter," then made the theatrical feature BLACK GOLD, and the TV series "Alaskans" and "The Dakotas" from the story.

Whittington became friends with Sid Fleischman, another Fawcett novelist and screenwriter who was working at Warner's. "He was affable and affectionate," Fleischman described him. "A true Southern gentleman!" Whittington was comfortably overweight (5'11", 210 pounds) and he brought flowers when he was invited to dinner.

Whittington felt like he was unable to function within the studio system. He said the process killed his creative juices. "Nobody in Hollywood knew a writer's name unless he'd won the Nobel Prize last week—late last week," he wrote in 1963. "Nobody in Hollywood ever read anything except the analysis prepared by studio readers."

In 1959 he mortgaged his home and raised $20,000 to produce THE PHANTOM OF STAGE 13, later retitled FACE OF THE PHANTOM (Whittington Productions, 1960). He wrote a screenplay from his novel *Backwoods Hussy* (Paperback Library, 1952), intending to make it his second production, SWAMP ANGEL.

Whittington planned at least seven more productions, including TEENAGE VAMPIRE and adaptations from stories by Gil Brewer and W. T. Brannon. Whittington, Brewer, Sid Fleischman and Burt Kennedy would prepare the screenplays. Whittington announced that the veteran director Lew Landers would direct his screenplay, A WOMAN POS-SESSED.

This was the summit of Whittington's career, the culmination of his dreams, as both a novelist and filmmaker. Fleischman wrote to him from Santa Monica, California: "Just came from the downtown newsstands. My God, Harry, you've taken them over!"

After this success came the fall. Bad news from all over.

Whittington couldn't set up a distribution deal for FACE OF THE PHANTOM. He was in debt and the market for paperbacks was changing. He was increasingly estranged from his agent, who had nothing but rejections for him. The markets were overstocked. No one was buying.

Whittington was in his mid-forties, at the height of his ability. His storytelling skill had lead him to success as a steady performer but now it was looking like he might never sell a book again. He wanted to keep going. He just couldn't seem to sell a book.

The whole business of publishing was becoming more difficult for Whittington. The market was changing and so was his writing. He was moving closer to realism and his characters were becoming philosophers. He was trying to break out of the restraints of genre to consider racism and other social issues while keeping all the twists and pyrotechnics that made his plotting so exciting to read.

A Night for Screaming (Ace, 1960) and *Any Woman He Wanted* (Beacon, 1961) were published during this period of adjustment and discontent. Both had been shopped around for months before they found buyers. Along with a handful of contemporaneous titles, they represented what appeared to be Whittington's last efforts in the field of crime and suspense.

A Night for Screaming is one of the gems, a novel that has become an expensive prize for paperback collectors. For Whittington, the sale to Ace meant considerably less income than the Gold Medal books. Though it featured a classic lurid cover, its original sales were unexceptional and it was limited to a single edition.

A Night for Screaming takes place within a population of migrant farmworkers, though Whittington's readers learn little about the laborers from this first-person narrative. Whittington was no Upton Sinclair, no reformer. In style this was more like a Midwest CABINET OF DOCTOR CALIGARI. His description of the other workers serve mostly as examples of what additional humiliations might still befall his hero. There's little sense of color or landscape, just barbed wire, isolation and brutality.

In *Any Woman He Wanted* Whittington was trying to create a series character. He revived his tough, amoral city detective, Mike Ballard, from *Brute in Brass* (Fawcett, 1956), in a new novel originally titled *Bier Date*. When Fawcett turned the effort down, he considered changing the character's name, to keep him available for another shot with Fawcett. Ultimately it was published with the Whit Harrison pseudonym but with the Mike Ballard character intact.

Unfortunately, Whittington and series characters really did not mix. The trouble with a series character was that no character with any smarts would agree to go through these agonies twice. His characters would have to learn something from the experience of just showing up in a Whittington novel. Couldn't they finally keep up their payments on the appliances, or say "No Thank You" to a seductive wanton?

One of the editors who rejected *Bier Date* noted: "It's hard to tell what he's trying to do... maybe a detective-mystery, maybe a modern novel."

Another editor complained that the Whittington effort was neither a sex book nor a suspense but something in-between. It seemed that Whittington, so much a product of his time, was now suddenly out of step, either ahead of his time or perhaps slightly behind it.

Though Whittington was no stranger to happy endings, it's tempting to argue that the end, the last paragraph of *Any Womaan He Wanted*, was tacked on as a late add-on. It would be interesting to consider the fate of these characters between the time this novel was first published, 1961, and the date of this new edition. A passionate reader might want to consider laying out his own finish. How long would these iconoclastic Whittington characters survive, anyway?

Late in 1961 Whittington quit his agent and because of threatened litigation, he was blacklisted by the major paperback houses. He sold no novels during the first six months of 1962 so he wrote seven "true confession" stories for "Secrets" and "Real Confession," as Kay Whittington. He sold seven novels during the second half of 1962, including three westerns and a nurse novel. In 1963 he sold three contemporary novels to Beacon Books and was hired to write a novelization of THE FALL OF THE ROMAN EMPIRE for Fawcett. None of these were for big paychecks. It wasn't enough to keep the family going.

It was over. A fantastic writing career appeared to be at its end. Some readers assumed Whittington had died. After one last effort for Gold Medal, the Hollywood novel *Don't Speak to Strange Girls* (1963), and three westerns published by Ballantine, *High Fury* (1964), *Hangrope Town* (1964) and *Wild Lonesome* (1965), Whittington's next ten years would be a career of compromises, with little published under his own name.

But Whittington hadn't died, and he hadn't given up the writing trade, not yet, but now more than ever, his career would be determined by economics. Whittington was trying to pay off his creditors. His slow start in 1962 had already made things worse.

Help arrived from an unexpected source. It had something to do with the Sexual Revolution and a new agent, Scott Meredith. Our sexual mores may or may not have become liberated during the sixties, but there was no question that American sexuality was becoming big business, and several paperback publishers began specializing in sexual themes. These publishers represented a new market that allowed dozens of established pulp and paperback writers, masters of westerns, crime and science fiction, to keep working in their trade. Many of these writers were represented by the Meredith Agency. Today these stories are sometimes violent, sometimes coquettish, sometimes clueless, but seldom are they shocking to contemporary fiction readers.

Whittington was one of these writers. Late in 1963 he accepted a work-for-hire contract with a publisher of "adult paperbacks." The bookkeeping was simple: every month Harry would receive $1000 for one 55,000 word novel. It was, he noted, the only work that he seemed able to get.

Under the terms of the agreement he wrote what he called "simple suspense plots." Some were not unlike his "legitimate" work, with noir situations and intense, hard-boiled action. The agreement offered steady income but no credit and no secondary rights or royalties. The books were published under various house names. It was a keep-your-head-above-water sort of agreement and the beginning of what Whittington called "The Lean and Savage Years." In essence, he was taking a pay cut. He was also giving up a good piece of his freedom for the guarantee of steady work. He'd be working at home, writing novels from his own plots, but it was the closest he would ever come to working in a factory.

Whittington hoped to finish the contracted novels quickly enough to continue writing books under his own name but the job quickly became "a real grind." The rest of his sales were unimpressive, at least by Whittington's standards. Between 1964 and 1967 he worked on *Above All Gods*, an unpublished novel intended for Putnam. He contributed nonfiction crime stories for "True Police Cases" and short fiction for "Mike Shayne Mystery Magazine" and the "Man From U.N.C.L.E." digests, based on the television spy series. He wrote six novelettes, under the name Robert Hart Davis, for the "Man From U.N.C.L.E." magazine, but only four were published. When the spy genre lost some of its steam one of the stories was rewritten as "The Ship of Horror," for "Mike Shayne." The other disappeared unpublished. *High Fury* was filmed in Italy as ADIOS, GRINGO (1966).

He wrote *The Doomsday Affair* (Ace, 1965), the second book in the "Man From U.N.C.L.E." paperback series and two Vietnam novels, *Doomsday Mission* (Banner, 1967) and *Burden's Mission* (Avon, 1968). He tried to sell screenplays based on *Saddle the Storm, A Trap for Sam Dodge* and the original story, "Savage Stallion," for "Bonanza." BILLY THE KID—TEENAGE KILLER was another idea. Whittington produced a Young Adult Bonanza novel, *Treachery Trail* (Whitman, 1968), a novelization of the Elvis Presley movie CHARRO! and he sold the film rights to *Brute in Brass*.

While the book-a-month job bankrolled his debt, Whittington was still contacting dozens of distributors trying to sell FACE OF THE PHANTOM. One of the New York distributors complained that there was not enough horror and no sex.

Whittington scripted a promotional film for the Tupperware company. He also tried to produce a horror film. In 1967 he finally sold FACE OF THE PHANTOM to G. B. Roberts, an exploitation filmmaker whose best known feature was THE WEIRD WORLD OF LSD. Scenes from Whittington's feature would be combined with footage from a nudist colony; Whittington Productions would receive half the revenue.

Whittington made the most of the contact, analyzing stories and working on a handful of screenplays for Roberts. In 1966 he was hired to write a narration to salvage the feature PLEASURE AND PAIN. One of his screenplays became FIREBALL JUNGLE (Americana Entertainment, 1969), featuring Lon Chaney Jr., in one of his last, discouraging performances as the alcoholic owner of a junkyard. Whittington wrote unproduced screenplays for HIGH SCHOOL HELL SQUAD and THE CROWDED BIKINI.

In 1967, after 38 months of hard labor, Whittington quit the novel-a-month work. The pace of the past twenty years was finally beginning to take a toll. After so many years of knocking out words, Whittington was exhausted, depressed and still in debt. Worse, he felt that the marketplace was demeaning his talents, not allowing him to grow or deepen as a storyteller. According to his wife, who could be as direct as one of Whittington's heroines: "He'd written his brains out."

In April, 1968, Whittington gave up his career as a freelance fiction writer. That same month he moved to Virginia and began working in Washington D.C., at the Rural Electrification Administration, a division of the Department of Agriculture. He'd work as a writer and editor in the Information Services Division.

For the most part, Whittington stuck to his agency's work during the next seven years. In 1970 he rewrote the CROWDED BIKINI screenplay. In 1972 he wrote three more "adult" novels for Greenleaf Classics, *The Mexican Connection* (Whittington's title was *Hot Dust*), *Midnight Alibi*, (originally intended for "Manhunt" magazine) and *Another Man's Claim.* At first Whittington was enthusiastic. His editor urged him to attempt a series character, perhaps continuing with his character Harry Welch, a disbarred lawyer in *The Mexican Connection.* Another option was a motion picture press relations man, "old enough to have worked under the studio system." Unfortunately, even without the same financial pressures, completing these three books in three months brought back all the unpleasantness of the three years of writing a novel-a-month. Nor was Whittington particularly fond of the genre. He wasn't ready to return. Once again he retired from fiction writing.

At the Department of Agriculture Whittington wrote press releases, speeches and skits on the subject of rural electric power, traveling to Arkansas, Indiana and other states. One of the conferences he attended was in New Orleans, where he and Kathryn took in a Sonny and Cher concert. Whittington didn't have to compete with his own pseudonyms any longer, to carry a reputation or expectations. The state of the marketplace was of no concern. The money pressures had lessened. Gradually the act of writing became fun again.

In 1974 Whittington left government employment for a second time and began what he called his "second act" with the rewriting of *Sad Lovers*, a short novel from 1936. This one remained unsold. His next project was *Golden Stud*, finishing Lance Horner's last novel for Fawcett and the Lance Horner estate. This was the first "Ashley Carter" book. Whittington considered it a one-time rewrite job but soon he was writing the "Lance Horner" novels *Master of Blackoaks* (1976), *Sword of the Golden Stud* (1977) and *Secret of Blackoaks* (1978). Whittington would also continue the Falconhurst series begun by Kyle Onstott.

These historical romances took a different tone and length (well over 400 pages) than the terse originals of twenty years before. Whittington would write movingly about the human dilemmas of slaves and their masters. Ultimately Whittington would sell more copies of his books as Ashley Carter than he had ever sold under his own name.

In 1977 Whittington fulfilled a lifelong dream of seaside living by moving into a four bedroom home at Indian Rocks Beach. He began teaching a night course in writing and he prepared a home-study course in plotting and storytelling. In 1978 he published *Rampage*, the first book with a Whittington byline in almost ten years. A year later, *Sicilian Woman* became the last new paperback with the Whittington name. "Blaine Stevens" was the name he used for the historical novel *The Outlanders*, (Jove Publications). He began research on *The Rich and the Damned*, an incomplete novel set within the beer industry. In 1980 and 1981 he contributed six novels to the Longarm western series.

In his seventies Whittington tried to promote a science fiction screenplay, SURVIVORS OF THE FROZEN PLANET. He pitched a television series, "Personal Column." He considered *Saddlebred*, a novel which would have been set within the Kentucky breeding and horse racing farms. Another idea was going to be *Feedback, or You Ain't Heard Nothing Yet!*, about Hollywood between 1928 and 1930 and the changeover to sound. He lectured at the Tampa Art Museum on the WPA and its assistance in his career. He traveled to Hawaii and Reims, France, where he was the Guest of Honor at the Fourth Festival of Suspense Novels and Films. He assembled a collection of his short stories titled *False Starts and False Stops, or Why A Writer?* and requested a copy of the "Writer's Guidelines" from "Cracked" magazine. He tried to put together a film magazine.

In 1987 Black Lizard Books reprinted six of his Fawcett suspense novels, all of which were optioned for film rights. Whittington had survived to see some of his best work rediscovered.

Despite an enthusiastic reception to his "return," Whittington never saw the great Harry Whittington Productions that he had sketched in his creative leisure, so many years before. He was worn out, suffering from congestive heart failure. He died June 11, 1989, following a stroke, two weeks after sending off his last, unpublished Blaine Stevens manuscript, *Lord of Kauai*. Whittington was just seventy-four years old. Several of his best novels were back in print and there were movie deals pending. He had not run out of stories, only time. He left behind pages of titles and story ideas. He had never really stopped writing.

It is from his earlier career, from 1951 until 1965, that Whittington is best known today. He was a cornerstone of postwar noir fiction, a tense, claustrophobic and sexual branch of the genre that also included his friends Day Keene and Gil Brewer.

Whittington wrote nightmares; he wrote about the strange and dangerous shadows that lie just below the surface of familiar and commonplace scenery. Doorways become caves; shadows contain enemies and Whittington's plots obeyed the protocols of dreams. He created his stories by mechanically piecing together his plots, settings and characters. His memories of poverty and social slight are what gave them unexpected depth.

Whether he was writing a western or a contemporary suspense novel, Whittington's romantic, downbeat characters remained about the same. He wrote lurid, primal stories about swamps, hired guns and dishonest cops. His flawed heroes were forever pursued by police and criminals through Spanish moss and cliffhanging plots. A Whittington character could—and would—take punishment. Usually they were prepared to expect it, running desperate, crazed. In the rare moments of rest they were able to understand, somehow, that they were lucky just to survive.

"My hero cannot put on the happy face," Whittington wrote. "He is pushed to the place where he can trust only himself, even when he recognizes the impossible odds he faces. This does not stop him because he would rather die fighting than to surrender to greed, corruption and mean heartedness."

According to Whittington, who enjoyed advising young writers: "A story is not 'about an innocent man framed by his own government' but how—with what special, carefully foreshadowed strength, skill, knowledge or character trait—he overcomes this terrifying situation. That 'planting' and a preconceived 'emotional effect' which will gratify, shock and involve the reader is truly what the novel is all about."

Stripped away from glamour or any rewards which would have been proportionate with Whittington's effort or talent, this scrambling for a marketplace, the highs and lows and ultimate disappointment is the essence of what it meant to be a paperback storyteller. Whittington could be cast as the prototype. It was hard enough just to make a living as a writer and Whittington did it twice, as both Harry Whittington and Ashley Carter.

He was a common man, a working-class high school graduate with a passion and skill for words. It wasn't surprising that he could sometimes write a story that became bogged down, or veered away from Whittington's particular symphony of violence. It's amazing that he wrote so many excellent stories, scores of them. He called the novels his "hundreds of little bastards." He never lost his style, an easy, accumulative rendering of setting and character. He was smooth and tricky; he could write about old situations in a new way.

The cause of the "little guy" came easily to Whittington. He was not, by nature, a writer of the lurid and brutal. His model was F. Scott Fitzgerald. Whittington became a Fitzgerald transformed by the marketplace for a post-depression, postwar generation preoccupied with loyalty oaths, spies and "The Bomb." Whittington may have been the poet laureate of that era. He was both light and blunt, witty when he wrote about situations where the gift of wit wouldn't be any good at all. He returned from World War II with eyes made more sensitive to social ills, racism and corruption. He wrote about the domestic front of the Cold War, with Americans fighting or suspecting the loyalty of their neighbors.

Suspicion, deceit and manipulation were Whittington's storytelling tools; he took paranoia and made it entertaining. Writing fast, for a hungry marketplace, he caught the spirit of the time.

Downieville, CA
May 2006

A NIGHT FOR SCREAMING

BY HARRY WHITTINGTON

1

I said it again, and when she realized I'd asked her for a handout, she stared at me as if I were crazy.

We stood facing each other on the sun-struck main drag in this village that was a careless sowing of shacks and one-story buildings clustered around that phallic symbol of the Kansas plains, the district grain elevator.

"A quarter? For a cup of coffee?" she said, parroting me, and looking as if she was about to laugh in my face.

She'd paused when I spoke to her, all right. I'd figured she would stop because like every other woman she'd be curious to know what some man, even a stranger, mumbled at her as she passed him on the street. Anyway, this was rubesville where everybody spoke to everybody else, and she looked like the busty, leggy brand of chick that got spoken to by any man with energy enough to open his mouth, which was just about what I had left.

The look of controlled laughter and contempt angered me and I said, keeping it cold, "That's right. A quarter. If you haven't got it, forget it."

Something happened in her face; the taunting smile didn't falter, and the contempt around her mouth didn't fade, but I felt her looking me over. She was used to being spoken to, but not in that tone.

"I've got a quarter." Her voice was even. "But you won't get it from me by begging."

I shrugged. "So good-by."

"If you want to work for a quarter, why..." She opened a smart handbag she must have bought in Denver or Kansas City, took out a business card and extended it toward me between polished, manicured fingers. "See my husband at this address."

I took the card, dropped it in my shirt pocket without looking at it. "Thanks. If I ever get that hard up," I said.

Now she did laugh. She had the arrogant look of the spoiled babe who has learned to take everything that isn't freely rendered to her; laughter didn't come easy to her unless there was the knife in it.

"You're already that hard up, mister. You just don't know this town. If they arrest you for panhandling, you'll end up working for my husband for nothing."

"Thanks," I said again.

"It was nothing," she said.

She turned away. When I said, "Very nearly," she turned, looked straight into my face and laughed again. She was a lovely doll, no use playing that down. She got her arrogance from her certain knowledge of this. It was in her walk, the tilt of her head, the upthrust of her breasts, the curve of her sulky mouth.

You have to see these rich, young, small-town dames to know what she was really like. They might have come out of a family of migrant workers, subsistence farmers, or maybe the bankers' home. They went to school in these small burgs, growing into something so lush, so luscious that every woman hated them and every man coveted them. They had everything they could ever want long before they were ripe. It made them hard and demanding, and looking for the big take. They had love when they were thirteen, and now they wanted everything their beauty would buy. And when they got their hooks in the richest man in the area, they truly began to live. Shopping trips west to Denver, east to Kansas City and St. Louis, and at least twice a year into New York and Chicago to see the shows. They believed their beauty indestructible, the fun was going to last forever. Only it didn't work that way. The oldest saw was the truest: when you've seen one circus, you've seen them all.

That was my judgment of her, my snap judgment, and it pleased me to believe it.

She looked me over one more time, then she went away along the street, seeming somehow taller and more tightly packed than the grain elevator.

I glanced around: drugstore, hardware, department store, movie theatre, grocery, couple of filling stations, the Kansas Pacific Railroad station, the bus depot. Nothing much worse than being stranded and broke in a prosperous small town among straight-ticket Republicans. The only more evil situation would be to be in trouble with the law besides. So I was bucking a stacked deck.

I checked the walk again, but the good-looking doll had disappeared into a store, or in a car.

I took another tuck in my belt. Panhandling was a misdemeanor in this burg. I had to get out, and on an empty stomach.

I wiped the back of my hand across my mouth. I'd purposely limited myself to female touches, telling myself it was the hard way because women are tough to get money away from. But I had another, bigger reason.

I didn't want any man checking me too closely. Men listened to car radios, paid attention to faces flashed on TV screens, noted mug shots in newspapers. But I figured women never looked anywhere except in the society section for Ann Landers, the horoscope and the divorce listings. And these were about the only columns I'd not been in recently.

I walked slowly west along the main street for no good reason except I'd been headed west for three days now.

I glanced around, feeling a sudden chill in the bright midmorning sun. I had the feeling cops were behind me, across the street, up ahead of me.

I should have been used to that setup by now, but I wasn't. I never would be.

My heart slugged faster. I'd been running so long that when I thought about running, I reacted in fear, like a conditioned mouse in a maze.

I trembled, wanting to run. Suppose the long-legged doll decided to get her kicks by casually mentioning to a cop that there was a panhandler defiling main street? Sure, she wouldn't. She'd already forgotten me. But on the other hand these dames had a cruel streak. Laughs were harder to come by for these babes every day. They had to look pain right in the face to really experience any sense of pleasure.

I turned and the word *café* struck the rods and cones inside my retina, and there was instant reaction in my brain. My mouth began to water.

I stared into the café, my gaze fixed between ice-topped letters: *Air-Conditioned*. A waitress was alone in there; young, blonde, in white smock, crepe sole shoes.

She was lazily wiping at the counter that ran along one wall, polishing the coffee urn, wasting time between the pancake special and the businessman's lunch.

I swallowed the saliva in my mouth. I could eat breakfast, admit I was broke and beat a retreat before she could summon a cop. I'd never tried it before, but I was doing a lot of things for the first time. If anyone had told me a week ago that an innocent man could run in just as much terror as a guilty one, I'd have told him he was nuts. I never thought I'd try to beat someone out of a meal, either.

There wasn't any haughty air of arrogance about this blonde. She might even buy a hard luck story.

I moved toward the thick glass doors, then stopped. She wouldn't be alone in there. There'd be a cook on duty, the owner might be in his office. If this girl served me food, called the law and I was caught, all the running bought me nothing. I'd be on my way back, handcuffed to Fred Palmer. I exhaled heavily and turned away.

I saw the cruiser then, parked a block away, door opened on the driver's side, a uniformed cop slouched on the far side of the seat.

I couldn't locate the other cop. He might already be moving toward me, watching me.

I glanced around. I had to get off the panic button. That cop was sagged hot and bored and sleepy in the cruiser.

Still, I didn't want to walk past that cruiser. I hadn't shaved since yesterday; the freight car had rumpled my jacket, wrinkled my slacks. I had begun to look like what I was—a man on the run.

I took a quick peek over my shoulder. Nothing for me back that way. I'd been there.

The waitress glanced up from her polishing when I sat on a stool halfway along the counter. I checked the rear exit; swinging kitchen doors. If I moved that way, no cook could stop me before I hit the alley.

She set iced water on the chilled counter top before me, waited. Her blue eyes were unimpressed. She was accustomed to seeing young men, with beard shadows, rumpled slacks.

I took a swallow of cold water, felt it to the pit of my heated stomach, for a moment the room wheeled before me.

I replaced the glass on the counter, closed my fist around it, clinging to it.

She waited, pad and pencil poised.

"Look, Miss," I said. "I'm broke."

She registered no astonishment. She shrugged, replacing pad and pencil in a smock pocket that was heavy with tips. I stared at the money bulging against the fabric.

"So. What else is new?" Her voice was mild.

"I'm hungry," I said, trying to make a joke of it. "What will a hard luck story buy me in here?"

She nodded toward the water glass. "You're holding it," she said.

My shoulders sagged. I felt new ruts around my mouth.

I pushed the glass away, turning on the stool. That was when I saw the cruiser parked outside the café, two cops in it, very pointedly not even looking toward me.

My hands trembled and I dropped them to my side. My gaze moved back from the blue-tinted front window, touching the cash register, gleaming coffee urn, tips bulging in the blonde's smock pocket, double doors to the kitchen.

"Mister, I better tell you something," the waitress said in a flat voice.

"Panhandling is a misdemeanor in this town," I said.

"If you knew it, why'd you try it?"

"I made a mistake. I thought you had a kind face. From outside. Through the window. Probably the shadows, or something."

"We all make mistakes," she said.

"You haven't got a copyright on that, have you?" I stared around the room, feeling helpless. "I'd like to use that sometime. It's real clever."

She stared through the window at the cruiser. "They're coming in here," she said.

"Why not? Free coffee. Happy quips with the waitress."

"I'll bring you a cup of coffee first, and a bowl of cereal. That's fastest."

"Why? I told you. I'm broke."

She moved in a smooth, effortless way, not wasting a motion. By the time the cops crossed the walk and entered the café, she'd spread napkin, silverware, coffee, cereal before me, poured milk and pushed the sugar toward me. The expression on her face did not alter, but she had the props set so it looked as if I were already five minutes into my breakfast.

She walked away from me, going to the front of the café where the two cops had squatted on stools beside the cash register.

I didn't hear what she said to them. I saw they were wearing lightweight slacks, short-sleeved blue shirts with town police emblems on the sleeves. They'd pushed their summerweight caps back on their heads. They looked completely relaxed.

There was only one thing wrong: they didn't even glance toward me.

The waitress set coffee before the two cops, let one of them hold her hand for a moment while he stroked her inner arm, elbow to wrist.

"Purr, pussy," he said. "Let me hear you purr."

"Not during business hours," she said, pulling away from him.

I had all the woe I needed trying to keep my hand on my coffee cup from trembling. But I saw the cop tickling her arm was angered. He'd wanted to demonstrate to his buddy how this waitress reacted to him. They probably whiled away many dull hours with him going into detail about what happened when he got her out in a car somewhere. It teed him off now when she made a liar out of him.

He laughed. "Dot's a sweet girl, Arnie. She can give it to you like she was taking something away from you."

"Sure she is," Arnie said.

The waitress's face was white, rigid. She came back to me. "I'll see if your pancakes are ready, sir," she said.

She walked away behind the counter. The two cops whistled. "Look at that, Arnie. More bounce to the ounce. And what's best of all, that girl's French. Ain't you, Dot?" He lifted his voice, laughing, but she didn't hesitate. Her shoulders hunched just slightly as if they were throwing something at her and she was setting herself against it. Otherwise, it was as if she didn't even hear them.

We all waited, but she didn't come back.

Finally the two cops drained off their cups, and then Dot's lover turned on the stool, and it squealed under his two-hundred pounds. He set himself with his feet wide apart and stared at me.

I concentrated on the cereal. My coffee was inside me now, and I felt better. The panic was there, but the milk and cereal and the coffee diluted it slightly.

"Howdy," the cop said.

My stomach muscles tightened. The word struck against the side of my face as though he'd spat on me. There was belligerence in his tone. I knew they'd come in here because I was in here, but it had been routine, something to check because there wasn't anything better to do in the hot morning.

But now the waves this boy was sending out had the rage in them that he felt against the waitress. Rage was like acid. It had to burn out of you in some direction. He didn't dare vent it on Dot; he had intelligence enough to see he'd gone too far there already. He had to strike out at something. I was nearest. I was a stranger. I needed a shave.

Hell, it was easy to follow his reasoning. I knew how men like him reacted. I knew all about it, too much.

I nodded without looking up from my cereal. It was almost gone. I couldn't stall over it very long.

"I said howdy," he said again. He turned his head. "He ain't a very friendly cuss, is he, Arnie?"

"Maybe he don't like policemen," Arnie said.

"You like policemen, mister?"

"I got nothing against cops," I said, bearing down on the word. "When they mind their own business."

"Tough. He's tough, Arnie."

Arnie pushed away his cup, his mouth twisted. He got up, came around his partner and stood beside me.

"What's your name?" Arnie said.

"Why?" My cereal was gone, the coffee cup was empty, except that the waitress had said she was bringing me an order of pancakes there was no reason for me to stay on that stool. The backs of my legs were weak.

"I asked you your name. You want to take a little ride down to police headquarters?"

"No."

"Then get smart," the other cop said. "What's your name? Show me your wallet."

I felt the tightness in my throat, the trembling in my legs. I went on sitting there. I turned just enough to look up at them. I pulled my mouth into a savage kind of grin.

"Sure," I said. "You show me your warrant."

Arnie laughed. "He wants to see my warrant, Cotton. How about that?"

"You got one?" I said.

"You're in a mess without getting smart-off," Cotton said.

I felt the increased pumping of my heart. Had that dame reported me? God knows there isn't much to do in a small town, but what could that act buy her, except a brief laugh, and she wasn't even around to see it?

"You're a stranger in town," Arnie said.

"What ordinance does that violate?" I said.

Arnie shrugged. "Depends. We got a lot of ordinances. Where's your car?"

"I don't have a car."

"How'd you get in town?" Cotton said.

"On the train." I neglected to mention that it had been a freight train, going west between three and four A.M. today.

"Which train?" Cotton said.

"Hell, I don't know. I bought a ticket. The conductor punched it. We got west of the tree belt—"

"Where'd you get this train?"

"Kansas City."

"What time you get in here?"

"Hell, I don't know. I slept. I told you. We got out of the tree belt. The country looked the same. The dames on the train were the kind you guys would go for. All the towns looked alike; a grain elevator and a few squatty buildings. I fell asleep."

"What'd you get off here for?"

I began to think about why I had gotten off that freight, the way I had gotten off of it. I was afraid it would show in my face. I grinned up at them some more. "Now that I've seen it, I'm damned if I know."

"How long you expect to be in town? What'd you say your name was?"

"I didn't say."

Cotton was looking over my head toward the double doors to the kitchen. They were closed, leather-padded, still. Nothing happened back there. He jerked his gaze back to Arnie.

"Think we ought to take him in, Arnie?"

"Sure."

"What for?" I said.

"We need a reason?" Cotton said.

"Yes." I clenched my hands on the edge of the counter, watched my knuckles go white.

"How about this?" Arnie laughed and nudged Cotton with his elbow. They both grinned, having a ball. "There's an ordinance in this town against panhandlers, bums."

"Ordinance 718, paragraph *b*," Cotton said.

"Right. That's the one. Loitering in the streets, in public places, begging, soliciting funds. It's pretty complete." Arnie was pleased with himself.

"There's just one little thing," I said. "I'm not on a public street. I'm on private property. I'm having breakfast. For all you characters know, I have a thousand bucks in my wallet."

"You don't look like you got the price of a shave," Arnie said.

"Still, I might have it."

"Sure," Cotton said. "So let's see your wallet."

"You try to take it in here," I said, "without a warrant, and you'll be back jockeying a reaper in the wheat fields."

Arnie and Cotton looked at each other, grinning.

"He talks tough," Arnie said. "Like a road bum should."

Cotton nodded. He looked me over. "It'll be a pleasure to arrest you."

Arnie licked his lips. "You'll resist, won't you?" His eyes looked hot with anticipation. "Kind of mild, even? Just a little bit? Knot your fist, or lift your hand? Please."

I swallowed, but I kept my voice level. "Why don't you try it and see?"

Arnie and Cotton looked at each other again, and laughed. They hadn't had so much fun since they'd clubbed a sixty-year-old drunk.

"Oh, not in here," Arnie said. "We wouldn't think of disturbing your breakfast, Mr.—what did you say your name was?"

"I didn't say."

He shrugged. "We'll be outside on the sidewalk. Okay? When you come out. No hurry. Right, Cotton?"

Cotton was watching the kitchen doors. They were shoved open and Dot came through with an order of pancakes, syrup, butter, side order of bacon, and a bowl.

"Sure," he said, not giving it much attention.

The waitress set the bowl down on the rear shelf, then turned as if she and I were alone in the café. "Sorry I took so long, sir," she said. Deftly she removed the cereal bowl and set the pancakes and bacon before me. The odor of the food assailed my nostrils and I was afraid I was going to be sick. I gripped the counter hard. I'd never realized before that the smell of bacon and pancakes on an empty stomach could make you ill. For a moment she spun around my head like a blue fly.

"Thanks," I managed to say. Neither of the cops noticed what was happening to me. Cotton was staring at his waitress, trying to force her to meet his gaze. Arnie was enjoying his own cleverness.

"We'll be out front," Arnie said. He tapped Cotton's arm with the backs of his fingers, and turned to walk out. He shifted his gunbelt on his thick hips as he walked.

Cotton hesitated a moment. He seemed to have forgotten I was alive. He was staring at the waitress, his face rigid. "Dot," he said.

She looked up at him, hating him for what he'd said as she went into the kitchen. She met his gaze, but didn't answer.

"Dot. I'll see you. Tonight. When you get off."

She didn't say anything. She didn't even appear to be breathing. She just stared at him.

The doors closed behind the cops. My queasy stomach settled slightly and I buttered the pancakes, poured syrup over them.

It was quiet, the chilled, air-conditioned silence settling over the whole room. Outside, the two cops lounged against the front fenders of their cruiser. Cars passed on the street, and people moved along the walk, calling to each other, laughing, but none of the sounds penetrated into the café.

"Nice town," I said at last, chewing.

She pulled her gaze from the front window, looking at me as if she'd just awakened standing there, as though she'd never seen me before in her life.

"Wonderful," she said.

"Why do you stay here?"

She shrugged. "I got a job. Why did you come here?"

I shook my head. "You weren't born here?"

"God, no. My God, no." Then she laughed suddenly, in an abstracted way, as if remembering something. "But the town I was born in—" She shook her head and laughed again.

"Worse than this?"

"Just like it."

She brought me a fresh cup of coffee. She smiled, pushing the backs of her fingers along her blonde temples as though strands of hair were loose on her forehead. But they weren't.

"You were really hungry," she said. "How long has it been since you ate?"

I shrugged. I motioned with my fork toward the pancakes, bacon and coffee. "Why'd you do it?"

She exhaled. "You had a pretty face." She was staring through that window, as if sick, as if she'd lost her last tipping customer. "Does your mother love that face?"

"I don't know. They took her away. Screaming. When I was born."

She managed to smile. "I'll bet they did."

She began to work with the polishing rag. I ate, beginning to feel almost human again. Finally, I realized she was speaking, talking to herself more than to me.

"A girl comes to a town, new town, nobody knows her, and nobody knows a thing about her. And everything is fine. For the first time. For the first damned time everything is fine. She can get a job, go to church, feel like she's just as good as other folks. Then there's this guy. Nothing much. But he's got a steady job—"

"With a pension." I glanced through the window. Arnie leaned against the cruiser, waiting in the white sunlight, but Cotton stood stiffly, back to the café window. Only he couldn't stay like that. He'd glance over his shoulder at Dot, lips set and gray.

"With a pension," she agreed, barely hearing me. She scrubbed hard at the aluminum ice cream covers. "She tells herself she could do a lot worse."

"We all make mistakes," I quoted.

She looked up, stopped polishing, and smiled. "You want some more coffee?"

"No. I may as well go out there and face it. Thanks. I can take it now... I don't think I could have before."

She didn't say anything. She turned, picked up the bowl she'd brought from the kitchen and set on the rear shelf. She brought it to me, leaned against the counter and pushed the bowl toward my plate.

My heart sank. The bowl was almost full of change, dimes, quarters, fifty-cent pieces and two one-dollar bills. Her smock pocket that had been bulging with tips, sagging out of shape with the money, was empty now.

I stared at the money in that bowl.

"Why?" My throat felt raw and tight.

She ignored that. "Lucky you came in this morning. Couple men in who always tip me a dollar when they buy a dime cup of coffee. They think it's going to buy them something extra."

"Sort of a living trust," I said.

"Sure. Annuity."

I pushed the bowl away. "You fed me." I still didn't look up at her. "You didn't adopt me."

"Don't be a fool. Feeding you won't get you out of town." She glanced through the window again. "I better tell you something looks like you don't know. You ever hear of the Great Plains Empire?"

I shook my head. "Sounds real melodramatic."

"You better listen good," she said in that flat voice. "It covers about two or three hundred sections. You know how much that is out here?"

"About twenty-eight acres to a section? Big."

"A man named Cassel owns the Great Plains Empire. Wheat. Cattle thick like fleas. Truck farm—"

"I'm not looking for work here."

She laughed in a flat way. "That's what I'm trying to tell you. If Cotton and Arnie arrest you for panhandling, you'll get thirty days at labor—"

"And Cassel pays the sheriff for prison help?"

She nodded. "He has a big place. Needs a lot of help. If you went out there, he'd hire you. You'd live in a barracks, he'd pay you. But you get arrested in town, you'll sleep in a different barracks behind barbed wire fences, and the sheriff will get paid for your work."

"You've been reading Daphne DuMaurier."

Her expression didn't alter. "Not unless she writes for the local paper."

I remembered the leggy, busty dame handing me a business card. I fumbled in my shirt pocket, pulled out the card. It was senseless, but my hands trembled when I read it:

BARTON M. CASSEL
Great Plains Empire Farms
U.S. Highway 40 East of Fort MacKeeney, Kansas
Phone 404 - Blue

2

I dropped the card with its face up on the counter.

"So you see how it is?" she said, barely glancing at the card. She'd seen cards like it before. She moved up the counter to the cash register where the box of mints, the bowl of toothpicks and a card holder were grouped on top of the cigar case. She brought a business card to match mine and laid it on the counter beside it.

"Gin," I said.

"Bingo." She smiled.

I glanced through the blue-tinted window at the cops in the sunlight. They were getting impatient. Arnie was standing up now, mopping at the sweat on his forehead and around his thick neck under his open shirt collar. His blue shirt was discolored at the armpits. He was staring into the café, his face muscles set and rigid.

Cotton was saying something coldly and emphatically.

"Mr. Cassel is a good customer of ours," Dot said.

"A dollar tip?" I said.

She shrugged. "Sometimes five dollars. Especially if he's been drinking. And he doesn't come in very often unless he's been drinking."

"I thought this was a dry state."

She shrugged. "He leaves a stack of cards for us. Likes us to give them out to men looking for work."

"You keep talking about work," I said. "I don't want to work. Not around here. I'll never forget what you've done for me, Dot. Never. I'll send you some money to pay for it, but I can't ever thank you—"

"I'm all heart," she said. "I fed you to keep those two goons from arresting you. Now I'm telling you to take that money and buy yourself the biggest bus ticket it'll buy. You got no chance of getting a job at Great Plains, even if you were fool enough to want it."

"I don't want it. But why not?"

"Stop wasting time with stuff that don't matter, mister. They're not going to let you get a job out there, because if they arrest you, they'll get paid for the work you'll be forced to do. Put that money in your pocket. Walk up front, pay me a dime, wait for some change and walk out of here."

I scooped up the money, closing my fist over it and dropping it in my jacket pocket. I put the two singles in my wallet and stood up. She had moved up to the cash register and was standing there, waiting.

I moved slowly toward her, disliking the idea of facing those boys even with money in my pocket.

I leaned against the cigar case, looking straight at her.

"I don't think your friends are in any mood to let me leave town," I said. "Even with a bus ticket. I better go out the kitchen door and make a run for it. I'll repay this. I'll send you a letter: 'Dot, care of the Fort MacKeeney Café, with love—from Mitch Walker.' What's the last name, Dot?"

"What difference does it make?" Her eyes were cold. She took the dime at the side of the register, punched a key on the cash register and handed me two half-dollars in change. "Dot. That's enough. It's all you need to know."

"What's with the cold shoulder all of a sudden? I thought you were a friend of mine? You don't think I'll repay you?"

"I know you won't if you try to run out that back door. How smart are you? How'd you ever get this far?"

"It wasn't easy."

"I'll bet it wasn't. Don't you know Arnie and Cotton are waiting for you to make a run through that back door? Either one of them would shoot you in the back in that alley. Resisting arrest."

"They're about to have an orgasm out there thinking about getting me in a cell."

"You can take a beating," she said. "You're young. You'll get over it. Besides there's nothing more they can do to that face of yours."

I shook my head, my voice hurried. "What's with this face bit, honey-lamb? You feed me, you fill my pockets with gold, and you act like you hate my guts."

Her voice was bitter and her eyes were chilled. "All right, you're a handsome guy. Is that supposed to make me feel better? A guy walks in here and I act like his fairy godmother, just because he's young and pretty?"

I looked around, trapped. I could not deny a sudden painful sense of relief. I could not get out of here. Those cops were hovering, waiting. It was over. It was ended. All the running, and the hiding out—it had ended. Highway 40. Fort MacKeeney, Kansas. Dead end.

"There's one way," she said.

I didn't believe her, but I looked up, and from the corner of my eye saw Cotton move toward the thick doorway. But I didn't think he'd come back in here. They wanted me on the street, they wanted me stripped of defenses.

"The men's room," she said. "A window in there. Opens on the alley. It's locked, but you're a big boy. You can go in there. They'll buy that for two or three minutes. Everybody has to go, sooner or later. Even those goons know that."

"Two or three minutes," I said, grinning at her. "An eternity. A bigger headstart than I ever had before. God bless you, you hear me?"

"God," she said in a bitter way. "He don't know yet that I've left Salina."

I was already moving at an angle through the tables toward the men's room. I paused, turned, seeing Cotton and Arnie straighten out front, troubled. I stared at her and tried to smile. "If He doesn't," I said, "He ought to get on the ball. Damn few saints left on this earth. He ought to keep better track of them."

I was running.

I ran east along that narrow alley, not knowing why. West was my goal; anywhere west. But I tried to figure Arnie and Cotton. When they first spotted me I'd been headed west. Inside the café, I'd admitted coming here from Kansas City which was east. The city limits lay only two blocks to the west. A stranger in town might feel some safety lay beyond the city limits, but I'd been warned these two boys worked for the sheriff and they could trail me as long as I ran their county—a barren, treeless land where you could see a jackrabbit jump a mile away.

Far behind me, at the west end of the long block, I saw that cruiser whip into the alley, speeding toward me.

As its front bumper, grill and engine hood came into view, I lunged out of the alley, landing on my knees between two frame shacks.

The shack on my left was set on brick foundations and under it was the darkness of a cave.

I went scrambling under the shack, sprawling forward in the breathless darkness. If anybody the length of the alley had seen me duck in here, I was dead. I didn't waste much time worrying about it. I wasn't fooling myself. Who could hide in a town this small? And who could hide outside it when there wasn't a tree or rock to conceal you? It was just a matter of time.

I lay there, breathing into my palm.

The cruiser raced past in the alley. I could count the minutes remaining to me now. They would go to the end of the block, maybe along the next block, slower, checking the openings, and then they would retrace along here.

Because there was nothing else to do, I lay in the sand. I couldn't hope for much now, not anything really.

These cops would come back, close in, arrest me, check the files at headquarters.

They would find the wanted dodger on me, and they would call in Fred Palmer, and no matter how hard I'd tried, the whole thing would be over.

I lay still and grinned coldly in the darkness, thinking about what I hoped would happen when Arnie and Cotton came back looking for me. I hoped Cotton came alone between these two shacks. Sure, he was tough, big, a trained cop. I'd fix that mouth so it'd be a long time before he detailed any more dirt about the little waitress. I owed her so much more than money could ever repay. And it wouldn't take long.

I heard the rasp of speeding tires on the pavement alley. The cruiser went speeding along, heading west.

I pushed deeper under the shack, moving between brick supports, away from the alley, wondering what sort of place this was and if the people in it could hear me wriggling under it.

I peered through the lattice between the front foundation supports. A short arid yard was bare. The street was silent, swimming in heat waves. Front stoops of other houses were empty, doors and windows gaped open as if the houses were gasping for breath, and no one was in sight either way along the block.

I heard the cruiser speeding east on this street and I wriggled backwards. I watched the police car race past, Arnie at the wheel, both searching each side of the street.

Cotton supported his arm on the window frame, a police special gripped in his fist. It was in their faces; they were pleased with me. I had done what they hoped I would do, I had run, resisted arrest.

The cruiser made a tortuous U-turn at the corner, tires wailing, then straightened and bucked to a stop. As it settled, Arnie got out on one side and Cotton stepped out on the other.

Cotton leaned against the fender, looking around, gun at his side against his leg. He moved his gaze slowly across the shack I was hiding under, and I felt our gazes clash and lock, even though I knew better. The house sat too close to the ground, and I was too far back. He couldn't see me. Not yet.

The street came alive. Men, women and children spilled out of all the doors when that cruiser screamed to a stop. Fort MacKeeney, Kansas saw damned little excitement. When the cops came, everybody turned out to see the fun.

Arnie moved among them, questioning them, describing me. They shook their heads, but glanced around, eagerly. Nothing is as intoxicating as the smell of blood.

I looked around. I had to get out of here, and before they started a house-by-house search.

Something nagged at me. I watched them out on the street, and there was something I should know, but I couldn't think clearly with the panic eating at me.

Some of the people turned, went back to their houses. They moved warily. Arnie had gaudied up the story: I was a dangerous criminal, armed.

But nobody came near this house. Whatever it was, it was vacant. There was not even the whispering of mice above me.

I crawled toward the rear of the shack. I saw what a fool I had been. I had left a clear trail scraped in the sand as I writhed under this house. Little oversights like that could get me killed.

I moved my hand around, found a short block of wood, smoothed over the sand. It looked too smooth, but after a couple bystanders ran across it, it would look fine.

I moved back into the darkness under the house. It was like an oven. My clothing was wet with sweat, thick drops leaked out of my hair and ran down my face.

I heard them running beside the house, saw their legs when they stopped.

"Hey, Arnie. Look at this."

Cotton's voice had excitement in it, the kind that's in the baying of hounds at the foot of a tree. "He's in this house, Arnie."

They tried all the doors. Arnie was telling Cotton he was simple, there were no broken windows, no forced locks. How could anybody get in?

"It don't matter. He's in there, all right."

They smashed a window, I heard the crash of stone on the glass, the pieces raining on the floor.

Then they pushed up the window.

"Push the kid in." Cotton was the take-charge boy now, excitement crackling in his voice. "Open a door for us, kid."

"We've fooled around here too long," Arnie said. I heard them hoist someone through the window, and he ran across the house, opened a door, calling to them.

The footsteps were loud in the house. I lay there, tried not to breathe. I had run so far. They said I had killed a girl, only she had been dead when I got there. But I couldn't prove that, and I had run; a lung-bursting, throat-scorching running, and no sense in it. I couldn't even remember just where and when I'd started running. I felt as though I'd been running all my life. I couldn't even remember now how it had been before, in that time before I started running. Worse than that, in all these endless hours there hadn't been a chance that I could make it. They'd been too close behind me all along. Right from the very first, I hadn't had time to stop long enough to think, to plan. I was bursting with weariness and they weren't even breathing hard.

I needed to gasp for air through my parted lips, but didn't dare open my mouth at all.

"Hell, that guy doubled back," Arnie said. "We've covered this here alley, just like he figured we would, and he went back through that café, and I bet you he's ten miles out of town this blessed minute."

"The hell." But there was doubt in Cotton's voice.

"You don't see nothing, do you?" Arnie said. "Not even the dust has been stirred. We're wasting time in here. Come on, let's check the highway."

"He's in here," Cotton said. "I know it. It's a feeling I got."

"You got a feeling, all right. Hell, you're letting him get away on that highway. If he's around here, he can't get away now without somebody seeing him. They can get word to us. But if he gets away on that highway, we've shot it."

"Okay," Cotton said after a moment. "But I'm leaving the Ludkins kid here to watch this place. He's around here."

"Well, damn it, if he's here, show him to me," Arnie yelled.

"Hell with you," Cotton snarled back at him. "We'll do it your way. I'm just telling you. I know he's around here. Come on. Let's go."

Arnie cleared all the bystanders out, but warned a boy to stay around the shack, to watch and listen.

"Sure I will, Mister Arnie."

They walked out, trooping through the front door, going down the steps. I listened to their voices receding, heard the cruiser start up and blast off as if Arnie's rage furnished the propulsion.

My throat was raw and I felt as though my lungs would burst if I didn't drag in one deep breath of air. But before I could even move my legs I heard the Ludkins boy walking around above me, going slowly, all through the shack.

3

I lay in the breathless heat and silence.

I felt myself drawing up in a neat tight knot of panic all over again. For half a second there had been the exhilarating sense of outsmarting the two hick cops, even temporarily. But now I was trapped under this shack and I heard that boy moving around inside it.

Sweat coursed down my face.

Suddenly I heard something. It was a strange hissing noise in the silence. It came from east of me along the alley and I sweated trying to think what it could be.

I waited. Twenty slow minutes crawled past before I heard it again. This time I recognized it. It was the sound of air brakes.

I nodded, pinning it down. These were the big air brakes of the Greyhound buses. The buses pulled into the depot at the corner east of me, less than a quarter of a block away. I touched the money in my pocket, thinking about the ticket the waitress had urged me to buy. It was as if she were giving me the gift she most wished someone would give her, a way out of this town.

There was the roar of an engine as the bus pulled out of the station.

I began to see one chance of getting out of here alive, not only from beneath this shack, but out of Fort MacKeeney.

There were two ways to work it, and neither of them were very good, but offered the only opportunity I could see. One, I stayed where I was, hoping the cops would not get back here until the kid got tired and left, and that they would overlook checking under this house. There was the slim chance that they would leave again, finally. Then I could lie here until dark, and when I heard a bus enter the terminal at the corner, I could sneak out, wait in the shadows, and board that bus in the last moment before it departed.

But I couldn't fool myself that the sheriff didn't have somebody watching that bus depot by now.

If I had any hope there, it was that his deputy would be guarding the ticket window. But the loading platform was at the end of the alley, and I could board the bus there, saying I'd arrived too late to buy a ticket. And that would work.

I mopped more sweat out of my eyes. It occurred to me that I couldn't figure by the swish of air brakes which bus was going east and which west. But this seemed of no significance. The direction didn't matter. I could change buses at the first rest stop. The important matter was to get out of this town.

In the darkness I could hide, I could stay hidden. Night. That was the answer. If only I could somehow hang on in this oven until nightfall.

I shook my head, beginning to see what was wrong with this plan. Everything was wrong with it. Once Arnie and Cotton checked out the highways and satisfied themselves I was hiding inside town, it wasn't going to take them long to pin me down here under this shack. And I was as helpless as a turtle on its back under here.

Wait until? I couldn't even wait until those two cops returned.

I held my breath, listening. The next time I heard the sigh of air brakes in the bus terminal, I had to make a run for the loading platform and then leap into the bus in that instant before the driver closed his doors to pull out.

I waited for the hiss of air brakes. If I could reach that loading platform, I could find a corner and stand there until the bus was ready to leave.

I accepted the fact the sheriff would have a stake-out in the terminal waiting room. But I was gambling they would never think to cover the loading area.

I sweated, praying for the hurried beautiful whisper of huge Greyhound brakes.

I didn't deceive myself. Somebody would be prowling the alley now. They would see me. Somebody would. I had to count on that. I had to cut it close, so close that I could just make the bus before the alarm went up.

I had carefully counted the minutes between arrival and departure of buses in that terminal. This was all in my favor. Fort MacKeeney was even smaller than you think, a quick stop for the big Greyhounds. There were not more than six minutes between stopping and starting of those buses.

Six minutes can be an eternity, but on the other hand, if I shaved it close enough, there wouldn't be time for anything more than a yell from a bystander in that alley, and I'd be gone.

The town grew quiet in the hot early afternoon, almost as if it were prostrated from the heat.

The hiss of air brakes reverberated inside my head.

I forced myself to remain cold, deliberate. All I had to do was move fast, attract attention of the kid in the shack, and I'd have outsmarted myself.

I crawled painfully slowly toward the rear of the shack.

I came out from beneath that shack, paused for the space of a breath and slapped the sand from my clothing. I didn't even look around.

I ran along the alley. I heard the terminal P.A. system crackling, but the starter was calling the town names in some foreign tongue. I couldn't decipher one of them.

At the corner of the wide drive behind the loading ramp, I stopped. I pressed myself against the wall. There was one little item: I had to know which way this bus was going before I boarded it. Boarding without a ticket was one thing, but being unable to name a destination might be ruinous.

I pressed hard against the wall, keeping out of view of the waiting room and also pulling myself out of the alley.

It was the smartest move of my life.

Pressed there, for the moment concealed, I stared across that ramp toward the bus.

I went sick.

I saw where the bus was headed, all right. It was bound for Denver. The last of the passengers were aboard. The driver was checking his manifest, about to step inside. The moment was perfect. All I had to do was to stride across the cement drive, enter that bus and I would be safe again; could rest, could breathe.

Only it was never going to happen.

The driver stepped into the bus, and the doors hissed closed. He started the engine, checked his rear-view mirror, straightened his cap, made all those last minute adjustments, scratched his crotch, and engaged the gears.

I didn't bother watching him.

I barely saw the bus at all. Instead I stared at the man leaning against the wall just outside the waiting room exit doors.

Palmer.

Sure, the sheriff's deputy was inside that waiting room, watching that ticket window, just as I'd known he would be.

But Palmer didn't work that way. Palmer wasn't Palmer when he was on a case. Palmer liked to tell you you had to think like a criminal to catch a criminal. Only you had to know in advance what the criminal was going to think; you had to think the criminal's thoughts, faster. But that was always easy because a criminal had to keep a hundred things in his mind, while the detective on his trail had only one thought on his brain: the criminal.

I sagged against the wall. I watched that bus pull out into the alley, make a left turn and go toward U.S. Highway 40 West.

Hammers pounded behind my eyes. Palmer had been on my tail from the first. If he hadn't been, I'd never have run. I'd have taken my chances with anyone but Palmer. But I knew him too well. I had lost him in Kansas City.

I panted, my mouth against the brick wall. It didn't make sense that Palmer could be standing here in this hick burg, this grain depot in the middle of the plains. Why Fort MacKeeney? Why not a hundred other towns?

I clenched my fists, knowing rage wasn't going to buy me anything. Palmer was thinking ahead, as I would think. He was standing there, relaxed and cool, going over in his mind what Mitch Walker, fugitive, was going to do next.

I exhaled heavily. Okay. So now I had to think like Palmer, even if it did make me want to wash my mind out with soap.

I pressed deeper into the niche between depot wall and adjoining building. I still couldn't breathe any fresh air, but I calmed down enough to answer one question. Palmer had checked with the railroad detectives this morning. Any tramps booted off the freights during the night? Where? Outside Fort MacKeeney on the Kansas Pacific?

And here he was.

4

He stood there against that doorway for what seemed like a screaming eternity after the Denver bus pulled out. He was smoking a cigar, rolling it on his lips, savoring it.

Palmer was a big man, in his early thirties, maybe four or five years older than I was. He was square in the shoulders and flat in the belly. This may not seem like anything extraordinary in a man of thirty, but he liked rich foods washed down with beer, and the only exercise he ever took was on the pistol range. He'd go white with rage any time he got more than a half an inch away from dead center on any target.

He looked at the cigar for a moment and then flipped it across the cement driveway almost as though he were throwing it at me. He straightened up, and I could see he'd finally let the women convince him: he was as handsome as they told him, in that dark, rugged way. He always told them that's why he'd never married. But I knew why he never married: a wife would be in the way when he started on a case, started hounding some poor devil twenty-four hours a day.

I stared at him across that twenty feet, thinking he was the reason I'd gone sour on the police department. After I'd completed my probation back home, I passed first man on the detective examination. They made a big thing of assigning me to work with Fred Palmer. With my two years of college, and what Fred Palmer could teach me, I'd be a big man in the department: Fred Palmer was everything a good detective should be. In just three months I had the urge to vomit every time I looked at him, and I knew I'd never make the detective list, and all I wanted was out.

He was the reason I'd run. I was innocent of any crime, but I couldn't prove it, and I knew what Fred Palmer could do to a man. I'd seen them beg to be allowed to confess after a session with him.

He re-entered the waiting room. I stared after him, thinking. I was out of the department and now Fred Palmer was going to brighten his record with me. Pursuit and arrest. Interrogation and conviction. The whole thing was inevitable. It was in the way he walked. His whole manner said, "You're around here somewhere, Mitch, breathing scared like a rabbit. Why not make it easy on yourself? Why don't you come in and surrender to me?"

I heard men yelling in the alley west of me. Someone had seen me running away from that shack.

Their shoes were loud, pounding toward me along the narrow alley. I glanced once toward the depot to be sure Palmer had gone inside the waiting room and then I pressed deeper into the narrow crevice between wall and building.

"He got on that bus," one of the men was yelling as they ran past me. "I know that's what he done. He made a run for it and got on that bus."

They went along the alley toward the street. Somebody was yelling that they had to get word to the sheriff, maybe they could stop the bus on the highway.

I crept back slowly toward the opening, glanced cautiously up and down the alley.

I couldn't stay here, and I couldn't walk abroad in the daylight, either. I pressed against the wall, feeling the pound of my heart, looking around, trying to think, searching for one break.

My gaze raked across the phone booth, moved past it and darted back.

I stayed there for a long time, or what seemed a long time. Maybe it was less than a minute, but I solved this immediate problem for myself. I found an answer. I figured it was the smartest decision I'd ever made in my life.

I felt myself grinning, felt the muscles ache around my mouth with the angry pull of that grin. I glanced toward that waiting room, thinking, "Think fast, Palmer."

I thrust my hand into my jacket pocket, sorted out a dime from the pile of change the waitress had given me in the café.

I stepped boldly out from the wall and walked across to the phone booth. What I loved about this particular phone booth was that it had been placed on the ramp for the last second convenience of bus patrons; that hurried final moment call. It was around a corner from the waiting room, and a building wall shut it off from the alley.

I entered the phone booth, closed the door behind me. A small fan dried the sweat on my forehead.

I punched the dime into the slot and didn't even hesitate as I dialed. *Phone 404 - Blue.*

The phone rang a long time. Finally a man answered, his voice sounding almost reluctant. "Hello," he said. "Great Plains Empire Farms."

"Is this Mr. Barton M. Cassel?" I said.

"No. Mr. Cassel isn't here right now. I'm his foreman. Any message? Anything I can do?"

"Well, I don't know," I said. "I was in the Fort MacKeeney Café and they said you were looking for farm help."

"Oh, yes. We're always looking for help out here."

"My name is Mitch Walker," I said, not bothering to lie about my name. It was a thousand to one chance anybody out there had ever heard of me. A ranch as big as that had its own woes.

"Yes, Mr. Walker. What can we do for you?"

"Well, it's like this. I'm on my way west. But I'm not in any hurry. I've heard a lot about your place. I thought I'd like to work out there a while."

"We're in tomatoes and watermelons right now, unless you know something about dairy cows."

"I better stick to watermelons," I said. "I don't promise to make a career out of it, but if you'd hire me, I'd stick it out for a while and give you a day's work every day."

"Sounds fair enough. We pay a dollar an hour, and we pay by the day, so you can stay as long as you like, cut out when the notion hits you. We find migrant workers like this plan best. We feed you, and you can stay on the place in the men's barracks if you want to. So your eight bucks a day is clear."

"That's all right with me. How do I get out to your place?"

"Drive east on Highway 40 until you see the sign over our gate. There's a man on duty there. Tell him your name and he'll let you in."

"I don't have a car."

"We could send for you if you're in Fort MacKeeney."

"You do need help."

He laughed. "Oh, yes. We can always use all the help we can find."

I glanced around me. "If you could pick me up at the rear of the bus station," I said.

"You got yourself a deal, Mr. Walker. We got a man in town now. In a jeep. I'll call in and tell him to pick you up. Ten minutes all right?"

"Boy, you do need help," I said.

He laughed and hung up.

I stayed right there in the phone booth with the receiver against my ear, my face turned toward the wall, and the breeze from the fan riffling my hair.

The minutes dragged. I saw three men move west along the alley, growling at each other. I kept waiting for a bus to come in. If Palmer stepped out on this loading platform, I wouldn't be able to get to that jeep.

Eight minutes. A jeep skidded to a stop at the end of the wall on the alley, and the driver slapped his horn.

I replaced the receiver. I stepped out of the booth, went over to the jeep. The driver was a thin, sun-darkened man in khaki shirt and trousers, boots and a battered five-gallon Stetson back on his sweated hair.

"Your name Mitch Walker?" His voice was high, almost a whine.

I slid into the seat beside him. "Right."

"You got no suitcase or nothing?"

I glanced around, taut. "I'm ready to go if you are," I said.

He studied me a moment. "You look kind of messed up."

"Been traveling on the bus," I said.

"Inside it or out?" he said.

"Like amusing," I said. "Let's go."

He slapped the little car in gear and laughed. "The way you look is like a joke on Evans, all right."

"Evans?"

"The foreman. Don't you know him? He said he hired you."

"Oh, Evans. Sure. Yeah. Mr. Evans hired me."

We had swung around a corner and were streaking east on the highway.

"Not Mr. Evans. Mr. Howell. Evans Howell. If he hadn't been in such a rush to hire you, you'd of been picked up by the cops and he could of got you for half price and the county would have had to feed you." He laughed. "That's a real good one on Howell. Only I hope the old man is feeling good when he hears it."

"The old man?"

"Cassel. He owns the place. But don't think he misses a trick. He knows everything that goes on out there... well, almost everything." He shook his head and laughed again as we drove out of the town limits. "What you want to do this kind of work for?"

"Getting low on money."

He laughed again. "Either you don't know where we're going, mister, or else you're real desperate for money."

I inhaled deeply. I couldn't tell him it didn't matter where we were going. I was breathing again, that was all that really mattered. A few minutes ago I had been dangling on a string, and now I was off that string.

There didn't seem a place on earth I'd be as safe as I'd be out at the Great Plains Empire. Was the sheriff going to look for me on a farm where he supplied prison labor? When you wanted to hide, you went to the one place nobody would think to look for you, didn't you? Not even that little waitress would ever think I'd go willingly to work at the Great Plains Empire. She'd warned me against it, and I was most grateful to her for that above everything else she'd done for me.

In that moment back there at the bus station when there was no place to hide, I'd thought of Barton M. Cassel. Great Plains Empire. Phone 404-Blue.

I couldn't think of a better place to hide than in the middle of prison labor.

He held the car on sixty. "You got any money?" he yelled at me.

"A few dollars. Why?"

He shrugged. "Poker game tonight. You might want to get in it."

"Sounds real merry," I said. I glanced at him, the sharp features, the thin hands gripping the steering wheel. "What's your name? Or don't you give out that information?"

He gave me a quick glance. He shrugged. "You won't be seeing much of me. I'm off the place most of the time—"

"Picking up labor?" I said.

"Yeah. Either the free man, like you, or them that Sheriff Mason sends out in cuffs. But my name's Buster Kane."

The little car raced along the highway. We didn't speak for some minutes. There was nothing to see in any direction except the flat unbroken plains. Jackrabbits and ground squirrels raced across the highway. Infrequently we would pass the small white triangles of the oil pumps.

"You got a lot of those things on the farm?" I said, nodding toward the small pumps.

"We got a lot of everything out there," Buster said.

A car was racing toward us, and I saw it was a police cruiser with red roof light blinking. My hand gripped the seat rail. Buster slowed and I held my breath, waiting for him to stop, but the cruiser sped past, and the two cops in it waved back at Buster.

I sagged in the seat, recognizing those two cops.

Buster said, "Couple real swell guys. Lots of fun. Always anything for a laugh with them two. Arnie Vallon and Cotton Powell. They been hunting some bum that gave them the slip. And—" Then he stopped talking, letting the car slow as he turned, staring at me. He let his gaze rake over me, and he got it. He knew now who I was, who those cops were looking for.

I set myself, ready to take him apart if he made a move to turn this jeep around.

After a moment, he burst out laughing. "Well, I'm damned," he said. "So you think you're like real clever, huh? You knowed if them two guys arrested you, you'd work out your sentence for us anyway—"

"Only I wouldn't get paid for it."

He slapped his leg laughing. "Oh, man. This gets better all the time. You figured you had to work out here one way or the other, it might as well be for pay. Huh?"

"Something like that."

He shook his head, laughed again. He stepped hard on the gas. He glanced at me. "At first, you didn't look like too much to me, Walker. But you pulled a good one. Only one thing wrong with it. You'll wish you'd picked a better place to hide."

"I didn't have much choice."

He laughed again. "There's always the French Foreign Legion," he said.

I watched the dust cloud boiling toward us, thinking we were in the path of a small but violent cyclone. It came on so swiftly I didn't even have time to yell.

I didn't need to. Buster saw it, and he began to curse. He jerked his foot from the accelerator, clung to the wheel with both hands.

A white Cadillac convertible materialized abruptly from the dust cloud. It was coming down the wrong side of the highway doing better than a hundred miles an hour.

"That bitch!" Buster yelled.

I hung on waiting for the driver to see us and jerk the car to the other side of the highway.

It didn't happen. Whoever it was at the wheel was going so fast that he had the instinctive knowledge that turning that wheel at all would send the big car wildly out of control.

But it didn't slow down. It came directly toward us, wavering slightly as if caught on the wind and barely touching the ground.

Buster didn't hesitate. He jerked the jeep hard to the right and we bounced off the highway, across the hard-packed orange shoulder to the stubbled field.

The car whipped past and the back wash from it shook the jeep.

Buster had stepped on the brake and for some moments he sat there clinging to the steering wheel, saying one thing over and over. "That bitch. Oh, that bitch."

My voice shook slightly. "You know her?"

Buster swallowed and wiped the back of his hand across his mouth. "Know her? Everybody knows that bitch." He laughed. "You work for her now, friend."

"Mrs. Barton M. Cassel?" I said.

He shrugged. "Who else?"

5

The man at the gate had a rifle across his arm.

My sense of shock must have showed in my face. Buster glanced at me and laughed. "The boss had to give him a gun," he said. "We're bothered all the time out here. You know? Tourists wanting to take pictures. Kids throwing things out of cars. Don't worry about that rifle." He laughed again. "It don't mean a thing."

"Sure," I said. "I'll bet it isn't even loaded."

He had pulled the jeep to the gate and he stopped there waiting while the man, dressed as he was, in khaki, boots and Stetson, came out of the small house inside the fence and walked out to the gate with that rifle across his arm.

I looked around. Only the fence and its posts broke the landscape along the highway as far as I could see in either direction. I began to see how smart I hadn't been. And I knew something else. This was the moment of decision. There was one thing to do: step out of this jeep and keep walking east. But it was already too late for that. Inside that sentry box beyond the fence I could see the telephone on the shelf. There wasn't much else. Comic books scattered on the floor, an old wicker rocking chair, pegs for the rifle, that was all. But the telephone was all that mattered. If I tried to walk away, they could get in touch with the sheriff's office almost instantly. Alexander Graham Bell's little miracle.

I stared east along that sun-blasted highway. This wheat and farm country was flat and dry and barren under the pitiless glare of the sun. Stubbled grass covered the land like thick hair on the back of a man's fist. A hawk sailed against the faded, cloudless sky. I had no idea how far east of me was the county line, and without that knowledge I was helpless in a land where one farm was larger than the state of Rhode Island. This farm.

I exhaled heavily, and Buster laughed in a dry way as if he had been following my thoughts.

I pulled my gaze back. The gate was swinging open, whining dryly on its hinges.

The hard-packed orange road stretched like a line into infinity across the bare unbroken fields. Distantly, I could see the sprawling massive buildings of the farm.

There was nothing elegant about the gate, or the simple wooden sign hung above it on two skinned willow poles.

Inside the gate, Buster stopped the jeep again, waited until the keeper had closed and locked it behind us.

He walked toward us, squinting. He bent his knees, sighting in at me.

"Got a new one," he said. "He a free man?"

"Yeah, that's right," Buster said. "He can leave any time he wants to."

They both laughed.

About a quarter of a mile from the farmhouse we entered a long avenue of cottonwood trees. In the distance I could see the tan hides of grazing cattle; there were thousands of them but they seemed only peppered against the sprawling graze land.

I counted six windmills strung across the farm. This man was pumping enough water to supply a small city.

The farmhouse was completely isolated from the rest of the buildings by a squared setting of tall cottonwoods backed by a cyclone fence topped with three strands of barbed wire.

Beyond the fence the milking barns were as large as plane hangars and built with the same rolled roofing. They were all freshly painted with gleaming cement ramps at each end. There were corral areas of carefully heaped manure; there were feed barns, and stables, fertilizer barns, one long red building which housed the farm machinery, huge reapers, plows, harrows, tractors. Everything was brightly polished, painted and washed down.

A man came running when Buster slapped the jeep horn. He opened a gate, touched his cap in a gesture right out of Sir Walter Scott as we rolled past.

Buster drove slowly between the barns and stables, speaking casually to the men who paused, looking up from their work.

We passed the last of the barns, struck another cyclone fence. Buster punched the horn and a man came running from the unpainted barracks beyond the fence. He pulled open the gate, running with it, and we rolled through. Out here, completely hidden from the farmhouse by the smartly painted barns and hangars, were two barracks. Except that they were separated by more cyclone and barbed wire fence, they were identical in shape, lack of paint and general disrepair.

At the end of the two barracks was another building with two sets of double doors on either side of the dividing fence. This was the kitchen and the messhall.

"How you like it?" Buster said, watching me.

I had a knowledge that this boy didn't. He knew what life was like at Great Plains Empire Farms, but he didn't know what awaited me a thousand miles back east.

"Looks charming," I said. "Too bad they ran out of paint before they got back this far."

"Yeah. You're right. It's a shame."

"Which one of these barracks belongs to the free men and which to the jail labor?" I said.

He laughed, "Why man, look around you. Can't you tell?"

"No. There doesn't seem much to choose from between them. That barbed wire fence works both ways."

"Oh, man, you're wrong. That barbed wire fence is just for them on the other side of it. Out here, you're as free as any bird. You don't see nobody with guns on this side of the fence do you?"

Evans Howell was maybe two years older than I was. He was tall, well over six feet in his spit-polished boots, but he was slender, angular and knobby in his freshly pressed khaki. His hair was dry, blonde and wavy over a narrow, thin face. He was the kind of man women thought handsome, and it was obvious they never got any argument from him on this subject. He seemed to have a horror of dirt and wiped his hands four or five times on his handkerchief in the first ten minutes he talked to me.

He was waiting just inside the free men's barracks when Buster and I came in from the messhall. We'd had coffee and a sandwich. I felt better.

Evans Howell winced when Buster told him who I was. Buster's mouth was twisted in a grin, and I knew Howell recognized the silent ribbing he was getting from the driver. Howell had hired too many migrants not to see instantly that if he'd left me to roam loose in Fort MacKeeney for another hour or two, I'd have showed up out here as county-paid labor.

But there was one thing I had to give the foreman. He saw immediately that he'd been had, hiring me for pay, but he spent no time in regret.

He looked me over. "You look kind of mussed up, Walker," he said.

"Bus travel," Buster said, grinning.

Howell ignored the little man. "Well, Walker, take the rest of the day. Walk around, get the feel of things. Buster will assign you a bunk. Rest up. We turn out at five A.M. tomorrow for breakfast."

"And we're loaded on the trucks at a quarter to six. Right, boss?"

Howell ignored Buster Kane again. He looked me over. "You're a strong-looking man, Walker, better than we usually get around here. If you want to leave any time, that's your choice. But if you like the work, or—" his pale blue eyes narrowed and I saw he knew I had good reasons for showing up here, "—or if for any other reason, you want to stay on here, we'll be glad to have you as long as you do your work."

Buster snorted with laughter again, but Howell paid no more attention to him than he would to a fly.

"Sure," I said. "I'll be all right. Soon as I've had a shave and a shower."

Now Buster did burst out laughing. But Howell did not even smile. His face pulled in a cold way, and I saw that though he was terribly thin, there was nothing weak about him.

"No showers," he said. "We don't waste water, Walker. Not on showers. Not out here."

"My God. Men work all day in this heat and don't even take a bath?"

Buster laughed. "Hell, man, week or ten days, you'll get used to it. Most the workers like it that way. You don't see anybody but each other anyhow. What difference does it make how you smell?"

Howell said, "We pump a lot of water, Walker. But I want you to see how it is. Every drop of water in the state of Kansas is a drop of gold. We got wells sunk down to two-fifty, three hundred feet. We don't work that hard so a bunch of stoop-laborers can look spic and span. We got a lot of expensive dairy cattle, a truck farm. It takes a lot of water. And wheat. Sometimes a year or even two years pass when that wheat don't get a drop of rainfall. Lot of wheat people take the wheat that matures from the snow in winter, whatever rain they get. But not us. We don't raise that kind of wheat. When we send a cutter out in our fields we know the wheat is going to sprout high enough so the blades can reach it."

"So you can see how it is," Buster Kane said, grinning at me.

Howell glanced at him now. "Why don't you get back into town, Buster? Must be something you can do in there."

Buster stared at him, his face set, mouth pulled as far as he dared.

"Yes sir, Mr. Howell."

I found a razor in the men's room at the rear of the barracks. Iron cots were pushed against the wall with an aisle down the middle of the frame building separating them. There were a hundred and twenty of these cots on each side of the aisle.

The first thing I noticed in the men's room was that the shower spigot handles had been removed and the fittings had been twisted out of shape and soldered at the pipe nipple. Nobody was even going to steal a bath out here.

I washed my face in the tin basin, scrubbed soap into my beard, scraped the razor over it until my face burned.

I felt better after I'd shaved.

I dropped my jacket across the bunk they'd assigned to me. Then with my sleeves rolled up and my collar open I went out into the bunkyard.

I went through the first gate, prowled the implement barn, the stables, the milking barns. All the latest machinery was in use here. The stalls were scrubbed, hosed down, gleaming. In the cattle barns were men sprawled sleeping in the shade. I found out they had one job. They jumped a cow when it lifted its tail and stood ready to clean up after it before it hardly finished, scrubbing, hosing, polishing, until even the cow was uncomfortable. They swore some of the cows were housebroke.

I went through all the barns and finally found myself at the cyclone fence where the cottonwoods grew like a windbreak and a cyclorama over the ugly facts of life behind the farm house.

I paused at the locked gate, staring up at the house. There was a small sign beside the padlock: *Laborers wishing to visit at the house, please get written okay from foreman. Signed, Evans Howell.*

The sign was so politely worded that you almost believed a laborer could visit the big three-story white house set in the cottonwoods.

"Where you going?" I heard the voice at my shoulder, but I hadn't heard anybody approach on the hard-packed gravel. I looked over my shoulder at the boy in denim shirt and Levis. He had a key ring hooked on his black leather belt. He had black hair and black eyes, looked to be about eighteen. I shrugged and grinned at him. "Nowhere. The foreman said for me to look around, so that's what I was doing. How much farther can I go?"

"You got a pass from the boss?"

"Nope."

"Then this is it."

"Suppose I wanted to get out of here? Suppose I wanted to leave?"

He stared at me. "Where would you want to go?"

"Hell. I don't know. Just anywhere."

He shrugged. "That's easy. You just collect your money and they drive you out to the highway. No trouble."

"But nobody walks out there?"

He shrugged again. "Not since I been here."

I stood there a moment just for the hell of it, looking at the big house, seeing the gardeners working around it, the people scurrying around in the rear cooking area.

Then I turned toward the barns, the second gate and the free men's barracks. The boy was still standing there, squinting at me in the sun.

"See you around," I said to him.

"Sure."

I kept waiting for Evans Howell to ask me where I was from, what work I had done, what I could do. It didn't happen.

As I walked back past the milking station, he came out of the huge hangar-type building carrying a clipboard. He paused and stared at me, as if surprised to see me, as if he didn't even remember me.

"You said look around," I told him.

It took him another second to come all the way out of it. I had seen men like him before. Nothing organically wrong with them. What men like him suffered was a virus of the soul.

He smiled. "Oh? Sure, Walker. Good idea." He exhaled heavily, as if there were so much on his mind, he had to clear it all away before he could enter in the simplest discussion. He looked around, seeing the brightly painted barns, the rows of farm machinery, the men bowed over them, working, painting, scrubbing. "Quite a place," he said.

"I never saw anything like it."

"No." He smiled again in that abstracted, blonde way. He glanced around. "Kind of fact nowadays. Just one way to run a farm, any enterprise. Big business. If it ain't big business, you might as well shut down. Lot of work to this place. God knows. But the profits are big. Really big. If a man likes this sort of thing, he can really make something.... What do you think of it?"

I was startled at the sudden interest in his voice, the depth and life that abruptly appeared in it. It was as if he had finally emerged from his funk and was aware that I was standing before him, a man almost as tall as he, much heavier, shaved now, practically presentable.

I jerked my head up and looked at him, warily. What was the pitch here? Was this it? Would he start asking now? Where did you come from, Walker? Why are you here? What do you want? What are you running away from?

One thing we can pin down hard: He hadn't been fooled from the first minute he saw me in that barracks. He knew there was plenty of trouble wherever it was I'd come from. He knew I was running. He knew I was up to my ears in it.

I frowned. I couldn't help it. As I've already said, he was a nice looking young guy, and when he smiled, he looked very friendly.

I warned myself to be on guard, but even so, his smile was warm, disarming. He just looked like a pleasant, personable young guy. Look out, Mitch, you haven't run into much friendliness lately, you'll be spilling your guts.

He gestured again, "What do you think of all this, Walker?"

"Oh, hell," I said, "I don't know. Doesn't mean much to me. I won't be around here long."

He shrugged, still smiling, still looking at me as if I were an honest-to-God human being. "That's up to you. But... well, I came here a few years ago, Walker, just like you did today."

He paused, and stopped smiling for a moment, and I saw he meant that literally.

He exhaled. "For the right man, this can be quite a place. Quite a place. It... it was for me."

He winced, turning his head quickly as if he was afraid I'd see the sickness in his face.

He smiled again. "A man with intelligence, and some strength. A man like you, Walker. He doesn't have to stay down there with the stoop-laborers. Those men down there—" he shook his head. "They're not really human. They're kind of subhuman.... They're better than animals. But not much."

I grinned coldly at him. "Maybe if they had showers they'd smell better."

His smile was warm, but he shook his head.

"Don't fool yourself, Walker. They don't want to bathe. Most of them don't even bother to shave. We put razors down there and they steal them to sell. I've tried to find out. Honest to God, I've tried to find out what it is any of them want. Any of them. But they don't want anything. They get up in the morning. They eat without even looking to see what it is they're eating. They do just exactly what they are told. Just exactly." His mouth twisted. "Just exactly like a herd of dumb, stupid animals."

"What else can they do?"

He frowned, looking at me. "They can have anything they want for breakfast. I mean just for instance. Eggs, any way they like them, all the cold fresh milk they want. Pancakes, rib steaks, beans. Now, don't get me wrong. We're not the Waldorf, but Cassel learned a long time ago that men work better on a full stomach. It's just plain good business. Big business.... But you know what happens? If they go in that messhall, and their breakfast isn't sitting right on the tables waiting, they're confused, don't know what to do. If a cup of coffee was set there, they'd drink that and get up, ready to work. They'd grumble among themselves, but that's all. So, you know what we've had to do?"

"Something big business, I'll bet."

He grinned. "We set out dishes of oatmeal at each place every morning. The best protein we can give them, the best possible breakfast. There's a man stands at the entrances everyday telling them as they come in that they can have anything they want for breakfast, all they've got to do is ask the servers for it. You know what happens? They slink in, eat the oatmeal ladled out to them, and then file out, ready to go to work."

"Nobody can call this Sunnybrook farm," I said.

He smiled again. "No. It's hard work. But a man with brains can get himself a good job, and good pay—and a private room in those quarters beyond the machine shop."

He nodded his head toward a painted two-story frame building, square and red-roofed, but gleaming and clean in the sun.

"You live there?" I said.

He smiled and nodded, "That's right. I've a suite up on the second floor. Parlor, bedroom, dinette, kitchen. Food brought out from the big house kitchen and served up here. You see there's no fence between that place and the big house."

"Very swank," I said. "You have your own shower."

He laughed and nodded again. "All the water I want. Hot and cold."

"You make this ambition kick sound very appealing," I said. "I'll give it a lot of thought."

I was sitting on the barracks steps, watching the nothingness in the sun-bleached sky, and the nothingness to match on the unbroken land all the way to the horizon.

It troubled me. That Evans Howell was friendly, easy-talking. But I got a sense of wrong. He was the boss. He ran this place, or all of it this side of the farmyard fence. Why wouldn't he want to know where I came from, what I was doing here?

It didn't make sense.

He seemed anxious not to learn a damned thing about my life before the moment I dialed 404-Blue in Fort MacKeeney today.

I watched the big gates swing open up near the painted barns. Three big yellow buses rolled through. They looked like school buses except they were paint-scabbed. And painted along the sides of them in bold red letters was: BARTON M. CASSEL'S GREAT PLAINS EMPIRE FARMS. PRIVATE. NO RIDERS.

Another gate opened and the prison-labor bus drove through it.

I sat there and watched it stop outside the jail barracks. Two county guards stepped out of the bus with rifles across their arms. After a minute the workers began to spill out, they were yelling and laughing and jostling each other. The guards yelled at them, leather-lunged. They shouted, ordering the men to shut up and fall in line.

I felt my mouth pull in a grin. It took a long time to get those men in two lines outside the bus and headed toward the barracks steps where two more armed guards stood waiting to take over. The men fell in, but only when there was nothing else they wanted to do. They stopped talking then because the guards patrolled the lines, rifles extended ready to slam a gun-butt across the face of the first man that spoke.

The other two buses of free men rolled slowly along the fence to the barracks where I sat. I got up and moved away from the steps.

I leaned against the front of the house, watching them unload.

They came out of the buses silently, shoulders round, heads lowered. Their clothing was sweated, gravel-crusted. The two strawbosses wore denim shirts and Levis.

There were almost two hundred men in the buses. They trooped tiredly up the steps without talking and plodded along the aisles to their bunks.

When all were inside, the strawboss nearest me turned and looked me over.

"You a new one?"

"Yes. That's right. Mitch Walker."

"Okay. Inside, Walker. Nobody hangs around out here."

He was set on his parted legs, waiting for me to answer back. I shrugged. "All right. I didn't know."

I went up the steps. They stood there looking at me. The man who'd spoken first said, "Walker."

I stopped. He said, "My name's Handecker. This here is Tom Potter. We're in charge down here. You give us a fair day's work, do what you're told, you have no trouble with us."

"I don't want any trouble," I told him.

He nodded. "Okay. Anything you want, you got any gripe, you come to Tom or me. Right?"

"Anything at all," Potter said. "You don't have to bother nobody else. Handecker and me will take care of everything."

They stood there at the foot of the steps smiling, sweating and smiling. But they knew I read their message. Loud and clear. There was a chain of command here. And nobody went over their heads.

Twenty minutes later the front doors were shoved open and chocked wide. Potter and Handecker entered. Potter leaned against the doorjamb swinging his billy stick. Handecker blew a shrill police whistle three times.

"All right, men," Handecker shouted. "Chow's down. You guys washed up, let's go. No lagging. Huh? Okay?"

The men got up from their bunks, talking quietly among themselves as they moved along the aisles toward the front doors.

Outside in the waning sunlight we lined up. We made two rows. Across the barbed wire fence I saw the prisoners were lined up also, smaller lines, but noisier, once in a while there would be a burst of laughter from over there.

We marched into the chow hall first. There was a rafter-high wire fence that separated the long narrow hall from outer walls to serving counters.

Potter stood just inside the doorway of the messhall. As the two lines came in, he directed them to benches on each side of the door, filling the far tables and then the nearer ones.

I sat down on a bench. The plate before me was already served, steaming. There were two lamb chops, cooked carrots, mashed potatoes with lamb gravy, a fresh salad and dried white beans. Servers in white aprons moved between the tables with pitchers of coffee and iced tea. Beside each plate was a slice of white cake.

The men around me didn't even check to see what they were being served. It was a well-prepared, generously portioned meal, but these men didn't care. They didn't have energy enough to care. The food was good, but it could have been slop for all they knew or cared. They began to eat noisily, rapidly, faces close to their plates. They looked up only to grunt when the servers came along asking if they wanted coffee or iced tea.

I got up from the table. I picked up my plate and sidled through the rows of hunched men to the aisle. Carrying my food, I went over to the serving counters.

One of the servers came from the big urns in the cooking area. He was frowning.

"What's the matter?" he said.

"Nothing. Nothing. But they told me I could have anything I wanted to eat."

He frowned again, looking around, "Sure. So what's wrong with what you got?"

"I said nothing. I just want a steak, that's all."

I felt somebody standing close against my shoulder. I turned. Handecker was there. Potter was just behind him.

"What's the matter?" Handecker said.

"Nothing," I said. This was something I had to test for myself. It seemed urgent that I know what kind of a man Evans Howell really was. Anybody could smile, especially on the first day you were on the place, and especially since I knew now that Handecker and Potter were in charge of the stoop-laborers and that Howell very infrequently came in personal contact with them. Perhaps he didn't even know what went on down here. Maybe he didn't want to know.

Maybe he even avoided knowing, the way he had avoided learning anything about who I was.

"So?" Handecker was waiting, eyes narrowed.

"So, they said I could have anything I wanted to eat."

"That's right," he nodded. "So what's wrong with the food you got?"

"Nothing. I just would like a steak, that's all."

The server across the counter looked ill. He said, voice shaking, "I'll have to call the cook."

He turned before Handecker could stop him. He called, "Ling."

From a rear room, a Chinaman in white clothes and white apron came through the cutting tables to the serving counter.

"This fellow," the server said, nodding at me. "He wants a steak."

"Don't like lamb?" The cook looked at me, puzzled.

"It's all right. I just want a steak."

The cook nodded. "Sure. All right. Take just little while. Hokay?"

"Thanks," I said.

The cook jerked his head toward the server and they went back to the stoves. Now that I knew a man actually could order anything he wanted, I didn't care anything about the steak. But I couldn't back down now.

Handecker stepped closer. "What you trying to pull, Walker?"

"Nothing."

Handecker's voice was very soft. "I hope I'm not going to have trouble with you, Walker. A man makes his own life on this here farm. He gets just what he asks for."

I turned. His eyes were narrowed, cold. He was staring at me as if he were trying to memorize every feature of my face, as if he expected to remember me and this moment the longest day of his life.

6

Precisely at six-thirty that night, Handecker and Potter pushed open the barracks doors. Handecker blew his whistle. The men stood up at the foot of their bunks in a spiritless kind of silence.

There had been a sense of impatience inside the barracks after supper. It was nothing you could pin down, but the men were edgy, awaiting something.

When we were all standing in two lines down the center aisle, Potter opened the barracks doors again. Evans Howell in a fresh white shirt, dark trousers and black shoes entered, followed by a small, balding man who looked as if he wanted to hold his nose when he stepped inside the long room.

Handecker snapped an order and the two men nearest the front door pushed a small pine table and a straight kitchen chair out into the center of the doorway area. The little man, nostrils distended, sat down in the kitchen chair, placing a black tin money box and a ledger book on the table top before him. Potter and Handecker stood at each end of the table and Howell leaned against the doorjamb, watching.

Potter gave a signal and the men stepped forward to the table. Each mumbled his name. The little man checked the ledger, handed the laborer eight one-dollar bills in a paper clip.

The pay line moved silently and swiftly.

The only thing that happened to disturb the smooth execution of the daily pay-off was when the door at Evans Howell's back was pulled open. Howell straightened, and both Handecker and Potter leaped around, ready to clobber the intruder.

It was the dark-haired kid who guarded the gate between barnyard and the farmhouse. He looked at both Handecker and Potter, smiling in a frightened way.

"Just a message," the boy said. "Just a message. That's all. Message for Mr. Howell."

"All right, Chick," Howell said. "What is it?"

Chick tried to smile at Howell. "From the big house, Mr. Howell. From Mr. Cassel. They said tell you Mr. Cassel himself sends word. Mr. Cassel wants to see you up at the big house. Right away."

I saw Evans Howell's fair face flush to the roots of his dry blonde hair. He glanced around at the paymaster, at the strawbosses, at the men in the room. There was a sickness in his face.

Puzzled, I saw Potter grin toward Handecker on one side of his face.

Handecker looked wise. Some of the men along the aisles glanced at each other, but none of them said anything.

Handecker leaned against the table, waiting.

Evans Howell straightened. He looked at Chick, shook his head. "No. Mr. Cassel is—" He stopped. "You tell him I'm sorry. I... I can't come up there right now... I'm busy."

Chick now looked as ill as Howell had a moment ago. Here was a message he dreaded delivering. "Please sir, Mr. Howell," he said. "They said it's very important."

Howell shook his head again. "No. You tell them no. You understand? Tell them I'm too busy right now."

Chick looked twenty years older than he had when he walked in. He no longer made any effort to smile. He nodded, not looking at Evans Howell any more, then he turned and went through the doors.

Howell's voice was sharp. "All right, Reeder. Get on with the paying. Get on with it."

When all the men were paid, Reeder closed the box, gathered up his book and stepped through the doors, hurrying.

Howell stepped up to the table, looked along the aisle at the stoop-laborers lined at the foot of their cots.

"Anything you men want to say? Anything on your minds?"

None of the men moved, none said anything. I glanced at Potter and Handecker. Their gazes were fixed on the men in front of them.

Howell shrugged. "So. Okay. We're all one happy family. Any of you men want to leave tonight? We'll run any of you down to the gate that want to go."

He waited. A couple of the men shuffled their feet and looked around, but none stepped forward.

Howell gestured with his lean-fingered hand. His gleaming white shirt contrasted with the sweaty clothing of the men around him.

"All right. So we got nobody leaving tonight. Remember, you can't leave now, with pay, until after pay time tomorrow night. You understand? Mr. Barton M. Cassel pays all of you by the day, in cash, so you can leave when you want to. This is an inconvenience and extra expense to him, so his rule is that no matter what the emergency, there's only this one pay time a day. You all understand?"

The men shifted from one foot to the other. This was the daily routine. They heard this every night.

"Okay," Howell said then. "I guess that's all. Except one word of warning. Don't let me catch any of you men gambling down here. That's one thing I won't permit. It's not that we're trying to tell you men what you can do. But Mr. Barton M. Cassel has found out that when as many men as there are in this room start to gamble, the next thing is fighting and brawling and knifing. We won't permit it. We won't allow any cards, dice, betting. If that's clear, good night."

He stood there a moment. There were grumbles of assent from the men, whines of inarticulate protest, but that was all. Howell nodded in a curt way, stepped back and left the barracks. The men shuffled between the cots, sitting down, sprawling across them, the springs crying in a hundred voices at once. Potter and Handecker pushed the chair and table against the wall.

The men slumped there, only a few of them talking in whispers together, as if they were waiting for something when they all knew there was nothing to wait for.

It was barely dark at the barracks windows when the jeep stopped outside the front doors. The men came to life on the cots, Handecker and Potter came out of their sleeping-cubicles at the front of the barracks. The doors opened and Buster Kane came in, carrying several packs of playing cards and half a dozen pairs of dice.

Most of the men got up from their beds, displaying the first signs of vigor since I'd seen them this afternoon. Potter stopped Kane just inside the barracks doors. "Everything all right?"

Kane laughed at him. "The best. Our loyal leader is being taken care of the way we want him handled."

Handecker laughed. "All right, you guys. Who wants a little action? Kane and me will set up a nice little stud game back there."

The men laughed, some of them crowded around Kane and the straw-boss.

Potter said, "Anybody else would like a little action with the ivories, see me in my office."

He pushed through the knot of men, laughing, shaking a pair of dice in his fist as he walked toward the rear of the barracks.

It was only a matter of minutes before the two operations were set up, ready for action.

I lay on my bunk, watching. Handecker set up the pine table between two bunks and dozens of men crowded around.

In the cleared space at the rear of the barracks, Potter was clattering dice against the wall. Warming them up, he called it.

Then Kane moved along the aisles speaking to all the men. They turned when he spoke and each of them tossed a knife or a closed straight razor into his basket. He had quite a haul by the time he stopped at the foot of my bunk.

He set the basket on the end of my cot. "You got a knife?"

I touched the knife in my pocket, nodded. "But I am not going to get in any of the games tonight."

His face tightened for a moment, then he smiled again. "Oh, hell. You think you won't. Everybody plays. And we can't have no knives floating around here loose. You see, we try to give you guys some entertainment. But the first time we have a knifing down here, good old Johnny Handecker, me and Potter get fired and some of you guys end up in jail—and no more fun these long nights. Now, nobody wants that. So let's have your knife."

I was aware that all the men in the room had paused and were watching me. The talk about my steak supper had spread fast. None of them had missed the way Handecker had looked at me in the messhall. The way these men saw it, I was asking for trouble, and begging for it every step of the way.

Handecker pushed his way along the aisle. His voice was hard. "Let's don't have no trouble, Walker. No one guy spoils the fun for everybody. Toss in your knife. The games end, you get it back, just like all the rest of us."

There was a murmur from the men in the room, an impatient buzzing sound.

I glanced around at them, shrugged. "Sure," I said.

I pulled the knife from my pocket, stared at it on my palm a moment.

"Wow! Switchblade," Buster Kane said.

I heard the whisper run across the room. Here was a tough guy with a switchblade.

I tossed the knife into the basket, hearing the men laughing and talking among themselves.

I lay back on the straw pillow, staring at the ceiling, not thinking about Kane, Handecker, any of them, but remembering the kid I took that knife from. It was like something from some other lifetime, like something that had happened to two other people.

My hands clenched at my sides. I'd been working with Palmer then. Plainclothes. A sixteen-year-old had been knifed in the park. Palmer was gray around the mouth. He was going to smash those stinking juve punks. There was one way to handle them. Smash their rotten mouths, break their arms, take their switchblades away from them and carve them a little bit with their own knives. It was suddenly a crusade with Palmer, twenty-four hours a day. Frisk every tough kid in that end of town, stop every one you saw on every street. Bring in every kid that had a switchblade on him. These kids were tough. Palmer was tougher.

I was with Palmer that night. One of his personally planned raids. I found this kid hiding, sweated and trembling on a tenement roof. When I asked him what was eating at him, he could hardly talk. He was about seventeen, skinny in white bucks, Levis, the leather jacket, acne, sideburns below his ear lobes, thick-lensed, black-rimmed glasses and visored cap two sizes too small on thick, curled hair.

It took a long time, too long, to find out what was chewing him. Palmer was pounding up the roof stairs as I took the switchblade from the kid and dropped it in my pocket.

Palmer looked at the trembling kid. "You frisk him yet, Mitch?"

I nodded. But as usual, nobody's word was good enough for Fred Palmer. He told the kid to turn around, brace his hands against the vent wall. He went over him good, socking with the side of his hand as he frisked him. The kid was ready to crumple by the time Palmer was through with him.

"Okay, kid," Palmer said. "You're clean. You stay clean."

The kid looked at me once, those eyes distended, magnified through those thick lenses. He was nodding at Palmer, trying to get past him and down those steps.

I stood there with that switchblade in my pocket. I didn't mention it to Palmer, then or ever, just as I didn't say anything about why the kid was half insane with fright, and hiding up here.

The kid had finally spilled it all to me just before Palmer joined us. Palmer had once picked the kid up on suspicion of car theft, taken him to headquarters. The kid had never known before what a man could do to your body if he tried. He had never even realized there was the kind of pain that Palmer inflicted on him. And the kid had been innocent. He had slobbered, begging me to tell him what Palmer would have done to him if he'd been guilty.

I couldn't tell the kid.

But the kid did say he'd rather jump over the side of that roof than ever be arrested by Detective Palmer again. And why did I have the knife with me?

I stared at the ceiling, shaking my head. The night when I had known Palmer was looking for me and I knew I was going to run, I had picked up this knife from my dresser. The crazy kind of thing you do when you're too fouled up to think straight. I had brought that knife with me when I ran. It was a kind of symbol. The kid had been deathly afraid of being arrested by Fred Palmer, he'd rather leap off a building first.

And that was exactly the way I felt.

There was a fast turnover at the poker table. A man would sit in with Handecker, Kane and a half-dozen others, lose three or four dollars and then get up, leaving the chair for the next man.

There were only three of us in the whole barracks who didn't crowd immediately into either the poker game or the crapshoot. One was a Mexican kid they called Jose. Some of the men kept telling him, almost in a tone of warning, to get in the action, but he shook his head. The whites of his eyes showed, and his mouth was taut and gray, but he would not get off his cot.

On a cot beside Jose was a man who looked to be sixty, with sunken eyes, wispy hair, so thin his bone structure showed through his skin and even through his denim shirt. Nobody asked him to play, but when they called to Jose, the old man would shake his head, grinning vacantly as f they were speaking to him.

I got up finally, stood at the rim of the crowd around the poker table. I watched man after man lose half his day's pay on that table. Kane was smoking cigar after cigar, eye squinting against the burn of the gray smoke, other eye fixing on nothing but the cards they dealt him. I never saw a man concentrate so intently on a hand of cards. Most of the chips were stacked before him or Handecker.

Kane glanced up, saw me. "Wanta get some action, keed?"

I shook my head. "I don't think so. Craps are more my speed."

Handecker looked up. "That's the old spirit. Have some fun. Everybody have fun."

In four rolls of the dice, I had five dollars worth of fun. At least, fun was what Potter kept telling me I was having, and five bucks is what it cost me. Most of Dot's tips were gone in less than two minutes. I stood up, slapped the dust off my knees.

"Man, you quitting already?" Potter grinned at me, money tucked between all his fingers.

"I had no pay day," I said. "I'll take you next time."

"That's the spirit," Potter said. "Have fun."

"Everybody have fun," I said, quoting Handecker.

As I turned around, I heard Jose's Mexican accent protesting something. Handecker was standing beside his cot. The kid had been writing a letter and now he sealed the envelope, looking up at Handecker, shaking his head.

"Come on, Jose. You don't want to send all that money home. Hell, they'll throw it away. Don't you want to have no fun, kid? Everybody has fun. Lose a little money, what the hell?"

"No," Jose said. His voice trembled. "Not tonight."

On the cot next to him, old man Hogan was shaking his head, too.

Handecker stared down at them a moment, his face taut, then he forced himself to laugh. He shrugged and strode away toward the front of the barracks and Jose sank on his cot as though the sound of a man's laughter was a terrible thing.

I sprawled down on my cot, wondering when they would turn out the lights in this place.

I pressed the uncased pillow over my eyes. At once I saw Howell smiling, talking about everything in the world except who I was, where I was from. Then I could see Fred Palmer watching all the buses and trains pull out of the Fort MacKeeney stations. You got to think like a criminal. Only faster. You got to know what he's going to do before he does it, and be there waiting for him.

Somebody came by with the basket, tossed my knife on the cot beside me. I put it in my pocket, but didn't move the pillow from over my eyes. I didn't like what I was seeing in the darkness, but there was nothing in this barracks I cared anything about seeing, either.

7

The noon sun was like a blast-swollen blister in the center of a livid yellow bowl.

The whole free men gang of us assigned to the fields were doing stoop work in the rows of truck vegetables. When we'd started work at seven the deep trenches between the rows were still damp from the irrigation flooding, but by nine the land itself was crusted hard as rock with the sun reflected on it.

About five minutes before Handecker called the noon break, I was on the verge of wild laughter. I had thought I could take it. The fields were whirling around me. Half the time the vegetable rows were streaked across the stark sky. Every time I bent over, I was afraid I was going to fall flat on my face.

We staggered over to any inch of shade we could find beside the old buses. The ones that got there last were out of luck. Servers from the messhall came out with cold meat sandwiches and iced tea or iced coffee.

The only way I'd endured working all morning in that heat was by glancing around, trying to figure the best way to walk off this place when the time came. I didn't think it would be very long. If Buster Kane mentioned me to the two cops in Fort MacKeeney, though my name wouldn't mean anything to them, it would mean something if they checked, or if Fred Palmer had gone to the sheriff's office for local co-operation. Fred wouldn't do that until he'd exhausted everything else. Asking help was an effeminate symptom of weakness. But he would accept help as a last resort, even from hicksville cops for whom he had nothing but contempt.

Now I sprawled in the shade of the truck, trying to figure what would happen if Barton M. Cassel found out that Mitch Walker, fugitive, was working as a free man at Great Plains Empire. Howell had acted as if he didn't want to know anything about me, had even hinted that he'd been on the run those years ago when he found this place.

I tried to swallow my sandwich through my parched throat, thinking about Howell. He could stay on here, with whatever that soul-sickness was that was eating at him worse than any ulcer ever could. I wanted to hide as long as I could, and then I wanted out.

I heard Handecker's voice near me and I tried to close my ears against it because the heat had made me giddy and that voice scraped my nerves raw. I couldn't do it. He was talking to somebody less than two feet away from me.

I turned over on my back. Under my breath, I cursed. Both the little Mexican named Jose and old man Hogan had flopped down beside me to eat their lunch. Wasn't it bad enough they bunked beside me at night? I wanted no trouble of any kind, and everybody knew these two were swimming in trouble with Handecker and Potter.

"Sorry to send you back there, kid, but I got to have that roster. I can't check off the payroll without it."

Jose's dark face was sickly pale. Beside him Old Man Hogan was shaking his head back and forth. I decided it was an involuntary reaction. Old Man Hogan began shaking his head every time Handecker or Potter came near him.

"All the way to the barracks?" Jose's mouth quivered. "It'd take me an hour, Mr. Handecker."

"I know that, kid, and I'm sorry. But you better get started. You ought to be back before the lunch hour ends. You don't want to get docked for missing any work time. Huh?"

He stared down at the kid, letting him chew that over. Old Man Hogan went on shaking his head.

Handecker laughed. "If you hurry, Tamale, you ought to get back before the work whistle.... You know, kid, I wouldn't dock you, but it's Mr. Barton M. Cassel's rule. Everybody's got to be on the job when that work whistle blows. Better not waste no more time, kid."

He was still smiling, but his voice had hardened.

It seemed to me it had taken Jose one hell of a long time to read Handecker's message, but at last he got it. He stood up and trotted across the rows, going toward the farm buildings that were hazy in the heat-distorted distance.

I hadn't realized I had stopped eating until my iced tea spilled on my fist when I gripped my paper cup so tightly I crushed it.

Handecker glanced at me. He grinned, mouth pulling, "How's them sandwiches, kid?"

I just stared at him, didn't speak.

He went on grinning and spoke to Hogan. "Pop, there are some stakes at the end of all these rows. Somebody should have checked them stakes this morning. Everytime they irrigate, some of them stakes get washed out. I want them checked, right now. Should of done it this morning. There'd be hell to pay if Mr. Barton M. Cassel was to come out here and find some of them stakes down. Get with it, will you, old-timer?"

Hogan's narrow head was shaking now as if he had palsy.

He glanced once at me, but I looked away. Then he lifted his head, watching Jose go across the sun-blasted fields. He looked up at Handecker finally and stood up.

"Sure, Mr. Handecker," he said. "Sure."

He dropped the remainder of his sandwich and his paper cup where he stood in a childish gesture of defiance.

"Pick that up, Hogan." Handecker's voice lashed at him.

"When I come back, Mr. Handecker. Got to check them stakes. Got to check them stakes right now."

Handecker took a step after the old man, fists knotted.

Then he stopped. I still hadn't moved. I wanted to, but the rage in me had chilled me. My stomach was tied in knots. Handecker turned, staring at me, as if waiting for me to lift my voice. What was the matter with him? Did he think I'd taken those two derelicts to raise? Did he think I was going to stand up for them, or did he think in his own guts that somebody ought to?

Our gazes touched for a moment because I hadn't realized I had been staring up at him so intently. The hell of it was, for the moment he didn't look any more like a strawboss named Handecker than he did like a cop named Cotton calling a waitress a slut as she walked away from him, or like a detective named Palmer rupturing a suspect's spleen in routine questioning.

I jerked my head around, searching the country. There was only one thing I wanted: a sure way out of here.

When the men began staggering in the rows at two-thirty, Handecker blew his whistle and called a twenty-minute break.

I straightened up slowly because I could no longer straighten up with any speed. It was as if the blast of Handecker's whistle had taken the final twist in my back tendons to keep me knotted over.

I saw Handecker coming down the rows toward me.

I set myself, hoping he had intelligence enough not to cross me in this heat. He didn't know I'd learned everything you could do to a man to cripple him in the space of two breaths. I had learned from the master. Hail, Fred Palmer! Everything a good detective should be. Also hail Spanish Inquisition. Also hail all atrocity reports since time began.

He moved past me, and I looked over my shoulder. Jose and Hogan had started along the rows behind me. He stopped them, the two party-poopers who wouldn't join in the gambling last night. The spoil-sports. Everybody have fun.

Handecker's voice was amazingly quiet, and I have in me reserved an especial hatred for people who can speak softly and sweetly while white with rage inside.

"You was about twenty minutes late gettin' back here at lunch, Josie-kid," Handecker said, pronouncing the J instead of the Spanish H sound. "You better keep working. We wouldn't want Mr. Barton M. Cassel telling me to dock you. Huh?"

Hogan's head was moving and his mouth trembled. He knew he was next. He should have known in the hour and a half since noon, Handecker would have figured out some way to deal with a spoil-sport like him.

"Keep working, pop," Handecker said to Hogan.

"Why?" The old man's voice quavered, sounding as if he were going to cry.

"Hell, old man. You know I keep you on here when you ain't worth a damn to Mr. Barton M. Cassel. Why, if Mr. Barton M. Cassel knowed I was keeping a man like you—at full pay—why he'd skin me. If he knowed how you barely move.... Hell, old man, these men around here got bets about you. Ever time you bend over they bet amongst theirselves whether you'll make it or not, and after you get bent over, they make new bets on if you'll ever straighten up again."

"I do the best I can, Mr. Handecker."

"Ain't good enough. Now if I'm going to take a chance on gettin' myself in Dutch with Mr. Barton M. Cassel over keeping you on, you got to give me a little work in return. Now hit it, old man, or walk off right now."

"No, sir, Mr. Handecker, I'll keep working."

Handecker heeled around and almost bumped me. I hadn't even realized I was standing there. I looked around, dozens of other men were ringed around, too, but there was a difference. They were grinning.

I realized my face was bloodless, rutted.

Handecker said, "What's the matter with you?"

I shook my head.

He laughed. "Hell, man, you best make a run for that shade up at them trucks. You let them other boys beat you to it, you'll have to sit out in this here sun."

I used all the water the barracks-master would allow me and washed my face and neck and arms to my elbows. I tried to buy a second basin from him for a dollar, but he had a gravy job and he wasn't about to jeopardize it for a buck.

I walked out to my bunk and flopped across it. The body heat from the hundred-odd men packed in this old barracks was worse on me today than it had been yesterday. I could feel the heat still radiating from my body as if I were still reflecting the rays from the sun.

I pressed my eyes closed, then opened them. I was thankful it was a couple hours yet to chow time. I had to cool down some or food would make me ill.

"Got to get out of here."

I turned my head. Old Man Hogan was sitting on the side of his bunk, his back to me. Beyond him, Jose was composing his daily letter in awkward Spanish letters. "Just got to get out of here."

Jose stopped writing, looked up at the old man. He asked the question everybody asked, "Where would you go?"

"I'm old. What's it matter? How long you think we can stand that sun? No rest? I got to get out."

I'd had it. I sat up on the side of my bunk. "You ever shot craps, old man?" I said.

He and Jose looked up at me. He nodded. "Most of my life."

"Then what in hell you got against losing a couple bucks every night to get off Handecker's list?"

He looked at me, shaking that head. "Why don't they just rob us? Why don't they just come along and take it out of our pockets?"

I shrugged. "Maybe they haven't thought of that gimmick yet. Give them time. Meantime, they're offering you the pleasure of being robbed, seeing all your friends robbed every night. You got to pay something for pleasure like that."

"You ever stop to think, mister, what three or four dollars from a hundred and twenty men amounts to every night?"

"They should have it so good in Las Vegas," I said. "And no overhead."

"I need my money," the boy said. "Bad."

"You need to stay alive, too, don't you?" I asked him.

His mouth trembled. "But to be robbed, mister. Every night. When the need is so terrible."

"We all got our woes," I told him.

"Got to get out of here," the old man said.

"Why don't you tell Howell what's going on?" I said. They both stared at me, bloodless with fear.

"No," Jose whispered. "Please. Somebody will hear you."

"He'd help you."

Jose looked ill. "Sure. Señor Howell would fix.... But we'd never get out of hell then. You can see that, can't you?"

"We got to get out," Hogan said.

I looked at them, shook my head. "Either that," I said, "or learn to play poker."

The milk barns were cool, fresh, clean-smelling at eight-thirty that night.

When I walked up the ramp, Chick, the gate guard, pointed to where Evans Howell was sitting under a shaded lamp working over his clipboard on a small pine table. "There he is," Chick said.

Howell looked up, his blonde hair was toppled dry and lank over his high, narrow forehead. He managed to smile, but it was as if it were something he had to remember to do.

He nodded toward another straight chair beside the table. "Sit down, Walker. How'd you like your first day out there?"

I looked at him, and had the sudden compulsive urge to tell him about what was happening to a Mexican kid named Jose and a battered old derelict named Hogan. I knew better. I wouldn't help them any. In the long run they'd lose to Handecker and Potter, no matter what happened.

I sighed. "Hot," I said. "I guess I got along all right. Except for a slight case of heat prostration."

"How'd you like a better job?"

"What?"

"That's right. Working with me. Like I say, those men down there are animals. We get a good man once in a while, we're willing to step him up and give him a chance."

"Thanks," I said. "But no thanks. I won't be around here that long."

Suddenly he asked me the question they asked each other in the barracks. "Where would you go?"

"This is a big country."

He winced, and tried to smile, gave it up. "I thought that too, once. But as long as there's people who won't keep their goddamn noses out of other people's business this whole blasted country's no bigger than that—" He held up his palm, fingers cupped tensely.

I shrugged. "I never planned to stay here."

Now he did manage a sick smile. "Neither did I. Not when I came. But where do you think you can go where you'll be as—" he narrowed his eyes for a moment looking at me, "—as safe as you are here?"

"Am I safe here? Nobody's even inquired who I am, where I came from."

He ignored that as if I hadn't said it. "Nobody talks about who's working here, on either side of that fence. As long as a man does his work, doesn't start any trouble, he gets along fine. Nobody talks off this farm about who is here. Not even Buster Kane."

Chick, the dark-haired gate-watcher, came through the wide doorway. I saw Evans Howell get a glimpse of Chick from the corner of his eye, and then turn away, actually trying to pretend the boy wasn't there. A shudder ran convulsively through Howell's thin body suddenly.

Chick stood beside the table, looking almost as ill as Howell, twisting his hat in his hand.

"Mr. Howell, sir—"

Howell shut his eyes tightly for a moment, then opened them. He spoke very softly. "All right, Chick. What is it?"

"Message from the house, Mister Howell, please. Mr. Barton M. Cassel wishes to talk with you up there. Double quick."

The pencil snapped in Howell's long-fingered hand. For a moment he didn't speak. Then he said, "Chick, you know Mr. Barton Cassel isn't in the house."

"Yes, sir, Mr. Howell. I do. But the house girl said it was sure urgent. He sure wants to see you at the house. Right now."

Howell shook his head. "Is the girl waiting at the gate?"

"Yes, sir."

"Then you tell her you couldn't find me. You tell her I said to tell Mr. Barton Cassel that I was down at the barracks with the men."

We sat there a long, slow, silent ten minutes after Chick walked back down that ramp. I stared along the cool, washed-down stalls, the shaded lights stirring easily in the light draft. Limber shadows wriggled on the scoured white walls.

After a long time, Howell glanced at me as if becoming aware of me for the first time.

"Uh... that's all, Walker."

"You wanted to talk to me?"

He shook his head. "No. Not now. Some other time, Walker. But if you stay here, Walker, think over what I said. We can always use good men. But not laboring in the fields."

He stopped talking. I got up and walked out. I glanced back. He'd forgotten me before I got as far as the big doorways.

The sudden glare of headlights stabbed huge gaping yellow holes in the night, appearing from behind me and lighting up everything around me.

I was almost back to the barracks yard gate, but suddenly I felt as though I were in the middle of a highway and a car was about to run me down.

I leaped to one side and whirled around.

That was when the big white car plunged into the gate under the cottonwoods.

There was an explosion when that speeding car ripped into the cyclone fence, the engine roared, the link-fence squealed and broke under the driving impact of the big white convertible. The gate folded forward and the car climbed up so it was almost to the barbed wire when the fence supports finally held and the car stalled. It hung there, three or four feet off the ground, the shattered headlights pointing into the sky.

Every man in the barracks poured out through the front doors. Handecker's leather-lunged yelling was lost and finally he gave up and ran with them. They came through the gate as every light in the barnyard, including huge floods, were snapped on, making the yard around that smashed gate as bright as day.

Beyond the prison fence there was a mild riot. The men over there spilled out of their barracks in their underpants, screaming, yelling, laughing and throwing anything they could get their hands on.

They surged against the fence, pressed against it, staring across the two yards to where the woman was standing up on the front seat of the white convertible, yelling.

I turned and moved just ahead of the first wave of laborers back to the broken gate.

The woman I'd asked for a handout the day before in Fort MacKeeney was waving a whiskey bottle. Her hair was loose, long about her shoulders. She wore a sheer powder-blue nightgown and a matching negligee.

She was so drunk she could barely stand up.

"Gentlemen," she cried, swinging the bottle in her arm. "Gentlemen, I greet you. Greetings to all of you from Barton M. Cassel and wife. Greetings."

She toppled forward and I thought she was going to fall, not that I moved a muscle to catch her. But she only braced her hand against the top of the windshield and stared at the men ringed inside the fence, gaping up at her.

"We need some fun!" she yelled. "Let's have some fun around here. What's the matter with you men? Can't you make no noise around here?"

Suddenly, her eyes focused on me. Her head moved and then jerked back. She wiped her hand across her mouth, spouting laughter. "Well, look who's here!" at the top of her voice.

She brought the bottle overhand and smashed it against the outer windshield glass. The windshield shattered in long spidery lines but the bottle didn't break.

"You," she said to me. "What's your name?"

"Walker," I said.

"Walker what?"

"Mitch Walker, Mrs. Cassel."

She laughed. "You know how to have fun? You know how to make some noise? No. Not you. Mitch Walker. Wait a minute, Mitch Walker. You're a tramp. Like all the others. All of them. Wait a minute, Walker. I got something for you. I got a quarter for you."

And she flung the bottle at me, hurling it across the front of the car with all her strength. She stood there raging with laughter. "You're all tramps," she screamed. "All bums. All of you out here."

She stopped laughing and looked around wildly, searching for something, somebody in that crowd of men. She didn't find it, and this made her laugh even louder, wilder.

By that time, two housemen had come across the yard. One of them was trying to get Mrs. Cassel to get out of the car and the other was shouting at us. "Get out of here. Go on, get back to your barracks."

Mrs. Cassel screeched with laughter. "Yeaah. Get out of here. Circus over. Go on. Get out of here. Trash."

The houseman spotted Potter and Handecker in the mob. "What's the matter with you two men, Potter? Handecker? Can't you handle these men? You like for me to tell Mr. Barton M. Cassel you can't handle these men?"

Handecker went into action. His voice cracked like whips across the backs of the retreating men. Potter began pushing and herding the men back toward the barracks. They had them lined up and marching by the time they reached the rear gate. The prisoners were still yelling at the tops of their voices for Eve Cassel to come down there and open her circus.

I thought of something and glanced around. Every man that worked on the Great Plains Empire was in that barnyard at the moment except one.

Evans Howell was nowhere to be seen.

I came up out of a nightmare with somebody's hand gripping my shoulder, shaking me.

In my nightmare I was being interrogated in a room alone with Fred Palmer. I was on my knees, already paralyzed by his expert questioning. I knew my kidneys were ruptured, a disc was cracked in my spine and the side of his hand across my neck had stunned me so I could not move my arms or legs. But I was still conscious, I could still feel every new agony when he struck me in every vital zone of my body.

I opened my eyes, protesting. The only light was from the two twenty-five watt bulbs that burned all night at each end of the barracks.

I recognized the face of Bub Turner, the barracks-master, the man in charge of doling out water in the men's room.

"Hey, Walker. Hey. Get up."

"What's the matter? What you want? What time is it?"

"About two. They want to see you."

"Who?" I sat up.

"Mr. Handecker. Mr. Potter. Out front of the barracks."

I swallowed at the sudden hot water that formed around my tongue, the taste of gall. I nodded, and stood up, slipping into my slacks.

They were waiting in the dark, about ten feet from the barracks entrance. The wan shaft of the twenty-five watt bulb reached almost to their feet on the crusted ground.

They stood on each side of me when I reached the end of the light shaft and stopped.

"Walker," Handecker said. "We want to talk to you."

"You look like trouble, Walker," Potter said.

"You went up to see Mr. Evans Howell tonight," Handecker said.

"You didn't ask us," Potter said.

"He sent for me."

"Still, man, you got to know better than that."

"When you go see anybody up front, you tell us first."

"What did he say to you?" Handecker said.

I shrugged.

"Did you say anything to him?" Potter said.

"About what?"

"Like get smart, man. We don't want no trouble. Like the fun we try to help these poor guys have."

"Cards? Craps?" I said it innocently.

"Yeah," Handecker said, losing his temper. "Like cards. Like craps. Like Old Man Hogan. Like the Mexican kid. Like anything."

"What'd you tell him?" Potter said.

"You ain't going up there no more," Handecker said.

"Why not?" I set myself on the balls of my feet, reading their slow-burner minds.

"Because next time you're gonna be smarter." Handecker spoke with a grunt, setting himself to swing.

I moved backwards before Potter could jump me or Handecker could swing that big fist. They laughed in the darkness, liking this. I wasn't going to stand still for it.

As they set themselves again, I figured it was Handecker who'd be most enraged. And the madder a man was, the poorer fighter he was. For that moment I let Potter move as he liked, knowing he would wait for Handecker to clout me first.

I waited until Handecker started that thick arm up. I brought up my right arm just enough to ward off the blow and I caught his pants and belt buckle in my left fist, twisting it and jerking upward. He came up on his toes, grunting and I bounced him like that. For a moment his body was between Potter and me.

Handecker swung with his left but I chopped the side of my hand across his Adam's apple and his fist fell before it even touched me.

Potter was trying to get at me around Handecker. Handecker was hanging helpless, unable to breathe. I danced him along with Potter, driving my extended fingers into his solar plexus with such force that he went insane with agony, forgetting the terrible agony in his throat.

Handecker sagged, sobbing and gasping for breath. Potter paused for a second, shocked that Handecker was hanging there helpless already. Why not? Hadn't I learned all this in my nightmares? Hadn't I watched that old master, Fred Palmer, cripple and paralyze men in interrogation rooms for three months? Fred Palmer. Everything a good detective should be.

As Potter paused, I doubled my fist and drove it full into Handecker's face, releasing him at the same time. His two-hundred pounds toppled against Potter and Potter cried out, trying to untangle himself before I got to him.

He didn't make it.

As he came up, I chopped him across the side of his neck, and he straightened, sprawling out on the ground. He struck on his face without even breaking his fall.

I stood there looking down at them a moment. Potter moved his head, mewling. I kicked him in the face and he stopped that. I turned and walked back toward the barracks, feeling good, feeling clean for the first time in a week, feeling cleaner than a shower would make me feel.

8

Barton Cassel was leaning against his desk, awaiting me when the houseman showed me into his office.

For a moment he didn't move after the houseman closed the thick oak door behind me. He stayed where he was, propped against the desk, ankles crossed, arms folded over his chest, a smile I made no attempt to understand pulling at his mouth.

He looked me over and I stared at him.

I know my eyes widened, my mouth drooped slightly at the sight of Barton M. Cassel.

I know what I'd expected, the sort of picture I'd built up in my mind. I figured him a man in his late forties, his early fifties, graying, arrogant with money, influence and power.

I wouldn't even have believed this man was Barton M. Cassel if the houseman hadn't said, "Here's Mitch Walker, Mr. Cassel," and then closed the door behind me, leaving me alone in this office with him.

"Sit down, Walker."

That smile stayed on his wide-lipped mouth, but he unfolded his arms, stood up, went around his desk and dropped into a gleamingly polished brown-leathered judge's chair. He rested his head against the back and went on studying me when I sat in the straight leather chair across his desk.

It was quiet in this big room. None of the sounds of the farm or of the house penetrated these walls. There was the gentle purring of an air-conditioning unit somewhere. It was the only sound except the creak of his chair springs when he moved.

The office was large, at least twenty by twenty, but looking at Cassel you knew he had to have a big room or he'd bump things when he moved around. Cassel was about an even six feet tall, which was my height, but he outweighed my one-seventy by forty pounds at the least, and if there was an ounce of fat on him, it didn't show.

But the muscled bigness of Cassel didn't knock me off balance as much as the fact that he wasn't a year older than thirty at the most, not more than four or five years older than I was, and yet he was the nearest approach to a feudal lord that I had ever seen. Sure, I had it all set up in my mind, Eve Cassel, married to an older man, bored, chasing after the foreman. God, how wrong could you be? Barton Cassel was a younger man in every way than Evans Howell, he could have snapped Howell in his hands like a matchstick. He was big, vigorous, with the driving kind of energy that never let him sit still.

"Been hearing about you, Walker," he said, not changing his expression.

I sat there waiting for the ax to fall. Either he would fire me, or he'd have me arrested for assaulting his two strawbosses last night. Sitting there, I began to see how much power of life and death he had over human beings in this part of the state. Not only his farm employees, but the people in the surrounding towns depended on his trade and his payrolls.

"I've heard a lot about you, too," I said, refusing to bow on one knee until I had to.

He smiled. "Yeah. Saw the look on your face. You expected a man old enough to be my father, eh?" He waved his arm to the large oil painting of a retiring-looking man framed on the oak-paneled wall. "That's my old man, Walker. You know why I got him framed up there? So all I got to do is look at him, and nobody even starts to walk on me. Nobody. My old man was a living doormat for half the people in this state. Sure, he made some money, but he kissed bottoms to do it. I built this. All this. And I don't kiss their bottoms. They kiss mine. Where the hell do people get the idea a man has to be forty before he can accomplish anything? You take it from me, Walker, a man can do what he wants to when he's young—if he wants to; if he's got the guts and the energy. You can get anything you've got the energy to take. That's all that matters. Not another damned thing. Men smarter than you? You meet them all the time. Only you keep moving and they don't. So maybe they're not really smarter than you after all. Hell, I meet guys all the time. Chicago. St. Louis. New York. They look at me and they say, hell, they could accomplish all I have and more. So I laugh and take another drink. You know what I tell them stupid sons? I tell them, 'So you *could* do it. And I *have* done it. That's the only difference.' No. It don't matter. You got the ever-loving energy to do something and you want it bad enough, you'll do it." He laughed suddenly. "So much for the Dale Carnegie course for today. I called you in here because I wanted to see you too. You got two of my men in the infirmary."

I stared back across that desk. "You want me to get off the place?"

Even here in this house, in this swank, deep-carpeted, polished office, I got the words I got down in the barracks; that same old question that nobody at Great Plains Empire could answer: "Where would you go?"

I grinned, because this was the question nobody believed could be answered. I slapped my slacks pocket. "How far would eight bucks take me?"

He laughed, "You're a cool customer, eh, Walker? Nobody walks on you, either."

"I wouldn't say that. But sometimes I bite at the soles of their feet."

He laughed again, swinging back and forth in his judge's chair. "Yeah. Like Handecker and Potter, eh? You got some bite. Where'd you ever learn such tactics?"

"Once I worked in the—"

"Okay." He held up his hand, halting me. Here it was again, just the way it had been with Evans Howell. Both of them let me know they weren't deceived, there was trouble behind me. But that was as far as either one wanted to go with it. Not only did they refuse to question me, they appeared anxious to know nothing about it. "Well, it don't matter where you learned it. Huh? You're quite a scrapper. Nobody will deny that."

"So what do you want me to do?" I said.

He smiled. "You got eight bucks and you're willing to walk out, eh?"

"That's right."

He leaned forward, propped his thick arms against the desk top. "Why leave?"

"Why kid about it? I was in trouble down there, and that's what you don't want. I been hearing that since the first day."

"Hell, man, don't worry about me. I can stand a little trouble. Depends on who makes it. Why, Potter and Handecker will be out of the infirmary tonight, back on the job in a day or so, better workers than ever." He laughed. "They'll be careful now. I hate a man makes a fool mistake, like overmatching himself, or going into a fight outnumbered like they were."

He sat there and laughed about this for a moment, and then he stopped laughing as abruptly as he had started. It wasn't that he was arrogant about it; he was too busy even to spend more than seconds on laughter.

"Stick around, Walker," he said. "You might work into something good around here."

"I won't be here long, anyway—"

"Well, let's look at it this way. Evans Howell can handle those stooplaborers for a day or so until Handecker and Potter get back on the job—if you will help him."

"Me?"

"That's right. Seems to me you owe me that much, don't you?" He was watching me with his mouth pulled faintly.

"If you say so."

"Oh, I'll pay you. Same as I pay Handecker and Potter. But Evans will need help out there."

"Okay," I said. "Thanks for taking it like this."

He stood up. "Hell, how should I take it? You look like a pretty smart guy. Had any schooling?"

"Two years of college."

"Why'd you quit?"

I looked at him a moment, shrugged. "Easy. I ran out of money."

"I quit too. One year. It was all frat parties and drinking and some of the stupidest courses ever conceived in the minds of progressive educators. Fine for kids with nothing to do. I was in a hurry. Well, the hell with that.

You stick around, Walker. You'll be glad you did. I can use a man like you. Sure. You stick."

He got up, walked around the desk, taking long strides, his face pulled and cold.

He heeled around suddenly. "Sure. Stick. Howell's got a lot on his mind lately. Ain't worth what he used to be to me. Might need a man to replace him, Walker."

"I want it clear. Now. Don't count on me."

"Okay. For now. But think it over. You can't lose, Walker. Stick around."

I closed his door behind me, walked along the corridor toward the front door. The hall was like a cool passage leading toward the hell of those fields. I didn't hurry. A houseman stepped out of nowhere. He'd been lurking, waiting for me.

"I'll show you out, Mr. Walker."

"Thanks." I didn't tell him I could see the front door for myself. Everybody had to earn his keep out here.

She stepped from the last doorway on the right before we reached the front door.

"It's all right, Jerkins. You can go back to the kitchen. I'll show Mr. Walker out. I want to talk to him a moment."

She was wearing another sheer negligee and she had a cocktail glass in her right fist. Her hair was loose about her shoulders, but it glowed with brushing.

She also was wearing a fat, purple eye.

She saw me looking at it, and smiled, shrugging. "How you like it?"

"Matches the rug, anyhow."

"It's what I got for breaking down that fence last night. Kind of a medal."

"Oh, you can buy a car to match it. Nobody will ever notice."

She laughed. "Nobody will dare to notice anyhow. Nobody except boors like you. Most people around here know I'm Mrs. Barton M. Cassel."

"Fat eye and all."

"Fat eye and all, Mr. Walker."

"It won't happen again, Mrs. Cassel."

"But that's it. You make a lot of mistakes."

"Yes, Mrs. Cassel."

"Stop it you stupid jerk. Are you leaving here? Are you still working here?"

"I'm on my way to work now, ma'm."

"I want to ask you something."

"Do I bow or curtsy?"

"Try listening. Are you going to see the foreman?"

"Who, Mrs. Cassel?"

"All right. Evans Howell. Are you going to see him when you leave here?"

"Yes."

"All right. I've got a message for him. I want you to tell him I want to see him this afternoon. This afternoon. You tell him that."

"Do I tell him you want to see him, or do I say Mr. Cassel wants to see him?"

Her face flushed and something happened in her eyes. Her head tilted. There were a dozen things she almost said, vile and violent things, but she controlled them all. Finally she said in a flat, hard tone. "You tell him *Mrs.* Cassel wants to see him. You understand?"

"Sure."

Her face was pale now, and there was a stricken look in her eyes. It seemed to me I was looking at a woman getting the brush. Hell hath no fury.

I turned and walked to the door.

"Walker."

I turned. "Yes, Mrs. Cassel."

"Since you figure you're so smart. You know so much already you might as well deliver the rest of my message to Evans Howell."

"All right."

"Tell him—" she drew a quick sharp breath. "Tell him he's smarter than this—or he better be!"

I found Evans Howell sitting on a camp stool in the shade of one of the buses.

He whistled when I stepped out of the jeep. "Oh, man," he said. "You're in solid."

"It was parked outside the house after I talked to Cassel. Chick drove it up from the machinery pool. Told me Cassel said I was to use it."

Howell exhaled heavily, pressed his hands against his eyes. "You helping me?"

"That's what Cassel said."

"Good. I asked him for you."

"Thanks." I stared out at the laborers. "It carries a raise in pay."

There was a sudden bitterness in his voice, "Oh, you can do a lot better than this around here," he said.

I had the certain knowledge that he knew exactly what Cassel had said to me in that office. About Evans Howell.

After a moment, he grinned. "At least you can move out of those stinking barracks. I'll fix you up a room in my building. This afternoon."

"Look. I've tried to tell you and Cassel. I'm not staying around here."

"Okay. Up to you. But you might as well be comfortable while you are here. Clean sheets, clean room—"

"A shower?"

"I told you, didn't I?"

"I'll take it."

Howell blew his whistle, gave the men a morning break which was something they never got with Handecker. And Howell didn't even look around to see who sprawled down where. He just sat on that stool, lost in his thoughts.

I glanced around, saw Old Man Hogan still bent over the vegetable rows. I walked out into the sun. "All right, Hogan," I yelled at him. "Sit down for God's sake."

"What's wrong with him?" Howell said.

"Nothing. He's afraid if he stops working, you'll fire him."

"Fire him?" Howell said. "Hell, where would he go?"

"That's what troubles him," I said.

When the men went back to work, I leaned against the bus and stared at Howell's slumped, thin shoulders. He kept pulling his handkerchief out of his pocket and wiping his hands with it. He had it bad. He couldn't sit still, as though he could not stand to be in his own skin with himself.

I had put it off as long as I could. "I saw Mrs. Cassel while I was at the house."

His wide thin shoulders stiffened. For a moment he didn't move. At last he said in a voice tired of God, tired of living: "When does she want to see me?"

"Any time this afternoon, I reckon. That's what she said."

He shivered in the blast of sunlight.

"You could always quit," I said.

He turned, staring up at me, his blue eyes starkly naked, with pain in them. "Where would I go?"

"Hell. Why don't you try it and see?"

"Look. I know you don't give a damn. Why should you? You got your own woes. You know the day I became Evans Howell? The day I walked in here and asked for a job. And I've got a good job... it used to be a good job...."

"Sure. Until you got the hots for the boss's wife."

"Is that a halo you're judging me through?"

"I'm sorry. I thought I was just saying what you already knew."

He exhaled. "Okay. You tagged it. I'm not offering any alibi. I'm not the first guy ever got caught in a hair trap. She's young, not more than twenty-four now. I never met anybody like her before." He shivered. "I thought that at first. Now I know nobody else ever has, either."

"We all got our woes."

"This is a good job. Goddamn it. It's the kind of work I love. I was born in a tenement district. I never saw a cow, never saw a field of growing things, miles and miles of it, thousands of head of dairy cows. God knows, it's the kind of work I'd do for nothing. Only there she is, plowing into fences, sending messages by every bastard on the place, calling me, coming up to the—what the hell's the use? It's a good job, but she's a dame no ten men could ever satisfy. And you know why? Because she wants something and she doesn't even know what in the hell it is. All she knows is the next guy might have it. Cassel didn't. And I didn't. Only she don't let anybody go. She needs what she's got—whatever it is."

"Doesn't she know Cassel is going to kill both of you?"

He shivered. "Good God yes. Everybody knows that. He wouldn't think twice about it. Sometimes I think that's half the thrill with her. She's daring him. So what in hell am I supposed to do? Go on like we are? Let him kill me? Leave here? Hell, I got no place to go. In fact, I could go to prison once I'm off this place, once I'm not Evans Howell, foreman of Great Plains any more." He stood up, looking around him as if he were lost in a place he'd never seen before. "Around here I'm Evans Howell. Away from here, I'm—" he shuddered convulsively and covered his face with his hands.

At two-thirty, Howell blew his whistle for the afternoon break.

He'd been edgier by the minute since the noon hour. He had held a sandwich and a cup of iced coffee in his hand for thirty minutes without even looking at them, then dropped them in the disposal container.

When the men were sprawled around, panting like animals in the sun, he said, "I'm taking the jeep, Mitch."

"Okay."

"You can break this thing up about three-thirty. Okay?"

"All right."

He walked over to the jeep, moving like a condemned man. He didn't look at me. "See you when you get back to the house. I—I'll have your room ready."

"Okay."

I watched the jeep racing across the rutted tracks toward the distant farm buildings. Dust boiled up behind the jeep. Howell drove like a man in a rush to die.

Some of the men came near the bus, looking at me as if they'd never seen me before.

"You the new strawboss now, Mitch?"

"That's right. Temporarily."

"Potter and Johnny Handecker be back?"

"In a day or two."

"You moved up kind of fast, didn't you, Mitch?"

"I'm Cassel's bastard son, didn't you guys know that?"

They grinned faintly. One of them said, "What's going to happen now?"

I glanced after the racing jeep. "Hell," I said. "Who knows? Anyhow there won't be any crap game or stud poker tonight."

I'd thought these guys would be pleased, for one night at least they'd keep a full day's pay. But their faces clouded, they looked at each other, troubled, confused. God. Howell was right. They were like animals.

"Hell, Mitch," one of them whined. "What we gonna do for a little fun?"

I stared at them. "Why, you stupid jerks," I said. "Okay. You want action. You'll have it. Tonight. Same cards. Same dice. Same stakes. Same time."

They grinned then, and looked at each other, their faces pleased.

One of them nodded and even raised his voice in a cheer. "Okay, Mitch," he said, with a lot of feeling. "That's fine."

"You're all right, Mitch."

"I'm all heart," I said.

9

Cassel stopped the jeep on a knoll that looked south across the unend-ing flat land of his farm. Down the incline on the other side was a dry creek with willows and cottonwoods growing in its bed. A rutted jeep trail wandered across the dry creek and through the flat grazeland beyond.

He cut the engine, and when the sound of the motor died, the silence was almost as oppressive as the heat.

He didn't look at me for a moment but sat there with both his huge fists gripping the steering wheel.

I didn't say anything. We hadn't talked since we rode out of the farm-yard. His face was pale, tight with a scowl that seemed as full of self-hatred as much as anything else. Something was wrong.

He exhaled, picked up a pair of binoculars from a leather case in the crevice between our seats. More silent minutes went by while Cassel adjusted the field glasses to suit himself. The expensive black binoculars looked like a toy in his thick hands.

He pressed the glasses against his eye, trailed them across his grazing cat-tle, the stoop-laborers in the truck fields, the machinery at work in the wheat sections.

I sat there, looking along that snake-trail that led north across the creek and away from the Great Plains Empire. The road looked great to me. Maybe it was the escape I'd been looking for.

"That trail down there," Cassel said, as if following my thoughts. "That there's my private road out of these parts." He sighted along it through his binoculars. "It hits a secondary highway near Wild Horse."

"Wild Horse? What's that?"

He shrugged. "Hell. What you care? A settlement. A filling station, gro-cery, a church, a whorehouse. Nothing. Just a jog in the road and they call it Wild Horse. My trail hits the road about two miles above the settlement anyhow. I like to have a quick easy way out of here, so I can duck out in a hurry in case some company is coming that I don't relish yakking with, something like that."

I waited. I didn't say anything about this trail being a quick, secret way *into* the house as well as a fast exit. It was none of my business, and as he said, what did I care? The answer was that I didn't care. He hadn't brought me out here to show me the countryside.

I sat there watching a fly on the windshield, thinking I could wait as long as he could. But he surprised me. I didn't have to wait. There was no fencing. He removed the binoculars from his nose, leaving a red rut across its bridge, and stared at me. His face was cold with that unchanging scowl.

"Had a visitor yesterday," he said.

I exhaled, but held his gaze. "Palmer?"

He reacted. Something flickered in his eyes. "You're quick on the uptake, huh? Think fast—"

"You have to think like a criminal. That's Fred Palmer's philosophy."

"Yes. He told me. Palmer seems a dedicated man."

"There's another word. Psychotic."

"Well. Like I say, I quit school before we got to that word. But he appears to have one thing on his mind. That's his job. He's not a real warm character."

"It was Palmer," I said.

He nodded. He shoved his thick-fingered hand into his lightweight jacket's pocket and brought out a folded piece of paper. He took his time straightening it out against the steering wheel. For a moment we sat there looking at my printed picture. It wasn't new. It wasn't flattering. What it was, was accurate.

"According to this Palmer, you have got a couple of stiff counts against you. Unlawful flight to avoid prosecution. Murder—"

"You want to hear my version?"

He moved his head in a negative motion and made a sharp cutting gesture with his hand.

"No. That's between you and the cops."

I exhaled again, feeling that tightening in my stomach. I had that same feeling that had struck me the night I decided to run rather than face Palmer in an interrogation room. Nobody gave a damn whether I was guilty or not. But I *was* innocent.

My voice shook now. I couldn't help it. It seemed to me that somebody had to hear the truth.

"I'm innocent," I said. "I never murdered anybody. I—"

"Look. I'm thirty-one, and I've met a lot of people, a lot of odd-balls that come to this farm looking for work. I reckon I've had as much experience with different kinds of men as anyone in the country, and I met a lot of types of men. But there is one kind I never have met: a guilty man. I've never yet met a man that was guilty of anything. They're all innocent."

"Okay." The breath pushed out through my mouth. "The hell with you."

He laughed, a dry, level sound. "That's better. Now, like I said, if you committed this murder or not, that's between you and Palmer and the police and God. But it's got nothing to do with me."

I turned on the seat, stared at him. "Hasn't it?"

"Not one damned thing. However, if you want my opinion, and I can see you don't, it's this: If you were innocent, why this other charge, this one that says unlawful flight?"

I looked at my clenched fists, the knuckles white. How could I make him believe my reasons for running? How could I tell him that for three months of unvarnished hell I'd watched Fred Palmer wash confessions out of men with boiling water enemas? I'd seen innocent men with ruptured spleens? Cracked spinal discs? That I'd seen men helpless on their knees before him because he knew how to stun a man with the flat of his hand? What did a man named Barton M. Cassel care?

This I knew. Nobody cared back there in that town where Fred Palmer had a better conviction record than all the other men on the force combined. Maybe in all the history of the force combined for all I knew. And Fred Palmer believed me guilty.

I had to give him one thing: it was an honest belief. He *did* believe that I was guilty. I couldn't prove my innocence without finding the man who actually had killed Wendy Parker. I had been there. I looked guilty, especially to Fred Palmer who wanted me to look guilty. And I had known what would happen to me once he got me in handcuffs. Sure, I had run. I had run in terror, the way you run in your nightmares, looking over your shoulder in horror, and never daring to stop long enough to breathe.

I thought about that switchblade knife I'd taken from the terrorized kid on the tenement roof that night. That kid would rather leap off that building than face Fred Palmer in an interrogation room again. That kid was smart. I agreed with him right down the line. Unless I wanted to be subjected to every inhuman cruelty ever devised until I was begging Palmer to *let* me confess. I knew I had to get to hell out of there.

Didn't stoop-labor at Great Plains Empire look like paradise to me?

I didn't say anything, I just watched that fly circling nothing on the windshield.

"This man Palmer," Cassel said. "He said if I saw you, if you showed up at Great Plains Empire, I should get in touch with him. He offered me a twenty per cent split on the reward after he deducts his expenses."

"He's getting generous. Or desperate."

"Maybe he just wants you pretty bad. It seemed to make him ill that you've gotten away from him for even this length of time."

I exhaled again, looking around. "There's just one thing. You're a pretty husky guy, but I'm telling you, just don't try to take me back to him."

He laughed. "Who said anything about taking you back?"

I felt cold. The fly flew away suddenly. Smart fly. "You want something," I said.

He stared at me, turning the binoculars in his fists. "Why don't we get down to cases?"

I felt empty. "Yes," I said. "Why don't we?"

"I like a man that's in trouble, Mitch. Now you take a man who's got trouble. Why, you can talk to a man like that, Mitch. He understands easy.

He's good to talk to."

"Yeah?"

"Right. Now me. For some time now, Mitch, maybe you won't believe this, I been hoping a man just like you would come along. Looks like I got my wish. Huh? A smart man. Intelligent. Strong."

"In trouble," I finished it for him.

"That's right. A man I could talk to." He crumpled the picture of me in his big fist. "That's why I brought you out here where we could talk. I got a little job that's been needing handling for a long time."

I breathed out slowly. "Crooked, of course," I said.

Cassel shrugged. "What else?"

After a long time of silence, I swung my legs around over the side of the jeep, got out.

Cassel's voice was sharp. "Where you going?"

"I need some fresh air."

"I better warn you, Mitch boy. Don't try anything cute. Not with me. You're smart. Clever. But this is Barton M. Cassel. You try to leave here and I'll stop you. Like permanent."

I stared into the car at him. "Like a bullet in the back?"

"Better than that, Mitch. A bullet I could explain. This is my land. All my land. I could give a hundred reasons for my having to shoot you. Without even breathing hard, I could come up with a hundred. But if you try to get away, I'll run you down. With this jeep. It's one hell of a sport on these flat fields. And nobody would ever even know anything about it. As a matter of fact, I told Mr. Palmer I had never even seen a man resembling you. So run. Only I think you're too smart for that."

"I'm standing."

"Okay. So we can be friends. Hell, you're in trouble. I got my troubles." He swung out of the jeep, came around it, leaned against the front bumper. "You got any notion of the overhead on a place like this?"

I waited.

"Just feeding the crew. But I got millions in trucks, cars, machinery, combines, tractors, pumping equipment, generator power, maintenance. Hell, that just starts it. And there's an awful loss in farming. Sometimes it's hell. Drought. No matter how many pumps I got and then rain. Rain at the wrong time. Too much of it. A depressed market. Government interference. Taxes. Insurances. Loan interests, and a hundred other costs."

I shrugged. "So it's not paradise."

"That's right. So it's not paradise. But I could make it. I could have made it. But my wife has cost me another million in parties, and travel, and waste, and destruction. Well, the party is almost over."

"And that's where I come in."

"That's where you come in." He breathed out heavily. "I'm closing a deal on a hundred and forty thousand dollars' worth of my cattle. Tomorrow. Now I'm covered by insurance on every angle. The cattle. I'll be paid off in cash. That cash payment is also insured. Nobody thinks nothing of my collecting in cash any more because I pay off so many people and so many services daily in cash. They call it Cassel-type business."

He walked back and forth beside the jeep, his shadow short and stubby, seeming to run to keep up with him.

"Now. If I was robbed of the hundred and forty thousand, the insurance company would make it good. To the penny. If I split that first cash with you, after the robbery—say I'd pay you forty grand—I'd end up with almost a quarter of a million. Now I don't pretend that would save me, but it would keep me going until I can get on my feet again, get some of the creditors off my neck."

"Hell, if a quarter of a million would save you, you could buy time with that hundred and forty thousand just as quickly."

"Smart. Only what you don't know is that when I collect that payment tomorrow, I got about an hour to pay most of it out to one creditor. A robbery would take him off my neck for a while, make me an additional hundred grand besides. Now, time has run out for Barton M. Cassel, and if you don't think it has run out for you, try to turn down this little proposition. With forty grand, you can buy your way out of this country. That's what you want, isn't it? You can disappear without leaving Palmer a trace? Forty grand would make it easy. And I'd help you."

I walked around in circles until I began to remind myself of that fly on the jeep windshield. The fact that I was innocent of murder, but I'd no longer be innocent of crime if I robbed this character even in a rigged deal, didn't seem to hoist its own weight. I had no choice. I had run because I could not prove my innocence. I still couldn't prove it. Forty thousand dollars would take me a long way from Fred Palmer.

Cassel laughed suddenly. He reached into the jeep, brought out a bottle of bourbon. "Okay, partner. Let's have a drink on it."

I nodded. He extended the bottle. I turned it up, took a big pull at it. I hadn't had a drink in so long, the whiskey almost knocked me off my feet.

10

I didn't sleep all night. I stood at the window and stared north across that flat farm country, thinking there was one thing I could do. I could walk out of here, start walking and keep walking. Once I robbed Cassel, I'd reached the point of no return.

I scrubbed my face with my hands. Who was I kidding? I'd already reached that point a long time ago.

I was truly sick by the time the stoop-laborers marched up to the buses to load at seven the next morning.

Dust boiled across the whole farmyard, almost obscuring the sky.

There was a lot of action out here today. Huge vans were loading thousands of fine dairy cattle at the loading pens. At the buses the stoop-laborers were boarding like sheep.

I walked across the yard to where Evans was waiting for the men to board the buses.

Evans grinned at me, even through the gray sickness in his own face. Welcome to Sunnybrook Farm. My own illness was the empty-stomached kind. I had the helpless feeling that I was being shoved along, and there was nothing I could do, even to delay it.

"I won't be able to make it today, Evans," I said.

I must have looked gray. He frowned, troubled, genuinely concerned about me—and him with a sickness that could turn fatal at any minute.

"What's the matter, fellow? You better get to the infirmary. You do look bad."

"What's wrong here? What's the delay?"

It was Cassel. I had not seen him approaching in the smoking dust, but I realized he must have planned to be here when I goofed off from work for the day.

"Nothing's wrong, Bart," Howell said. "Mitch is a little under the weather. He's going to take the day off."

"Oh? He is, huh?" Cassel's voice was hard. The men stopped boarding the bus, trembling at the great man's wrath. "You got anybody else to help you?"

"I can get by," Evans said.

"The hell you can. That's a two-man job out there. You get on that bus, Walker."

"The guy's sick, Bart," Howell said. "I can get Potter. He can help me out there today. I can get by."

"I won't have it," Cassel said. His voice was loud. It was a good scene. He was getting the message across to the laborers. "Everybody works around here. Every day. Or no pay."

"Look, Bart. Mitch has worked hard. No trouble. He looks bad. Let him take the day off, and he can come back tomorrow. Better to take one day than lose a week for hell's sake."

"Okay. Okay." Cassel's voice boomed even above the loading of the cattle. "Stay in your room then, but you don't get paid for today, by God, and that's an order."

I paced the floor in my room. The sickness was worse than ever. It was like a knot in my throat now. Cassel had made it look good. Everybody in that farmyard knew I was ordered to stay in my room. He had played it well. Why not? He was playing for a quarter of a million dollars.

My watch seemed to have stopped. I shook it, stared at the minute hand. It was running all right. It was time itself that was slowed down. The minutes crawled past. I had never seen time go so slowly. I had never heard of so many cattle being shipped at one time. The trucks rolled in an endless line out of the loading area going down the road to Highway 40.

A hundred times I decided I couldn't pull the job the way Cassel had outlined it. A hundred times I went over every detail. Over and over. All the time I knew I was going through with it because I had to.

I tried to stop thinking about it, tried to concentrate on what forty grand would buy me in some Latin American country. And Palmer. He'd never find me. I'd beat Palmer. I'd be free. Hell, at that moment it looked worth it. Only what had happened to time? Why couldn't they get through down there, and get out of here?

The last truck rolled through the gates. I stood at the window, my heart hammering over the empty place in my stomach. Then Cassel went through the gate in his green and white station wagon. He did not slow down or look back. He was sure of what was going to happen, how it would end. I wished I had some of his confidence, or even a bottle of his bourbon.

I wiped my hand across my mouth. He was out of here. It was time to go. I looked around the room one more time, went to the door.

As I reached for the doorknob, somebody knocked on the facing. I stopped as if I'd been poled. I didn't know what to do. I had no time to waste on anybody. I had to get out of here.

I swallowed the gall in my mouth, opened the door. Somebody else had been waiting for Bart Cassel to barrel out of here in his station wagon.

"May I come in?" Eve said.

I stared at Cassel's wife. Even in a sleek, form-molded knit dress, and that thick hair bobbling around her shoulders, Eve looked like all my troubles packed into one neat bundle and left on my sill.

I tried to keep my voice level. "Howell's room is down the hall," I said.

"I know where his room is."

"I'll bet you do."

She looked past me, across my shoulder toward my rumpled unmade bed.

"Everything's a mess," I said. "Or I'd ask you in."

"I don't mind," she said. "I'll come in anyway."

"Look. I'm in a hurry. You got Howell. He's one swell guy."

"Salt of the earth."

"And Barton M. Cassel. More muscle to the ounce—"

"An ever-loving stud, that boy," she said, voice negligent. "Now, how about you, Mitch? Don't you know how to be friendly?"

"I'm nothing but a big friendly clown."

"You don't act friendly."

"It's just that I'm in a hurry."

The smile faded around her mouth, and her gaze moved over me slowly. "Don't rush out to do anything you'll regret, Mitch." Her voice had more meaning in it than sixty pages of scripture.

I swallowed, tried to play it cool. "What kind of talk is that?"

She shrugged, and turned on the smile again. The smile meant nothing. "I don't mean anything," she said in a voice purposely empty. "Only you. And Barton M. You two have been so friendly the last few days. Friendly. Friendly."

I decided to let her have it, sharp and cold. "Maybe he's been grooming me to take over when he shoots Evans Howell."

Something flickered in her eyes, but she tilted her head, went on smiling. "Just be sure who your friends are, Mitch."

"I'm a big boy. If I want to be friends with a millionaire like Barton M. Cassel, you can't call me anything but a snob."

She shrugged, moving those shoulders so the thick curls touching them bobbled slightly. "Snob, Mitch? Or slob?"

Now I shrugged. "Sticks and stones," I quoted.

She laughed. "Barton M. never had a friend in his life that he didn't skin alive."

"Well, think how charming I'll look mounted in your trophy room." I tried to move past her.

She touched my arm. Her fingers were chilled. "Why the rush, Mitch?"

"I told you. I'm in a hurry."

She did not move her hand. Instead, she tightened her fingers. "You'd have a lot more fun staying here."

"I'm too young to die."

"Who'd tell Bart? Nobody. They'd be afraid to. He'd kill anybody who said anything about me—even if it was true."

"That must give you a great sense of security."

"Money in the bank."

"Well, you better send a message out to Evans Howell. I'm too busy. Permanently, Mrs. Cassel."

She swung, her arm lashing upward, but I caught her wrist the instant before she connected with my face.

I parked the jeep near the bus station just off Fort MacKeeney's main street. I was near the bank, but on this side street were only the unbroken walls of buildings, only an occasional passer-by. This robbery was going to take place in broad daylight. But the way Cassel had figured it, it made sense to me. It had to happen fast, on a lightninglike schedule, and I had to get out of there, going back to the farm as if nothing had happened, returning by the Wild Horse entrance, as I had left.

Something was wrong. Cassel's green and white station wagon should have been parked diagonally across the street so that when he came out of the bank, I could accost him there. The sight of one of his own jeeps across the street should allay any suspicions, even if someone from the bank walked out with him. All I had to do was sit there, my hat shading my face, and wait until he was alone.

Only the station wagon wasn't there yet.

I sweated. This was bad. Of all the angles that Cassel had considered and nailed down, neither of us had even thought I'd get to town ahead of him.

I looked around. Traffic moved slowly on Main Street. Once in a while a car passed where I was parked. I didn't look up, but everything depended on my having not left the farm. We even had my using the jeep nailed down. I told them in the farm garage that Cassel had asked me to check on something in the lower section. No sweat there.

I reached for the key, wanting to turn it on and get out of there. Where was he? What could have delayed him? He'd had a thirty minute start on me. He had gone out the front gate and hit the highway. Nothing but an accident could have delayed him more than fifteen minutes on the run into Fort MacKeeney.

I mopped the sweat away from my eyes. Where was he? Had he pulled out? Changed his mind? I knew better than that. No matter what went wrong, he wanted to lose that cash, collect from the insurance people. But where was he? It had been rough miles across that farm road to the secondary highway. I'd been careful that nobody had seen me leaving the farm area.

The hell with sitting there. I'd drive away, come back in a few minutes.

At that exact moment the green and white station wagon skidded around the corner off Main Street and bumped to a stop against the curb.

I sagged back in the seat, staring at Cassel, alone in the station wagon across the street. I felt nothing except the sickness, the emptiness.

He swung out of his car as if this were just another day like any other in his life. He glanced around, not bothering to look at me. Then he strode toward the corner and around it into the bank.

Time stopped cold.

Suddenly this side street was the busiest thoroughfare in town. I gripped the steering wheel to keep my hands from trembling.

Two kids came out of the alley and started throwing a ball against the wall. I sat there not looking at them, hoping they would go away. If I didn't look at them, they would go away. Only they didn't. *Bop. Bop. Bop.* That ball against the wall. A car went by, moving slowly. I didn't look to see who was in it, what kind of car it was. The car was gone, but the kids were still yelling over there. *Bop.* The ball hit the wall.

Suddenly one of the kids caught the ball on the rebound, and in that spirit of clean, boyish cruelty threw it as far as he could up the alley.

This kid had been reading my mind.

The other child ran screaming along the alley, followed by his companion who was laughing and yelling at the top of his voice. I sat there, shaking, listening to their shouts mixing, vibrating inside my brain.

Then somebody came striding around the corner off Main. It was Barton M. Cassel. I sat up, tense, my hand closing on the short two-by-four on the floor beside me.

Then I stopped as if stunned.

Cassel wasn't alone.

He was carrying a satchel in which undoubtedly there was the cash payment for the cattle. The satchel banged against his leg.

But I was staring at the man with him.

It was Fred Palmer.

Hell. Who else?

Except for that moment at the bus station loading platform, this was closer to Palmer than I had been since I had started running.

I turned my head, tilting it so my hat shielded my face. I felt as though a thousand spots were fixed on me. Why did I think Palmer wouldn't recognize the very shape of my shoulders?

And the worst part of it was that I got an ache in the nape of my neck. It felt like the center bull's-eye in a target. I couldn't keep my head turned. I had to see what was going on over there.

I pulled my head around slowly, painfully. They were at the station wagon now, on the other side of it.

I saw that Cassel was at least smart enough to stand so that in order to face him, Palmer had to put his back to me.

I trembled, wanting to slide across that seat and walk around the corner. But any movement over here might cause Palmer to turn. I knew he'd recognize my walk.

I turned my head, gripping the steering wheel and forced myself to go on sitting there.

I heard a door slam on the station wagon, and I turned my head enough to see what was going on.

Cassel was inside his station wagon, sitting under the wheel.

Palmer was walking away toward Main, almost at the corner. I sat there and counted to five. Palmer rounded the corner.

I closed my hand on the short two-by-four, stepped out of the jeep. No cars approached on the side street, either way.

I kept the two-by-four just behind my right leg as I walked. I didn't even want Cassel looking at it, anticipating it, trying to ward it off, even involuntarily.

I started walking across the street.

There was a sudden terribly heightened sensitivity about everything. The sun had a fierce brilliance. The cars were louder on Main. Even my own footsteps seemed to jar my ear drums. The sweat prickled my flesh along my throat and on the backs of my hands.

I opened the back door of the station wagon and got in just as Cassel had planned it.

"You bastard," he snarled over his shoulder. "You took your own sweet time."

"Where the hell have you been?"

"Never mind me, you son of a bitch. You just do your part of it without snarling it."

"Hand me that bag," I said.

"Don't panic, you clown," he said. He handed the bag over the seat. I was building up a big hate for this boy. I hated him almost as terribly as I hated myself.

I brought that two-by-four down hard against the back of his head, harder than I'd intended, harder than he ever planned. It was as though I had to hit him as hard as I could.

I had to get that hate out of me some way or I'd burst with it.

I looked both ways along the street, stepped out of the station wagon, walked back to the jeep, got in, started it, and drove out of there without even looking back.

I had to go east on Main Street. Cassel had insisted this was the most important angle of all. If anybody saw his jeep headed out Highway 40 toward the Great Plains Empire main gate, they wouldn't give it a second thought. Nobody would recognize me in that town, but everybody would recognize his jeep. He was counting on that, banking on it. Anybody see any suspicious strangers? No. Nobody but one of Cassel's own farmhands, in Cassel's own jeep, going toward Cassel's own land.

I swung the jeep east on Main. I don't know how many people recognized that jeep, but I know I saw a man I knew. He was standing on the curb as I drove past. I tried to turn my head, but I didn't know if I'd been quick enough.

Fred Palmer was staring straight at me.

11

I held the jeep at a lawful thirty after I drove past the Fort MacKeeney city limits, but I didn't want to. I wanted to plunge that accelerator to the floor, I wanted to move faster than the wind, and keep moving, and go wherever it was the wind went.

I had to clamp my jaws tight to keep my teeth from chattering in the heat. I hadn't been a cop very long, but I had seen enough to know what can happen to a guy in trouble. I held the jeep at an even speed, trying to tell myself that a robbery didn't matter much when you were already wanted for murder. But that didn't help. I was innocent of murder, maybe inside I had been praying all along for the miracle that would clear me of that charge. But I wasn't innocent of theft, not any more. Maybe before there'd been a chance I could stop running someday, but not anymore. Then I thought, the hell with that, at least now I can afford to run. I can run in high style.

I glanced at the black satchel on the floor beside my leg. I tried to think about all the things I could buy, the places I could go. It didn't do any good. Nothing helped.

A car raced past, going toward Fort MacKeeney, the wash from it shaking the jeep. I stared across my shoulder at it, feeling an unexplained fright, and I was still shaking even after the jeep had stopped.

That was when I saw the police cruiser. It was behind me and moving toward me as though it were on a line and I was reeling it in with frantic speed.

I had to fight the reaction that slapped my foot down on the gas pedal. There was a chance they were after me, but there was the same chance they were on a routine patrol. If I ran, they might chase me. I looked at the satchel. If they stopped me and found this satchel, I didn't have a chance.

I glanced around at the flat, open country. The hot wind chilled my face.

I checked the rearview mirror. They were close back there now. I made my decision. I held the jeep at thirty. If they tried to stop me, I'd take off across the plains. They could follow me if they dared, but I could outrun them in the jeep. But that was the desperation move. Meantime, I had to lay off the panic kick.

They were behind me now, and then they slid past me as if riding a greased wind. They glanced toward me. I recognized Arnie and Cotton. I kept my head tilted as much as possible.

They did not even look back.

I swung off Highway 40, going south on the secondary road. I passed no cars on this road at all. I braked down when I got to the Wild Horse turn-off, checked the highway both ways. There was not a car in sight.

I went off the secondary road onto the almost invisible ruts across Bart Cassel's far sections. Ahead of me I could see the twisting growth of trees in the dry creek. I stared ahead at it as if it were the last hiding place on earth.

Once I was past that creek, I was safe. I kept whispering this to myself.

I approached the sump where Cassel had told me to bury the satchel until it was safe for us to bring it out and share the loot.

I was almost to the sump when the small nagging sense of wrong in my stomach became a big, deviling weakness. I had been going along trusting Bart Cassel, and I had no reason to trust him. Anyhow, I trusted myself more than I trusted him.

Why should both of us know where that money was hidden?

I swallowed hard, feeling a little better, a little more secure, and relieved that my mind was beginning to click again.

I drove right into the sump where the stones were, where trees, stones, the contour of the land itself made a natural pocket for the satchel of money.

I stopped the jeep, got out, walked to the spot Cassel and I had agreed upon. I was careful to leave heel prints in the sand.

Then I ran back to the jeep, got out of there. I drove back to the twisting rutted road through the plains and followed it to the creek bed.

I pulled the jeep into the concealment of the willows in the creek, then I got out, ran along the grassy bank until I found the spot I wanted. Lightning had marked a cottonwood for me, scarring it so it looked like no other cottonwood on earth.

I knelt with the satchel and tried to scoop out the ground near the tree. I couldn't do anything but scrape hide off my fingers. The earth was crusted, like rock. I had to break the top layer before I could dig any kind of hole at all.

I looked around, saw nothing. Then I slapped my pocket, looking for the switchblade knife I'd taken from that kid on the tenement roof.

I cursed. I didn't have the knife. Just when I finally needed the damned thing, I didn't have it with me. All these weeks of carrying it, and now I must have left it in my room at the farm. I hadn't been thinking clearly when I took off from there this morning. This morning? It seemed like a thousand years ago since I'd started out on this trip.

I ran back to the jeep, found a tire iron. I broke the ground in as large chunks as I could, setting them aside carefully in the grass. It wasn't likely anybody would be snooping around here, but if they did, I didn't want the ground to look broken.

I dropped the satchel in the small hole, covered it and set the chunks of rock-hard earth back in place. I found some of the heavy topsoil and spread it around with my palm so the sand seeped into the crevices between the chunks, filling them. In a moment or two even I was satisfied. The ground looked baked hard, untouched by human hand.

Carrying the tire iron, I ran back to the jeep.

I drove the jeep up the ramp into the machine hangar. Some of the mechanics glanced up, but went right back to work.

I wanted to peg it down that I hadn't left the farm so when the shop foreman came over, I said, "Hell, I don't know what Barton M. Cassel thought was wrong over there in the lower sixty. I sure as hell couldn't find anything."

He smiled, shrugging. "You know Barton M. Cassel," he said.

"Yeah."

"By the way, Mrs. Cassel just called from the house. She sounded upset. Wants you to come up there right away."

I nodded and walked out into the sunlight. I turned toward the bachelor quarters, thinking to hell with her and her messages.

Then I stopped. This was no time to play solitaire. I didn't want to be sitting alone in my room now. I wanted witnesses to the fact that I was on this farm today. Even a witness like Eve Cassel.

I went striding toward the house. Chick was grinning and holding the gate open even before I got to it.

Jerkins opened the front door when I rang.

He nodded toward the parlor to the right of the foyer. "In there, Mr. Walker," he said. He walked away toward the rear of the house. From back there I could hear the faint sounds of servants at work, talking in a subdued way to each other.

I walked through the parlor door, stopped.

Eve was lounging on a deep divan, sporting a martini in her right paw. She was wearing the same knit dress she'd slunk up to my room in earlier, but she'd put her hair up in one of those loose-looking French rolls across the crown of her head.

But I really didn't even give her more than a glance.

"Hello, Mitch," Fred Palmer said. "Long time."

I felt the backs of my legs go weak. It seemed to me somehow it had to be like this. It wouldn't play any other way. I could run a thousand miles, but when Fred Palmer caught up with me it just had to be because Eve Cassel set it up for him.

"Don't blame me," Eve said, as if reading my thoughts. She took a long drink of her martini. "Mr. Palmer said he already knew you were here."

"Sure," I said.

"Have a drink, Mitch," Eve said. "I need somebody to drink with me. Your friend Mr. Palmer doesn't drink at all."

"My friend." The bitter words tore out of me.

"I am your friend, Mitch," Fred Palmer said. "I've always liked you, Mitch. From the day they assigned you to work with me. You never liked me, but I was sorry about that. I always liked you, Mitch."

I watched Eve get up and pour me a martini. Then she got an olive very carefully from an iced container, touched it against her mouth with a faint smile on her face, and dropped the olive into the glass.

"Sure, Palmer. You always liked me. You liked me so much you were willing to railroad me for murder."

Palmer winced. "That's not true, Mitch." Eve brought the martini to me where I stood unmoving. Maybe I couldn't have moved if I tried. I took the drink, held it without looking at it. "I know how you feel about me. I know that you always hated my tactics, the way I did things. I never offered any apology. I been a cop a long time. After a while you get so you hate the guts of every criminal. You look in their sneaking, sniveling, lying faces and you feel like you can't stand to hear them mouth one more lie. But I never railroaded anybody, Mitch."

"Oh my God."

"No, Mitch. Never. They were guilty. They were always guilty. It was something inside me. I could *feel* it, Mitch. I knew they were guilty no matter what they said, no matter what anybody else thought. I just had to make them say so, that was all, Mitch."

Now I took a drink.

"I never tried to railroad you, Mitch. No. You were with that girl. Once she had gone out with me, but after you came along, Mitch, she fell for you. Wendy fell for you—"

"A hell of a motive for killing her."

"But she wasn't faithful, Mitch. Not even to you. Oh, I found out—after she stopped seeing me. I began to watch her. I spent a lot of time watching her, and I found out she was crossing you, Mitch. With several guys."

"Look, get this straight. It might be the last time I ever get to talk to you outside your torture chamber—"

"My God, Mitch—" he sounded deeply offended and hurt.

"—so get this straight. She was never crossing me because I never gave a damn. I never wanted her. She was never anything to me. Never. Nothing. I went there that night to tell her I didn't want her calling me any more, I didn't want to see her any more because I'd never cared anything about her, and it was no use kidding her. Only when I got there she was already dead. But you wouldn't believe that. You wouldn't believe anything except that I had killed her. I had seen what you could do to men once you got them in your torture racks, so I cleared out. That's the truth, and the hell with you."

He said, softly, "You never should have run, Mitch."

"No. I ought to have stayed there and gotten the rubber hose treatment, the scalding water enema. No thanks, it made me sick just to watch that happen to other poor devils."

"I never would have tried to railroad you, Mitch."

I took another drink. "For God's sake, you talking for Mrs. Cassel's benefit, or mine? You can save your breath."

"No, Mitch. I'm talking to you. I came after you, because the FBI could have got you for unlawful flight across state lines. You made a lot of mistakes, Mitch. I knew I had to take you back."

"The hell you say. Torture. That's all you live for. That's why you chased me out here where Eve Cassel could tell you who I was, where I was."

Eve laughed. "Oh, I'm a real hellion, Mitch. But don't give me any medals. He knew you were here."

"That's right, Mitch," Palmer said. "I got into Fort MacKeeney. I talked to a waitress at the Fort MacKeeney Café. A young blonde lady named Dot. I told her I was a friend of yours, looking for you, trying to help you. I showed her your picture. After she was sure I wanted to help you, she said you had been in—"

"Oh, this boy has got a way with the women," Eve Cassel said, moving the cocktail glass along her lips.

"So then I had to think what you'd do. And I kept hearing about this place. It seemed like an answer. I came out, and first Mr. Cassel said he didn't know you. I suppose that's because he has hundreds of migrants working for him. But then I told Mr. Cassel in town today to be sure and tell you—if he did see you—that a man named Mel Long confessed last night to the murder of Wendy Parker. So there's no charge against you any more, Mitch. You are free."

The room spun. One moment Palmer was on the couch and Eve was standing there jawing at me. The next moment Eve was on the ceiling and Palmer was sailing around with her.

I reached out, caught the back of a chair with my hands. That was the first I realized I had dropped the martini glass.

From somewhere I heard Eve saying, "You're messy, Mitch. Breaking glasses, spilling gin on my rug. Barton M. Cassel won't approve of that at all."

Barton M. Cassel. I stared at them wheeling around the room before me and suddenly it seemed that Barton M. Cassel was already in the room, skidding around it with them.

I hung on, gripping the back of that chair.

"He doesn't take freedom with any grace, does he?" I heard Eve saying to Palmer.

"Mitch. Mitch, what's the matter?" Palmer said. "Are you. sick?"

Sick? I didn't know what I was. All I could think was that Bart Cassel had known before I slugged him, before I took that satchel from him, that I was cleared of the charge of murder. That I was not guilty.

"Sit down, Mitch," Palmer was saying. "Everything is all right."

All that time I had walked across that street, gotten in that station wagon, Cassel had sat there, knowing I was not guilty of any crime. What had he said? Something about how long I took getting there.

"Mitch can do anything he wants to now, can't he?" Eve was saying.

"I hope he'll go back with me. It would be much better if he cleared everything up."

I pushed the back of my hand across my numbed mouth. I *had been* free. For a few hours this morning I had been in honest man, guilty of no crimes. But that was no good now. Now I was a man who'd stolen a hundred and forty thousand dollars.

I heard the front door open, but I didn't even turn around. I was staring at nothing. All I was thinking was that I had hidden that money where Barton M. Cassel was never going to find it.

I leaned against that chair and watched Eve Cassel run across the room, like a loving, dutiful wife. Sheriff Mason helped Barton M. Cassel in, let him down in a big chair.

Cassel's head was swathed in tape and gauze, and the bandages were tinted red. He sat down heavily and looked about, still groggy. But he was conscious enough that he didn't want Eve fluttering around him, and he spoke to her sharply: "Let me alone, Eve. Get away from me."

"Why, Bart, what's the matter?" She played the aggrieved wife very well.

Mason said, "Mr. Cassel was held up and robbed, Mrs. Cassel. In town. We been warning him for years about his habit of walking around with so much cash."

"Hell. He sneaked up. Nobody could take me," Cassel said. He rubbed his hands across his eyes.

"Did you catch the thief?" Palmer said.

"No. We might of got him, but Mr. Cassel took out after him, head banged up and all before he reported the crime to my office. We put an all points out, but so far we've drawn a blank."

"What kind of car was it?" Palmer said.

"Hell. I don't know. A Ford. I know that. Light blue, I think." Cassel put his hands over his face. "Sure dirty car. Four or five years old. I chased it, but—my head—"

"How about the license number?" Palmer said.

"I don't know. Mason's asked me all this, Palmer. I didn't get that close—"

"Not even to see what state the license belonged to?"

"No. I told you no. What difference would it make? Most of the time they steal a license when they're going to pull a job like that, don't they?"

"I don't know," Palmer said. "Do they?"

Cassel glanced up at him, face rigid and white.

Palmer gave him an odd smile, turned away, looking at Mason. "You know, somebody robbing him like that in town. Funny. I was just talking to him. I was telling him I no longer had any charges against Mitch Walker here. I didn't see any blue car around."

"You mean you didn't notice one." Cassel's voice was cold with contempt.

"Well, yes," Palmer said. "I guess that's what I mean. I didn't notice one."

But I knew what Palmer meant. He meant that if there had been a blue car he would have noticed it. Routine.

He looked straight at Mason. "I did see one of his own jeeps across the street when I talked to him."

I felt, more than saw, Eve's face move, her gaze stabbing at me.

"So what?" Cassel said. "My jeeps are in town all the time. Mason knows that."

"That's right," Mason said. "But I see Mr. Palmer's point, Barton. It could have been one of your employees."

"Who else would know more about you carrying cash in big amounts, and when?" Palmer said.

"Nobody even knew when I was going to collect this money, Palmer, except me and the man that paid it through the bank. They got in the cash to handle the deal, and we closed it today. Now which one of my employees could know a thing like that?"

"You never know," Palmer said. "You never know how word like that can get around."

"I know it didn't get around, Palmer," Cassel said. "I don't operate that way. It was some guy figured to jump me for whatever I had on me—"

"And just happened to hit the jackpot," Palmer finished.

"That's right. Everything except your tone," Cassel said. "I don't like that."

"Now, now, take it easy, Bart. I'm sure Mr. Palmer is trying to help. But I admit that I go along with his idea that the robbery might have been committed by somebody right on this farm." The sheriff turned and looked at me. "We better question them, Bart."

"If you want to waste time," Cassel said, snarling. He pressed his hand against his head. He didn't have to act about that head wound. I had really clobbered him. But the way I felt at that moment, I hadn't hit him hard enough.

The sheriff had not pulled his gaze from me. "How about you, Walker? That your name? You were here on a fugitive rap."

"I was cleared of it," I said. My voice was weak. "Remember?"

I was staring at Cassel, but he didn't even glance my way.

"Still, the temptation of money is a big item in the mind of a man on the run," the sheriff said. "I'm afraid you're going to have to account for where you were all morning."

"He was here on the farm," Cassel said. "He was here when I left."

"I saw him here," Eve said. "An hour or more after Barton had left the farm."

"He wasn't around when I got here," Palmer said.

"Thanks," I told him. "Any time I can do you a favor. Mr. Cassel had me ride out to check an irrigation flow in the wheat fields."

"That's right," Cassel agreed.

"I'm not trying to get you in trouble, Mitch," Palmer said. "I'm trying to help."

"Who needs enemies," I said, "when they've got you?"

"I was just thinking," Palmer said. "You could prove that you never left the farm.... Do you keep a mileage record on the jeeps, Mr. Cassel?"

"No, we don't. That's for towns, and small runs. Besides, what in hell would mileage prove? It's farther from one side of this farm to the other than it is from here to Fort MacKeeney. You wouldn't prove a damn thing with mileage. I'll tell you how you can prove if Walker left the farm. Call down at the gate. Check with Lefty. He'll tell you if Walker was through there today."

"Good idea." Mason was already lifting the phone. He spoke into it, listened a moment, replaced the receiver. "Lefty says Walker never left the farm through that gate."

"And there are no other exits from this farm?" Palmer said.

"My good buddy," I said.

"It's going to come out sooner or later," Palmer said. "If we pin it down now, we can clear you, Mitch. And you can go back home with me."

"Well, I can answer that for you," Eve said. "There are no other gates off this farm. I'd know."

Palmer shrugged. "Well, that's fine. What do you say sheriff? You want to hold Walker?"

"We might want a few more questions answered," Mason said. "But I don't see why he couldn't leave here with you if he wants to."

"Leave?" Cassel sat up. "Where you going?"

"He's cleared of that murder charge, Mr. Cassel," Palmer said. "I explained that to you in town. He can go anywhere he wants to."

"Hell," Cassel said. "That's what I mean. Why should he leave here? Young guy. I can use a guy like him. He's got a great future right here on this farm with me. Hell, he's a young guy I've come to depend on. Why should he go anywhere?"

12

"All right, Mitch, where is that money?" Bart Cassel's voice struck at me like deer shot. It was the first thing he said when I walked in his bedroom just before three o'clock that afternoon. "I want it."

"Sure. Go and get it," I said. I stared at him on that bed, his head swathed in fresh bandages.

"No." His voice was cold. "You go and get it."

"You must be nuts," I said.

"I'm not nuts. And don't go making any other stupid mistakes about me, Mitch. I'm in bed for one reason. I want it to look good for the cops and the insurance adjuster. Don't think you can get cute with me because I'm in this bed."

"I'm not about to touch that money," I said. "You think they won't be watching? You think just because Palmer and the sheriff left and pulled the deputies out of the house they wouldn't be watching for just such a stupid move?"

Cassel's face was rutted. "Sounds real clever, Mitch. Sounds like you might think you've got all the angles figured."

"You know you can't walk out there and pick up that money."

"Yes. I know." His voice was cold, and his huge fists were clenched on the bed.

I stared straight at him. I suppose he could see the hatred that had been like a sickness since I'd learned he'd known before I took that money that another man had confessed to the murder of that girl back home. The bastard. He didn't give a damn what happened to anybody as long as he got what he wanted. Another skin for his trophy room.

I kept my voice level, with the kind of innocence in its tone that wasn't innocence at all, but told him to make what he wanted to out of it.

"Sounds to me like you're the one not being very smart, Bart. The great Cassel. God knows you ought to know you got to leave that money alone until it's safe to touch it."

"That would be fine. If I knew where I could touch it."

"What's that supposed to mean?"

"I warned you, you bastard. Stop playing cute. I tried to get that money. In the sump where I told you to leave it. It wasn't there."

"Maybe somebody stole it."

"You're damned right somebody stole it. Only you're not going to get away with it. You've made the dumbest move you ever made."

"Did I? How smart was it to go romping around in the sump looking for that money?"

"Get one thing straight. I'm Barton M. Cassel. I can go anywhere on these two hundred sections, and nobody can question it. If you'd been smart, you'd of left that money there, and we'd have something now."

"You'd have something now."

He stared at the backs of his fists. "And just what do you think you've got?"

"Well, unless the bank short-changed you, Barton M., I've got a hundred and forty grand."

"Decided you'd keep it all, eh?"

"Not when I planted it in a new place. No. I was still going along with you. But I didn't want you outsmarting yourself by trying to outsmart me. So I put it where it would be safe."

"Okay. Go and get it."

"No"

"Look, Mitch. I'm trying to keep my temper. You push me, and we'll blow this deal. Go and get that money."

"No. We're not going to blow any deal, Cassel. If we had any deal, it was off when you didn't deliver Palmer's message to me in town."

His laugh was a snarl. "So that's what's eating at you, is it?"

"That's what's eating at me."

"So you've decided to cut me out of my money, eh?"

"That's right. You crossed me. I been through hell. Plenty of it. I was clear. But you fixed me. Somebody has got to pay me for all that hell."

"So you elected me?"

"If you want to look at it that way."

His hand moved on the cover. "Do you think you can get out of this place alive if I give the order to stop you?"

"I think I can. Because as long as I'm alive, you've a chance to get that money. But the minute I'm dead, you'll never get it."

"Might be worth it to me."

"Sure. Only you're in a spot. You're in debt. You couldn't stand to have anything happen right now."

"You feel pretty safe."

"Rich, safe, young and lovely," I told him.

"I'd hate to be in your shoes."

"Maybe neither one of us would like to change. So why don't we just drop all this?"

"You think I'm going to let you walk out of here with a hundred and forty thousand dollars of my money?"

"You are unless you want the roof to fall on your head."

Now his laugh had a tone of cruel pleasure in it. "Oh, boy, I love this. I love it when you clever boys think you got ole dumb Bart Cassel by the short hairs. Ole country boy like Cassel. You think you can really take him."

"I think I'm going to try."

"Well, you better clean out your think pipes, buster. You think you been in trouble before, but you been living high."

"Not like I'm going to, Bart. And I want to thank you. If you'd told me what Palmer said in town, I'd be an honest man, but free. Now I'm almost as dishonest, as immoral and vile as you are. But I'm a rich man."

"Sure. You stupid clown. I could have told you, there in Fort MacKeeney. We could have danced in the street, sang happy songs. You were free. Cleared of all charges. How lovely? And what then?"

"You wouldn't be out of a hundred and forty grand, for one thing."

"Buster, this little game hasn't even begun yet. You try to take that money, and you're a dead little duck."

"It's a chance I'll take."

"This is my last offer, Mitch. I want you to think about it carefully. You bring that money to me, and when I get it fenced, I'll give you the forty grand I promised. We forget this little mistake you made."

I was staring at him. "Fenced?"

His mouth twisted. "Oh? Didn't I tell you? That money has got to be sold somewhere. Every thousand dollar bill of it is hot. Like radioactive. That's one reason the cops pulled back. They were all so sorry for me, but then the bank told us that we don't have anything to worry about. All that money will be recovered the first time any of it appears. They kept a record of the serial numbers. Just trying to protect good old Barton M. Cassel who wouldn't listen to reason, but insisted on dealing in cash. So now it looks like we're back where we started, and you've got to trust me."

I stared at the pictures on the wall, the drapes at the windows, the rectangle of yard I could see through the pane, white with the sun on it, silent and white.

I shook my head. "No. I'll still keep it. I might have to travel farther and oftener, but I'll make it."

"You'd never spend more than one of them."

"I might."

"Have you tried to imagine what it's going to be like? You trying to run from here to the Mexican border with a satchel of hot money?"

"Like you told me, don't worry about me."

"I don't. I'm just trying to make you see some reason before you hold a gun to your own head."

"Hell," I said. "I've had it that way so long now, I wouldn't be comfortable without it."

He lifted his fist, waved toward the door. "Okay. Get out of here. But let me warn you. When you walk out that door, I'm turning Palmer loose on you."

"What for? He doesn't want me any more. He told you that. What you going to tell him? That I robbed you?"

"If I can't think of anything else."

I jerked my head toward the phone beside his bed. "Be my guest. You tell them that. And I'll swear you waited for me in town until I took that money, that you met me afterwards—before you went to the sheriff and reported the robbery—and that you got a hundred thousand of that money. Hell, I'll tell them you got all of it."

"You think anybody in the state of Kansas would take the word of a tramp over Barton M. Cassel?"

I shrugged. "Maybe not. But you got the insurance people to think about. Maybe they won't even believe me. But they'll investigate you because I'll swear you told me you were on the verge of ruin—"

He laughed again. "Who'll believe that? I still got plenty I can sell off, plenty of ways I can hang on."

"Sure. Like I say. Maybe they won't believe me, but they'll have to audit you, they'll have to investigate. And right now you can't stand to be investigated. When they find out how deeply in debt you are, they'll know that you did plan a fake robbery."

He chewed that over for two full minutes. Neither of us spoke. His face got so white, it matched the sheet on his bed. But at last he smiled, his lips taut and gray.

He stared up at me.

"Go on. Get out."

I frowned. Things hadn't changed that much that he was now willing to allow me to walk out.

But I decided to play it along with him. He wasn't going to panic. Neither was I. But I had a feeling of wrong, of some gimmick that Cassel had come up with that I knew nothing about. Maybe things had changed more than I realized. Because suddenly he wasn't fighting any more.

We stared at each other another moment and then I shrugged, turned toward the door. I was walking out, but I had a hellish feeling, as if I were in a lion's cage, and the lion himself had politely held the cage door open so I could leave.

She was waiting for me at the foot of the stairs.

Eve had the honor of being runner-up to her husband in the person-I-least-wanted-to-meet stakes.

Her face was chalky and her hand gripped the newell post. She looked at me as if I were a fellow conspirator in some dangerous plot.

"We can't talk here," she said as I stepped off the stairs.

I kept my voice low. This was easy because I was drawn taut, my throat almost closed. I felt as though I was wearing a target on my back and Barton M. Cassel was drawing a bead on it. I had tried all the way down those steps to figure why it was he'd decided to allow me to walk out of there.

"No," I said to Eve Cassel. "You're right. We can't talk here. But we can't talk anywhere."

"Not here."

"It doesn't matter," I said. "Because we haven't anything to say to each other, anyhow."

"I've got to talk to you." I had never seen her like this. She was pleading.

"I'm on my way out of here," I said.

"You can't leave now."

"I've got to leave now. Barton M. gave me his okay. He might decide to rescind it."

She caught my arm, gripping it. "Please. Listen to me. It's after three. Stay just until the buses come in, until Evans gets back."

"Even if I was nuts, why should I do that?"

"He's going to kill him."

"Cassel is going to kill Evans?"

She nodded, her mouth trembling. "Please. Not so loud. Stay. Just long enough to warn him out of here. He'll be back with the men."

I stared at her. "I thought you got a large charge out of all this hell you were causing."

"Please. Not now. Maybe I've been evil. Insane. But Bart told me—he's known about me and Evans for a long time—he is going to kill him. Please, help me. Just wait until Evan gets back down there."

I walked out of the front door. I had been sweating inside the air-conditioned house. The yard made me as wet as a steam bath.

I felt as though Bart Cassel were standing at that upstairs window looking along a gun barrel at me as I walked across the yard.

Chick pulled open the gate and I went through it, hurrying toward the machinery pool. There was one thing I wanted. I wanted a jeep that would take me as far as the Wild Horse turn-off. I had to get that money and get out of here.

I still believed that if there was a hundred-dollar bill in that satchel, I could buy a plane ticket to Brownsville, Texas, or somewhere on the border. A hundred-dollar bill wasn't going to attract enough attention, even in a travel office, to have its serial number checked until it got to a bank. Anyhow, this was a gamble I'd have to take.

All I wanted right now was a flying start.

I was almost to the machine garage when I heard the buses rolling into the yard, coming around the milk barns.

I paused, looking over my shoulder. I didn't have time to waste warning Evans Howell out of here. Maybe even if I told him there was a bullet waiting for him, he'd look at me with that sick face and ask the Great Plains Empire stock question: "Where would I go?"

I'll never know why I walked through that lower gate and moved toward the buses as they unloaded. The men spilled out, glancing at me.

Potter stood alongside the buses, watching the men. He looked sweated down.

I didn't see Evans anywhere.

"Tom," I said. "Where is Evans Howell?"

Potter nodded at me. "He's not with us."

"Where is he?"

"Beats hell out of me, Mitch," he said. "Barton M. Cassel come out to the fields in his station wagon and picked Evans up right after we got out there this morning. Evans ain't been with me all day. It's been hell trying to handle it by myself. I don't know why Evans never did come back."

I looked around, wildly.

All I could see was fences topped with barbed wire. It seemed a mile back to that machine garage. Suddenly I had the feeling that Cassel had anticipated that move anyhow. I was sick, willing to bet they had orders to refuse me a jeep. Why should he help me rob him?

Just the, same, I wanted to get out of there, and there was no way out.

I heeled around and had to fight to keep from running toward that lower gate.

"Mr. Walker!"

"Señor Walker!"

I paused, chewing at my mouth, and looked over my shoulder. Jose and Old Man Hogan came running toward me.

"Please, Señor Walker," Jose said. "Just a minute."

"Some other time," I said. My voice was shaking.

"Señor Walker. Today we talk with Señor Howell—"

"When?"

"This morning. Just before he left fields with Boss Cassel. He said he was worried about you."

"I'm all right."

"You been good to us," Hogan said. "Since you come around, Jose and me been treated better."

"If you need anything," Jose said, "both Hogan and me got a little money. You can have it if you need it to get away from this place. Hogan and me want you to let us help you if we can. In our small way."

"No. I'm all right," I said. "Thanks. You two take care of yourselves."

They wanted to say more, but I turned and strode away toward the gate.

At that moment I heard the screaming from the messhall porch. I stopped as if stunned, listening. I knew that it was a man screaming down there, but the sound had the high keening wail of a terrified woman in it.

13

I stood there listening to the strange wailing scream of the man at the messhall.

Everybody in the barrack yards was running toward the messhall. Men near the gate ran past me, shouting. I heard the prisoners on the other side of the fence yelling as they converged on the messhall. When they reached it, they crowded up on the porch, pressed against the fence.

I did not move.

Jose and Old Hogan heeled around and ran with the herd toward the messhall.

I stared at the gate, but I did not move toward it, either. They were shoving it closed and I saw Handecker standing there watching them.

The gate slammed shut and Handecker began to blow shrilly on his whistle. The sound of the whistle was almost lost in the raging screaming of the prisoners.

I could see them milling around the messhall porch, leaping against the fence. Those men didn't give a damn what had happened, but they were not going to miss a chance to scream at the tops of their lungs, add as much to the confusion as they could. The two guards stood helplessly, afraid to move into that crowd even to try to break it up.

All I could think was that I would have been out of the farm yard, almost to the last gate before the creek if I had not wasted those minutes coming out here looking for Evans Howell.

I stared at the closed gate, at the strands of barbed wire across it. I did not really believe that I would have gotten away.

I began to see I was never going to escape.

When I could move at last, I walked slowly past the buses and the barracks, going toward the messhall.

I reached the outer rim of the workers. They were staring silently at the Chinese cook who seemed to be in an hysterical state on the porch.

Ling was standing only because Potter and Handecker on each side of him were supporting his arms.

Ling's mouth was sagging open. His eyes were distended. He was trying to speak, but none could understand him because in his terror he had forgotten how to think in English.

I pushed through the closely packed rows of men. At first they grunted, protesting, but when they recognized me they stood aside. I walked up the steps to the porch when all I wanted was to run.

"He can't do nothing but spout Chinese," Potter said to me. "Let's take him inside."

Ling must have understood this because he began to shake his head violently. His body trembled and he tried to writhe free.

Potter and Handecker merely lifted his feet off the floor and pushed through the swinging screen doors. I turned and told the herd of men to stay where they were and I followed. The prisoners were still raving beyond the fence.

Inside the messhall, Ling quieted down some. He pointed toward the rear of the kitchen. I took his arm and the four of us walked past the serving counter and into the rear pantry.

When we stepped through the pantry door, we stopped.

Ling had opened a freezer door and Evans Howell's body had toppled out, and it was still sprawled on the floor, face up. There was a knife handle projecting out of Howell's solar plexus. He was rigid with cold and stiff in death.

None of us spoke. I heard the men talking outside and then the messhall doors were pushed open.

Maybe I should have been surprised when I saw Barton M. Cassel with the sheriff and a deputy come across the messhall toward us. Maybe I should have been, but I wasn't.

I stared at the pleased expression on Cassel's face and I realized that the sheriff had been on his way out here when I was up in that bedroom talking to Bart.

No wonder Bart had let me walk out of there. He had been trying on this frame for size. No wonder I hadn't been able to outguess him. And in that moment I knew why he'd been late getting into town to the bank this morning. He'd had a little matter of murder to attend to first.

Only I knew how far I could get trying to prove that.

The sheriff was bending over Evan's body. He glanced up, spoke over his shoulder, "Here's something that might be a final answer in this here killing, Bart."

"Yeah, sheriff?" Cassel could barely control the smug smile. He spoke to the sheriff but he was staring at me.

"This here knife that killed young Howell," the sheriff said. "It must belong to somebody out here. It's a switchblade. Anybody know this knife?"

I didn't speak. I didn't even glance at the knife handle sticking up out of Evans Howell's chest. I was staring at the chilled smile on Cassel's face. I didn't have to look at that switchblade knife.

I knew it.

It was mine.

I felt myself tighten up. No wonder I hadn't taken that knife with me this morning. It had already been stolen from me, and I was too fouled-up when I left my room to pay any attention to its loss. When I'd needed it out there at the creek, the explanation had seemed simple: I'd just forgotten it.

Now I knew better.

I stared at Cassel. No wonder he was barely able to conceal that cat-eating grin. He'd killed Evans Howell, and he'd decked me out in a neat, snug-fitting frame.

"Anybody know this knife?" Sheriff Mason said again.

I went on staring at Cassel. His mouth was twisted and he seemed to be waiting to hear me ask for a noose around my neck. I didn't move.

But I heard the stirring of the men around me.

I wasn't the only one who recognized that knife.

"Sheriff." It was Handecker speaking. I winced. His voice sounded apologetic, mildly reluctant.

Cassel said, before Mason could speak, "All right, Handecker. Speak up. What is it? Is that your knife?"

"My God no!" The words burst across Handecker's mouth. His lips were still split from our debate the other night. But he forgot any slight pain that speaking caused him. Any reluctance to speak up, to tell what he knew, disappeared at Cassel's suggestion that the knife in Howell's chest might belong to him. "No, sir. That knife ain't mine. But I seen it before."

"Where?" Mason said.

Cassel relaxed now, standing there, waiting. One thing he could not conceal was the anticipatory pleasure that glinted in his eyes.

"That knife is a switchblade," Handecker said. "The only one like it that I seen around here."

"Go on," Mason said.

"Well, sir. One night down at the barracks we had reason to take up all the hardware—the knives and razors—any of the boys might have on them. I remember because it was the first night that... that Mitch Walker showed up here."

I heard the slight exhalation as Cassel breathed out.

Sheriff Mason glanced at me.

"I don't know if that knife still belongs to Mitch Walker or not," Handecker said. I'll give him that. He didn't mind beating a man's head in, but nailing him for murder was something else again. Handecker wasn't happy with what he was doing. "He might of got rid of it since then. I mean he might of sold it, or give it away. But he had it with him that night."

"Is the knife yours, Walker?" Mason said to me.

"It was mine," I said. "But I lost it. Even if it is mine, I had no reason for killing Evans. He was good to me."

"We'll worry about that later," Mason said. "If Evans happened to learn the truth about you, that you were wanted for murder, that might be a motive—"

"But I was cleared of that."

"You didn't know you were cleared until after noon," the sheriff said. "Like I say, we'll worry about that one when we come to it. We'll have to wait until we find out just when poor Howell was knifed and shoved in here."

Cassel shook his head. "It's one hell of a thing. We take a man like Walker in—and have something like this happen."

The sheriff showed no compassion. "We've tried to warn you, Bart, you take men in, migrants, without checking on them, you're bound to have trouble. Just like the way you carried big sums of cash on you until somebody slugged and robbed you."

"I reckon I been wrong all right," Cassel said.

"Maybe it's taught you something," Mason said. "Maybe you'll listen to us next time."

"I'd sure be a fool not to," Cassel said. "Yes, sir, I reckon I've learned a lot today."

"I didn't kill Evans Howell," I said. My voice shook.

"Now, son, let's not have any trouble," the sheriff said. "You'll get your chance to testify in your behalf."

"I'm not going to get any chance at all, and you know it," I said. "I never had a chance from the day I walked on this farm. Hell, I had no reason for killing Evans. But Cassel did."

"Me?" Cassel looked shocked. "My God, boy, what are you trying to pull?"

"I had no reason for killing Evans. But you did. You knew he'd been crossing you with your wife for months."

Cassel lunged forward. His big hands came up and before I could set myself, before anyone could stop him, he had closed his fists on my throat and borne me over and down on the floor.

The sheriff spoke sharply. His deputies, along with Handecker and Potter pulled Cassel off of me. It took all of them to do it.

I stood up slowly, breathing through my opened mouth. "You son of a bitch," I said straight into Cassel's face.

He jerked free of them, but I was waiting for him this time, and he took a step forward before he saw that I was ready, and he paused.

They grabbed his arms, and he let them.

He said, gasping, "I ought to kill you. For talking like that, I ought to kill you."

"Sure," I said. "Why don't you? One more kill won't make any difference to you."

He tried to lunge free again. But the sheriff stepped between us. Mason stared at me. "You're in trouble enough, boy," he said. "Making wild accusations against the lovely wife of the leading citizen of this state ain't going to buy you much from people like us."

"Hell," I said. "I know that. So what have I got to lose?"

"I don't know, son. I'd kind of think careful, though. I'd keep my mouth shut."

"You might. But I'm not going to. Hell, Cassel killed Evans Howell. Ask Handecker. Potter. Potter told me that Cassel came out there this morning and picked Howell up at work, and Howell never came back out there. Isn't that true, Potter?"

Potter looked as if he were going to fall. He had never even thought anybody would ask him to accuse Barton M. Cassel of anything. He moved his head, and tried to speak, but there were no words.

I glanced at Cassel. I could see the wheels turning in his head. It was almost as if I could follow the way he figured. There were almost two hundred men on that field when he picked Evans up in his station wagon. Among them, one or two would have guts enough to tell the truth. It could not be concealed that he had picked Evans up early this morning.

"Hell, Potter don't have to answer for me," Cassel said. "Sure, I picked Howell up. What was so strange about that? Ain't he my foreman? Ain't I allowed to make decisions about the men that work for me?"

"And the one that goes to bed with your wife," I said.

The sheriff caught my shirt. "Shut your filthy mouth, killer."

Cassel looked as if he would shed tears of gratitude for the sheriff's intervention on his behalf. "Thanks, Mason. God knows what this killer thinks he can serve by defiling the fine name of my wife, but I reckon you got to expect things like this. But I brought Howell back to the farm, told him what I wanted done, and let him out. I had to get into town to close that deal for them cattle. That's the last time I've seen this poor boy until now."

"That's good enough for me, Bart," the sheriff said. "We'll have to have the coroner out here, but we don't need to have you subjected to vile abuse from this man. We'll take him on in and lock him up."

"I hate to see any man locked up for murder," Cassel said. "But I'll thank you for getting Walker off my land. Much more talk like that and I'm afraid I'd kill him. Sheriff, I want you to question the men on this farm. Ask any of them if they know of anything except the very finest behavior from my wife."

"No, sir," Mason said. "I wouldn't insult that lovely lady by giving any credence to the vile things this man has said here today."

"Not even if I could prove them?" I said.

Cassel looked as if he were going to jump me again. The sheriff's face was white. "You'd be a lot smarter to keep your mouth shut, man. You got all the woe that you need."

"Only I'm not going to take it. I wasn't even on this farm when Cassel picked Howell up out on that field."

"You're a vicious liar, as well as a killer," Mason said. "We've got witnesses that testified you never left this farm."

"Some of them don't know what they were talking about," I said. "Some of them were lying."

The sheriff's laugh was harsh. "Funny, everybody lies but you, huh?"

Cassel shook his head.

I said, "Bart Cassel is the only one who has truly lied, all the way. He knows I was in town because he blackmailed me into agreeing to rob him. I was in town before he got there. And he knows I was."

"Sheriff, I'm telling you. This boy is insane."

"Sure I am," I said. "So insane I wouldn't turn over that money I took from Cassel—which he handed me across the seat of his station wagon of his own free will, before I hit him with that two by four. But I can prove I didn't kill anybody on this farm, because I can take you to that money. I hid it. And that will prove I was not on this farm this morning."

The sheriff hesitated. He glanced at Bart, then at the deputies.

Bart said, "Hell, sheriff. It's a trick. He thinks he'll have some chance to get away."

"Sooner or later, sheriff," I said, "you're going to have to take me to the place where I hid that money, because you'll never convict me of murder because of it. That's one story I'll stick to as long as I'm alive."

The sheriff considered a moment. Finally he scrubbed at his chin with his fingers. "Okay. We'll take a run to this place. I'm in favor of getting this here lie nailed down for once and all."

The deputy parked his car beside the creek. After a moment Cassel arrived in the station wagon with Handecker and Potter.

The sheriff ordered a deputy to link me with him in handcuffs. Then I led them down the embankment toward the tree that had been scarred by lightning.

"First," I told the sheriff, "I better tell you this. This is part of Bart Cassel's land. But like you saw, we came through a maze of fences, cutting sections off from other sections. It's all very clever. We are now on open range. There is no fence at all between here and Road 27. There's a turn-off about a mile north of a place called Wild Horse. And if you know how to do it you can get on Cassel's ranch and off of it without going through any gate after you leave the farmyard."

"Well, if that's true," Cassel said, "it's news to me."

The sheriff laughed in a cold way. "It's Walker's fairy story," he said. "Let's go along with him all the way. We don't want nobody saying we didn't give him every fair opportunity."

"Sure," Bart said. "Let him hang himself. Only he's wasting your time."

I pulled the deputy along after me down the grass embankment. The tree stood, scarred with gray streaks. But when I got to it, I knew it was no good.

There was no gaping hole, but I knew how I had left that satchel covered. I could see already that the hole had been opened and carelessly closed, hurriedly.

I fell on my knees, grasped the loose chunks of gravel and jerked them from the ground. I threw them aside, dug with my bare hands. But the hole was empty. The satchel was gone.

I just stayed there on my knees, staring at the empty hole I had dug for myself.

14

When the sheriff got me in the cell at the county jail, he stood outside it looking in at me as if he could not understand a man like me.

"You make up your mind, Walker, to behave yourself in here," he said. "You'll have it a lot easier."

"Listen to me, sheriff. I robbed Bart Cassel. He planned it, and I robbed him."

"Look, boy. I got no robbery charge against you. Now forget it. If you robbed Cassel, like you claim, you'd have that money. Right? I gave you every opportunity. Seems to me I bent over backwards to give you a chance to prove what you said. Now, I'm sick and tired talking about that robbery. When you're ready to talk about how and why you killed Evans Howell, why you send for me, and I'll come any time of the day or night."

"I didn't kill him. I wasn't on that farm."

"Look, boy, we fought all through that. We got the testimony of both Mr. and Mrs. Barton M. Cassel that you claimed you was sick and you stayed right around that farm all day."

"Mrs. Cassel might have thought she was helping me to say that. But Cassel is lying, and he knows he's lying. He planned that robbery—"

"Lay off that robbery. I told you. You show me the money you are supposed to have taken, and I'll listen to you on that subject. But not until. And if I was you, I'd lay off that talking against Mrs. Cassel. It ain't going to help your chances with the good people in this here county."

"She admitted—"

"Stop it. Now, we got other witnesses that say that though you took that jeep you never left the farm in it."

"I showed you how I could have left that farm and nobody would even know anything about it."

"Oh, you had a getaway planned clever. You found out something that even Barton M. Cassel didn't know—"

"The hell he didn't. He showed that road to me."

"He says he didn't, boy. And his word is better than yours. His wife says she didn't know you could leave their land that way. Now we got witnesses that place you on the farm. We got people to swear that for two hours every morning after the breakfast is cleared away, there's nobody down at the messhall. You could of lured Evans down there and killed him. It looks like that's what we'll prove that you did."

"I wasn't there, damn it. I was in town, waiting to rob Bart Cassel. The way he planned it."

"You're charged with murder, Walker, and it's my duty to warn you that anything you say from now on can be used against you."

"Would it make any difference, sheriff? You think I got a chance?"

"You don't help your chances any by dirtying the names of highly respected people."

"Do I even get a lawyer?"

He shrugged. "Sure. Why not? You'll get a fair trial."

"Sure, I will. So send me a lawyer."

Now he laughed in a sharp way. "That might not be so easily done, Walker."

"Why not?"

"A lawyer that defends you won't make himself popular around here. Especially if you keep accusing the Cassels of wild crimes."

I prowled the cage, walked back to the bars where he stood watching me, that puzzled look still in his face.

"Maybe I could just hang myself," I said, my voice bitter, "here in my cell."

He shrugged. "You could confess. To murder. That would help."

"Don't sit up waiting for that to happen, sheriff."

He shrugged again. "Likewise to you, don't think it's going to buy you anything to keep talking about robbery and accusing a lady of Mrs. Cassel's position of ugly, vile things."

At seven that night Cotton Powell came on duty in the cellblock.

"What happened to your cruiser?" I asked him.

He shrugged. "Arnie and I had a little mix-up. So I got guard duty for a month." He dragged his nightstick across the bars and grinned at me. "I don't mind guarding you, Walker. It makes it a real pleasure."

I turned and walked back to my cot. I flopped down on it. I heard him walking away. I did not look up. I stared at a crack in the floor, going over all of it for the hundredth time.

I could still remember how Cassel had suddenly told me to get out, to take that money and clear out. I had thought at the time this was phony. Cassel wasn't going to give up like that unless he had a good reason.

He had dozens of good reasons.

He had known the sheriff was on the way. Maybe he was even amazed that Ling or one of the other cooks hadn't already discovered Evans Howell's body in the freezer. This would be one of the first doors the cooks would open in the messhall when they came in on the afternoon shift.

And then later, down at the creek, when I found out that the money and the satchel were gone, I had expected Cassel to show some emotion, but he had seemed scarcely upset at all. There was one explanation.

Cassel already had that money.

And that brought me around in that tight little vicious circle. How had he gotten it? I had not hidden it in the sump. He could not have trailed the jeep, even if he'd had the time to do it on that hard-packed earth. And he hadn't had the time. He had gone back to the sheriff's office. They had bandaged his head and brought him out to the farm.

Then I stopped. He hadn't had much time. If he'd had to search for that money, he would never have gotten it. But he had known where I put it.

How?

"Hey Walker."

I sat up slowly, troubled, sick. I turned on the cot.

"What you want?"

"You got a visitor. You want to see him?"

It was Fred Palmer.

Palmer sat down on the kitchen chair without its back prop. Cotton locked the cell door and walked away.

"I got permission from Sheriff Mason to see you," Palmer said. "I'm leaving in little over an hour. I'm taking the train back."

"Palmer, I need help."

"That's putting it mildly. I'm sorry. I'm washing my hands of you, Walker. Tell you the truth, all the time I was hunting you down for murdering Wendy, I couldn't make myself believe you had done it. But it looks like Howell threatened to expose you and—"

"But I wasn't guilty."

"You didn't know that, Mitch. You see, Howell was killed in the morning. They had some trouble pinning down the exact hour because the freezer had changed the condition of his stomach contents, as well as lividity, body changes. But they figured from the time he was last seen alive. He was put in the freezer after the noon crew left the messhall. You were back on the farm then. Everybody knows that."

"Fred, listen to me."

He smiled. "Oh, now I'm a friend of yours? Now when you got your neck in a noose, I'm not Palmer the killer-cop any more. I'm good old Fred."

I stood up. "The hell with you. I might have known you wouldn't listen."

"Oh, I'll listen. Only I've heard most of it from the sheriff, and it doesn't make much of a case for you. If you had been involved in the robbery, and had produced that money, it might have cleared you of the murder charge. Maybe—"

"I was sitting across that street when you walked around the corner with Cassel this morning."

"And you just went on sitting there, knowing I was looking for you?"

"Didn't you see the jeep?"

"I see everything, Mitch. But I don't buy it that you would sit quietly with me across the street from you."

"Still I know you were there. I was afraid if I started up the car, tried to leave, it would attract your attention. So I sat quiet. Then after I took that money, I stared right at you when I drove the jeep past you on Main Street. You were standing on the curb."

"You make a convincing picture, Mitch. I noticed the jeep. I even thought it looked like you in that jeep. But when I got out to the farm, you were there. And if you robbed Cassel, where is the money?"

"I don't know. If Cassel saw me bury it, he could have dug it up, hidden it again, then gone back to the sheriff."

"He could have. But how could he have seen you out in that flat country, treeless and open, and you not see him or his station wagon? You were in the creek, and he would have had to be in the open. I can't believe you would have hidden that money, if you ever had it, without checking to see that nobody was watching you. If he could have seen you, you could have seen him."

I felt my heart slug faster.

I stared at Palmer, walking back and forth. I was doing what he always had done, thinking like a criminal. For the first time I was trying to think what Cassel would have done.

"I know how he did it." My voice rose with the excitement in it. "I know how it had to be. He came out of it after I slugged him. He knew where I was going, and he drove out there. He knows that country better than I do. He knew how to watch me without my seeing him."

"Yeah?"

"Binoculars. Field glasses. I remember he checked on his whole farm one day through those powerful field glasses. I was with him. He could bring almost any spot right up close."

"So he got the money back and framed you for murder?" Palmer shook his head.

"Hell yes. I was the sucker he was waiting for. A man on the run. When I came over to the station wagon, after you had told him I was cleared of killing Wendy Parker, he didn't even mention it. He had me where he wanted me. He knew his wife was having an affair with Evans Howell. He wanted to get rid of Howell, and he wanted to frame me for that murder so he could keep all that money for himself. He had my knife. That would be easy enough for him to get. He told me in front of all the workers to stay on the farm, setting it up in their minds that I would be there. I thought it was because he was giving me an alibi for the robbery, but it was so I would have no alibi at all when Howell's body was found—with my knife in it. Hell, maybe he didn't even need that money. It might just be gravy. He had to throw me off so he could set me up in a frame for killing Evans."

"That's a pretty wild story, Walker."

"It's the truth!"

He shrugged. "I hope you have success with it. I don't see how you can make a jury believe it. I'm a friend of yours, whether you believe it or not, and I can't buy that story, You couldn't ever prove any of it."

"But maybe I could. If you would help me."

"Me?"

"You chased me out here, Palmer. I might as well tell you the truth. I was afraid of your torture chamber. I knew I was innocent, but I didn't know if I could stand up under your torture. That's why I ran. It's the only reason I ran. I was innocent and I couldn't prove it. I was scared to face you. I'd seen too many other men do it. But I know you can do a good job of investigation. Maybe the very best. And I'm desperate. I need you. Looks like you owe me this chance to prove I'm innocent."

He lifted his left arm, pushed his cuff back and glanced at his watch. I saw the wan light glint on something under his coat and I held my breath, my heart began to pound fast. He shook his head. "I'm leaving. On the train. In just a little while, Walker. I'm sorry. I'd help you if I believed you. But I don't believe you. It's that simple."

He exhaled and moved to stand up. I glanced along the cellblock. Cotton was not down there.

I set myself and brought the side of my hand down across Palmer's neck in a judo chop. I put everything I had into it, all the fear, all the terror, all my strength.

Palmer didn't make a sound, there was no outcry. He didn't even grunt. There was the sharp exhalation of his breath and then he plunged forward on his face near the cot.

I knelt beside him, feeling the panic making my hands tremble. I fought his small Police Positive from his belt holster. I'd seen it glint when his coat moved. I was thankful Fort MacKeeney was a small town and that Cotton Powell was a stupid guard. Almost anywhere else they would have searched a visitor to a jail cell and removed his gun.

I shoved the gun in my pocket. Palmer was out cold. I lifted him with my hands under his shoulders.

I set him back on the backless chair. But he sagged and would have fallen off again. I shoved the chair around so I could lean him against the side of the cot. It left him propped in an awkward position, but all I needed with Cotton Powell was a little time.

I stepped away from Palmer, left him in almost a crouching position on the chair, tilted toward the cot. I moved to the bars, standing between the light and Palmer.

"Cotton!"

The guard came around the corner at the end of the cell block. I held the gun behind my leg, and stood waiting until he was just outside the barred door.

"Yeah, killer? What you want?"

He was standing just beyond the bars. He hadn't seen Palmer yet.

I brought the gun up, held it where he could see it. His face showed his sickness.

"Open the door. Move fast or I'll shoot you."

I let him look at Palmer to convince him I was not joking. He began to nod. He found the key, and with his hand shaking, unlocked the cell door.

I stepped through it, took his gun from him.

"Get inside the cell," I told him.

"You're not going to get away with this, jerk," Cotton said as he stepped past me.

Something in his voice reminded me that I hated him, and I didn't even stop to think about it. I brought the butt of his own gun down across his skull, and then I stood there just long enough to see him crumple slowly to his knees and topple forward against Palmer. He knocked Palmer off the stool and both of them fell to the floor like toppling dominoes.

I turned then and ran toward the back door of the cellblock.

15

I was doing seventy in the sheriff's cruiser when I approached the Wild Horse turn-off on the county road. I was pushing the light car so hard that it swayed on the narrow, empty road. All I could think was that I was insane to be back out here. If they caught me now they wouldn't even try to take me back to a cell. It would be easier just to shoot me on sight.

I found that turn-off onto Cassel's land as if I were on radar. It was crazy to get back in that maze. Before I'd been a killer in the sheriff's eyes, now I was a fugitive killer who'd slugged a guard and stolen a cruiser.

I slowed enough to make the turn and that was when I saw those head-lights bouncing out on those flat fields, lunging in wild yellow shafts upward in the darkness.

In a reflex action I turned off my own lights. I didn't even stop to think why. All I knew was that I didn't want any cars out in those fields to see me make a turn off the county road onto Cassel land.

I let the car slow, keeping my foot off the brake. I didn't want even a red glow to attract the attention of the people out there.

I did not hesitate in making the turn, though. I went off the highway, found the ruts like a mole going hell-bent through its burrow.

I let the car continue to slow down, watching those crazy careening lights out on the fields.

Finally, I was barely moving, just giving the cruiser enough gas to keep it rolling.

Those two cars out there were moving as though driven by two hopped-up jalopy jockeys. They seemed to be racing. The first car was moving slowly, as if its driver were feeling his way along in unfamiliar terrain.

But nothing was slowing the second car. I couldn't guess what kind of speed it was making across the grass fields, but it was bouncing and never slowing.

It would come near the first car and then the first car would abandon that cautious movement and race forward. It was as if the first car were far more powerful, faster than the second, and there would have been no con-test if the driver in the first car had known the land out here as well as the second driver.

The second car overtook the first, the headlights raking along the side of it so that I recognized it as a convertible. Eve Cassel's Cadillac convertible.

The reflected light showed me that the other car was Bart Cassel's sta-tion wagon.

He brought the station wagon hard against the Caddy. The Cad was jerked hard away, but he maneuvered quickly, turning with it so the big car was forced around in a circle.

They had almost completed the circle when the station wagon moved faster and cut in harder.

The Cad was jerked around so suddenly that it skidded along for a moment and almost went over on its side. The station wagon stalked it, cutting sharper, sharper, like a trained cowpony herding a bunch-quitter.

Suddenly the Cad was given a burst of gas and it leaped past the front of the station wagon. The bumper on the wagon raked a long line along the Caddy, and then the Cad was caught on the wagon's bumper and I saw it going upward and then spilling out on its side.

At the very last instant before the wagon was caught in the overturning metal and whirling wheels, it was cut hard away and leaped free as the bigger car struck on its side, its headlights cutting strange wild paths in the darkness.

I was near them now, but the station wagon driver never saw me. He was too intent on that Cadillac.

He whipped the wagon around in a wide circle and fixed the lights on the overturned Cad, the dust boiling up gray around it in the night.

In the glare of the wagon's lights I saw a head appear at the upper door of the Cad.

It was Eve Cassel.

She stared around wildly in the light of the station wagon. She pulled herself upward through the window and toppled along the side of the car toward the ground.

As she slid along the side of the car, the station wagon raced in toward her.

When Eve let herself down over the side of the car so her feet were reaching for the ground, the station wagon came right at her, its headlights pinning her against the underside of the upset car.

For a moment she stood in paralyzed terror staring at the onracing station wagon and then she ran around the front of the car.

The station wagon skidded to a stop only inches from the car. If she had not moved, he would have crushed her against it.

The station wagon was reversed in a screaming of gears and then it leaped to the right, going after her around the front of the car, trying to drive her away from it, out into the open.

I wanted to yell at her to stay where she was. As long as she could keep moving at all, that overturned car was going to offer her the only protection she'd find on this field.

But she was too full of terror. She ran around the car again and when the station wagon raced after her, she stood for a moment undecided and then ran away from the car into the darkness. She was running into the open and by now I knew that Bart Cassel was at the wheel of the station wagon and that he would run her down in this open field. Great sport.

I didn't know what had happened between them, but I knew that Bart at least was completely insane by now. I could not even figure how he could hope to kill his own wife out here on the fields and get away with it. And then I knew that was because I was not Barton M. Cassel, accustomed forever to doing whatever he wanted to do, and getting away with it.

As I stepped down on the gas, driving toward his station wagon, the cruiser lights still killed, I began to see that he would replace her battered body in the overturned Caddy.... And he was driving right now, racing toward her without ever doubting for a moment that he would get away with this next murder; that he was going to come up like roses.

I saw Eve stop running suddenly and stand in the headlights. She brought up something in her hand, and I saw it was a gun. She fired toward the onrushing wagon as though it were a rhino and she were going to bring it down before it could crush her.

Her gun cracked, showing a blast of orange fire in the darkness. Her bullet smashed into the windshield of the wagon so it ebbed out in a thousand lines and cracks directly in front of the driver.

At the last moment she leaped wildly out of the path of the wagon and it roared past her.

Cassel was already slamming on his brakes. He was headed directly at me, and I stepped hard on the gas, reaching out at the same moment and turned on the cruiser lights, stepping on the bright-button. For a moment those lights would blind him. They might even scare him so badly for an instant that he would be off balance.

It happened that way.

It was all so fast it was hard to say how it did happen. I had my gas pedal pressed against the floor.

He was trying to brake down for a quick left turn and another run at Eve when my lights blinded him. He jerked the wheels hard, stepped down on the brakes with all his power, bucking to a crazy stop.

The cruiser plowed into the wagon. The sound was deafening, the impact of the two cars, the scream of metal. The wagon was thrust hard around and the cruiser plowed deeply into it before it stopped.

My headlights were smashed, one twisted so that it sent a beam directly upward. The other was fixed across the wagon and upon Eve who had stopped running in the field. She was staring at us as if a miracle out of heaven had suddenly spared her life.

The door on the driver's side was thrown open by the impact of the crash. In the moment after the cars stopped, Bart Cassel was already moving out of the car.

He landed on his feet and wavered there a moment. Maybe he was only barely conscious. He staggered as though he didn't even know where he was. But conscious or dazed, he made a fatal mistake. He lunged toward Eve, stumbling in wild drunken steps.

She brought up the gun and shot him.

She stood there and pressed the trigger. The sound of that gun was louder even than the crash of the cars had been. For a moment I did not move.

I saw Bart Cassel straighten and then go backwards under the force of the bullet, and then he caught his balance, lost it again and fell forward on his face.

I jumped out of the car, ran around it. Eve did not move. By the time I got to Bart Cassel he was dead.

I knelt beside Cassel's body a moment, then I heard Eve moving in the grass behind me.

I straightened slowly, standing up. When I had knelt over Bart's body, Eve had stood as if in a catatonic trance. Now she turned and ran toward the Caddy.

"Eve!" I yelled.

She didn't stop running. She didn't even slow down. My voice was loud in this flat open plain, and it was as if the sound of it made her run faster.

"Eve."

I ran after her, yelling her name.

Just before she reached the overturned car, she stopped running abruptly and heeled around to face me.

I slowed, staring at her stark, rigid face. Her eyes were distended in the light from the cars behind me. Her face muscles were stiff. Her eyes were as vacant as the deepest reaches of this black night.

"Eve."

She brought the gun up, and I yelled at her again.

Abruptly the lights behind me were like floodlights, many lights, all of them reflected in her black vacant eyes.

I stopped, legs apart, and turned staring over my shoulder.

There were four cars in a semicircle around the smashed cruiser and the station wagon. I didn't have to see who was in them. I knew that the sheriff and his deputies had followed me, and they had come out on this field in darkness just as I had, and I hadn't seen them because I hadn't taken my eyes off Bart and Eve.

I heard them getting out of those cars, heard the doors slam, and the voices, the crunch of boots on the crisp grass as they came toward us.

Then I heard Eve's voice, and I turned around. Even with the glaring lights in her face she was not aware of them. She was talking to me, wildly, warning me.

"Don't try to stop me," she said.

I stared at her, feeling the creepy sense of shock along my neck. She still didn't know those people were there. Maybe she didn't even know me. But she brought the gun up slowly.

Someone shouted at her from behind me, but she did not hear them. Nothing changed in her face. There was nothing there any more to change. There was nothing but death in her face. She was alive, but everything inside her had been killed.

"Eve." I lowered my voice, trying to hide the shock at what I saw in her face.

I was less than a foot from her. I had kept moving toward her because there was nothing else I could do. I saw her hand tighten on that gun.

"Eve."

She shook her head, wavering, and I snagged her wrist. I twisted the gun from her grasp.

She stared up into my face. I didn't know if she recognized me or not. Her voice was as empty and soulless as her eyes.

I heard the sheriff and his deputies surround us. She was unaware of them.

"He killed Evans," she said in that flat, soulless voice.

"It's all right, Mrs. Cassel," Sheriff Mason said. "We were here. In the dark. We saw it all."

One of the deputies had moved past us to the overturned convertible. He played his flashlight inside. Then he reached in and brought out the satchel I had taken from Bart Cassel in Fort MacKeeney that morning. I stared at it. It was in Eve's car, and she'd been running. No wonder Bart had tried to run her down and tried to kill her.

"Here's something, sheriff," the deputy said.

The rich leather of the satchel gleamed in the headlights, shining.

Eve turned her head, stared at the satchel. She lunged away from me, grabbing at it. Before anyone could move, she jerked it away from the deputy, hugged it against her.

"No," she said in that spiritless voice. "It's mine. He killed Evans."

"Come on, Mrs. Cassel," the sheriff said. "Let me take you in to town... to the doctor."

She tried to writhe free of his arm, and she would not release the satchel. I put my arm around her. "Come on, Eve," I said. "Let's go."

She glanced up at me, nodded, and did not resist. We walked slowly toward the sheriff's cruisers. The lawmen followed, silent.

Suddenly, she stopped walking. Her voice quavered. "Where are we going?"

"We're going into town, Eve. You're going to be all right."

"No." Her voice did not rise, but there was terror in it. She tried to pull away from me. "I can't go.... I shot Bart. You know I did. You saw me shoot him. I can't go to prison. I'd die.... I—"

"It doesn't matter, Eve. He tried to kill you. They saw it. The sheriff saw the way it was."

She smiled then in a strange vacant way that made me shiver. "Yes. He's dead. Bart's dead. He can't lie any more... You saw how it was, Mitch."

"Yes. I saw how it was. He can't hurt you any more."

"He can't hurt me any more?" She turned and looked up at me, eyes wide and empty. She was still unaware of the sheriff's men around her. She cried out suddenly, a heartbroken sound. "He doesn't need to hurt me any more. He's already hurt me.... Already hurt me.... He killed Evans. That's why I had to shoot him, Mitch. You see how it is."

"Yes," I said. "I see how it is."

THE END

ANY WOMAN HE WANTED

BY HARRY WHITTINGTON

1

When I got my first gander at the girl witness they were questioning, I lost interest. Ernie Gault and I had been on our way home that night when the cruiser radio crackled, ordering a prowl car to investigate a robbery-murder at Climonte's grocery, corner of Third and Halsey. I was tired, riding with my head on the back rest, hat tilted over my eyes, but I could feel Ernie tense at the wheel. Ernie Gault was a cop twenty-four hours a day. He slowed the black police sedan, pulled the speaker off the hook and told the dispatcher we were in the neighborhood and would meet the prowl car at Climonte's.

I sat upright, sighing, but not bothering to protest. Third was almost deserted in the pelting rain that danced off the Plymouth hood. Dim lights of street lamps and closed shops shone palely in the puddled gutters.

Ernie parked outside Climonte's grocery behind a cruiser, and was out of the car before the motor died.

I got out, checking the shabby, deserted street. This was Ernie's neighborhood, but I felt a cramp in my guts, the way I always did in a place like this. I shivered. The street brought back all the poverty and hunger and hell of my childhood.

I followed Ernie across the streaming pavement, feeling the rain pepper my shoulders. A bell rang when I opened the door of the dingy corner store. Two prowl cops glanced up, then turned back to question the girl.

Sam Reynolds, a robbery-detail man, had beaten us here and was trying to calm her enough to make sense of what she was saying.

She couldn't stand still; her splayed fingers wove nervously through her thick black hair, and when Sam turned from her to tell Ernie he'd called an ambulance, she tried to run.

Ernie touched my arm and I followed behind the counter and along the stacked shelves to where the grocer lay with blood gurgling from a hole in his stomach.

"Take it easy, Mr. Climonte," Ernie said. Mr. Climonte was breathing fast, like a hummingbird, because he had been robbed and shot and because every time he breathed, the spurting blood and the pain reminded him he was going to die, that he was almost dead.

"Can you tell us anything, Mr. Climonte?" Ernie squatted beside the man on the floor. Somebody had propped Climonte's head on an old jacket.

I leaned against the shelves behind the counter, checked the small store once for any signs of the armed thieves, knowing I wasn't going to find anything.

"Can't you tell us anything at all, Mr. Climonte?" Ernie repeated. He put his hand under the old grocer's head and lifted it gently. Ernie glanced up at me then, his face stricken, said, "Mr. Climonte is a friend of mine, Mike."

"That so?" I watched the rain oozing along the front window, large swollen drops spilling across the old-fashioned lettering: CLIMONTE'S CORNER GROCERY. It figured. Climonte would be a friend of Ernie's; this was the type of friend Ernie cultivated.

"Yes. A good friend." Ernie stared around the store. "Where's that damned ambulance? You said you called one, Sam." Realizing that his frantic tone was upsetting the old man, Ernie tried to smile. "We trade here with Mr. Climonte. Isn't that right, Mr. Climonte?"

Climonte was in his late sixties, a round man with a round head, and tufts of white hair over his ears. His clothes were shabby, even his apron was torn. The big supermarkets had put him out of business ten years ago, only he had refused to recognize the fact. He stared up at Ernie Gault, too full of agony to answer.

"Doctor." His voice quavered. He clawed at the blood-fountain in his pot belly.

Ernie tried to pull his hands away, but they scrabbled back.

"Doctor's coming, Mr. Climonte." Ernie nodded again and again. "Just hang on."

Suddenly the girl talking to Sam and the two prowl-car cops up front let out a scream. The sound ripped through the small store.

Ernie replaced Mr. Climonte's head on the folded jacket and jumped up, looking around.

"What's the matter, Mike? What's happened?"

I shrugged. "Relax."

"What happened?"

Ernie saw the girl was fighting at the cops, clawing and wailing. He hurried toward them, a small, wiry man in a cheap suit and scuffed, resoled shoes. He was very plainclothes. His collar was loose, his wrists hung from shrunken shirt cuffs and tight coat sleeves, his shoulders were round with the worries he dragged around on them.

"What's going on now?" he asked Sam.

"Girl's all upset, Mr. Gault," Sam answered. He was big, beefy and young, but he showed Ernie a lot of respect. Most of the men in the department did. Ernie was so honest you couldn't even laugh about it. Since he'd been promoted to lieutenant, I was about the only one with detective rank who called him by his first name. But then, I was the only one in the department he owed money to. A debt four years old and still plaguing the poor little bastard. I had told him to forget it, but I knew he never would.

"What's the matter, Miss?" Ernie put his hand on her shoulder, trying to soothe her.

"Don't touch me!" She trembled convulsively as she backed away. That was a laugh. Ernie was old enough to be her father, and all he ever thought of was his job.

"She's had a bad time, Mr. Gault." The detective nodded toward bruises on her arm. "She was in here when those young punks came in. They—roughed her up some. She—saw them shoot the old man back there. She's all shook up."

"I see." Ernie glanced around, as if looking for the ambulance that still hadn't arrived. "Take it easy, girlie. You're all right now. When the doctor comes, he'll give you a sedative."

"I'm—all right" The girl swallowed hard. She twisted her mouth, trying to smile at Ernie. "I'm sorry I acted up. It was so terrible, all so terrible."

I spent half a minute looking her over, fighting down a grudging admiration for the way she was laying it on. Thirty seconds was more than I would ordinarily have spent on her kind, but two or three things about her were off key.

She wore her thick black hair shoulder length. Its curls were snarled, partly from the rain and maybe partly because someone had waltzed her around the stacked canned goods with a grip on that hair. A cheap orlon sweater sagged on her. Though something in her face pegged her as sixteen at least, even without makeup—and she wore none—the sweater front was as flat as a boy's, or that of a girl under twelve.

I checked the hips in the cheap skirt, slim legs and feet encased in bobby sox and spattered saddle shoes.

I didn't bother looking at her anymore.

"Mister." Climonte was writhing on the floor. "Please—help me."

"Hang on. I told you. The ambulance is on its way."

"Mister. If—you—you'd ever been shot like this—you'd know—"

The rain was harder now at the window. "I had one, pop. Just like it. So I know the score, and I can do you just one favor."

His round head nodded, sweated. "Yes?"

"I can tell you. Calm down. The more frantic you are, the more blood will pump out of that hole."

He stared up at me, his eyes filled with silent panic. He didn't answer.

Ernie Gault came along the aisle behind the counter. From the street came the distant cry of the ambulance siren.

Ernie knelt beside the dying man. "The ambulance will be here in a minute, Mr. Climonte."

But Climonte couldn't pull his eyes off my face. He was staring up at me as if he were looking into the face of the devil himself.

Ernie touched the old man's shoulder in a soothing gesture, stood up. "One break, Mike."

"Yeah? What's that?"

"The girl. Thirteen. She saw it all. Got a good look at the two punks that shot Mr. Climonte."

I tried to keep my lips from twisting with the bitter taste of contempt in my mouth. "She giving your boys a full description, huh?"

"Like I say. She got a good look at them."

The front door pushed open and rain blew in. A man with a medical kit shut the door with his shoulders. He stood a moment, looking around in a nearsighted, muddled way.

Ernie saw him and hurried toward the front of the store.

Doc Yerrgsted recognized me. "Mike Ballard." He waved to me, smiling.

He was a slender man in his late fifties, with thick wavy hair deeply indented at the temples of his high forehead. His brows were thick and the nose over his heavy gray and brown moustache was large. His chin was strong but his eyes were weak, the color of bourbon, and focused with difficulty.

I nodded toward him and Ernie stopped him near the front of the store. "Doc. This girl here is in a pretty bad way. Needs a sedative."

"I'm no G.P., Gault," Yerrgsted said. "I'm just the medical examiner. Where's the stiff?"

"Back here, Doc." I grinned at him. "Only you're a little early. He's still alive."

Climonte moaned at my feet.

Yerrgsted scowled, paused long enough to glance at the girl. As his eyes focused I saw them grow cold. He had spotted the thing I had noticed about her. He shrugged, stepped around Ernie without speaking and walked back to where I stood over Climonte.

He stared at the man twisting on the floor.

"What the hell is this?" Yerrgsted said. "They told me there was a corpse. They got me out of a warm bar."

"They tried to kill him," I said. "But he's a tough one—he's hanging on. Is there anything you can do for him, Doc?"

"Not unless he's dead." Yerrgsted pressed his fingers against his eyes. "I don't have to remind you, Ballard, I'm the M.E."

"Please, Mister." Climonte raised a blood-streaked hand.

"See what you can do, Doc," I said. "Mr. Climonte is a good friend of Ernie Gault's. The Gaults trade here. Charge account."

Doc Yerrgsted winced. He glanced first at Climonte's round face that was becoming very white, then at his own trembling hands. He laughed in a dry, self-deprecating way. "He's a friend of yours, Gault, and you want me to touch him?"

Ernie stood looking down at the grocer. "God knows we'd appreciate anything you can do, Doc." His head jerked up and he glared at the front window. "That damned ambulance. Thirty minutes to get here."

Yerrgsted shivered almost imperceptibly. He knelt beside the man on the floor. His voice took on an old smooth bedside tone. "You understand there might be some trouble with the G.P.'s if I were to take that bullet out of you?"

"Please. Help me."

"They might charge I was drumming up trade for myself as medical examiner. No. Better leave that bullet where it is. Fleshy part of your belly." He opened his kit, took out a hypodermic and needle. "Few little things I can do to make you comfortable and stop that bleeding, fix you up so you'll ride safely to the hospital—after that I can't guarantee you a thing. Right?"

His voice was smooth, cheerful, as if there were some huge joke on himself, Climonte, and the world, and he was working swiftly as he talked.

The ambulance screamed into the curb out front.

A young intern, in hospital white, stethoscope around his neck, strode in, followed by two white-clothed assistants—they seemed unaware that thirty minutes had elapsed since they'd been alerted on this call.

The attendants moved directly through the store to us.

Doc Yerrgsted stood up. "Get a litter in here," he ordered.

They paused, almost ready to ask who he thought he was, but something in his face changed their minds. They moved swiftly toward the store front.

The girl stared a moment at the intern and wailed, writhing free of the two uniformed cops beside her.

Sam explained to the young medic that the girl was upset, asked if she could be given a sedative. The doctor looked her over, nodded.

"Will you hold her, please?" The doctor nodded at the two cops, then placed his kit on a counter. He said something to the girl. She tried to pull free, her hair flailing wildly. The doctor nodded toward the cops and they bent the girl over toward the shelves. Her skirt was pulled up above her waist and tucked under her belt line to keep it out of his way.

He caught her pink panties on both sides of her hips and rolled them down almost to her knees; I glanced at Ernie to see if he noticed the round fullness of those pink shining cheeks.... But Ernie was such an honest man, that he saw only a girl being attended by a doctor.

The intern got a hypo from his kit, slid one hand along the inside of her left leg to hold her steady. She screamed, trying to lurch free of the two cops.

The medic tightened his grip. "You'll have to hold her steady," he said to the cops. He thrust the needle into the soft pink roundness.

She wiggled, but he went on holding her with his left hand until she quieted down.

I glanced at Yerrgsted and the twisted smile around his moustache and bourbon-soaked eyes.

"Couldn't they have shot her in the arm, Doc?"

The countless wrinkles around his eyes tightened.

"You're an old-fashioned man, Ballard."

Ernie caught his breath. "God, Mike, what a dirty mind you have. That girl is only thirteen!"

"That so?" I grinned at him.

"Thirteen, eh?" Yerrgsted shook his head. "Interesting."

"You don't believe it?" Ernie said.

I shrugged, watching the attendants wheel Climonte out of the store toward the ambulance. "I just don't give a damn. I'll tell you what, Ernie. I've decided against going on home. Doc's got his car with him, I'll check out with him."

Ernie frowned up at me. "What are you talking about? We got a robbery-assault case here—"

I nodded, watching them push Climonte into the ambulance. "Robbery. Yes. But no corpse. This case is nothing to me without a corpse."

"Sometimes I don't understand you, Mike." Ernie shook his head.

"Nothing for me here, either." Yerrgsted snapped his ancient medical kit shut. "Come on, Mike. I'll let you buy me a drink."

"You make a hell of a lot more than I do."

"True. But I've many more bartenders to support than you do, my boy."

Ernie's face was taut. He caught my arm. "Mike. I need you here."

I glanced around the store. "What for? This is a case for the vice squad. Robbery detail. I haven't been on the vice squad in four years. I'm homicide now, Ernie. Remember?"

His voice was hard. "We got a witness. We can get descriptions, break this thing."

"I don't think so."

"What are you talking about, Mike?"

I thought carefully. I didn't want trouble with Ernie Gault. I didn't want trouble with anybody. "Do I have to spell it out for you, Ernie?"

"I think you'd better."

I wiped the back of my hand across my mouth. "Well, first, there's your witness."

"What about her?"

"Like I say, I been off the vice squad for four years. But I'd recognize her in a chorus."

"I'm listening, Mike."

"Boy, I do have to spell it out, don't I? Well, she's nineteen if she's a day. She's got her breasts tied down flat under that cheap sweater. She's lying as fast as she can talk and, more than that, she's hopped up on dope."

Ernie stared first at the girl across the store, and then at me, mouth sagging.

Doc Yerrgsted grinned. He slapped my shoulder. "One hundred percent my diagnosis, Ballard. You're becoming almost as observant as I am. Maybe I will buy you a drink, my boy—just one."

2

I parked my middle-aged Olds on the brown pebbled drive outside Tom Flynn's home on Country Club Road the next afternoon, just a little after three.

I sat a moment gripping the steering wheel and staring around at all the elegance money could buy, but really delaying the moment when I would go inside. My stomach was drawn taut, but my tension had nothing to do with Tom Flynn's call, inviting me out here. District Attorney Thomas Elliot Flynn. The hell with him.

I saw several things at once, and was glad, because gawking was better than thinking, better than remembering. I could sit there, surrounded by this cool, expensive elegance and ponder on what drive, ability—and an inherited fortune—could buy a man. This story-and-half ranch-type with red tile roof sprawled tastefully on a couple of acres of landscaping and overlooked the seventh tee of the golf course. Vines, deep-banked shrubs and velvety grass gave the whole a look of proper aging and permanence. Nothing could look as unfortunate out here as newness, even in a house built yesterday. One thing the Flynn residence definitely looked—it looked like what Carolyn had wanted seven years ago.

A chick glistening with sun-tan oil and wearing a beige bathing cap that had more material in it than her bikini, came running around the side of the house. She was smiling as she moved toward the MG's, Thunderbirds and Fiats parked in the drive, but stopped when she saw my sedate Olds. Obviously she had been expecting somebody, but not me. She turned to go back around the house, but at the last minute must have decided I was one of those eccentrics who pretended to like old cars.

"We're all in the pool," she called. "Come around this way."

I got out of the Olds, slammed the door. I knew damned well Tom Flynn had not invited me out to join the people splashing and yelling in the pool, but, perversely, I decided that was the way I would enter his house. The prospect of annoying Tom was pleasurable. Besides, a view of loveliness encased in a strip of bikini was a good preparation for an interview with the district attorney.

I went around the side of the house and there was the forty-foot pool, the nylon deck chairs, the bright umbrellas, the glass-topped tables and the people.

The sun-oiled chick had flopped on a blue rubber mattress beside the pool. She raised herself on her elbow, managing not to spill out of her halter while showing starkly white skin where the sun had not reached.

She stared at me as if slightly nearsighted and I looked her over, wondering whether we had met before—an unlikely possibility. She lost interest before I did and lay back on the mattress, dipping her toe into the pool.

"Well, for God's sake!" Jerry Marlowe tossed the medicine ball at the other man and came striding around the pool toward me.

In brown, skin-tight trunks, Jerry looked like something off Mount Olympus, unless you looked too closely. As he strode toward me, I was startled to see he was going to lard. He couldn't have been more than twenty-six. I had not seen him in six or seven years but the last time we had met he had looked like something hewn out of a stone wall.

"Mike Ballard!" he shouted. "Old man Ballard."

He grabbed both my arms, then turned and yelled over his shoulder. "Hey, you characters, come here. Here's your chance to meet a man of the people. And when I say man, I mean man."

The other three came toward us, no emotion showing in their faces. The second man rolled the medicine ball toward a table and came around the pool edge, yawning. The chick on the mattress rolled over on her side, pulled herself up.

"This better be exciting, Marlowe," she said. "Getting me up, sore as I am."

Jerry laughed. "Mike Ballard, you old son of a gun! This fat little girl is Jackie Palmer."

"Fat?" Jackie said. "Fat? Why, I'll kill you."

Jerry grinned at her. His eyes looked tired and the muscles were slack around his mouth. "Tighten your halter, honey, and shake hands with the only man who ever Indian-wrestled Jerry Marlowe to the ground. I may add that this was years ago."

She came nearer, peering nearsightedly. She did not offer to shake hands. "Hello, Ballard." She squinted. "Have I seen you somewhere before—or am I being wishful?"

"You never saw this man," Jerry told her. "He leads a clean, pure life among harlots and thieves."

"I thought it would have been too good," the girl said and went back to the air mattress. "Forgive me, Ballard, unless you want to lie down with me. I'm dying."

I was watching her, more closely than was absolutely necessary, until Jerry pulled me around to meet the blonde youth who'd finally made it around the pool.

"Mike Ballard, Morgan Carmichael."

I frowned slightly, looking Carmichael over. He seemed to be about Jerry's age, almost as tall, but not as muscular nor as tired-looking. Carmichael had sharply cut features, a jutting chin but a mouth twisted in sullen fashion.

"Morgan Carmichael," I said. "Are you Fred Carmichael's son?"

He nodded, not smiling. "Mother says I am. Maybe it's true. I've never proved yet she's as big a liar as my sainted father. Do you know him?"

"Not very well."

Jerry laughed. "What Mike means is, he's never arrested your father in a poker raid. Mike's a cop, Morgan."

"I see."

Morgan Carmichael went on staring at me, but now there was a faint interest in his eyes. The kind he might show at a caged puma in a zoo.

By this time the other girl had gotten up from a deck chair. She took her time, pushing her feet into high-heeled green sandals that matched her swim suit. Her red-gold hair was brushed back from her forehead and almost touched her shoulders. Watching her slip her feet into those shoes, I remembered hearing that walking barefooted lessens the charm and curve of a woman's legs. The most obvious thing about this doll was that with her, the thing of first importance was appearance. She came slowly toward us, placing one foot precisely ahead of the other as if she were a professional model or was just learning to walk in high heels. Only neither of these things was true.

She kept her head tilted back as she walked and just before she got to us, she peeled off the green-tinted sun glasses.

I caught Jerry's grin and smiled. "You've come a long way, Jerry."

He laughed. "Onward and upward. Kind of friends I've got now. They don't like me. I don't like them. They can't stand themselves."

"Why, I love you, Jerry," the redhead said, her voice low in her throat and paced very slowly.

"Sure you do," Jerry said. "Mike Ballard, this is Naomi Hyers. Nobody knows who's got more money than her family. She's the only girl I know that I can't get in bed with. Morgan swears he's never made it, either. He's gone ape. He's marrying her sometime next month. Admirable. But a sacrifice I couldn't make."

"I do love you, Jerry," Naomi Hyers said. She looked along her nose at me. She raised her sun glasses to replace them, then hesitated, still looking me over.

"He's a cop, Naomi," Morgan Carmichael said.

Jerry laughed. "I'm damned. Here I am. Six-three. Two hundred and ten pounds. All-Conference half at State U. And here's Morgan Carmichael, good-looking, tall, lousy rich—and who is the first character Naomi Hyers stares upon impolitely?" He stopped smiling, and for a moment his face was cold, blue eyes hard. Then he forced himself to smile again. This time the smile did not reach his eyes. "You people want the real scoop? My sister Carolyn. She of the impeccable taste. She was in love with this mug, once. She almost threw away her chance for all this—" he swung his tanned arm in a gesture to include the house, the pool, even the very white sunlight. His voice chilled again, despite his best effort. "What are you doing around here, Mike?"

"Hell, I was just looking for the service entrance," I said.

The chick on the mattress laughed. Naomi replaced her sun glasses.

Jerry glanced around at his friends. "Come on, Mike," he said. "Don't try to make me sound snobbish. You knew little Jerry Marlowe when he didn't have a rich brother-in-law to his name." He straightened his wide shoulders, sucked in his stomach. His chilled gaze moved over me, that forced smile still pulling at his mouth. "Come to think of it, why should I be glad to see you?"

"Beats me."

Jerry shook his head. "Funny. I always did like you, though. Even when you tried to push me around, keep me on the straight and narrow. Wasn't that the low-class name you used to give to pushing me around?"

"See you soon, Jerry," I said. I turned, looking over the pool and the lawn. Carolyn was not anywhere.

I had that to be thankful for, at least.

"Wait a minute." Jerry caught my arm. "Where you going?"

"To find your rich brother-in-law." I shook off his grip.

He smiled in a savage way. "Tom? What you want to see that stuffed shirt for? You can't have any fun with him. The original square from Plymouth Rock, that boy. Stick around. I'll show you how I've grown up."

"Show Jackie," I said. "I don't think you have."

"Still tough, huh? Still think you can handle me the way you did when I was a kid?"

"See you, Jerry."

"Wait a minute. Have a swim with us. How about that, Morgan? Doesn't Mike look hot? Think he ought to take a swim? Cool him off, huh?"

"He looks kind of sweaty," Morgan said and laughed.

"Throw him in the pool, Jerry," Jackie said from the air mattress. "We need some excitement around this place."

Naomi Hyers didn't say anything, but she had paused, her lips parted slightly, her breasts moving with her sudden deep breathing.

Jerry was staring at me, the grin hard and fixed on his face. "Want to take a swim, Mike? I think you ought to take a swim. How about that, Mike? In the pool. I'm going to throw you in that pool—and then we'll be quits for all the times you pushed me around."

The redhead licked her lips. Jackie sat up on the air mattress, hugging her knees.

Morgan said, "I've got a hundred bucks says you can't do it, Jerry."

Jerry stared at him, his smile flint-hard. "You nuts?" Then he laughed. "You're on. A hundred bucks if I can't. But if I do, I'm taking Naomi down to Cypress Springs for a weekend."

"You bastard," Morgan said.

"It's a deal," Naomi Hyers said in that slow, throaty voice.

Morgan heeled around. "Damn you. Don't talk like that."

Naomi gave him a slow smile. "Why, darling, you don't think he can really do it—if you did, you'd never have bet a hundred dollars. Not you."

Morgan's face turned a bright red. Jerry and Jackie laughed at him. Morgan's fists clenched. "It's a bet," he said. His voice was tight.

Jerry stepped toward me. "You see how it is, Mike? So much to settle. A honeymoon with Morgan's bride. Old scores. So let's go swimming."

I stared at him. I did not bother looking at the others. I was remembering the times I had done exactly what he accused me of—pushed him around to keep him in line. He was a wild kid in those years before Carolyn married the Flynn money. Nobody in his family could handle him. Nobody but I could handle him. A long time ago.

I kept my voice low. "Don't try it, boy."

Jerry laughed, aloud. "Still trying to tell me what to do, old man?" He flexed his muscles, sucking in his belly. "Don't you try it anymore."

"You won't make it, Jerry."

He was circling me now. "Gonna try to spank me again, old man?"

"If that's the way you want it."

Jerry's face was white, rigid. He glanced at his three friends watching him. His voice lashed at me. "It'll never happen. Not any more."

He lunged toward me, moving like a halfback. He may have been All-Conference on the playing fields of State U., but I never learned on the football fields. I learned in the alleys. I never fought for sport. I fought to stay alive.

I side-stepped Jerry, faster than he thought I could move, and when he snagged at me with both arms, his hands struck me just hard enough to give me a flare of anger. I forgot the redhead watching us down her nose, forgot the chick in the bikini holding her breath, and laid the side of my hand across Jerry's shoulder just below the neck—a sharp, hacking blow.

I heard Jerry gasp and when he turned, the pain was in his face, along with surprise and rage. I tried to step back toward the low patio wall, but he wasn't going to stop.

He held his head up this time, watching me. But I saw his left arm was hanging at his side. He was still trying to tackle me, though, bull me off my feet.

I set myself and let him hit me. At the instant of impact I twisted my hip so that when his shoulder struck it, the double shot of pain almost blacked him out.

I stepped back, carrying him with me. I bent forward slightly, thrusting my arm under his loosely dangling left arm and struck upward into his armpit with my elbow. The breath burst across his mouth. The toughest guy he ever met on a gridiron never hit him like that.

Still moving back and dragging him with me, keeping him off balance, I shoved my left hand across his broad, bare back and snagged his right arm when he tried to wrench free. I didn't wait, or give him time to set himself. My fingers closed in on his wrist and jerked his right arm up between his shoulder blades. His knees sagged and he cried out.

I struck hard against the patio wall. I threw my right leg across his sagging knees, pinning him down, raised my right arm high and brought the flat of my hand down across that skin-tight suit. I struck him three times as hard as I could bring my hand down. I had never hit anybody that hard with the flat of my hand before.

I felt my arm ache to my elbow. Jerry struggled, kicking, writhing, trying to fight free. He was raging at the top of his voice. I tightened my grip on his wrist, pulled up on his arm until he stopped yelling.

I swung him upward, shoving him away from me as we moved, but keeping that arm pinned between his shoulder blades. He was bent forward.

I moved, marching him across the pool apron. He tried to fight free and kicked the air mattress as he passed it. The shapely chick screeched and scrambled out of the way. I shoved him, releasing his arm and thrusting him outward into the pool.

I turned around, slowly, retrieved my hat, set it on my head. I waited, standing on the pool deck until Jerry burst, gasping, through the surface.

His face was white and wild. But after a moment, he grinned, treading water.

"Damn you, Ballard," he said. "I still don't believe it."

I exhaled, staring at him, remembering how he'd been when he was a kid. "You never would, Jerry," I said sadly. "You just never would."

I turned and walked along the flagstones toward the house. Jerry stayed where he was. Morgan Carmichael stepped aside as I came near him, but he didn't look at me. The babe in the bikini was crouched on her hands and knees on the air mattress, writhing slightly as if she were afire inside. I pulled my gaze across them. The redhead had not moved.

When my gaze touched hers, she slowly pulled off those sunglasses and pushed her hair back from her face with the same gesture. She touched her tongue across her lips. Her lips were parted and she was staring. She forgot to stare along her nose.

I winked as I passed her. When I pulled my gaze around, I saw Tom Flynn standing at the French doors across the patio. He was watching me, his face cold and set.

3

"Quite impressive," Tom Flynn said. His voice was flat. He had waited until I stood before him in the doorway.

I shrugged. "I'm an impressive guy."

There might have been a flash of pain behind Flynn's dark eyes. He closed the double glass doors behind us. His voice remained flat. "Perhaps you could be."

He waited, but I didn't answer him. I glanced around the large sun room, looking for Carolyn. Again I was struck by how exactly she had gotten what she wanted. The modern paintings on the walls were probably originals, and lost on me. Day of the Condemned. Small Girl Smiling. Third Avenue Sunset. Maybe somebody had switched the titles. The furniture was low, deep and wide; it looked comfortable—and unused. The only touch lacking was Carolyn herself.

"Want to come into my study, Mike?"

Tom Flynn turned and crossed the room, moving carefully on the gray carpeting, almost as though he hated to disturb the deep pile.

I followed him, still expecting to see Carolyn, still feeling that constriction in my stomach. Seven years was a long time ago—only sometimes time doesn't mean a thing.

We crossed a wide, sunlit foyer. Tom Flynn held open a thick oak door. Carolyn was nowhere. I felt my mouth pull into a mirthless, involuntary grin. Was she out of sight because she didn't know I was coming out here today? Or was it because she did know?

I entered Flynn's study and he closed the door behind us. I turned, saw him lock the door.

He straightened, ignoring my smile.

He stood a moment as if undecided about what to do now that we were here, behind locked doors. The study was lined with richly bound reference books—it held leather chairs, a hunting trophy, a golf cup. Country Club Pro-Am, 3rd Place. His flat-topped, oak desk was polished to a fine patina. A brief case stood on its blotter. Homework. Flynn was honest, conscientious, hard working. I looked around again. Not a laugh in the room.

"Sit down, Mike."

His voice revealed nervousness. I sat down, staring at him. He had changed in the four years since I had last seen him.

He moved toward the leather upholstered chair behind his desk, but paused before he reached it. He stood against his desk, his hand nervously caressing the briefcase. I had never seen him like this.

He was as tall as I, barely under six-feet, but he looked as if he'd lost weight recently, the hard, slow way. When a man's insides turn to crud, the process shows first in his face—Flynn's cheeks were haggard and there were thumb-sized shadows under his eyes.

You had to know Tom Flynn to be hit as hard by what had happened to him as I was. He had been born into five or six generations of wealth, a family no longer as impressed by money as by social position—its status had almost become a social responsibility. Tom had always stood up well under the burden. He had been a leader in prep school. In college he joined the correct fraternity, made the honor society, won a Phi Beta Kappa key. At Harvard Law School he was high in his class, but not as high as he felt he ought to be—that king-sized Flynn sense of social responsibility again.

"I guess you wonder why I asked you out here, Mike."

I shrugged. "I'm waiting for you to tell me."

"I asked you out here, because it would be unfair to burden any of the office staff with something as confidential as the matter I want to discuss with you."

I slumped deeper into my chair.

Flynn finally sat down, too, bracing his arms on the desk.

He tried to smile. "By the way, we want you to stay for dinner, Mike."

"Thanks. But I'm sorry—I can't. I've already got a date." Maybe I'd drop by the Greek's and drink a late dinner with Doc Yerrgsted.

"Really?" Flynn drew a plastic letter opener between his fingers, looking troubled, as though my refusal were a big matter. "I hope you can break the date, Mike." He shot his cuff, glanced at his wrist watch. "It's early. You've plenty of time to let them know. You see—" he winced as if speaking reluctantly—"Carolyn has insisted you stay."

I exhaled slowly. "How, then, can I refuse?"

He tried to smile again, tried to forget, I suppose, that seven years ago he had married a girl who almost eloped with a cop the night before the biggest local wedding in ten years. Carolyn had wept when her mother and her father and her brother had stopped us, and they had had to confess the whole business to Tom Flynn because it had required all the Flynn influence to keep the story hushed up and out of the papers. I had not seen Carolyn again except briefly on a street, in passing. I had not spoken to her. What could I have said? Ah, love, they're playing our song. The hell with it.

My voice was sharper than I intended. "You didn't ask me out here to have dinner."

He almost smiled, grayly. "No, Mike, I didn't. I haven't seen you in some time."

I met his gaze. "Not since you tried to have me fired and imprisoned after the Luxtro deal."

He sighed. "We all try to do what we believe is right, Mike. In the best public interest. I'm still not convinced that you weren't guilty of felonies during your years as lieutenant in the vice squad. You took money from Luxtro. A lot of money."

I shrugged.

He got up, came around the desk, rubbing his face with both hands. "When Fred Carmichael interposed in your behalf, Mike, I was shocked. And surprised. He had more influence than I did, and so you kept your job, despite everything I could do."

I smiled evenly at him. "You did pretty well. You broke me to the rank of detective, third grade, assigned to homicide. Except for busting me back in uniform on a night beat, or firing me, there wasn't much more you could do."

His voice was hard. "I felt defeated when you stayed out of jail."

I grinned at him again. "Well, we can't win 'em all, can we?"

"In the past four years, Mike, I've heard nothing about you. I inquired of Captain Neal Burgess, Chief Waylin and Police Commissioner Stewart Mitchell. For four years now, you've walked through a daily eight-hour tour of duty. You've had no promotions, no commendations—"

"And no headlines, either."

"No. You've kept quiet. Four years ago, you were the subject of editorials, you were on the front pages. I wasn't the only decent citizen out to get you—and now suddenly—quiet."

"Is this bad?"

"I don't know. You're a strong man, Mike. You could have been anything you wanted to be. As Carmichael pointed out at your hearing, when you decided to wipe out Luxtro's crime machine, you didn't leave a cog unsmashed and you did it alone, with a bullet in you. I had to admire you, Mike, even when I had to fight you. I knew I was fighting a big man. And now you're all but forgotten."

I shifted slightly in the leather chair. "But not entirely, it seems." When he failed to comment, I said, "Hell, you don't even know why everybody was after me four years ago."

He leaned against his desk. "What's that supposed to mean?"

"Hell, it's easy. I had a new Olds, two apartments and a kept woman in one of them. I had a good bank account. That was a hell of a way for a cop to live. But then as soon as it was all stripped away from me, nobody gave a damn about me any more."

Flynn was scowling, his eyes deeply troubled. "Don't you think a man in a public job ought to be honest, Mike?"

I got up, walked across the deep carpeting to the window. I looked out across the velvety lawn, the thick hedge, the rich view. How could I talk to a man like Tom Flynn, a man who could live extravagantly and idly on the interest of the trust fund his father had set up for him the day he was born? I couldn't remember a day when I didn't have to fight my way home on the block where I'd lived as a kid. If you won a fight it was worse, because then all the bigger guys had to make their reps by whaling hell out of you. Tom had been born with everything he could ever want, and I was born wanting every nice shiny new thing I saw. I grew up seeing people as they were, while he was in college studying what people ought to be. We could stand together in the same room, but we couldn't speak the same language.

He took a couple of steps after me. "Doesn't a man have a responsibility to be honest, Mike?" There was a lot more feeling in his voice than he intended.

I turned away from the window, from the platinum-cast sunlight beyond it. I don't know. I never discuss virtue in the abstract. "How did you earn your first buck?"

His voice hardened. "Every dollar I've earned has been honest. I've given the people good service."

I shrugged. "Me, too. Can you swear that you've never been influenced by the fortune you inherited—never accepted a favor from your society contacts? Can you swear that when you tried to steamroller me you had nothing but clean government on your mind—that you felt nothing personal between us? Wait—" I said when he would have spoken. "I've got one more question. Do you think I could have wiped out Luxtro's crime combo if I'd never let them do me a favor?"

He suddenly looked even more tired than before. "I've thought of the answer to that last question a number of times. Maybe I'm smarter than I was four years ago." He took a deep breath, studying me. "Ever since you walked into this room, Mike, I've been waiting for you to say something."

I stared up at him, waiting.

"You know what it is, Mike. We both know. This town was one hell of a lot cleaner four years ago than it is now. Four years ago, you did accept bribes from the crime bosses. You've never denied it."

I massaged my thumb across my knuckles.

"I realize something now I didn't know then, Mike. You kept those people in line. Perhaps even with their knowing it. And eventually you smashed them. Maybe it was dirty fighting and you made a buck out of it, but it was effective."

I glanced up. "Was it?"

"Stop being tough and bitter, Mike. You know damned well it was. Our crime rate is up. The FBI has called our city one of the dirtiest in the country."

"I haven't paid much attention."

"Haven't you? Don't you read the newspapers? Isn't the homicide squad bigger than it ever was, and still inadequate and undermanned? For one Luxtro, there are now five of him in this city. Juvenile delinquency is up over two hundred per cent. This whole city is in hell."

His hands were trembling. He shoved them into the pockets of his tailored summer cashmere jacket.

He laughed in a self-deprecating way. "Four years ago, as you know, I was an ambitious man. I was riding toward the governor's chair—on my record against rackets and vice in this town."

"You'll make a fine governor," I said.

He paused, staring at me, flushing, seeking irony in my voice. There wasn't any—I had meant what I said. The realization made him more uncomfortable than ever.

"Thanks, Mike," he said at last. "But I'll never be governor. Right now, today, I'm dead as far as state politics are concerned. This town is dirty and I'm the D.A. I haven't cleaned it up, and I haven't resigned. I don't give a damn about my personal failure. But this is my town, Ballard, and nobody knows how rotten dirty it is better than I."

"You do what you can."

"It hasn't been enough. I've got to do more."

"I wish you luck."

He strode back and stood before my chair, staring down at me.

"I've got that coming, Mike."

"Make no mistake. You're a good man, Flynn. I've got no hard feelings."

Flynn turned away, wincing. He swallowed hard, went back to his desk and sat down.

"The hell with that, Mike. I called you here to offer you a job."

"I've got a job."

"Only your heart's not in it."

"I can't help that."

He leaned forward. "I've given this a lot of thought. I can give you a job you can put your heart in. Special vice investigator for my office."

I had to laugh. "Me? Working for you?"

"With me, Mike. It's no eight-hour job. I work twenty-four hours a day—and you would, too. The danger would be all at your end. You could put your heart in a job like that, Mike."

"No."

He jumped up. "You can't mean that."

"I don't want it. I wouldn't touch it."

He leaned against his desk, the corners of his mouth sagging. Whatever else he had considered, it hadn't occurred to him that I would refuse to work with him.

"I don't know where to turn if you won't help me, Mike."

"I'm sorry."

"You think I gave you a raw deal, is that it? You'll let this town go to hell to hit back at me?"

I stood up "Why talk about it? I admire you, Counselor—everything you've done, or tried to do. Maybe I just want to stay alive. I could walk among those racket bosses, as long as they thought I was one of them. I'd be dead in an alley—if one of them could stop laughing long enough to knock me off—if they ever heard I came out of your office. No. I'm sorry, Counselor, I'm not ready to die the quick, painful way."

His lips worked, but at last he got himself under control. His eyes still raged at me but he was Thomas Elliot Flynn. School tie. Code. Ethics. He spoke, his voice low and even. "All right, Ballard. I hope you never regret this."

I stood up "You'll tell Mrs. Flynn I'm sorry I couldn't stay to dinner?" I straightened my jacket. "When she sees your face, I'm sure she'll understand why."

4

I sat at my desk and listened to this doll rage from half across the office. Our detective bureau is no different from any other in the country— women, when they come in or are brought in, are usually ready for hysterics.

I glanced at the clock, glad that Ernie Gault had to deal with her. The clock must have stopped; it hadn't moved five minutes in the past hour. The hands stood at almost five and there was only one thing I wanted— a drink in the peace and quiet of the Greek's.

I shoved a report pad in the top drawer of the cheap pine desk. I had hardly slept last night. On the way home from Flynn's, I had stopped by the Greek's for a bourbon and some gab with Doc Yerrgsted. I sometimes failed to follow what the old guy was saying, especially when he began to picture in intimate and technical detail a delicate operation he'd performed in some distant place and some other existence, but he always loved to talk and nothing he said irritated me. But after I got home and hit the sack, Flynn's proposition began to bother me. It must have cost him a lot to make—it was costing me a lot to turn down. The hell with Flynn.

"I'm sorry, miss." Ernie Gault's voice filtered through to my conscious mind. "There's nothing the police can do. I'm sorry." That was Ernie Gault, he really was sorry. But he was helpless trying to get rid of her.

The girl's voice rose. "Somebody has to help me."

I watched Ernie pat her shoulder. Some of the other men were watching him, grinning.

"Look. Why don't you go back home, honey?"

The girl burst into a liquid Spanish that blistered the walls. Finally she got tired of yakking and stopped, her full breasts heaving. She was winded, but she wasn't about to give up whatever it was she expected from the police department. "You got to help me!" she cried out, and Ernie looked around again.

His eyes found me. I shook my head at him, looked back at the clock.

Next I knew, Ernie was guiding her toward my desk, assuring her repeatedly that everything was going to be all right.

I pushed back my pine chair, let my eyes rake Ernie before I looked at her.

Ernie's face was red. He wouldn't meet my gaze. He half pushed the babe into the straight chair at the side of my desk.

"Miss Valdez, this is Detective Ballard."

"Homicide," I said.

This meant nothing to her. It seemed to mean nothing to Ernie Gault, either. His voice gushed on.

"Detective Mike Ballard is a fine man, Miss Valdez. Mike, this is Lupe Valdez, 2310 Hermano... that's right in the neighborhood where Detective Ballard was born, Miss Valdez. He grew up right there on Twenty-third. Isn't that right, Mike? You tell him what you told me, Miss Valdez. Detective Ballard speaks real good Twenty-third Street Spanish."

She nodded, snuffling, and looked me over, her mouth swollen with her crying. She was a chubby girl, with olive complexion, black hair, black eyes. I had seen girls like her all my life. Gault hadn't lied to her. I grew up on the edge of the Spanish section on Twenty-third Street. I remembered many like her, right down to those shapely ankles in crepe-sole white shoes, and plenty had been in trouble.

Her shoulders, in a cheap dress that she must have worn because it would look nice when she came downtown, were drooping. She could not have been more than seventeen, but she looked ready to die of despair.

She tried to smile. I looked her over, wondering why Gault brought her to me. Ernie patted her shoulders, walked away.

I leaned back in the chair, told her in Spanish to relax.

"Oh, God," she said. "Oh, my God."

"You should have prayed," I said, still in Spanish, "while you still had your pants on."

She pressed her hand against her mouth, sobbing.

"All right," I said in English. "Relax. Take it easy." She nodded, wiping at her eyes with a brightly colored scarf. She had worn it over her thick black hair when she came in, but now she blew her nose in it.

"You're a nurse?" I asked.

She nodded, still trying to get herself under control. "Yes. I'm in training. General Hospital—how did you know?"

I could have given her a hundred clues. The way she stood in her white shoes, the way she walked, the way her nails were cut. But the main thing was that I knew her neighborhood. Not many things could happen to girls there. If they were lucky they got married early. If not, they went in the factories, or the hospital. They made damned good nurses. It was as if they grew up bursting with love and desire and had to spread it around among people.

"I'll bet you're a fine nurse."

She shrugged and repeated, "How did you know I'm a nurse?"

"Those white shoes."

She smiled wanly. "I guess—well, I did think of changing them."

"Then you said the hell with it. That right, Lupe?"

"You really were born up there—up on Twenty-third, weren't you?"

I nodded.

"And you know all about me, don't you? I don't have to tell you, do I? It's all pretty cheap—and ugly—and you've heard it too many times, haven't you?"

"I know most of the lyrics."

Her eyes brimmed again. She kept her face tilted. "What am I going to do, Mr. Ballard?"

I spread my hands. "It's like Lieutenant Gault told you, Lupe. There's nothing we can do."

"It's not for me, Mr. Ballard. I got in it. I can take it. I'm not asking anything for myself."

"No? Who are you asking for?"

She looked straight into my eyes, olive cheeks starkly pale. "For my folks. My mother and father. They're good people. Even if they are—Spanish."

"You don't have to apologize to me. You don't have to apologize to anyone for being Spanish. So they don't speak perfect English—so what?"

Her mouth quivered. "It's more than that, and you know it."

"Twenty-third Street," I said, thinking how it sliced the town in two; the right side, the wrong side. "It's a pretty wide street, eh?"

"I—can't get across it, if that's what you mean."

"That's what I mean. But you said it—I didn't."

I sat there and ran my tongue around the inside of my dry mouth. I glanced at the clock. It was five minutes past five, and now, suddenly, the minute hand was racing. Damn Ernie Gault.

"I'm going to have a baby, Mr. Ballard."

I shrugged. "So what else is new?"

She bit her lip. Her black eyes flashed. "You already knew that, didn't you?"

I shrugged.

"You knew. Because you know girls like me. Don't you, Mr. Ballard? You were born up there. You knew a lot of us, didn't you? Cheap, Mr. Ballard? Easy?"

I moved in my chair. I could never remember having been so tired in my life.

"You're a beautiful girl," I said. "I never said you were cheap. I said there was nothing I could do to help you."

But I was hooked. She had raged at Ernie Gault because he had not really understood the depth and scope of her problem, though he had sympathized with her. Now, though her voice still shook and the tears still clogged her throat, she was calmer. As far as she was concerned, she was home. By now she knew Ernie had not lied—I was a boy right off her block. I had her pegged—and she had me. She was still worried, but she was not afraid any more.

"I'm in trouble, Mr. Ballard. Bad trouble. The kind that could kill my folks."

"Why don't you see some good, reliable, crooked doctor? You're a nurse, ask around. It's done every day."

She shuddered. "That isn't the kind of help I want. I want my baby."

"Good. Then what's the beef?"

She sat as rigid as if she'd turned to stone. She was seeing something I could not see, but something I didn't care about seeing anyhow. "I need help," she said at last. "It's not as simple as you think. Won't you please listen to me?"

It never was as simple as we thought. I looked at her, at the empty desks, at the few men remaining in the long room, the dust-thickened sunlight at the windows.

I spread my hands hopelessly. "Sure. You want to come along and tell me your story over bourbon and water? I'll listen."

She hesitated, bit her lip. Her hands were white on her purse. "I'll go with you," she said.

She walked ahead of me into the Greek's on Lafayette Street; the boys all eyed her, turning from the bar and at the tables, taking their time. Then they looked at me and grinned.

I chased a drunk out of the rear booth and by the time Lupe and I sat down, the bartender was there with my bourbon and water.

"Anything for the lady, Mike?"

"Yes." I didn't bother looking at her. "A glass of milk."

When I did look at her, she was chewing at that full under lip. When my eyes met hers, she smiled.

She said, "Can I tell you about it now? I don't want to waste your time."

You're already wasting my time, baby, I thought. I took a long pull at the whiskey and water. The bartender brought me a second drink, set it down along with Lupe's glass of milk.

When I looked up, Doc Yerrgsted was listing toward us. He carried his glass. He did not see Lupe until he was sliding into the booth beside her, across the table from me.

He stopped, bushy brows and moustache working. "Oh, I'm sorry," he said.

He looked Lupe over. Observant man, Doc Yerrgsted; he saw everything in a fleeting second that I had seen since I met her, and how much more I would never know.

"Doc usually drinks his supper here with me," I told Lupe.

"Oh," she said. She did not offer to move over and make room for Doc. This girl had her woes, and there was room for nothing else in her mind. She had me and she wanted no complications.

"It's all right," Yerrgsted said. "I can find another booth. I can always find another booth."

I grinned up at him. "Sure, you can."

Those wrinkles deepened around his eyes, and he got a roguish tilt to his moustache. "Just one little question, my boy."

"Yeah?"

"Are you entertaining jailbait these days?"

I laughed. "A man gets harder and harder to please as he get older, Doc. You know that."

Doc Yerrgsted smiled, apparently satisfied. He bowed to Lupe. "My child," he said, "you're young enough to be this man's daughter. But this I can tell you. If you had a father like him, you couldn't do better."

"You're spilling your drink," I told him.

"Plenty more where that would have gone," he said, listing back toward the bar.

I sat, watching him crouch on a stool at the mahogany counter.

"He's right about you," Valdez said. "You are a good man."

"His mind is a sponge."

"It would kill you if anybody knew how good you are, wouldn't it?"

I finished off my second drink. I motioned the bartender. He nodded. When I looked down, Lupe was frowning again.

I said, "All right, baby, get it off your chest."

She sighed. "I may as well tell you about it." And she began her story, talking slowly, her voice flat and dead. I stared at Doc's rounded back at the bar. A lost, lonely old man. A girl, possibly lost, looking for home in a stranger.

"...I fell so crazy in love with him I didn't even care what happened. What he wanted—that was what I wanted."

"Sure, baby. Happens all the time."

"But this was different. There was something different about the way I felt about Morgan. When I was a little girl I used to get the same funny feeling when I saw the sun look through the stained-glass windows at the church. Nothing could be bad about what Morgan and I did."

"That's what keeps it spinning, all right."

"I couldn't believe it—when he told me he was marrying this girl from Hyde Park."

"Takes a lot to cure you, huh?"

"I was his, for good and all, Mr. Ballard. I thought he felt the same way about me. We loved each other. We were faithful—"

"You were faithful."

She smiled again, a wry attempt at perspective. Her eyes brimmed.

"Mr. Ballard, there was nothing in the world I wouldn't have done for Morgan. I—I even promised to stay away from him. Because that's what he said he wanted. He told me to stay away from him, not to try to see him again. He said he was marrying this—this s-society girl. His family wanted him to marry her."

"I like that line. He dug deep for that. I wonder how he thought of it."

She bit her lip. "It sounds pretty second-hand to you, doesn't it? But I loved him so much I promised to stay away."

"But that was before you knew about the baby."

Her head jerked up. Her black eyes widened and she stared at me. After a moment, she nodded. "Yes. That's right. It was before I knew I was pregnant. Now things have changed. Everything is all different. You can see that, can't you, Mr. Ballard?"

"I can see it," I told her. "But I'm just an innocent bystander. The important thing is to get the message to your lover. What did he say? Did you tell him you were *enciente?*"

Her mouth quivered. She sat up straight, swallowed. "I can't tell you what he said. I—just can't."

"Hell, you don't have to."

She reached across the table, caught my hand, gripped it hard. "He said that the baby wasn't his. That I was loose, cheap—and easy. He said—"

"Never mind, kid. I know what he said. He hasn't come up with anything new yet."

She sank back against the booth, sighing, exhausted, still hard to convince that her boyfriend hadn't written the most original script in the world—simply because all this banality had happened to her.

At last, though, she came to the nub of the matter. "What am I going to do? Morgan ought to give me money for his baby—so I could go away to some hospital where nobody knows me. So the baby would have good care. After all, Morgan's father is rich. Why should the poor little baby have to suffer?"

Money. Almost everything came back to that sooner or later. Gimme.

I moved the whiskey glass around on the table. "Beats me."

"I tried to tell Morgan. I don't want anything for myself. But he's rich. I want a trust fund for his baby, that's all."

I was frowning. Now that I had begun to listen to her, to give all my attention to what she was saying, the name began to strike a chord. I felt the sweat breaking out across my neck.

"You told who?"

"Morgan," she said.

"Yeah. Now. Morgan. As in J. P.—with money. This is just a name you selected. No real names. Huh?"

"His name is Morgan Carmichael."

I drew in a deep breath. His name was Morgan Carmichael. Sure it was. What else? It was a small world. Until yesterday I'd never seen Fred Carmichael's son. Yesterday I met him and now was meeting his friends. The redhaired doll, looking along her nose, and then this chick crying in her milk.

"A lawyer might help you," I said.

She leaned forward, shaking her head. "I went to a lawyer. It's too much like blackmail, with a man as rich as Morgan. I've got to have somebody strong, somebody who can talk to Morgan and make him listen. Somebody like a good cop who understands what happened. I'm not asking anything for myself, but—"

"For the baby," I finished.

"Yes. That's all I want."

I pushed my drink away. I didn't want it. I knew it would be tasteless.

Now I reached across the table and covered her hands with one of mine.

"Honey," I said. "Baby. Sweetheart. Will you do me a favor? Will you listen carefully to me? At first you were a nuisance, and all I wanted was to get rid of you."

She smiled, turning her palm upward under mine, clinging to my hand with her fingers. "I know," she said.

"All right. But now, I'm from up there on Twenty-third. I'm telling you straight. The father of that boy is the most powerful man in this town—maybe in this state."

"I know that. But it's for the baby, not me."

"It's no good, sweetie."

Her fingers tightened. "Please, Mr. Ballard. Mike. Don't turn me down. Everybody's afraid, but you're not."

"Honey. I'm trying to tell you. Being afraid has nothing to do with it. What's the point of fighting if you can't win?"

She scrubbed the tears from her eyes. Her voice went flat. "You won't help me?"

"I can't"

She looked at me again, as if she still could not believe it, as if she still would not give up.

She stood up suddenly, knocking over her glass of milk. She ran swiftly out of the booth and toward the front door. She did not look back. I watched her until the door hissed closed behind her. Then I stared down at the spreading white puddle of milk on the table. The bartender came running to wipe it up with a bar rag.

5

At four-thirty the next afternoon I was leaning back in my chair. Another long day. I had had no trouble sleeping last night, though. Doc Yerrgsted, the Greek and I had sat in the booth for three hours after the bar had closed, drinking and talking. Doc had relived the days of his greatest glory. The Greek had remembered the evil time he once had getting started in the restaurant business because his English was poor. I remember Doc laughing until he cried because we could hardly understand the Greek now, twenty-four years later, when he tried to tell us about it.

The phone rang, ripping at exposed nerve ends left dangling from this morning's hangover.

I grabbed up that receiver quickly—and was instantly afraid the caller might be Lupe. Girls can be hard to discourage.

"Homicide. Ballard."

There was a slight pause, curiously dead at the other end of the line, as if whoever had called had simply ceased to exist. I heard nothing, not even breathing.

Then, a woman's voice asked, "Mike? Mike Ballard?"

"Yes."

"Mike—this is Carolyn."

Like that. After seven years, the phone rings on the tail end of a misspent life and a voice says, *Mike—this is Carolyn....*

I pulled in a deep breath. "This is a surprise."

"Is it, Mike?"

"What do you think? Why would you be calling Homicide?"

She laughed. "I used to think about calling you, Mike. A long time ago. Once in a while I'd get as far as the telephone. You know?"

"Yes. I've been that far myself."

"It's sweet of you to say so, Mike. We were very young—and very foolish, weren't we?"

"Psycho."

"How are you, Mike? I wanted you to stay for dinner the other day. I truly did. I was so afraid it would be awkward—and yet all the time I was looking forward to it."

I made my voice laugh. "You always were a troublemaker."

"Yes.... Jerry says to say hi. He's sorry he tried to show off."

"Jerry hasn't changed much. Maybe he ought to stop feeling sorry."

She laughed. "I guess he always wanted to beat you—beat the champ. Is there anything wrong with that?"

"That depends. Is he sore?"

"You mean angry with you? No. He's always admired you, Mike. Even when he tried the hardest to put you down. But he was physically sore the other night—he ate dinner standing up. He says you haven't changed, Mike. I'm glad about that."

I glanced about the office. There was the usual festering bustle—the average plainclothes bureau is a scab over a running sore of society. It didn't seem real, talking to her from a place like this.

"Mike?"

"Yes?"

"I don't want to waste your time—"

"My God. After seven years? I'm glad you called."

"It is important, Mike. It's—about Tom."

"Oh."

"I'm sorry, Mike. Must you sound so—flat? Don't hate Tom. He's unbending, straitlaced. But he is a good man, Mike. He has a goodness of the kind that never gets in the newspapers."

I put my foot against the desk, avoided kicking it. The breath was tight in my chest. "Make no mistake, Carolyn. I never hated Tom Flynn."

"But you won't work for him."

I let my foot slip off the desk, sat up straight. "Did he ask you to call me, Carolyn?"

"Of course not. He'd be furious if he knew I had called. But he's desperate, Mike. Can I make you understand that? He's a good man, up against something he can't fight. He thinks you could. I don't even understand all of it. I only know he needs you, Mike. Terribly."

My hand tightened on the receiver. I could see Lupe Valdez's tear-streaked face. I thought of Fred Carmichael, whose son had got her into trouble. What would Tom Flynn say if I brought some of the city's filth right into his swimming pool? I'd had my share of trouble.

My hand sweated on that phone. I ached, wanting to replace the receiver, and break this connection, quick, clean and final. Mike Ballard had fought his battles, and had his scars to prove it. I had loved Carolyn seven years ago. But four years ago I had also loved a girl named Peggy. I was a wise, tired old bastard of thirty-three who wanted just one thing, to be allowed to drink with the Doc and the Greek, and never again have to look at tears.

"I'm sorry, Carolyn."

"Tom's been almost ill for weeks, Mike. He won't talk to me about it. Isn't there anything I can say to change your mind?"

"There isn't."

"Mike, I've always loved you. But I'd owe you everything if you would help him."

I felt the sweat across my forehead. "Don't do this, Carolyn. I don't want you to beg. If I could help, I'd do it—for you. You wouldn't even have to ask. But there's nothing I can do."

"Mike—I don't know where to turn. I don't know what to do. Can I come to see you, Mike? At your apartment?"

I replaced the receiver gently. I didn't want to hear more.

Ernie Gault came over and sat on the corner of my desk. I looked up. He was grinning. His lean, dour face was exercising muscles long atrophied.

"You look like you just lost your last blonde," Ernie said.

Coming from him, the words were crazy. I stared. Hell. Gault would pick this moment for levity.

"What's eating you?" I asked.

He smiled again. If you've ever seen a bloodhound chewing briars, I don't have to tell you what his smile looked like.

"Mike, you remember four years ago? Christmas?"

"No."

"Sure you do. Grace was in the hospital. Female operation. Remember?" He glanced around to see if he were overheard, lowered his voice, flushing faintly. "Hysterectomy."

"No."

"Aw, come on, Mike. I was up a stump. Borrowed from every bank, loan shark and credit union. You let me have a hundred bucks. If you hadn't, those three kids of mine wouldn't of had any Christmas at all that year. You told me I could pay it back any way I wanted to."

"I also told you to forget it."

"It's been a long time, Mike. Four years. I've felt like a dog. Hell, I remember when you were shot after you cleaned out Luxtro, and were giving yourself up to the police. You called me to come and get you. I felt like hell, Mike. You'd been good to me and the kids and I had to turn you in. But like you told me that day, it was my job."

"I remember what I really told you that day was you talk too much."

He laughed again, an odd, unaccustomed sound and thrust his hand in his pocket. He brought out four crumpled five-dollar bills.

"Mike. This is from Grace and me. By God, this is from Grace and me and the kids. The last twenty bucks. Grace's been saving dough out of her grocery allowance. I want to thank you, Mike, for being so damned patient with us."

He thrust the crumpled bills out toward me and when I didn't take them, he laid them out on my desk, smoothing them with his palm.

"We're all even, Mike. And it only took four years. Go on, Mike. Take it. Grace'd flog me if you didn't. You know you're a hero to her. When you cleaned out the Luxtro mob, she wouldn't even believe you'd ever been on the take—she wanted to go down and tear that hearing apart."

I took the money, stuffed it in my jacket pocket. I had to shut him up somehow.

But not Ernie. "Hell, boy, this is just part of it. Grace says I got to bring you home to dinner tonight."

"I'm sorry. I've already got a date."

"Some blonde? Break it."

"Blondes aren't that plentiful any more."

"Mike. Grace won't take no for an answer. This is a big moment in the Gault house. Another debt paid off. She and the kids have planned a celebration."

6

Grace Gault and the three kids were waiting for us in the four-room apartment on Eighth Street just off Third Avenue. Grace introduced me to each of the kids. They shook hands and giggled. They were nice, if you like kids, but I was uncomfortable because I couldn't think of anything to say to them.

After a while my strangeness didn't matter. Grace chattered until dinner was ready and then talked all the way through it. She served a pot roast, with plenty of potatoes and gravy, and you could tell it was a feast. After dinner, Grace went off to put the kids in bed. Ernie and I sat in the front room, not saying anything. The silence was fine. He asked me if I wanted the TV on and I shook my head.

Ernie sighed. "Thank God. If cops really acted the way they do in that box—" he shook his head and laughed.

I looked around, wondering how soon I could get away. The dinner had been fine, but I hated the thought of another three hours of talk about kids, costs and the neighborhood. Just as I was ready to bolt Grace came back, straightening her apron.

"I had to listen to their prayers," she said.

She was a stout woman, with dark blonde hair, a clear complexion, deep blue eyes and a look of contentment about her. She had nice ankles. I wondered mildly if either she or Ernie knew how nice her ankles were—and would it have mattered if they did.

"I'd better get along," I said, but neither of them even heard me.

Grace sat on the divan, smiling at me. "Guess whom I saw today, Mike?"

"Rock Hudson?"

She laughed. "Peggy Walker."

I felt the tightening in my throat. For an instant I couldn't talk.

When I finally made it, I kept my voice even. "That so?"

I stared at the backs of my hands. I felt the old illness, the old bullet wound, the old need. The bullet wound alone had healed.

"She and I should form a Mike Ballard admiration club," Grace said. "Ernie, did you know that Mike saved Peggy's Earl—right out of the death house?"

"Honey, I know all about it," Ernie said.

"She looks fine, Mike," Grace said.

"Have they moved back here to town?"

"Oh, no. She and Earl moved away. Four years ago. Right after you got him out of prison. He's a salesman again. They're getting along fine. She just happened to be in town on some kind of business. I just ran into her. She looks lovely, just lovely."

"I'm sure of it." I stared at Grace, wondering if there was any way to shut her up.

"She looks older," Grace was saying. "She has a streak of gray in her hair, Mike. Right across from her widow's peak. But no wonder, I say, all she went through while Earl was in the death house. It's a wonder she isn't completely gray."

I stared. Grace was a nice woman. It would be a sin if someone shot her. About an inch above her eyebrows.

I thought they had me hanging on the ropes, but I didn't know my own endurance. Grace talked for another hour, and then Ernie gave her some kind of silent signal, and she began yawning. I had to forgive her, she said. She had been up since six this morning. But I wasn't to think about leaving. Ernie and I could have a nice long talk after she was in bed.

When Ernie and I were alone in the living room, I frowned, wondering what he and I were going to have a nice long talk about.

"Mike, I been wanting to talk to you."

"You had a lot of competition tonight."

He smiled, sucking on a pipe. "Grace is a good girl. A hell of a lot too good for me."

"Well, as long as you know it."

"Mike, you ought to get married."

"My God. That isn't what we're going to talk about, is it?"

"No, pal. It's a lot more serious than that. A lot more urgent."

I felt my thoughts grow tight. I searched back in my mental catalogue of debts, errors and trespasses, wondering what Ernie was going to preach to me about. Ernie was his own type of cop, serious, plodding, conscientious. Lately, I hadn't been much of any kind of cop at all, but I could never be a cop like Ernie.

"I've got a message for you, Mike. Tom Flynn called me into his office yesterday. Personally. We had a long talk. He asked me to use all my influence and friendship with you to make you accept an assignment with his office."

"My God. You too?"

"What?"

"The hell with Flynn. You know better than to ask me, Ernie."

"No, Mike, I don't. Yesterday a taxi driver got killed when he tried to collect on numbers. A teen-age girl walked in front of a car—she was so full of dope she didn't even know where she was. And two punks killed old man Climonte because he wouldn't pay them protection money. Sure, Climonte lived to die in the hospital. The punks didn't kill him. Sure, these cheap young hoods do the muscle work, but crime's gotten to be a big business in this town, Mike, and it's getting bigger every day. And it's organized. It's so damned well organized it's reaching out into the best families, the best kids in town. They think they can wreck, and destroy and maim, if it gets them what they want. Hell, I thought we had a witness who saw the two killers shoot Climonte in his grocery. We let go of her—nothing to hold her on. When we went to look for her again, she'd never lived at the address she gave us."

"I could have told you that."

"Sure. You tried to. What you did tell us was that she was on dope, that she was nineteen at least, and lying all the way."

"Wasn't she?"

"Right down the line. The descriptions she gave us were as phony as she was."

"Sure. They planted her in there. She was supposed to sell you a phony bill."

"But that was no kid gang job. An organization with brains was behind it. A grown-up syndicate. Listen, Mike. You've still got a rep as a crooked cop. Even Tom Flynn knows by now that you're not—but there's nobody else in town can work into the syndicate the way you could."

I shrugged. Ernie scowled, ready to go on with his oratory, but at that instant the phone rang. He laid his pipe aside, got up and went to answer it.

Grace came into the front room. Her hair was in rollers. She had used cream to wipe the rouge from her face and mouth. Her skin looked pasty. She wore a thick robe that she gripped in tense fists. She was barefooted. Her eyes were distended. A phone call after ten o'clock at night in this apartment meant just one thing. Trouble.

Ernie stood listening for a long time with the receiver pressed against his ear. When he replaced it in its cradle and turned around, he looked like a man in shock.

He crossed the room to the foyer, got his hat. He did not look at Grace.

He said, "You can come along, Mike. It's your department this time. Homicide."

7

When Ernie and I got out on Essex Turnpike, a misting rain gave the night a gray sheen. Cars were parked along both sides of the highway and more were coming, like jackals to meat.

We got out of my Olds, and right away I felt the wrong in the chilled, wet night. I had seldom seen so much police brass in one spot. Captain Neal Burgess stood marking the spot on the highway's shoulder and halfway down the embankment Chief Waylin was directing things. I glanced around for a black Caddy, found it. Police Commissioner Stewart Mitchell was staying in where it was dry, but he was out here. Only an important death brought the top echelon out on a night like this.

"Over here, Ballard." A uniformed cop motioned to Ernie and me. "The car's down in the ditch."

I nodded, hunching my shoulders against the chilling rain.

I glanced around. Criss-cross headlights webbed the mist. The cop who had called to us was holding things down at a wide curve in the road. He motioned us toward the big, blue convertible squatting tails up in a boggy sump off the pavement. The convertible hadn't made the curve, had chewed deep ruts across the shoulders and down the embankment.

More than a dozen uniformed cops were sloshing around in the mud and stagnant water, keeping the people back. They were even refusing to allow reporters anywhere near the overturned car.

Chief Waylin stopped Ernie and me on the incline. His face was grayer than the night. "Just a minute, Ballard. Ernie. No sense getting down in that bog. They're moving the body out of the car now."

We stopped beside Waylin, watching. I saw Doc Yerrgsted standing knee-deep in the water, directing the removal. Three interns, hospital whites muddy to the hips, worked the body from beneath the steering wheel and staggered out of the muck. A state trooper tossed a tarpaulin on the muddy embankment beside the deep-plowed ruts and the interns stretched the remains out on that.

"Okay. There it is, Doc," one of the boys in white said. I stood looking down at the dead man.

He was Tom Flynn. I felt as though someone had struck me with a fist full in the face. There it was. The body. The corpse. The stiff.

Ernie said something to me, but I didn't answer. I didn't even hear what he said.

I heard Chief Waylin and Captain Burgess talking beside me, but the words they were saying didn't reach me.

Doc Yerrgsted knelt beside Flynn's body and pressed the eyelids shut.

That was all he did. He stood up, peered through the lighted mists at Waylin. "I'm through here, Chief." He picked up his medical kit. "Anybody wants me, I'll be in my office."

"Sure, Doc. Thanks."

"Just send me my check." Yerrgsted shrugged his raincoat higher on his shoulders and moved up the embankment toward the roadway. He looked straight at me. His face was gray. He did not speak.

I watched an intern bring a sheet from the ambulance and stretch it over Flynn's body.

"How'd it happen, Chief?" A reporter pushed through the line of cops. He stopped where Waylin stood.

"We don't know yet. Doc said he was drunk. The investigating officer said he was driving over ninety. Probably hit the shoulder, couldn't control the car."

Another reporter came down the embankment. "No matter who they are, they never learn."

"Well, we don't know yet," Waylin said. "Flynn was one of the finest men this town ever had. We'll have a fuller picture in the morning."

I stepped away from them and started down the embankment.

Waylin said, "Ballard."

I didn't stop. Abruptly, out of the mist, two young cops stepped in front of me, blocking my way.

"There's nothing you can do, Ballard," Waylin said from behind me.

I didn't bother looking at him. I just stared at the two who were barring my way.

One of them tried to smile. "We're just following orders."

I said nothing. I kept walking. The two stepped back. Burgess spoke my name from up the embankment beside Waylin. He came striding down the incline to where the two patrolmen stood. He said something to them, his voice low but crisply accented.

One of the two said, "We're sorry, Captain. We tried to stop him."

I hunkered down beside the body on the tarpaulin and turned back the cover. I heard Waylin shouting at the ambulance attendants to get a litter down there and move the body into town. I did not look up.

When I turned the cover back, the light rain pattered on the dead face, running off the rigid cheeks in long streaks.

I took a deep breath. The smell of whiskey was strong near the corpse.

I slid my hand under Flynn's head, lifted it. I bent closer. The odor of liquor was weaker around his face. I let the head back gently to the ground and withdrew my hand. My palm was wet, sticky and smeared with blood.

I clenched my fingers over the blood and stood up, facing one of the uniformed men holding a flashlight.

"You investigate this?"

"We'll get a report from Hogan, Mike," Burgess said.

"Did you?" I ignored Burgess, stared at young Hogan.

"Yes, sir. Clemmons and I were the first ones out here."

"The car turn over?"

"No, sir. It went straight down into the ditch. We figure he was doing better than ninety. These new jobs pack a lot of power."

"What kind of skid marks did he put down?"

"None. Ain't no sign he tried to put on brakes. Road is clean. He just got to this curve in this rain without slowing down. Without even trying to slow down. Not like a guy that didn't make a curve. Like a guy who didn't even know there was a curve—or didn't give a damn."

"Was he dead when you got to him?"

"Yes, sir. He must have crushed himself against the steering wheel. That's what the ambulance doctor said. Said he did all his bleeding inside."

"What did the M.E. say?"

"He didn't say anything. Just pronounced Mr. Flynn dead and took off. You saw him go."

"Was Flynn sitting up behind the wheel when you found him?"

"Yes, sir. Slumped over the wheel. Smell of whiskey was terrible in that closed car. We figure he never knew what hit him."

I kept my blood-smeared right fist clenched, shoved it into my jacket pocket.

The ambulance men moved a wheel-litter past me.

Waylin said, "All right, you people. Stand back. Take Mr. Flynn's body to the morgue."

One of the interns glanced around at Waylin, frowning. Then he shrugged. The attendants lifted the body to the stretcher and panted up the incline to the ambulance. Cops started clearing cars away so a wrecker could come in and hoist Flynn's Chrysler out of the bog.

Ernie came down the incline to me. "Going to stay until they check the car, Mike?"

I shook my head. "I'd stay if I thought they'd find a steering failure, or a stuck accelerator. But they won't."

Chief Waylin, Burgess and Ernie trailed me up the incline. I thought they would leave us at the roadway, but they followed us along the lane of parked cars to my Olds.

I got in under the wheel without looking at the chief or the captain. Waylin said, "Get in the back seat, Ernie, you and Neal." He got into the front seat beside me. He closed the door. He shivered. "Start your engine and run your heater, Mike."

I started the motor, turned on the heater.

"What do you think, Mike?" Waylin said.

"I think just the same thing you do, Clyde. Somebody killed Tom Flynn."

Waylin looked astonished. "Murder? How? In a car going eighty miles an hour?"

I held my breath until my lungs felt hot. "When the call came to Ernie's place, they were calling it murder."

"My God," Neal Burgess said. "That was just a mix-up at headquarters. You know how they foul things up like that on a first report. By the way, Clyde, now that Mike mentions it, I think they reported a homicide when they called me."

"They reported a murder." Ernie's voice was low.

Waylin tried to laugh. "It was murder, all right. Murder the way that man hit that bottle. Murder the way he came off that highway. Either Flynn was drunk, or he tried to kill himself."

"You think he tried to kill himself?" I asked.

"What else? And he made it. Drinking. Driving too fast. Never even touched his brakes. And he's dead. A fine man. But we all make at least one mistake."

I sat there a long time watching the wrecker falter up that incline. "I can't see a short drop like that killing a man. Even at ninety."

"Why, that car rolling over would beat him to death. Very likely, crush him."

"Only the car didn't roll over. I asked that. That car went straight down that incline in deep ruts and into a ditch."

Waylin sat still for some moments. Finally, he said, "Mike, maybe there are a few things you don't know about Tom Flynn."

I stared straight ahead through the windshield, waiting.

"If you knew as much as I do about Tom Flynn, Mike," Waylin said, "you'd agree that he committed suicide in that car."

"A man with a future like his?"

"What future? His future was all behind him. This is between us, but we've been getting bad reports on him, Mike. He was in trouble. Taking bribes, offering bribes. There's been talk lately about an investigation of his office. If some of his malpractice had come to light, he'd have been ruined. You know the Flynn name. A scandal would be something Tom Flynn couldn't face. When the threat of exposure came, he knew he was finished and took the easy way out. Fast car. Rain-slicked highway. A bad curve. And liquor to kill the pain."

I turned slightly on the seat. "You feel that way, too, Neal?"

Burgess shrugged. "I don't know as much about the inside of this mess as Clyde does, Mike. But there was whiskey. He was drunk."

"He killed himself, and it ends there," Waylin said. "Naturally, we're going to try to soften this as much as we can, for the family's sake. We're going to call it an accident as far as the public is concerned, but officially it's a suicide, and Doc Yerrgsted will sign his report that way, closing the whole regrettable incident."

I turned to stare at Ernie Gault. He raised his head but his gaze did not touch mine. Finally he turned his head and stared into the rain-filled night.

8

The Greek's was closed when I got there, but I rattled the door until he opened it, cursing. He stopped when he recognized me and held the door open. Gusts of rain followed me in before he could slam it shut behind me.

"What a night," he said. "Don't you never sleep?"

"If you don't like the weather here," I said, "why don't you go back to Greece?"

"Greece?" He limped through the dark saloon behind me. "Greece. She's like a mother to me. But I hate my mother."

"Who you kidding? You never had a mother."

"You hungry, Mike? How about a nice salad?"

"No. I want a drink. You know how bad I want it when I come to this place for it."

He glanced around his polished, richly upholstered saloon with Greek scenes in giant paintings alternating with huge, tinted mirrors around the walls. He spread his hands and sighed. "You and Doc Yerrgsted. You don't care where you drink."

"Is he around?"

He nodded toward the rear booth over which a small lamp glowed. He shook his head. "He don't want to talk to nobody. He sits. I speak. He growls. He hates me, hates this place so bad I sometimes wonder why he never goes home."

"You mean he don't live here?"

"He don't live—period. Except here." The Greek tapped at his heart with his cupped fingers. "Tonight it's worse than ever. I ask. But he won't say."

I leaned against the bar while he went behind it, poured me a double shot, filled another glass with water.

"A man died tonight," I said.

"A friend to you and Doc?"

"He wouldn't have spat on either of us. They say he committed suicide."

"Ah? A sad way to die. Do I know his name?"

I took a quick drink at the bourbon. "He never came in here to drink, if that's what you mean. His name was Tom Flynn."

The Greek stared. "Mister Thomas Flynn." He breathed deeply. "A great man."

"A regular Steve Canyon," I said. I held the bourbon glass in my fist. "Or maybe a Li'l Abner."

He swallowed, frowning. "I see. You make a joke. You don't care, huh?"

I shrugged, pushed my empty glass toward him. "Maybe I don't blame him. He was a good man in a rotten town. "Sure. Give me that bottle. I'll go back and speak to Doc. You talk like one of those Greek comedies. I hate to see a grown bartender cry."

He pushed the bottle across the gleaming bar to me. "Why don't you go somewhere else to do your drinking, huh? Do me a favor. This town got mighty few good men like Thomas Flynn. It's time to stop and think about it. Talk about it. We should feel sad. Even you. Not for him, but for you. For this town."

"You know Ernest Hemingway?"

He shook his head.

"You talk like he invented you."

He leaned against the bar. "Nobody invented me, you dumb cop."

I stood very still, watching him, until he looked away. He must have been really worked up to talk to me like that.

I paused beside the rear booth. Doc Yerrgsted sat slumped over the table, his head on his arms. He lifted his face slowly and looked up at me. His moustache twitched slightly. He said nothing. Very carefully, he lowered his head on his arms again.

The Greek brought himself a small glass of wine. He pulled a chair to the end of the booth and sat down. He glanced at the Doc and then at me without saying anything.

After a long time, Doc Yerrgsted raised his head again. His eyes, glistening like bourbon, focused on me with difficulty.

"Well, Ballard, see you got back from the scene of the crime."

"Crime?" I poured myself a drink. "What crime? Flynn committed suicide."

Doc laughed. "Very unlikely. I have been a man of medicine for many years—witnessed many phenomena. However, one I've never seen. I've never seen a suicide shoot himself in the back of the head."

I laid my hand on the table top, opened it. It was still streaked with the blood that had smeared it as I drew it away from the back of Tom Flynn's head out near the Essex Turnpike. I stared at the blood on my palm until Doc turned his head, refocused his eyes upon it. The Greek leaned forward, staring at my hand.

I felt icy inside as I asked Doc, "Are you going to put that in your official report?"

For some moments it was quiet in the Greek's bar. Doc stared across the table at me, a twisted smile pulling his moustache out of shape.

When he did speak, he ignored my question. "You two. Both of you are fine men. You understand, I drink only with men I trust, and respect. You, Greek—and you, cop—" he could really make something nasty out of that word—"I feel a great attachment to both of you. That's why I can tell you this. I—I'm going to tell you men something I never told anybody before—in my life."

He licked at his moustache, stared at us as though he had never seen either of us before. He said nothing for a long time, and seemed to have forgotten he had promised to reveal untold secrets.

"Doc is an after-dinner speaker." I winked at the Greek. "He throws out a promise to get your attention and falls asleep on it."

"Sleep." Doc wiped his hand across his mouth. "Perchance to dream. Ah, there's the rub. I can't endure all this, cop. Can't you understand? You're an intelligent man. You must be, cop, though in your racket you've never had to exercise any mental powers. There must be acres of intelligence in that ugly head of yours—unused, untapped. Then try to understand what life has done to me? I was at Yale Medical. I made quite a record there. They—they invited me to—intern at Johns Hopkins—I didn't have to beg, to apply, to stand in line.... Oh, no. Later they invited me abroad—I worked with great surgeons in Austria.... I learned, cop, what a glorious, glorious science I was picking at with my little brain—" He sat up straight suddenly, flinging out his arms and staring at us with wild eyes. "Of course, I've failed... we've all failed. We've made compromises—"

He stopped talking, shuddered convulsively and sat staring at his hands, trembling before him. He dropped them suddenly hiding their tremors under the table. "But I'm no tramp to be pushed around, cop. You understand that? What are those lines—?

"Give me to drink Mandragora

That I might sleep out this great gap of time....

"This evil time. I'll have no part of this ugly business. I've compromised before. I—I am nothing. But my profession—my—" He jerked his head up suddenly, his face twisted, staring at me. "They sent you here to find me, didn't they?"

I shrugged. "They thought I might be able to find you."

"Look at him, Greek. Young. Strong. Intelligent. And yet what is he? What are you, Ballard? A messenger? A call boy? Errand chaser?"

"I chase errands when they tell me to."

"Are you proud of yourself?"

"I never bother to think about it. I just collect pay checks. The same as you. You ready to go?"

"No!" The word burst from him. "Why, I'll never do it. I'll never sign a false statement about Tom Flynn's death—they could never force me to do that."

I shrugged. After a moment I said, "How long do you think the Greek would let you sign tabs in here, Doc—if you weren't the M.E. any more?"

Doc shivered. We both turned to look at the Greek. He held the Doc's gaze for a moment, then dropped his head, looking at the empty wine glass in his fist.

9

They were waiting for us when Doc and I got to Room 817 at City Hall. Doc had said nothing after we left the Greek's and as we walked in silence up the paper-littered marble stairs to the elevator I thought of a small proud spaniel coming in out of the rain. He pushed off his hat, thumb under the band, slapped it against his leg. He shrugged his jacket up on his shoulders, stood straighter. Somehow, it didn't make him look taller. For the first time I saw how small and old he looked.

I knocked once, then pushed open the door to 817 and let Doc enter ahead of me.

Three men sat at the wooden conference table. Except for littered ashtrays and a single sheaf of papers, the tabletop was bare.

"You took your own damned sweet time, Ballard." Chief Waylin was sweated, his collar was limp and his black tie was awry.

"Never mind, Clyde." Police Commissioner Stewart Mitchell had silvery hair and a silvery voice. He was small, round-bellied and wore a tailored suit and custom made shirt. He was holding a cigar and looked completely unruffled. However, he did not intend to let me think I could get away with keeping him and Mayor Landon Bibb waiting. "This is a serious matter, Ballard. Naturally, we're all anxious to have it quickly disposed of."

I gestured to Doc. "There's your man."

Mayor Bibb, Mitchell and Waylin were sitting at the head of the table, facing the door. I went around the table and sat down as far from them as I could get.

His shoulders parade-rigid, Doc Yerrgsted walked to the empty chair facing the sheaf of papers. He stood looking at the papers, but did not sit down.

"They're all there, Leonard," the Mayor said to Yerrgsted. The Mayor was in his early fifties, had a large, balding head, gray hair. He was a troubled man. He was not sweating, as was Waylin, but neither was he as calm as Mitchell. The ashtray before him was piled high with butts. "The report has been filled out completely by your assistant. All it needs is your signature."

"And let's get it and get out of here, for God's sake," Waylin said. "I've been up all night."

"I can't believe it matters," Yerrgsted said. He pressed his knuckles against the tabletop, bracing himself. "I can't believe you could sleep, anyhow. Any of you."

"What kind of stupid talk is this, Leonard?" Bibb said.

"How drunk is he, Ballard?" Mitchell stared at me through his cigar smoke.

I shrugged.

"I'm not drunk at all," Yerrgsted said. "I'm appalled. Shocked. I saw a man tonight with a bullet in the back of his head. And now I am told I am to certify that death as a suicide."

"It was a suicide, Doctor Yerrgsted," Mitchell said. "And we're all saddened by it. We only want you to certify the death."

"Then we can all go home," Waylin said.

Yerrgsted shook his head. "What about his family?"

"Never mind the family, Yerrgsted," Bibb said. "We've removed Flynn's body to the morgue. As you know—after the accident, the body was in such condition that—well, we were thinking first about his family when we ordered his casket sealed."

Yerrgsted slapped the back of his hand down on the medical examiner's report before him. "I can't affix my signature to a paper like this."

Mitchell leaned forward. "Why not?"

"Because I'm the medical examiner in this town. It is my trust, my job to decide cause of death. You men don't seem to realize my position. My place of trust."

"Why, you damned old souse. Stop making speeches."

Bibb spoke quickly. "We feel as badly about this as you do, Leonard. We're all troubled. But this is a poor time for a scandal."

"He hasn't got a brain left unpickled enough to see that," Mitchell said.

"I want an investigation," Yerrgsted said. "I'm going to have to demand an investigation."

"You're not demanding a damned thing," Mitchell said.

"I'm the medical examiner, sir. I can demand an investigation by the police, by the sheriff's office—or conduct one of my own. Why, a thing like this—I can't believe it's happening."

Bibb stood up. "All right, Leonard. You've made your speech. Now listen to me. You sign that paper, or you'll find yourself on your ass in the street. Is that clear enough?"

"I—" Yerrgsted frowned, looking at them. His shoulders sagged. He ran his hand through his thick gray hair, and jerked his head around, staring wildly at me.

I just looked at him. I did not move.

At last he sighed. He seemed to shrink inside his clothes. He pulled his gaze from me.

At last he said, "I'm wrong, I suppose. You're our civic leaders. You certainly—more than I, perhaps—know the welfare of our town and have it at heart. Of course—suicide." He worked a fountain pen from his pocket, almost dropped it from trembling fingers. "In the death of Thomas Elliot

Flynn. Suicide."

The three men stared as one when Yerrgsted finally signed the last paper, steadying his right hand with his left as he scrawled his signature.

He did not look at them again, or at me.

He placed his hat carefully on his head, went around the table and through the door. He closed it carefully and quietly behind him.

"Well, thank heaven, that's over," Bibb said.

I stood up, strode to the door. There I paused, turned.

"There's one thing about a man who drinks," I said. "He's unpredictable. You never really know about him. You can't know when he's going to drink, whom he's going to talk to or what he's going to say." I smiled at them. "Good night, gentlemen," I said. "Sleep well."

I found Doc at the elevator. His hand was shaking so badly he couldn't press the down button.

He looked up at me. "Any more errands tonight, Ballard?"

"Not that I know of."

"Fine. Should we go somewhere and have a drink?"

"Why not? Any particular place?"

"Perhaps the Greek's?" His voice shook. "He serves a fine domestic liquor."

"Sure," I said. "And he's fast, too."

The Greek was waiting for us.

"How did it go?" he asked.

"Fine," I said. "Doc signed his name. He needed two hands to do it, but his credit is still good. He's got a job."

"Ballard here could have done it with one hand behind his back," Doc said. "Get me something to drink, Greek, I'm freezing to death."

He walked away from us, hurrying toward that wanly lit booth in the rear where I had found him earlier. When the Greek and I got there with bourbon and water he was slumped behind the table as though he had never left it.

"I would like to prescribe for you, Ballard," he said when I sat down across the table from him. "A nice long voyage. A trip somewhere. A vacation. Why don't you get out of this town?"

I shrugged. "Why don't you?"

He twisted the cork from a bottle with his teeth, drank with the cork pushed to one side of his mouth as though he were so thirsty he couldn't wait for the glass the Greek placed on the table before him.

"I'm trying to tell you, Ballard," he said at last. "You've got a terrible disease. You walk around with the pain carefully concealed inside you, and all the time the disease is eating up your insides. You were hurt tonight, perhaps more than I was. Why don't you buy a ticket on the first train out, Ballard? It doesn't matter where."

I tried to laugh. I said to the Greek, "Doc is angry. He hates me because I wouldn't stand up with him over there tonight."

Doc shook his head. "That's where you're wrong. Why should you stand up with a man who was bound to let you down? I was sorry for you."

I laughed, slid across the seat and got up. "I'm getting out of here. You've been drinking some of the Greek's private stock."

10

The next afternoon at five when I got off work and left police head-quarters, I wanted a drink as much as I ever had, but I didn't want to sit around in the Greek's bar with Doc. I climbed into the Olds, and sat gripping the wheel, staring at the windshield. I was tired all the way to the soles of my feet.

It had been a clear day, but now the skies were blackening and before I had backed out of the police parking lot, the rain had begun. Hell, I thought, there were plenty of places a man could get a drink.

I turned west, moving slowly with the five o'clock traffic, drove to the Third Avenue entrance and out to the Essex Turnpike. I kept to the inside lane, moving at snail's pace, and the cars behind me honked and snarled. My windshield wipers were going and the rain beat loudly against the car top.

I told myself I was looking for a bar, but when I reached the country club exit, I turned west and kept slowing down until I reached the Flynn house. Three or four cars were parked in the pebbled drive as I pulled up.

Lights were on in the house, glowing yellow against the rain and early darkness. I remembered how Carolyn hated and feared the thought of death—yet what choice had she had? Perhaps she, at least, should know that Tom had had no choice, either.

I did not know what I would tell her as I slogged across the walk to the front door and rang the doorbell. There was a long silence. This place had servants to open doors, answer bells. Maybe today nothing was working right.

When the door was finally opened, Jerry Marlowe stood framed against the light. He wore Italian straw shoes, dark slacks, a white shirt open at the collar. A cigarette hung from a corner of his mouth and his left eye was squinted against the sting of smoke.

His face showed some small surprise, then a touch of color. It was as though he had to dig back into his mind to remember to smile.

"Hello, old Mike. Come on in." He didn't shake hands. Instead he plucked the cigarette from his lips and flicked it across the veranda to sizzle out in the rain. He closed the door and when he turned again, his smile looked genuine. "Just follow me," he said.

I followed him across the foyer into the sun room that Tom Flynn and I had crossed so cautiously the last time I was here. The room did not look the same—it was no longer unused. The cute black-haired chick was sprawled out on the divan in yellow halter and slacks. She had one knee up, the other foot resting on it. Bright cosmetic bottles littered the floor beside the divan.

She was painting her toenails.

"Hi," she said. "You hunk of man. You beautiful hunk of man. Can I paint your toenails—or something?"

Her voice had an odd, loose quality and there was a light to match in her dark eyes. And again it itched at me that I might have seen her somewhere before meeting her here. Maybe in some expensive cathouse somewhere.

"Shut up, Jackie," Jerry said. "Don't mind her, Mike. There's just one thing Jackie wants. A year's subscription to any man who might be willing."

I glanced at her, and winked. "I'm flattered, but a year is a long time."

The man in the big chair laughed. He was Morgan Carmichael. "Some years are," he said. "You really have a way with women, don't you, Ballard?"

"Some of us do," I said. I felt myself getting tense.

But he wouldn't let it go at that. "Oh, but you have a special way. Women look at you, just once, and they have you on their little brains forever. Give you much trouble, Ballard?"

I stared at him and felt my hands clench into fists. He met my gaze for a moment and then his eyes moved away.

Jerry was leaning against a club chair, legs crossed at the ankles. I asked, "Is Carolyn seeing anyone, Jerry?"

He shrugged. "She'll probably talk to you." He glanced at Morgan, and his mouth twisted slightly. "Anything particular you want to see her about?"

"Come off it, Jerry. I guess Tom didn't mean much to you—"

"For God's sake, Mike. Did he mean much to anybody? Did he mean much to you?"

"Maybe he meant something to Carolyn. She married him."

He straightened. The smile around his mouth deepened. "Want to tell me how much loot you drag in per year in the cop racket, Mike? I'll present your case to the young widow. Sorry though—but, you weren't quite the first to come calling."

Maybe I could have taken it some other time, some other place. But tonight everything about the people in this room bugged me—I still did not quite know why I had come.

I said softly, "Talk out of the other side of your mouth to me, kid. Or I'll paddle some sense into your head."

Morgan Carmichael emitted another burst of laughter. "And he'll do it too, Jerry."

Jackie swung her legs to the floor, sitting up. "Wait till I get the top back on this bottle. I don't want to miss a thing."

"Get back in your kennel," Jerry said to her. He nodded toward the foyer.

His face was starkly white. "I'll tell Carolyn you're down here."

I nodded, followed him out to the foyer. Carmichael laughed again—there was no sound from Jackie. I didn't look at them.

Jerry stopped outside the closed door of the sun room. "I still like you, Mike," he said. "I always have. But don't ever put your hand on me again. Not even in fun. Clear?"

I shrugged. "No comment. Tell Carolyn I won't stay five minutes. But I would like to see her."

The man with Carolyn stood up as I entered. I barely saw him. Carolyn wore a lavender housecoat and rested a damp cloth across her forehead.

She peeled the cloth away and sat up.

I had sensed no grief, no sense of loss in the people I had just left. Here sorrow hung like a pall. Carolyn's face was bloodless, her eyes looked stricken.

"Mike. I'm so grateful you came."

Even with the grief like a veil over her, Carolyn was lovely, lovelier than she had been as a girl—for she was a woman now. Sorrow became her. She was slender, even with the indrawn quality the shadows under her deep-set eyes and high cheekbones gave her.

"I was hoping there might he something I could do to help, Carolyn." Surprisingly, I felt the old strong longing that I'd thought time-diluted.

Fred Carmichael moved away from the wing chair near the window and walked to the lounge. That was when I first really saw him. He stood behind Carolyn and put his arm about her shoulders. I tried not to see the way she reached up and touched his hand with caressing fingers.

"It's a good thing I've friends like you and Fred, Mike—or I wouldn't know what to do."

"We'll do anything we can for you, Carolyn," Carmichael said. He was a big man, taller than his son, bigger in the shoulders and chest. He was in his middle forties, but he was flat in the belly, trim in the hips. The tailored suit didn't hurt him any, or the imported linen shirt, or the close-cropped iron-gray hair. He was a handsome man, even with the broken nose and the faint scar tissue that quirked his right brow slightly so that no matter what he intended, he always looked slightly supercilious. "I don't know you as well as I'd like, Detective Ballard, but I've always admired you. A strong man. I admire strong men."

"I know that you used your influence to keep me on the police force four years ago," I said.

"You belonged there. Every man makes mistakes. Few of us ever rectify them quite as completely as you did when you wiped out the Luxtro mob."

"I was in love with Mike once, Fred," Carolyn said softly.

"I know, my dear." Carmichael still had his hand on her shoulder. I began getting a subtle feeling that he was trying to get some message across to me.

"It was a long time ago," Carolyn said. "Sometimes it seems to me, whenever I think of any happiness at all, that it was always a long time ago."

"This is a bad time, Carolyn." Carmichael's thick hand caressed her shoulder. "You'll be happy again."

Suddenly I was very tired of this house, these people. The very air seemed stagnant here, still and purposeless. The thought of the Greek's bar seemed pretty good. I had not said any of the things I had come to say—nothing I thought or felt seemed to fit, quite. It was as if death existed here only as a reaction, a feeling, a mental state—not as a fact.

"I'd better leave now," I said. "I just wanted to tell you how sorry I was about Tom."

Carolyn stood up. Her eyes brimmed suddenly with tears. She touched at them with her handkerchief. "I—I'll walk downstairs with you, Mike. Do you mind, Fred?"

"Of course not. I'll come with you. I tell you, Ballard, I appreciate your coming like this. It's helped Carolyn. By God, it really has."

Carolyn had moved across the room. She took my hand, pressing it.

"I never knew I'd miss him so terribly, Mike."

"Tom was a great man." Carmichael had followed her and touched her shoulder again. I tried to remind myself that it was a gesture of sympathy. "Essex City has lost a valuable citizen. We've all suffered a great loss with you, Carolyn."

I wished three things—that Carmichael would take his hands off her and shut up, and that he would leave us alone. He trailed us to the door.

Carolyn still held my hand. "Mike. They—won't let me see him. They won't let me see Tom's body."

"I'm sure you understand, Ballard," Carmichael said. "I've tried to tell her. The wreck—ghastly—Tom wouldn't want the woman he loved remembering him so. Or his friends either. Right, Ballard?"

"I don't know," I said. "I saw him at the scene of the crash. He just looked dead to me."

Carolyn's fingers tightened briefly on my hand. She said nothing. Neither did Carmichael.

Jerry and young Morgan Carmichael were waiting in the front hall. Jerry had heard me say I had seen Tom Flynn's body at the wreck. He laughed in my face. "I heard Tom was supposed to have been driving while drunk, Mike."

"That was in the report," I said.

"Hell, how dumb can you be? What is there about being a cop that attracts the worst of men to the force?"

"Jerry!" Carolyn's voice was sharp.

"What the hell, sis? How dumb can those cops be? Everybody in town knows Tom Flynn never took a drink in his life."

Carmichael's voice was very soft. "Maybe that's why drink hit him so hard this time. He wasn't used to it."

Jerry laughed again. "Sure. Tell it that way. It'll sound great to everyone who didn't know Tom. It won't even damage his memory much. But it won't bring him back to life, either."

Carolyn stared at him, her eyes helpless. "Jerry, you've got to stop talking like that."

"You're in very poor taste, young fellow," Carmichael said.

"Why?" Jerry moved his gaze from Fred to Carolyn. "Why? Even the cops ought to stick close to the truth when a man like Tom is killed. Everybody knows he never drank."

Carmichael stared at Jerry a moment. His voice was low. "Don't you think your sister is suffering enough, young man?"

Jerry laughed again. "I think she just got a reprieve from prison. That's what I think—if she just had sense enough to realize it."

Fred Carmichael's face was white, fists clenched and he was almost upon Jerry before he could stop himself. He got his temper under control just in time.

Jerry stood smiling at him.

Carolyn, shaking her head, took my arm.

At the door she said, "I wanted to ask you something, Mike."

"Sure."

"The funeral. Tomorrow afternoon. I'll be alone, unless—would you come with me?"

I glanced over the top of her head, wondering why she needed me with big Fred Carmichael in the house apparently ready to plug up gaps in her life. But I didn't argue with her. I told her I would be there. She pressed my hand and I went out the door and crossed the yard to my car. The rain was whipping in now, harder than ever.

11

I was unarmed. I yelled at them that I didn't have a gun. They laughed. They would have died laughing, but they were too busy trying to kill me. There were six of them and they were taller than the buildings, and all had guns and behind them stood Luxtro like a human skyscraper, yelling at them to shoot and keep shooting before I could get away. I looked around. A moment before I'd been on a wide highway, but now the boulevard was a garbage-littered alley, and the buildings of the alley were closing in on me and there was nowhere to run....

I woke up, sweating and shaking.

Somebody was pounding on my door.

I reached out and turned on a light beside the bed. The nightlight was weak. The room was thick with shadows, and I had not shaken off the dream when I could hear somebody calling my name at the door.

"Mike—Mike! Wake up!"

I glanced at the electric clock on the bed table as I swung my feet off to the floor. The hands pointed to three in the morning. I had been asleep for an hour.

"All right." I looked around for a bathrobe, failed to find it and crossed the apartment in my shorts.

Ernie Gault stood outside the door. He wore a rain slicker. His hound-trouble face was sicker than ever.

"Sorry to wake you up, Mike."

"Thank God you did."

He frowned. "Could you get dressed, Mike? It's pretty urgent."

"Homicide?"

He shrugged. "Would I wake you up for anything else?" He followed me into my bedroom, watched me step into my trousers and shrug on a shirt.

Trying to keep it light, he said, "Why can't people knock each other off during the day shift, huh?"

But his voice shook.

There were a half-dozen cops at Ed Clemmons' place out on Pine Street by the time Ernie and I got there. Normally, Pine was a quiet neighborhood, bargain-priced homes with green-stamp lawns, cheap roofing—a place where young couples bought when they were just starting out, or older couples who couldn't make the fast pace. But now lights blazed in every window for two blocks, and neighbors shivered on their front stoops or stood crowded in doorways. But they kept their distance. These people knew that trouble could be contagious.

Ernie and I got out of the police Plymouth and walked along the short driveway to the one-car garage Ed had turned into a gunroom and workshop. When we got nearer, I could hear a woman sobbing.

"Must be Ed's wife," Ernie said.

Norma Clemmons was on the verge of hysterics and the ambulance doctor was giving her a hypo as Ernie and I walked in. When she saw us, she cried out, "Mike—Ernie—"

Ernie went over to touch her shoulder. "Try to take it easy, Norma. I know it's a hell of a thing."

Her mouth quivered. "Ed's dead, Ernie—"

Young Ed Clemmons was sprawled out on the garage floor. He looked as if a gun had exploded inches from his face.

They were getting ready to move his body, but paused to see if I had any suggestions. I shook my head, told them to get it out of there. They lifted his body on the wheel-litter. Ed was still wearing his police uniform.

"How did it happen?" I asked.

A young patrolman spoke from the doorway. "Ed shot himself."

I turned. "Oh?"

"He was cleaning one of his guns." The cop nodded toward the collection on the wall of the garage, next to Ed's tools.

"At three o'clock in the morning?" I said.

"He was a nut on guns, all right. Everybody knew that," the young cop said.

Ed's wife cried out again, sobbing. She jumped up and Ernie tried to catch her, but she writhed free of him and ran after the ambulance men who were wheeling Ed's body out to the ambulance.

I snagged her in the doorway and we had a real waltz before I could quiet her down. But suddenly she sagged against me as if all the life had gone out of her.

"Open that door," I told Ernie. "I'll take her back in the house."

I carried her through the small kitchen, the apology of a dining room, crossed a hall and went into a lighted bedroom. The bedcovers were thrown back violently.

I put her down on the bed. "Is there anybody who can stay with you?" I said.

"I'm all right."

"Sure you are. I didn't ask about that."

Despite the sharpness of my tone, she managed a wan smile. "My mother. I'll call her."

Ernie spoke from behind me. "Give me her number, Norma. I'll call her."

She told Ernie the number and he went into the living room. It was so quiet in the house I could hear him dialing. Norma Clemmons shivered and I pulled the covers over her.

I asked, "Were you asleep when it happened?"

She nodded. "Ed was on the late shift. He—was in a prowl car with Carl Hogan. You know Carl Hogan, Mike?"

I didn't know many of the later rookies, but I said sure, I knew Carl.

"Well, Ed came in so late every night that I just went on to bed. I used to wait up for him, but he didn't want me to. He said—no use everybody staying up all night, just because he had to."

"Was he in the habit of cleaning his gun before he came in to bed?"

She shook her head. "He—never did before."

"Well, there's always got to be a first time."

"Mike, I heard something. I didn't tell anybody else. I was afraid to—"

"Why were you afraid?"

She scrubbed at her face with her hands. "I don't know. But Ed was upset all day. He wouldn't talk about it. Something was bothering him. I was asleep and I heard this shot—from the garage. I didn't even stop to think. I just screamed for Ed and I jumped out of bed and ran through the house to the garage—"

"And when you got out there he was dead."

She covered her face with her hands, nodding. "But there's something else."

"What?"

"I never told anybody. I was afraid to, like I said. But just after I heard that shot—before I got out of this room—I heard a car drive away out front. It was going fast. You think I should tell anybody about that car, Mike?"

"Don't worry about it," I said. "Now you've told me. It could have been just a neighbor. But I'll look into it. There's no point in your saying more about it."

But why had it frightened her that the killer had possibly come and gone in a car? Many of them do.

I rode in a black Ramsey-Angell funeral Cadillac with Carolyn that afternoon at three. We were the first car behind the hearse. Her face looked starkly white against her black dress and hat. The youthful chauffeur kept his eyes straight ahead.

"Thanks for coming with me," Carolyn said.

"I wanted to."

"I don't know what I would have done. Tom has such a large family— yet I felt completely alone. I hope you never feel as alone as I have been, Mike."

I watched the small blue fender pennant whip in the wind. "Biggest funeral I ever saw," I said. "If that means a damned thing."

"It doesn't," Carolyn said. Her chin tilted. She looked even more gaunt than she had yesterday. "They're all here. Not only his family, but every-body who ever hated Tom Flynn has shown up today. I never saw so many black suits, and black ties—and black dirty hearts."

"It's a winning combination this year."

"Even Jerry. He should be with me today, but I know how he disliked Tom. They lived their lives at opposite poles. But it's Jerry I'm worried about, now Tom is dead. Tom was a good influence on Jerry, no matter how contemptuously Jerry talked to him—and about him. Jerry's bitter. He keeps saying that Tom asked for it—and got it. Almost as if he knew all along it was going to happen."

"He doesn't mean that, Carolyn. He only means that Tom was fighting some powerful people and lost. Maybe he figures Tom must have known all along he was going to lose."

She nodded. "I suppose he did."

"He was doing what he believed in," I said. "There are worse deaths."

My God—Doc Yerrgsted had said that.

The funeral director had reserved a canvas chair for Carolyn near the open grave, under the green striped canopy where the Flynn clan had gathered.

She shook her head, and stood to one side with me while the minister read the final words of the burial ceremony. She barely seemed aware that I was beside her, and yet I had the damnedest feeling that she was leaning on me, clinging to me, and that behind the stark white mask of her face she was weeping uncontrollably.

I was glad to have her to think about. I stared at the black suits, black ties—and black hearts she had mentioned. Fred Carmichael had a black band on his sleeve. His face was rigid and set. Mayor Bibb's eyes were red. Stewart Mitchell, the Police Commissioner, was leaning on his son's arm.

I moved my gaze beyond them—to men from the local bar association, Tom's college fraternity, the veterans' organizations. I saw Police Chief Clyde Waylin and Captain Neal Burgess, their faces set, eyes straight ahead.

"Oh, God!" Carolyn whispered. "Oh, my God!"

I turned quickly and looked at her. But she was all right. She was stand-ing tall and straight in her black dress, her gloved hands clenched togeth-er before her.

Across the grave I saw Ernie Gault and Grace, and beyond them stood Doc Yerrgsted in a shabby gray suit. Beside him slouched the Greek.

I felt slightly better seeing Doc and the Greek. They made the whole affair a little cleaner.

The chauffeur drove swiftly on the way back. He still kept his eyes straight ahead, but now he used the Cad like a hot-rod.

"I know now what it was that Tom wanted to tell me," Carolyn said. She seemed unaware of the way the car jockey handled the Cad, unaware of anything outside her own thoughts.

"Yes," I said.

She turned and looked at me. "Do you know, too, Mike? Have you figured it out?"

The funeral pennant on the fender was snapping in the wind. I nodded. "It was easy."

He had been threatened. That was what he had wanted to say to me that afternoon in his library, what he almost said to Carolyn—his life had been in danger. But he had not been able to bring in the issue of his personal safety in a public campaign. That was the Flynn pride. He could plead with me to help him clean up a dirty town. But he could not ask anyone to save his life in that same connection.

"They threatened him, Mike," Carolyn said. "They threatened to kill him, unless he stopped."

"Yes."

She pressed her hand against her mouth. "He thought—he thought he would be all right—if he could get you to help him."

"Yes," I said. "I guess he did. But believe me, Carolyn, I couldn't have saved him. He helped make the police force in this town what it is today. He didn't mean to, but he did. He was, in some ways, an outsider and he made mistakes. But he wasn't wrong. Believe that."

Carolyn nodded and then it was as if she went away from me. She sat beside me in the back seat of that swift moving car, but she seemed far away, out of reach.

I watched the fender pennant snap in the wind. The sound did not reach into the silence between us.

Big Fred Carmichael's car was parked out front of her house when we got there. I did not even get out to go to the door with her.

12

"Mike. Mind if I sit down?"

I scowled even before I looked up. It was a little after five the next afternoon and I was enjoying a double bourbon in the peace and quiet of the Greek's. Maybe enjoying is a slight exaggeration. I had found scant enjoyment in the days since Tom Flynn's death. Suicide on the highway. Murder was the better word—the only word.

I stared up at Ernie Gault. The illness inside Ernie had turned his face a nice ash-gray.

I shrugged. "Sit down."

He sat. "I wanted to talk to you, Mike. I had something on my mind."

"Will you have a drink?"

"No, Mike. You go ahead."

"What's burning your ulcer tonight?"

He pressed the tips of his fingers against his solar plexus and belched. "God. My own hot plate. Mike, do you think Tom Flynn committed suicide?"

I watched the bookmakers at play along the bar. "Do you?"

"I don't know what to think. But I do know this. Ed Clemmons, the boy that was—the boy who shot himself cleaning his gun. You know he was with Carl Hogan in the prowl car that reached the scene first when Tom Flynn died on the turnpike?"

"Yeah, I remember that."

"How can you be so calm about it?"

"Why not? If Tom Flynn can kill himself, why can't Ed Clemmons?"

"Two nights later? Cleaning a gun at three in the morning?"

"That's the report."

"There's more to it than that. It's been eating me up. I haven't slept. The night Clemmons was killed he had left a note for me on my desk at headquarters. It was there at five o'clock when I was checking out. All it said was that he wanted me to get in touch with him and that it was urgent. Well, I know how these kids are, all of them have something urgent on their minds. Mostly it's a gimmick that'll get them a commendation or a promotion. So I went on home, tried two or three times to get in touch with him during the evening, but he was out prowling with Hogan and never called back."

"All right. Forget it. You tried."

"Can't you guess what he wanted to talk to me about? Can't you, Mike?"

"No." I stared at him coldly. "I can't guess. And you can't guess. And you better leave it like that."

I decided against having another drink after Ernie left—instead I ordered a steak. When the Greek heard about that he came running out of his office where he had hibernated all afternoon.

"You eating a steak, Mike? I'll cook it myself. It'll melt in your mouth."

"Stop licking my hand," I told him. "You're wetting my cuffs."

He nodded, smiling. "You begin to see, huh? A steak seems pretty good, eh? You begin to see bourbon for dinner all the time don't get you so very far, huh?"

"Not around here anyhow," I said.

I walked back over to police headquarters and wandered into the ready room just for the hell of it. I was looking over the patrol assignments when I felt someone standing close behind me.

I glanced over my shoulder. It was Captain Burgess.

"Hi, Neal."

"What you doing around here, Ballard? You're off duty. I thought you were a prowler."

"Always call a policeman when you see anything suspicious," I semi-quoted. I turned back, running my hand along the roster.

"What are you looking for?"

"Nothing vital. A kid named Hogan. You probably never heard of him."

I heard Neal's sharp intake of breath. "Carl Hogan? What about him?"

"Nothing about him. I just got curious. I wondered who was riding with him since Ed Clemmons shot himself the other night."

Neal pulled the roster away from me, checking it himself. "You know Hogan?"

"Not very well. Do you?'

"I think he has a pretty good record. A couple commendations—mostly an average rook. Why?" He paused reading. "Here he is. He's not riding patrol car. He was reassigned since Clemmons died."

"Oh? What's his assignment?"

Neal checked again. "Walking beat. Halsey and Twenty-third area."

"Tough section."

"Somebody has to do it. We moved a new team into the prowl car. We had to find something for Hogan."

"Naturally."

"Look, Ballard. I don't have to explain this department to you."

"That's right. You don't."

"I follow orders, Ballard. I assign men as I'm told. I see nothing wrong about assigning Hogan to a walking beat."

"So let's forget it."

"I am interested in what you think about it, Ballard. What's the gimmick? You know, as a matter of fact, Police Commissioner Mitchell was asking for a report on you today."

"How about that? Did he say why?"

Neal Burgess hesitated, but after a moment he smiled. "As a matter of fact he did. He said that Fred Carmichael had asked about you. Wondered how you were getting along in the department recently."

"How thoughtful of him. I wonder why he gave a damn."

Neal's mouth tightened. "He's a public-spirited man, a leading citizen. Don't ever forget how much you owe him."

"I won't," I said and walked out.

I drove crosstown to Halsey. No matter how many street lights they set out in the Halsey section, the streets were dark, the doorways like inhabited caves. I drove slowly. Girls stood at lighted corners, smiled expectantly and then moved on, hips tight in cheap skirts. I parked near Maistre's Bar, hearing the blaring of the juke box.

I went into the bar, asked if they had seen the new cop on the beat. None of them had. No one even realized there was a new cop.

I spent another hour walking the dark streets in the old neighborhood. Cats slunk in the shadows, people whispered from the black caverns of the doorways. I stumbled over a wino at the corner of Twenty-third.

I was really back in my old neighborhood.

I was already sick of this place. I glanced at my watch, decided to give myself another twenty minutes. Hogan was in none of the eating places, and there was no sign of him on the street.

I walked back along Halsey slowly, going toward the Olds, parked near Maistre's Bar. Far away, across town somewhere, I heard a siren scream. Nearer a cat squawled. Suddenly I remembered my dream—all of Luxtro's men and all of Luxtro's guns cornering me in a garbage-strewn alley where the buildings kept closing in tighter.

I felt a sudden sickness and wiped the back of my hand across my mouth. It was as if I were suddenly suffering from claustrophobia. I stood at the black mouth of an alley and the very thought of walking into it was terrifying. I sweated, staring into the darkness.

I knew I could not walk away from it. I had to walk through that alley. I knew better than to start running away from the things I was afraid of.

I sucked in a deep breath. The yawning hole looked suddenly darker, narrower. I made up my mind. I'd walk through this alley, go around the block to my car and call it a night. Hell, Hogan was a big boy. I was the kid shivering at shadows.

I glanced once along Halsey toward the brightly lit front of Maistre's Bar. Then I stepped off the walk and moved into the alley. A cat slithered through the shadows and I caught my breath.

When I stumbled over the wino, I almost yelled. I had to clamp my teeth shut to keep from yelling.

I stared down at the man sprawled at my feet. Only it was no wino.
I had found Carl Hogan.

Ernie Gault knelt beside Hogan's body. The alley was now lighted with
police car headlights.

"In the back of the head," Ernie said, looking up.

"Just goes to show you," I said. "Never turn your back on your friends."
Except that here no one had even admitted knowing Hogan.

Ernie walked with me to my car. "Well, Mike. I can't pretend any more,
can I? Hogan was murdered. Clemmons was murdered. And Tom Flynn
was murdered. As sure as you and I are standing here."

"Looks like it."

"But that's only part of it, Mike. Men in the department. Men over us.
Fellows I've known almost twenty years. They know it's murder, too. Just
like we do. You know they do."

"You're shooting into the wind," I said.

He stopped in the middle of the walk, staring at me in the street light.

"What's wrong with you? You know I'm telling you the truth."

"Listen to me. Once it wasn't safe to talk about anything in this damn
town. That's been changed. Now it's not even safe to think it."

"I can't keep still about a thing like this. Three men have been murdered.
Two of them were cops. And men in the department have known about it,
they've gone right along with it, they've hidden the truth."

"And you don't think they're as sick about it as you are?"

"I don't know. I only know about me. I can't take it, and I'm going to
make a stink."

I caught his coat roughly in my fist, twisted him up on his toes.

"Don't ever think anything like that again, Gault. You understand me?
What's the matter with you? Isn't your ulcer killing you fast enough?
You've got no proof of any kind—and until you have, you're going to keep
your mouth shut, or I'll shut it for you."

The life went out of him. He sagged, relaxing. I released him. "All right,
Mike. I know you're right. It's just that I don't see how I can go on living
with what I know inside me."

13

The guys in the detective bureau office were licking their lips and whining a little inside when I got in the next afternoon at five. They were whispering as I passed their desks.

"Sweet Jesus."

"And I got to go home to my old woman."

"Just one night with that and let me die."

Lupe Valdez was sitting rigidly in the chair beside my desk so filled with her woes and indrawn she had no idea of the commotion she was causing. I couldn't blame the guys. Even with woes she lighted the place up like a torch.

She saw me and tried to smile.

I sat down behind my desk, my swivel whistling dryly at her. "Hello there," I said. "Long time. I've been looking for you to show around here."

She sighed. "Why? Did you want to help me?"

I shrugged. "Let's just say I had you pegged as a girl who wouldn't give up easily."

"I can't give up," she said. "And you're the only one who can help me. I've stood out in front of this place—and in front of the Greek's bar—every day, trying to get up my nerve to talk to you again."

"And now you've made it?"

"Or else." She glanced at the clock. So did I. It was ten past five. She tried to smile again. "Shall we go to the Greek's and get you a drink while we talk?"

I didn't bother to ask her what she thought we still had to talk about. "This is all right. I can live without a drink."

She inhaled deeply, glanced about the room. She still didn't see the hot eyes melting and running all over her.

"You've thought over—what we said last time?"

"Yes."

"You know I'm right, don't you?"

"All I know is just what I told you before. You're fooling with a powerful man—the son of a powerful man."

"It's for my baby."

"Yes. That's what you said." I shook my head, stared at my knuckles. "Let me get it straight. You're willing to let Morgan Carmichael off the hook, but you think he ought to be forced to make some kind of settlement on you"

"Not on me. On—his baby."

"Okay. On his baby. What kind of settlement do you think would be right?"

Her mouth twisted, she sat straighter. "His father owns a huge corporation, is director of a bank. I don't know what else—"

"Never mind that. I do."

"What kind of settlement do you think would be—right?"

I grinned at her. "We'd never get that much."

For the first time, hope glimmered in her black eyes. She pushed her hand through her thick hair. "I thought you said the police couldn't help me."

"Technically, they can't." I shrugged, and she almost smiled again. I glanced at the clock. "But I'm off duty. Maybe we could work out something."

"Have you forgotten how powerful you thought Morgan's father is?"

"No. I remember all that. Clearly."

She did smile now. "Thank heaven I met you, Mr. Ballard." She gathered up her purse, started to get up.

I touched her arm. "What's the matter with you? Where are you going?"

"Maybe you'll be fired, blacklisted—even killed. I don't want that—not after you said what you just did." Her voice quavered. "I've changed my mind, Mr. Ballard. Thanks anyway."

"Dammit," I said. "Sit down. You came back here. I didn't come looking for you."

"I know. But I—"

I stood up. "If you're going to learn to think about your baby, the first thing to learn is to admit you're not the only one with problems. Maybe I've got my own reasons now for playing on your team." I took her arm, led her out. "Come on."

She did not say anything until we were downstairs in the parking lot. We got into my car. When I parked in front of my apartment house, Lupe was paler than ever.

"Where are we going?"

"Up to my place. Come on."

She breathed in deeply. She was very pale under her olive skin. "All right—if that's what you want."

We were on the walk. I grabbed her shoulder, heeled her around. "Look, kid. Don't get ideas about me. If I want a lay, I can get women."

She looked as if I'd backhanded her across the eyes. She took a step backwards. Her voice was low. "All right, Mr. Ballard."

I turned and strode ahead of her into the apartment building. I fumbled through the bills in my mail box for a moment, letting her get used to the idea of going up to a man's apartment. We went up in the elevator in silence. I wondered how Morgan Carmichael ever got her in this interesting predicament if she were so afraid of being alone with males.

I let us in, went around opening up the apartment. A breeze off the river riffled the curtains.

She sat down on the divan, knees together, looking at me.

The phone rang. It was Ernie Gault. "You busy, Mike?"

"Right now I am."

"Another blonde?" His voice sounded troubled.

I glanced down at Lupe who had leaned back on the divan, trying to relax. "A brunette this time." She looked up, startled, met my gaze, then smiled. She relaxed again.

"Well, I'll call you later."

"What is it, Ernie?"

"Nothing. Just wanted to gab. Hell, there's no hurry."

I replaced the receiver. I went into the kitchenette, found a glass, filled it with milk, brought it back to Lupe.

She smiled. "I don't like milk, Mike."

"You should."

"I'm all right."

I went to my small bar, poured myself a drink. "Sure you are. That's why you're here. Drink your milk."

Obediently she took a drink of milk, made a face. She watched me over the top of the glass. "You—drink liquor quite a lot, don't you, Mike?"

"I do a lot of things quite a lot, kid."

She was looking me over. "Yes. I guess you do."

I pulled over a straight chair for her, sat down and sipped my whiskey, studying her. "How would you like to see lover boy again tonight? Say for one last time?"

"Morgan?" Her mouth trembled. "I never want to see him again."

"You want some money though, don't you?"

"I—I've got to have it."

"Then get on that phone. Call your lover boy and don't take no for an answer. If he hangs up on you, call back. Tell him you've rented an apartment. This apartment. Tell him he's right about the things he said to you. Tell him—hell, tell him you'll call it quits, never bother him again, if he'll come over here tonight. One last time."

"Must I?"

I shrugged. "What made you think I was kidding?"

She sat there for a long time, long enough for me to finish the bourbon and get dry. While I was making a fresh one, she put through the call. It wasn't easy. At the Carmichael house, they tried to give her the runaround. It was easy to see Morgan had put her name on a list, even with the servants.

When she finally got through to Morgan, he was too busy to yak with her. She stared at me in desperation. I just kept looking at her, nothing in my face. She hung on.

She kept talking, whispering, wheedling, promising, dealing. I began to see how she got in this predicament after all. There was more sex in her voice than most women project with their whole bodies. I remembered Naomi Hyers, looking along her nose, and I grinned to myself. If young Carmichael passed up Lupe for Naomi, he deserved what he got. Hell, I could feel a stirring in myself just listening to Lupe.

Finally she glanced up, eyes stricken, but giving me a wan smile. She had heated young Carmichael past his boiling point—he was coming over.

She replaced the receiver and sank back against the couch, spent.

"Fine," I said. "Now get out of that dress."

She started to protest. Then her eyes touched mine and she changed her mind.

She gave me a scared smile, nodded. "All right, Mike."

She slipped out of the dress. I walked to the window to let the breeze touch me. I did not make a point of not looking at her—and she was even lovelier than the boys in the bureau had imagined she would be out of that dress. Her full curves looked swollen, as if they needed to be loved. She was lush and dark and beautiful.

I finally looked away. "Now take off that bra and your pants," I told her across my shoulder. I stared out at the darkening river. Lights winked, reflected in it. I winked back.

At last she said, "All right. I've done it."

I glanced across my shoulder. I caught my breath. "For hell's sake, kid, I meant leave your slip on."

She blushed and wriggled into her slip, pulling it down over her head and undulating up into it. I thought how tough it was remembering why she was here at all.

I drew in a deep breath and turned around, trying to keep everything natural and easy. Her slip didn't help matters. It only seemed to accentuate her desirability.

"Now, when he comes in," I said, "act as if you're hot as a rivet. You can't resist him. No matter what you think about him now, no matter what he says, get him down on that couch."

She looked miserable and forlorn, as if she wished she had never started this. "I'll try," she said.

I laughed at her. "Hell. It'll be the easiest thing you ever did."

"I feel so low," she said, shivering. "So vile."

"Good. If you feel vile, then Morgan Carmichael has finally dragged you down to his level. So just keep that thought in your mind—that and the way you want your baby to be taken care of."

We waited forty minutes, during which I kept coaching her; then we heard him at the door. I stepped into the darkened bedroom.

Lupe crossed the apartment in her slip, and I heard castanets. She hesitated. Carmichael rang again, an impatient sound. He was in a hurry to walk into our little trap.

She opened the door and Morgan strode in. I studied him through the partly open bedroom door. Even at twenty-six he looked like a spoiled lost kid who had no idea of the score, who had not even bothered to figure out the rules of the game. I failed to see what about him had excited Lupe.

His breath caught when he saw her. His headshake was unconvincing.

He said, "It's no good, Lupe. I told you. It's no use. I'm marrying Naomi Hyers. It's all over. God knows you're lovely. But—it's all over, baby. Why don't you be a nice kid—and forget it?"

All this time, judging by his eyes, he was not forgetting a damned thing.

Lupe breathed raggedly. Her breathing did something to the front of that slip. The castanets started again in my mind. I was pretty sure young Carmichael was hearing them, too, by now. Lupe managed to keep smiling.

"All right, Morgan. That's exactly why I wanted to see you. I wanted to tell you—you were right."

"You could have said that over the phone."

But something had happened to his voice. Lupe moved closer to him and the violins were coming in under the castanets. She was getting to him. It must have been easy—she had done this before. "I wanted you here—" her voice poured down over him like Cuban syrup—"because I had to see you—one more time."

"Okay then, baby." Big shot, he was doing her a favor. "That's the way it's got to be, then."

He got her sprawled on the couch almost before I could get my camera set up. He knew what he wanted, and she knew what she was doing. It was in her blood. She was still crazy about him, too, no matter how terribly he had made her hate him.

I had to act fast. I didn't give them any time together. I had worked up a real dislike for this boy. When my flashbulb went off, Morgan Carmichael sprang up from Lupe as if he had been shot. He moved fast, but not fast enough. I beat him to his clothes.

He was shaking all over. Typically, like a spoiled brat, he turned away from danger. What he needed was someone to blame.

"You damned little Cuban bitch! A blackmail trick won't buy you a damned thing."

Lupe jumped up from the couch but before she could speak he backhanded her across the face so hard he knocked her to the floor. He stood over her. His face was wild and frantic—and sick. I threw him his clothes.

"Put 'em on," I said thickly. "Then get out of here—fast."

When he was gone I went to Lupe. She was still on the floor. Her slip was pulled high above her hips. I knelt beside her, pulled it down. She was crying softly into her hands.

"Don't worry, *querida mia*." I kept my voice as low and soft as possible, the way my mother had crooned to me when I was a kid and hurt—hell, a hundred years ago. Lupe needed to be reminded of all the things her mother should have told her—of her baby, and everything she needed for it.

After a while she said, "Oh, how this is going to cost that *pudrise*. Oh, how it's going to cost him."

She sobbed for a moment, then turned and hurled herself against me where I was hunkered beside her. She struck hard against me, throwing her arms around me, thrusting her face against my chest, sobbing. I held her and let her cry it all out, the weeks and months of it when she had wanted to cry and had had no one with whom to share her tears.

I felt not the least ashamed—not even when I realized that being a young girl's idea of a strong man can be the hardest thing in the world.

14

At three the next afternoon, I began calling around trying to locate Morgan Carmichael. It came as a mild shock when I found he was at his desk in his father's offices. He would not talk to me and I had to put pressure on some top Carmichael Corporation officials to wangle an appointment with Morgan for four.

He was faintly puzzled as to why I would want to see him. So I had my picture, but who was I fighting? He even tried to buy me off.

"Anything particular you want to see me about, Ballard?" he kept saying, as if we had not met last night and I were there just to ask him to sponsor me in the Wednesday Squash Club, of which he was a member.

I did not actually say so, but I finally let him nurture the impression I wanted to talk to him about a block of a hundred tickets for the Policemen's Ball.

I knew he was muddled, trying to think of his way out of this jam as his father might have, but without letting the old man know.

Finally he blurted, "Look, Ballard—I haven't been exactly idle since I saw you last. I went through my old man's files, without his knowing. I found this picture of you—I'll trade it for whatever you got on me last night." He picked up a glossy print from his desk, held it in his hands.

I looked straight at him. "I'm not selling, buying or trading," I said.

"Do you have any idea what my father can do to you for trying a stunt like blackmail?"

"I know what your father could do to me for spitting on the sidewalk. I just don't give a damn—he could have told you that. But I haven't said a thing about blackmail."

"Well, I'm not going to pay you anything. Not a damned cent—not even for tickets to the Policemen's Ball."

He flipped the glossy toward me. It fluttered to the floor at my feet.

I glanced at it, then moved toward him. He stared at me a moment, his eyes wild, and wheeled around, leaping toward the row of buzzers on his desk. He never reached them. I snagged his collar, brought him up and around.

He swung at me once, but half-heartedly, as if he knew better than actually to hit me.

I beat him about the face—then lowered my blows to his midsection, until he sagged to the floor like an empty sack. He lay at my feet, bleeding into the expensive carpeting. One of his eyes looked bad. What the hell? He could afford the best medical care.

He didn't yell. He knew better.

I stood waiting until he finally stirred slightly on the floor. He had no idea of what else was going to happen to him. I bent over, caught his lapels in both hands, lifted him bodily and shoved him into one of his bright green overstuffed leather chairs.

He talked through the blood in his mouth. He wiped at the crimson stuff with the back of his hand, but it kept coming. He pulled a handkerchief from the breast pocket of his English-tailored jacket, pressed the white linen oblong against his nostrils.

His voice shook. "My father will break you for this. We'll get you for this. I'm sorry for you. You're out. You hear me? You're dead, or you'll wish you were—"

I caught his tie in my left hand and backhanded him across the face.

"You know what's dead? That picture you showed me. It's more than four years old. It shows me with one of Luxtro's whores. I've seen it before—hell, Tom Flynn was going to use it when he tried to break me off the force, send me to jail—but decided against it because it didn't prove anything. I've seen it before. What the hell do you think I am—a brat like you?"

"What do you want?"

"You figure it out, Morgan."

He tried to writhe free and I backhanded him again. For a moment he couldn't see anything. Gradually his eyes focused again.

"I begin to get an idea, Mike."

He whispered, sick in his guts with fear for the first time in his life. He began to get it. Nothing his father could do to me later was going to help him now. He was scared, and for the first time, he couldn't pay some money and stop being afraid. His father couldn't help him.

"I'm a police detective, Morgan," I said. "I don't blackmail people. Do you understand that, Morgan?"

He was crying suddenly. He began to cry helplessly, unable to stop.

"I didn't mean it—I was upset. I hardly knew what I was saying."

"Sure you knew. It just didn't work. I can see how you thought it might. A man like you, twenty-six, saddling up with a seventeen-year-old chick. I can see how you'd be mighty upset. That's rape."

"Oh, hell, Ballard! She begged me to come over."

I shrugged. "That makes it statutory rape. You got any idea what that can buy you? It can get you a lifetime lease on a jail cell."

"I've got lawyers. My father's got lawyers."

"Sure. And you both have money. Would you like to ask your old man how many kids he left on the sidewalk? Or would you like to make good on the kid you made with Lupe?"

He sat there a long time. "My God, Ballard—Mike—what do you want? What do you want me to do?"

I released him, thrusting him back in the chair. I sat on the edge of his desk. "First of all," I said. "Forget about calling me Mike. Next, don't say Ballard. Try to get used to Mr. Ballard—we'll never be friends. Then figure out what it cost your old man to raise you, and double it. You'd want your kid to be at least twice the man you are, wouldn't you?" I smiled. "He'll be born about a block from where I was."

Morgan looked as if he might vomit. "Oh, hell," he whispered. He drew a deep breath. "It could be anybody's baby."

I shrugged. "Another crack like that could cost you new bridgework. However, I can have witnesses to swear in court Lupe was a chaperoned, protected, revered and untouched virgin up until the moment she first shacked up with you—and that would be the truth. You see, Morgan, you're in a bad spot. All you've got is money. The kid's got me."

He sucked at his bloodied lip for a moment. I let him suck. It was his blood.

"What—if I gave her twenty thousand for her baby?" He said it without much hope.

"One thing," I said. "You're beginning to see the point. Your thinking is a lot better."

He said, "Forty thousand—"

I waited.

"Tax clear, Mr. Ballard. You understand. Invested. A living trust. He—the baby'd always have something."

I let him sweat himself up to seventy-five thousand, tax clear, then I cut him off, told him to write a check.

"I have lawyers," he said. "I'll have them fix up a living trust for the baby."

"I know some lawyers, too. You just give me the check. I'll have the trust set up. In your name."

He wiped his hand across his mouth. "I don't have that kind of money in my account. It'll take me a couple of days. I'll have to get it."

I shrugged. "You'll have to get it. That's up to you. But for right now, write out a check to Lupe Valdez. She can't deposit it until morning. That'll give you plenty of time to cover it. And you'll cover it—or I'll see you in the state pen for statutory rape."

He wrote out the check, looked up at me. "There's just one thing, Ballard. I'm going to have to tell my father about this. You understand? All about it and all about you. And then, God help you, Ballard."

"I figured you'd do that, boy. I'm prepared for it. You see, I found out a long time ago that nothing is ever easy."

"You've never had it tough the way you're going to." He blew on the check, held it out to me. "Take it and get out of here."

"Oh, there's a little more," I said.

His face went white. "What now?" He lost some of that arrogance he figured the seventy-five grand entitled him to.

"If I ever have to come up here again, Morgan, I'll have to be rough. I was easy on you today, because I like you. Hell, I figure you're just a spoiled kid. Just a twenty-six-year-old mixed-up kid."

"Why should you have to see me again?"

I shrugged. "I don't know. Let's just say if anything happens to Valdez, or her baby—if they even die of pneumonia or are killed in an accident—I don't give a damn if you're in Europe when it happens, I'll want you, boy. If they're hurt, you'll be hurt, bad. If they die you'll die, too—but slowly."

Young Carmichael jumped up wildly. His voice rose, frantic.

"How can I protect that girl? Dammit—how can I guarantee nothing will happen to her?"

I shrugged. "We've all got our problems, Morgan. Looks like you've named yours."

I turned and walked across the deep carpeting toward the outer door. Morgan stood frozen a moment, then wheeled and almost ran toward his father's suite of offices. He was wasting no time, but I had not expected he would.

I looked his secretary over as I went out. She gave me a smile, and tired as I was, I knew what I wanted right now. Lupe Valdez had gotten me all stirred up and what I wanted was a girl—any kind of girl.

15

When I got back to the detective bureau, it was almost five o'clock. There was a note on my desk. It said to call Carolyn Flynn at once. Urgent.

I crushed the slip in my fist, sat down and the swivel sighed dryly under me. I reached out, pulled the phone to me, and dialed her number before I had time to think about it and decide not to. Talking to Carolyn right now was the last thing I wanted.

The phone rang three times before Carolyn said, abruptly, "Mike?"

I laughed. "Hell, no. This is the third assistant secretary of the Junior League. Suppose I'd been the chairman of the Red Cross. Secretary of the Service League. Or Fred Carmichael."

She wasted no energy on worry. "I knew it was you, Mike. I could tell by the ringing of the phone. Haven't you ever felt that way?"

"No."

"I want to see you, Mike. I need to. I know I have no right to lean on you, Mike. But since Tom's death, I've been completely alone—except for you."

I wondered what Fred Carmichael would have thought of her saying that.

"How about eight o'clock?" I said.

She hesitated, then said softly, "Eight will be fine, Mike. I'll be waiting. Please don't mind—whoever may be here."

I replaced the receiver, thinking she probably meant that Fred Carmichael would be there. Then I thought about the scene that might ensue if Fred and I met at the Flynn house after what young Morgan must have told him this afternoon.

I sat up, glancing at the clock. There would be no way for me to avoid meeting Fred Carmichael. You can hurt a man almost anywhere except in his pocketbook and have some hope for forgiveness.

I touched the check made out to Lupe Valdez in the breast pocket of my jacket.

It was three minutes of five. I got up and got out of there.

As I pushed the key into my apartment doorlock, I could hear the soft strains of sentimental love ballads from my Magnavox console—a relic from my fat years as a vice-squad lieutenant.

I stepped in. Lupe Valdez was sprawled out on my divan. This did my libido—whatever the hell that is—no good because her position, except that she was wearing more clothes, was much like the one I had captured the night before with my Rolex.

She sat up, smiling wanly. Her cheeks were starkly pale, her black eyes lusterless.

I grew aware of something else—the place was beginning to smell like her. There was nothing wrong with the scent—a combination of mild bath soap, faint toilet water and youthful cleanliness—nothing wrong at all except for its effect on me. I had nothing but sympathetic understanding for Morgan Carmichael's rash need for this chick.

"Hello, Mike."

She gave me the kind of adoring gaze a young girl fixes upon a father who is above human frailties, and who is just a little stronger and better than the next man. One thing her look did. It switched off my libido button, fast.

I felt as gray, suddenly, as she looked.

I smiled back at her, moved toward my portable bar, and at the faint frown in her eyes, stopped. The hell with it. My God, what were people doing to me?

I went over to the couch, pulled the check from my inside coat pocket and dropped it in her lap.

I don't know what I expected her to do. What she did was burst into tears. She stared at the check, touched the amount, the scrawled signature with her fingers. She looked up at me and sat there sobbing, her eyes dripping, nose running, mouth trembling.

I tossed my handkerchief into her lap on top of the check. She picked it up and blew her nose.

"You're all right now," I told her. "You see an investment man at my bank tomorrow. You hear?"

"I hear you, Mike."

"I'm sure neither the kid nor Morgan will mind if you use some of this to go away a few weeks before you get too outstanding. In fact, Morgan insisted that you do."

"He does have some feeling," she whispered.

"Oh, yes, he hurts for you."

"Oh, Mike. You're so wonderful. I knew you would be—that first day I saw you."

"Sure. Only you hear me good. I want that kid to have a living trust. Understand?"

She nodded.

"I don't want to pick him up some time for stealing something he couldn't afford to buy."

"Oh, no!"

"I don't want him ever joining the cops, either—there are better jobs he can get."

She reached up, touched my face. "There are worse things than a good cop. Mike, I—I think I love you. Oh, Mike!"

"You're a doll, Lupe. You love everybody."

"Mike, I mean it." She jumped up, began to pull off her dress. "Take me, Mike. All I have to give you is myself. You want me, don't you, Mike?"

"Sure, but not because you're grateful to me, or trading favors." I patted her on that sweet fanny. "Now get that dress back on and beat it. Go ahead. Scram."

So I sat there, my libido snugly buttoned down in my back pocket. What had happened to me? I wanted a woman who could laugh, and what did I have? A grieving widow and a pregnant teen-ager. Great.

Carolyn was alone, waiting for me, when I got to her place. She answered the door herself, led me into the once more immaculate sunroom.

She sat on the smartly modern, rigidly uncomfortable divan.

"Come sit here, Mike. With me."

"There must be a more comfortable room in this house."

"Oh, Mike." She smiled sadly. "I really have missed you. All these years. Even when I was happy with Tom. And I was happy, Mike. He was good. And he loved me. And I learned one lesson. Love can be learned."

"Sure it can."

She smiled. "You're so violent, Mike. I can see in your face what you think of a love that has to be learned.... It isn't really thunder and lightning. Not all the time."

"Sure. And castor oil is good for you, too."

I stared at her and remembered how she had looked seven years ago. She had been lovely then. Perhaps the loveliest girl I had ever seen. Now she was the loveliest woman—every promise of her girlhood had been fulfilled—in spades. And I thought of what she was saying about love—as though she had never met it, had never trembled with need of it, had never known what it was like—or what she had missed. Maybe she was lucky. Under her grief was a look of serenity, as if innocence were bliss.

Also, maybe she was right. Perhaps the careful, decorous, sane life she had shared with Tom Flynn was the right answer. How would I have known? But watching her now, knowing that she had never really been touched, never been reached by passion, I thought of her as having been asleep—that there was in her seven years of violence she did not even know about.

I felt the sick longing in my loins, felt the silence of this big house pressing in on us, the darkness at the tall windows—these all became part of the need that had been building in me until I was ready to burst with it. I stared at her and wanted to touch her, to hold her against me. What I felt was worse than desire. It was a sick need, and I had to remind myself that she was full of grief. I had to put everything else out of my mind.

"You wanted to see me," I reminded her. "You sounded worried."

I was astonished at the flatness of my voice.

"I'm worried about Jerry."

"I've learned some things about him over the years. And since Tom's death I've kept my ears open. He's been doing a lot of gambling and he's in pretty deep. The boys carried him as long as Tom was alive. They had an idea that Jerry was some kind of insurance, which proves they didn't know Tom Flynn very well."

"Tom would never make a deal with any racketeers."

"I know. And like John Brown, he lies a-moldering in his—I'm sorry, Carolyn. It's just that I found out a long time ago that you've got to compromise. No matter who you are."

"Tom was a good influence on Jerry when he was alive."

I shrugged. "Maybe he was. Maybe Jerry just played it cagey."

"What do you mean?"

"There's nothing new about these gambling tabs on Jerry, Carolyn. You might as well know the truth. They're old. Tom was alive when Jerry made them. I'm afraid Jerry was giving Tom the con—making him believe he was impressed by Tom's unbending honesty."

"Oh, Mike, please—"

"What's the matter?"

"I'm so alone. I don't know what to do. I kept thinking Jerry would settle down. That Tom would influence him—for good. And now I don't even have that. Could you talk to him, Mike?"

"He wouldn't listen to me. Not any more. My talking to him might make him worse. He has some idea he has to prove I can't influence him at all."

"But I've got to do something. Mike, you're the only one I know who's ever been able to control Jerry. Down deep, I know he has real respect for you—even affection." She hesitated and presently I knew why. "Maybe you could talk to the gamblers he owes money to—make them see he can't possibly pay them, that they're just wasting time helping him destroy himself."

There seemed to be a sudden chill in the sunroom. "Nobody can talk to gamblers, Carolyn. What you mean is that you want me to scare hell out of them to protect Jerry."

"You could, Mike. Tom felt you could. I believe it—with all my heart."

"Well, stop deceiving yourself. Gamblers are protected in this town, better than any taxpayer you'll ever meet. They're entrenched, and they're organized, and they are protected. They have been for a long time now."

She seemed to grow more rigid; her cheeks became paler than ever. "I don't believe that, Mike. Tom would never have permitted such a terrible state of affairs in this town. He loved this town. It was his life—"

I gestured helplessly. "He couldn't help it, Carolyn. He couldn't stop them. He was a good man—maybe that was his weakness. He tried. He just couldn't beat them. Once I might have—with a few others on the force who could move among the racketeers. Tom stopped me and without meaning to, threw the town wide open. Now the gamblers and racketeers are in the saddle—and nobody can stop them."

She sat a long time without speaking. "You wouldn't help Tom," she said finally. "I don't know why I thought you'd help me." Her voice was chilled.

"I'd help you, Carolyn, if there were anything I could do."

She stood up, her face lifeless, her smile distant, cold. "I'm sure you would, Mike. Will you forgive me? I have a terrible headache."

I stood up, staring into her face, knowing the gap between us was wider than seven years now. She barely remembered me at all.

I wondered if she heard me leave the house.

Yet I wanted her. I wanted her. I wanted to touch her soft breast. I wanted to kiss her. I wanted to love her.

16

They were waiting for me the next morning in Captain Neal Burgess' office. When I didn't look surprised to see them, poised and ready to pounce, we had a quorum. We all knew why we were there.

Neal Burgess was Captain of Detectives, and next to me, low man on the totem pole. He was the only man in the room who looked sick. Chief Clyde Waylin looked troubled, but there was no illness in his face. Commissioner Stewart Mitchell sat at Neal's desk, a thick briefcase across his short, fat legs, his face pink under his white hair.

When we had all acknowledged it was a good morning, Mitchell was the one to raise the hammer and drop it on the nail.

"Ballard, I thought you'd learned your lesson four years ago."

"What lesson was that, sir?"

"Four years ago, you were a tool of Luxtro's in this department. A disgrace to the honest men in police uniform. A paid cop. A crooked cop. Delinquent in your office, taking graft, and bribes. I felt then that you should have been dismissed, prosecuted."

"I remember, sir. You told me."

Mitchell leaned forward, his face burning. He, too, remembered. We had had quite an interview. I had known four years ago that he, too, was playing footsie with Luxtro. He had tried to call my bluff because he doubted I could prove my facts—and had backed down when I showed him I could. We had agreed on a compromise. He reminded me of the terms now.

"We were lenient with you, Ballard. We allowed you to stay on the force. You were disciplined at my orders by being dropped to lowest rank in the detective bureau. We felt that you had paid, perhaps learned a lesson, and even your bitterest enemies admitted you could be a good officer, and a credit to the department. However, for four years, you've earned no advancement, no commendations. You've done nothing. Are you trying to make fools of us?"

Burgess leaned forward. "What are your specific charges against Detective Ballard, Commissioner?"

Chief Waylin said softly, "Never mind, Neal."

Neal's voice was sharp. "Nobody gets at my men except through me. On that I insist. It's always been that way, and it will continue that way as long as I hold my job."

"A commendable attitude, Captain." This from Mitchell, who smiled a little, sickly, but continued to grapple with the bull while making his passes on a powderkeg. "Commendable as long as you protect the honest men in your command. But do not involve yourself with a man like Ballard—"

"I still want to know, Commissioner, what he has done."

Mitchell's hands moved on the brief case. "We're not sure of what he might be doing, Captain. He hasn't been working for a promotion in the department. This is strictly my way of being fair to him, as I try to be to all you men. He knows what he has been doing. I had better warn you, Ballard, if you are accepting outside gratuities again, this time there will be no leniency shown you. I want this man on probation, Captain Burgess."

"Where did the complaints come from?" Burgess said.

"I'll tell you this much. I had a call at my home last night from Mr. Fred Carmichael, and later from Mayor Bibb. The activities of Detective Ballard seem once again to have attracted unfavorable attention—enough so that two civic leaders have been moved to complain. We're not going to tolerate it this time, Ballard. That's all I need to say to you. Behave yourself, or you're in desperate trouble. Do I make myself clear?"

He had made himself clear—at least to me.

There was more discussion. Burgess continued on my side—it was also his side. I answered questions, volunteered nothing. The questions were unspecific and I sensed they were fishing. What was I after, if anything? I wished I had the answer to that one.

In the end it was decided that, despite some evidence that Ballard, the bad cop, was stirring again, my probation would not become effective immediately.

I got up to leave when Mitchell and Waylin were going, but Neal shook his head. "I want to talk to you, Mike."

I shrugged, slumped back in the chair. The other two men went out. Waylin closed the door behind him.

Burgess said, "What are you pulling, Mike? What's the gimmick?"

"You tell me."

"All right, I will. I've heard that you have been questioning people around Halsey and Twenty-third about who shot young Hogan."

"Shouldn't I? He was killed. I am a homicide man."

Burgess shook his head. "We made a thorough investigation, Mike. Hogan was mixed up in some small-time racket on the side—that was why he was killed. None of us believe it would be to the best interest of the police department to have all that brought out in the open."

I stared at him without speaking. I needed no words. He knew what I was thinking. The investigation had been ordered pigeon-holed. After Ed Clemmons' death had been called an accident—which occurred while Ed had been cleaning his guns at 3:00 A.M.

"Do you believe that about Hogan, Neal?"

His face went white. His voice was very low. "If I didn't, you know damned well I'd order men kept on the case."

"And you believe Tom Flynn committed suicide while drunk?"

He moved in his chair. "That's enough, Mike. Flynn's death was a suicide."

"And Ed Clemmons' death was accidental?"

"Yes."

"And Carl Hogan was a crooked cop that got what was coming to him?"

He leaned forward. "For God's sake! Yes. Why don't you do your job—stay out of trouble with the commissioner, and stop asking questions? We've all got a job to do. You've got your own woes, now the commissioner is after you."

"And you don't think there's any connection?"

"Good lord, Mike. What kind of accusations are you making? Against me. Against Waylin. Against Mitchell."

"You mean I have to take it, but I can't dish it out?"

"Listen to me. Whatever it is you're doing that's got Mitchell upset, cut it out. Do your job. That's all we ask."

There was agony in his eyes, and his face muscles were rigid.

Somebody knocked on the door. Before he could control himself, Burgess yelled, "All right, come in! Who is it? What the hell do you want?"

Ernie Gault came in with a slip of paper in his hand. I hadn't seen him in three days. He looked as if he had aged ten years.

"What is it, Ernie?"

Burgess calmed down when he saw Ernie. Here was a guy everyone respected. He had given his life to the department.

"Protection racket, Neal," Ernie said. "What else?" He glanced at me, and looked sicker than before. But I knew it was not because he was troubled about me. Ernie had his own woes and since the death of Tom Flynn, the dishonesty in the department had been poisoning him like his ulcer. He knew Tom Flynn had been murdered, that Clemmons' death was no accident and that there had been no honesty in the Hogan murder investigation, and he also knew he had to keep his mouth shut. It was all inside him. Like some terrible disease.

"What now?" Neal said.

"We had a call this morning, few minutes ago. Spyrous Papolous has been threatened."

The name rang a faint bell. I had to dig around in my mind to realize it was the name of the Greek. I had forgotten he had a real name.

"What about Papolous?" I said.

"He's been threatened a couple times before, but has laughed it off. But now he thinks they mean business and he's worried. He wants police protection."

Neal shrugged. "Can you stake him out?"

Ernie's face was rigid. "I need more men. Like I told you and Clyde. We need some special assignments."

Neal said, "We told you, Ernie. You'll have to get by on the men you have."

"You mean you're not going to give Papolous protection?" I leaned against the desk.

"Never mind, Mike," Ernie said, troubled.

"Of course we'll give him every protection we can," Burgess said. "But we can't hire extra detail men. If we get somebody we can put over there, we'll do it."

"The Greek would never call you if he weren't in bad trouble." I was sitting on the edge of my chair.

"I'll run this department, Mike," Burgess said. "You got your own woes."

"We'll do what we can, Mike," Ernie said.

Burgess tried to laugh. "I know the Greek serves your favorite booze, Mike, but we have a department to run. We'll run it our way."

I glanced at Ernie. He was staring at the floor.

I left the building without even checking the assignments on my desk and walked over to the Greek's. It was only ten in the morning, but Doc Yerrgsted was in his favorite booth in the rear.

He stared up at me over his glass. "Well. Ten A.M. When a man drinks before noon, Ballard, his problem has become bigger than he is."

"Hell, I'm taking the day off."

"Are you? You can do that when it pleases you, can you?"

"Why not? You do."

"I'm farther down the road than you are, my boy. You come in for a drink at ten, but I must have my first drink before I can bear to put my poor, sore feet down on the floor. You have a career left to you but I have only this booth in the Greek's bar."

The Greek came over. He looked as if he had not slept. His hand on the tray trembled. He put a drink before me. "On the house, Mike."

"How are things, Greek?"

"Who can complain? This is a fine country. The finest in the world."

I gestured toward him with my drink. "Sure it is."

"Sure it is," he said. His face was cold. He turned and walked away.

"Poor Greek," Doc said.

"What's eating him?"

"Never ask, Ballard. Remember what I once told you about Moses. He let things trouble him and wound up with forty years in the desert. He asked questions to which there was only one answer—and never found the promised land."

"Booze is the only answer," I said. "And the hell with you, Doc."

I had lunch at the Greek's. He insisted on making me a filet mignon. I told him I never ate that heavily in the middle of the day, but he said a man who drinks a lot should eat a lot.

"You can get beriberi, heart damage from drinking and never eating," Doc said. "This is a medical fact. Beriberi doesn't occur only among the underfed Chinese, Ballard. It happens right here among people who drink all the time and never eat."

"Always take the advice of a fool," I told him.

He nodded. "It's starting. That wisdom. It must have been like this for Moses—the slow sure beginning of wisdom."

"Oh, for hell's sake."

The Greek pulled up a chair. "Mike. I got a small worry. You mind I trouble you?"

"No. Go ahead. You can't hurt this steak after what you did to it in the kitchen."

"The steak is on the house, my friend. My trouble is that I have been threatened twice. I must pay off for protection of my business—or my life is endangered."

"Hell. Why don't you pay?"

The Greek shook his head. "Twenty-four years I have been here in this country. I don't believe I must pay anything."

"It's your life."

"I got to live with myself. I should snivel and beg from these punks the right to stay in my own business?"

I glanced at Doc Yerrgsted. "You ought to start on the Greek, Doc. It's taking him longer than it ever took Moses to get even a little bit smart."

"This man is right. You know he's right," Doc said. He sat up straighter. "And you are a cop."

"The police," the Greek said. "I asked for protection. Twice. They promised. But nothing."

"You want me to try to jack them up?"

The Greek stared at me, then smiled, nodding. He snapped his fingers and a waiter came running with a telephone, plugged it in.

"Use my phone," he said.

"On the house, of course?" I said. I dialed police headquarter, asked for Neal Burgess. "Neal, I dropped in at the Greek's."

"I'll bet you did."

"Put it in my folder. But in the meantime, he says he's asked for police protection and hasn't got it. There's no stake-out here."

"We're rushed, Ballard. You know that. We're doing the best we can."

"Aren't you going to send a stake-out?"

His voice was rasping. He was a man pushed. "Dammit, Mike—are you telling me my job?"

"No, sir. Simply confirming a report."

"Of course we're sending protection. As soon as we can. We have a schedule, Ballard."

"I hope these hoods are on the same schedule—"

"Damn it, Ballard. I'll take care of it. Now, why don't you get back to work?"

"I think I'll just stay here until your stake-out shows up, Neal. Okay?"

He didn't speak. He just slammed down the receiver. I hung up, too.

"You're going to stay?" The Greek leaned forward, showing a little color in his face.

"Why not? As long as your liquor holds out, I couldn't do better."

"Them punks swore they'd be here today. They warned me not to call the police. If I don't pay, they wreck my place." His fearful gaze moved across his huge, framed paintings, the deep, tinted mirrors, the expensive white gleam of his tables, the glowing polish of his bar. "How can this happen, Ballard?"

"I don't know," I said. "Maybe we'll find out."

He offered to furnish me with more bourbon, but I told him I could exist on coffee. "After all, Greek," I told him, "I'm on duty. A cop shouldn't drink on duty."

At four the telephone rang. It was for Yerrgsted. His office was calling. He had not reported in today and several matters required his attention and signature.

He laughed into the phone. "The hell with you. I'm with Moses and the Greek, and about to witness the parting of the Red Sea, and I wouldn't miss this for a million kronen." He let the receiver strike its cradle loudly.

It had never occurred to me before that a bar quieted down so completely between four and five o'clock. The afternoon breaks are over, and the before dinner drinking has yet to begin. The bartender was alone, polishing glasses. Only one waiter was on duty and he was reading a newspaper near the kitchen doors.

We three—Doc, The Greek and I—sat in the booth, none of us saying much.

I was on my second pot of coffee. I had put sugar in my cup and was reaching for the cream when the Greek coughed. There was nothing spectacular or new about this signal, but it was effective. He got up, pushing back in his chair, staring toward the front door.

The boys had arrived for their protection money.

I sat there, waiting, until they'd had plenty of time to get well inside the thick doors. I found myself sweating.

I glanced at Doc. He took a deep, long pull at his whiskey, the ice clinking in his glass. I had never seen him look calmer.

I put the cream pitcher on the tabletop, slid my hand under my coat to ease the Police Positive from its shoulder holster.

The gun was in my hand when I stepped out of the booth.

There were two of them, both with hands covering guns in jacket pockets. The Greek was trembling and looked as if he were about to fall.

I saw the faces of the hoods. They were wild, desperate, as if they were either hopped up, or expected resistance. Their consciences were on their faces. I could have stopped the show by pressing the trigger of the Police Positive—I wanted to do it for the Greek and found my finger frozen.

There were only two of them, but one was Jerry Marlowe.

17

These was no sound in that dim room except the clink of ice in Doc Yerrgsted's glass. Doc kept swirling the cubes. A moment ago the Greek had been panting, but abruptly he was silent, as if he had stopped breathing at all. The whisper of drying cloth on goblets as the bartender worked behind the bar was silenced.

I stood staring at Jerry Marlowe. I don't know what went through my mind—perhaps nothing at all—perhaps a last faint fleeting thought that I was a fool to wait. I had learned the fast hard facts about Jerry from the men in the know—men he had dealt with over the past years. The gamblers, the racketeers. I had learned something from Jerry himself when he wanted to fight me beside Tom Flynn's pool. But, perhaps, far down in my mind, where I could not instantly reach it, was the thought of Carolyn.

I tried to press that trigger and could not do it.

Jerry faced me squarely across the room. The tables gleamed whitely beside him, the indirect lighting put his face in shadow, but I could see his eyes as though we stood in metallic sunlight, and his eyes were raging, partly with dope, partly with hatred.

The hood with him moved to one side, drawing his gun, and my finger tightened then without hesitation.

He fired first—and missed. I held my gun steady, pressing the trigger coldly, knowing I would not miss, and I didn't. I had been a cop too long, and I had long ago forgotten to be afraid of punks like him. I could hit a man like him as I could drill a dummy on a police range. And that was all I did.

The hood was moving forward. The impact of the bullet stopped him, turned him slightly, knocked him off balance. But he was on the needle, sure of himself and his gun. He took two long steps toward me before he knew he was dead. Then he listed slightly, sagged in the knees, toppled against a table and sprawled on the floor. He did not move.

I jerked my gaze up to Jerry. A professional hood would have thrown in the rag right there, called it quits. A pro knows when to work and when to call it a day. But Jerry was no pro. Not yet.

He had pulled his gun free from his jacket pocket. I yelled at him as he fired. They must have had some sort of plan, because the bright, sick, lemon-colored flame from his gun ignored me completely—I doubt Jerry had really even seen me—he aimed at the Greek.

Spyrous Papolous was knocked against the gleaming bar. Twenty-four years ago he had come here to keep a date with this bullet. The Greek was a courageous gentleman. He grabbed at the wound in his chest, collapsed, but did not emit a sound. I wasted a full moment, staring in horror at the little man crumpled on the floor—gaudy shirt, sleeve garters and bald spot like a monk's cap.

When I recovered, Jerry had spun around and was racing toward the doors. An early five-o'clock drinker had pushed through those doors, unaware of the excitement. Three gunshots would be muffled outside the Greek's air-conditioned, thick-walled saloon. They would not sound real. Whoever heard of gunfire in the Greek's place?

But he was inside the door, and when he saw what was happening, he turned to stone. He stepped away from the thick glass doors, standing pressed against the wall, not even breathing.

Jerry snagged the door before its oil pressure allowed it to close. He swivel-hipped between door and jamb, on his way to the street.

I had a split second to shoot him in the back and did not. I went between the tables, leaping over the fallen body of the hood. As I slammed through the door, I heard a patrolman's shrill whistle from across Lafayette Street.

Jerry and his friend had parked a Jaguar in the reserved zone directly in front of the Greek's sidewalk awning. There was a black-haired girl at the wheel of the Jag. I saw her reach over, open the door for Jerry.

The uniformed cop was racing across the street, blasting away at his whistle. Cars had bucked to a stop both ways, and he came running through the snag-toothed path they cleared.

Jerry slid into the Jag, half crouching, bringing his gun up to fire at the cop in the street.

The cop had not yet thought of his gun. His hand stabbed down to his belted holster.

I said, "Jerry—" as I fired.

My voice reached him. He was turning his head as my gun exploded. He was looking over his shoulder at me when my bullet ripped into him. At that range, I couldn't have missed, any more than Jerry could have missed the cop in the street.

Jerry's body was thrown on top of the girl in the Jag. She began to scream, trying to fight her way out from under him.

A police car skidded into the curb behind the Jag. The black-haired girl turned, saw the cruiser. She stopped trying to push Jerry's body from her and fought at the gears. All she could think of now was that she had to get out of there.

Ernie Gault leaped from one side of the black police Plymouth, a uniformed cop jumped out the other side. The two uniformed patrolmen converged on the Jag, grabbing at the girl, wresting her hands from the gear lever. One of them reached over her and twisted off the ignition key.

In the silence the girl went insane with her screaming. As one of the patrolmen put his shoulder under Jerry, lifting him, she began to fight, scratching and striking at anything in reach. As she leaped up in the seat of the Jag I saw she was wearing a baggy sweater and slim jims and knew where I had seen her before.

I walked slowly to the curb. Ernie was the first to notice I was there.

"I got here as soon as I could, Mike. You got to believe that."

"Sure," I said. I was staring at Jerry's black-haired chick. It was Jackie Palmer, the girl on the air mattress, the babe who painted her toenails in Carolyn's sunroom.

"My God." Ernie Gault's whisper was shocked, awed. "This is the dame that was in Climonte's store the day he was killed."

"That's right," I said. "And very likely the same two boys were with her that day, too. Only we'll never know unless we can make her tell us."

Ernie watched her fighting the cops, cursing them, spitting into their faces.

"We'll make her talk this time," he said. "We can make her talk all we want to."

He moved around the Jag. The two young cops were in trouble trying to quiet the black-haired Palmer chick. They were trying to be halfway gentle with her, and she was taking advantage of it. When they pulled her out of the car, she began kicking at them, aiming her pointed toes at masculine vital spots. Yelling, screaming, cursing and kicking, she almost spun free.

As she turned around, she came full face to Ernie, and for the first time I saw Ernie Gault forget to be the mild little gentleman.

He said, "Shut up, you bitch," and when Jackie screamed at him, he clipped her across the jaw, neatly, precisely and expertly.

Things quieted down then. Jackie's eyes rolled upward in their sockets and she sagged, stunned, out cold.

18

By the time Ernie and I got to the headquarters interrogation room, the black-haired chick was alive and kicking again. There was one chair in the room and they told her over and over to sit in it. But she was everywhere, all over that room, when we got there. Two detectives, a uniformed cop and a matron were making efforts to control her. The matron was present so there could never be any kick-back on what happened to Jackie Palmer during the questioning. She seemed more interested than effective. Neal Burgess had been summoned from his home and leaned against a wall, looking ill.

The girl was raging around the room, snarling and cursing, when Ernie and I came in.

"Stupid bastards," she screamed. "All of you. I want to get out of here! Do you hear me? I want to get out of here right now. You can't keep me here. I'm afraid of this place."

She thrust her splayed fingers into her wildly disheveled hair, yanking at it.

"What kind of deal is this, Ballard? Ernie?" Neal stared at us.

"She's hopped up," Ernie said. "She's on the needle."

"You lie!" the girl screamed. "That's another rotten filthy lie. You wait till my people get through with you dirty rotten liars."

"Sure," I said. "Just wait."

At the sound of my voice, the girl stopped, tense. Her hands were knotted in her hair. Her shoulders were straight and she poised a moment on her toes.

She turned slowly, looking up at me.

"You know me, Ballard," she said.

"I know you."

"You better tell that to these flunkeys, these overpaid garbage men."

"What do you want me to tell them?"

She breathed rapidly, her lips parted. "You better tell them who I am. You better tell them what my friends are going to do to them."

"Maybe you'd better tell them, Jackie."

"What's the matter with you?" she screamed. "You know they can't keep me here in this dirty place. You know I'm a friend of Morgan Carmichael's. I'm a friend of his father's, too. And my own father will fix all of you. And if he can't do it, he'll get Fred Carmichael to do it. You can't keep me in this vile place. I'm afraid in this place."

This chick didn't look afraid. She looked more vicious than frightened. Her hands were clenched into tense claws. Her mouth was twisted and rouge was streaked across her cheek where she had dragged her hand. The pupils of her eyes were pinpoints and even when she glared at me her eyes did not really focus.

"You better help me, Ballard." Her voice rose into a keening wail. "They killed Jerry. And now they're trying to keep me in this place. Mr. Fred Carmichael and Mayor Bibb—they're going to break all these dirty men—and they'll get you, too, if you don't help me."

"Sure." I took a step toward her. "The Mayor and Fred Carmichael. They're going to fix the Greek, too, huh?"

She shook her head wildly. "I don't know what you're talking about."

I took another step. She turned her head, looking around as if trying to find a place to run. "Sit down, Jackie," I said.

She shook her head, but took a backward step, sat down hard on the straight chair.

"Damn you. They'll fix you, too, Ballard."

"You let me worry about that, Jackie. Right now I'm worried about a little Greek. Never did a soul a bad thing in his life. He may be bleeding to death. Maybe he's dead already."

"I didn't do it."

"You were there, baby. You would have done it if you could have. And for what? For kicks?"

"I don't know anything about it. I want to get out of here. I'm no tramp you people can push around. I know people and I know what they can do to you."

"Sure, you know everybody, Jackie. Only they aren't going to help you. When this needle wears off, you won't care about the people you know. The only soul you'll really give a damn about is the one who can give you a fix—and I'll tell you now when you're going to get that next fix, baby. You want to know when?"

She was glaring up at me with those off-focus eyes, her chest moving with her rapid breathing.

"You'll get your next fix, baby, when you decide to tell us the name of the man you work for."

She screamed, clawing at her face. "I don't know what you're talking about. I want to get out of here."

Her voice rattled against the walls, shook up everybody in the room except the matron and me. Neal went to the door, hurried out.

The matron came over to Jackie. Jackie stared at her, pushing out her lip like a child in a tantrum. The matron lifted her hand as if to backhand her across the mouth.

"You want it, chick?" the matron said. "Or you want to shut your mouth?"

Jackie said no more. She sat trembling, breathing wildly, staring up at us.

Ernie and I were at his desk waiting for a call from the hospital. Doc Yerrgsted had promised to let us know as soon as there was anything on the Greek.

When the phone rang, Ernie lunged for it.

"Detective bureau. Lieutenant Gault." He looked up at me, shook his head. It was not Doc Yerrgsted.

He sat a moment, listening. "No," he said.

After a long time, he said, "All right, Commissioner. All right."

Neal Burgess came out of his cubbyhole at the end of the long room. Chief Waylin was with him.

"Was that Commissioner Mitchell?" Waylin said.

Ernie stared at them. "Didn't you know it was going to be?"

Waylin and Burgess had reached Ernie's desk by now. Waylin looked white around the mouth.

"What kind of talk is that, Gault?" He moved close to Ernie's desk, stared down at the little man. "I might expect something like that from Ballard, but not from you."

"Maybe you'd better expect it from me, too," Ernie said.

Waylin tensed, but Neal Burgess caught his arm. "Take it easy, Clyde. Ernie's upset. This has been a hell of a time."

"It's been a hell of a time for all of us," Waylin said. "He doesn't have to take it out on me."

"What did the commissioner want?" Burgess said.

"He didn't want anything. He called in to tell me that Mr. Judson Palmer will be down here with his attorneys in about ten minutes, and that Palmer's daughter is to be released into the custody of her father."

"All right," Waylin said. "That's what we'll do. We obey orders around here, Gault. All of us."

"And what about our material witness in a murder and attempted extortion case?" Ernie stood up. He was not as tall as Burgess and much thinner than Waylin. He didn't look like a match for either of them. But what he had they couldn't touch, a record of service and honesty that made him ten feet tall.

"Nobody's letting her get away." Waylin gestured with his clenched fist. "Her family is one of the finest in this town. She'll be where we can get her. When we want her."

"When that dame walks out of here, you'll never see her again." Ernie's voice shook. "She was the moll along when Climonte was killed. She was there today when two hoods were killed, and Spyrous Papolous was shot—and Papolous may be dead by now. I don't give a damn who this dame is, or who her family is. She's on dope, she's mixed up in this racket—a big thrill for her. But it's murder."

"We follow orders, Ernie," Waylin said again.

"I'm damned if I do. I've followed orders. From you and from Neal. I've followed them, by God, until I'm so dirty rotten filthy I can't live in my skin. I won't do it. Not any more. You let that dirty-mouthed little bitch walk out of here, and I'm going to resign. But I'll be damned if I'll resign quietly. Everybody in this town will know why I quit. I've given my whole life to this damned police department. I've gone into debt trying to give my wife and kids the few basic things they ought to have, but I've never taken a cent above my salary. And I've worked twenty hours a day when I had to."

"You're all upset, Ernie," Waylin said.

"You're damned right I'm upset. I'm telling you again—you let that thrill-crazy slut out of here, and you get my resignation. And I'll see that the story makes every paper in town."

I caught Ernie's arm. "Take it easy."

"Leave me alone, Mike. God knows I'm a hell of a lot smarter than I was four years ago when I thought you were a crooked cop—I don't think that now. But I've had a bellyful, Mike. I know what I've got to do and you can't stop me."

"You've got three kids to feed, too," I said. I kept my voice flat.

Ernie stopped. He seemed to shrink into himself. Then he shook his head. "I can't help it. I can get some clean job. I can scrub sewers. But I can't stomach this dirty dishonesty—not any more."

Waylin had calmed down now. He seemed to grow calmer the more agitated Ernie Gault became.

"We're only following orders, Ernie. You know what discipline means in the department. Both Neal and I would do anything for you. But we've got to do as we're told."

"Not like this, Clyde." Ernie heeled around, pleading with Burgess. "Neal? For God's sake. Tell him. This is too rotten. We can't go on taking orders like this."

Neal wouldn't meet his eyes. "I'm afraid we've got to, Ernie. I'm sorry."

Waylin actually forced himself to laugh. "Mike Ballard knows the score, Ernie. My God, if you don't know it, what can I say to you? You mean a lot to all of us, Ernie. To the whole department. But one thing doesn't change. We just work here, Ernie. Go on home and sleep this off. You'll see it all differently tomorrow."

Waylin's voice was soft, almost gentle. But his words were like fists hitting Ernie Gault in the face. Ernie retreated, braced himself against his desk. He would not look at any of us. He did not move.

19

Neal Burgess drove Ernie home in his car. Waylin vanished into his own office and I sat at my desk for an hour, waiting for the call from Doc. It didn't come. Finally I called the hospital.

I learned exactly nothing. Doc Yerrgsted was not in the hospital Out Ward. He had disappeared more than an hour ago. The Greek was getting every attention, but had not yet regained consciousness.

I slapped the receiver back into its cradle, hating the whole world almost as much as I hated myself. I went out of the building, got into my car. I drove past the Greek's bar on Lafayette. The bar was locked and dark, and I wondered where Doc Yerrgsted had holed in. Padlock the Greek's and Doc might die of exposure.

I found a liquor store, bought two pints of bourbon, then I drove back to City Hall. I supposed Doc had a room somewhere, but I didn't believe he would go there until there was no chance he would find himself alone with his thoughts.

There was a light in the window of the M.E.'s office. I parked and went up the marble steps, carrying the bourbon.

I knocked on the door marked Medical Examiner. Doc's voice called, "It's unlocked. Come in."

I entered his office, closed the door behind me. "You mean you sit alone in this place at night without locking your door?" I said.

He shrugged. "You wouldn't do it, Ballard, because you have something to live for."

"I'm loaded with happy reasons for living, all right."

He shook his head again. "If you weren't, you wouldn't be afraid of death. I'm not afraid. Suppose somebody walked in here and filled my carcass with lead. I might leak bourbon all over this nice carpeting, but—what you got there?"

He had seen the bourbon. I set it on the desk before him. He reached out for a pint, his hands trembling. "You're a good boy, Ballard." He grinned up at me. "Why don't you get out of this town?"

"I thought you were going to call me from the hospital."

He was removing the cork with his teeth. "I'll bet you did."

"What's the matter? Didn't you have a dime? Couldn't you con a hospital phone?"

He took a long drink. "I decided the hell with it."

"Why?"

He shrugged and took a drink.

"Doc. How is he?"

"The Greek? What do you care?"

"Good God. Why wouldn't I care?"

"I don't think you care about the Greek, Ballard. It was good of you to bring me this bourbon. I'm sure there are gold stars beside your name in heaven. Why don't you just leave this stuff here with me?"

"What's eating you, Doc?"

"Nothing. The Greek is still alive. He was still alive when I left him at the hospital in the hands of the young butchers they employ there. He may survive. He comes from a hardy people—it may take more than our modem medical graduates to kill him off. I devoutly hope so."

He took a long drink, glanced up after a moment. His thick brows wriggled as if he were surprised to see me still standing there.

"Good night, Ballard."

"Doc. I don't get this. What could I do? I did all I could at the Greek's."

He took a long drink. He got up, went to his window, stared down at the quiet streets. He shook his head.

"No. You barely did what you had to do. He was the Greek, a friend of ours. A close friend. You could not let him be killed. So you came to his place early and stayed to protect him. But you had done nothing about all this organized evil and murder in this town. Climonte, Flynn, Hogan. And the poor devil—whoever he is—who gets it in his gut tomorrow night? You didn't do much for the Greek, Ballard—only what you had to do."

I sat for a long time at the wheel of my car in the deserted parking area outside City Hall. Doc's window continued to glow. The streets were dark caverns.

Suddenly I knew just what I needed. What I needed was a dame and a bottle. Nothing wrong with me that a dame and a bottle wouldn't cure.

I started the car.

It was two A.M. when I got to my apartment. I had found a bottle, but I had not found a dame. I know plenty of them, but tonight none had suited.

When I saw the light in my apartment windows, I felt a surge of anger. If Lupe Valdez was hanging around again, I would kick her out. I didn't take her to raise. If she wanted the truth, all my sympathy was with Morgan Carmichael. She had enough to tempt any man—and if she was going to give it away, she had to learn to take the consequences.

I was still angry when I pushed the key into the lock and pushed the door open. The sound of music, whispering and insistent, filled my living room and I caught a whiff of perfume—but a strange scent I didn't recognize.

I closed the door behind me, leaned against it, staring at the couch.

Naomi Hyers, Morgan Carmichael's redhead, got up slowly, stretching, yawning, looking deliciously warm and sleepy—and completely naked. The doll who had stared along her nose at me beside Flynn's pool. I had to admit the absence of a bathing suit made her even lovelier tonight than she had been then.

Morgan Carmichael's fiancée— Morgan's women seemed to have developed quite a penchant for my couch.

"Hello, Mike," she said. Her voice had a breathless quality.

I managed to pull my gaze away from her for a moment to glance around the rest of the room. Her clothes were nowhere in sight—she must have undressed in the bedroom. Her eyes followed mine to the bedroom door.

"I didn't know if you were a subtle man, Mike, and decided not to take a chance. There's nothing subtle about the way I feel about you."

"What do you want here?" I gave myself an Oscar for the stupidest line of dialogue of the year.

"I've been thinking about you, Mike." Her voice trembled slightly. "You haven't been out of my mind—since that day you taught Jerry Marlowe a lesson at the pool. Have you remembered me at all?"

"I guess any man would remember you, having seen you."

She smiled languidly. "No other man has ever seen me like this, Mike."

The heat was building up inside me. My clothes felt tight, constricting. I wanted to be free of them, to be with this redhead and let the ache and frustration in my body that had been plaguing me for days go up in fire. Fire? A conflagration. We'd singe City Hall.

I knew now why just any doll would not have done for tonight. I needed something special—and there was nothing more special than Morgan's redheaded chick. I wanted to bury my face in her flaming curls, suck at her throat with my mouth. She was part of the nightmare that had enmeshed me—but the only part that had wanted to be on my side. Doc was against me—I had killed Jerry Marlowe, and Carolyn was never going to forgive me. Grab this, Mike, I thought. Grab it, take it, use it—for tomorrow she may hate you, too.

She was turning slowly before me, her face flushed and expectant, lips smiling slightly. She kept her arms at her sides. She was lovely and wanted me to know how lovely—and she was as artful in her movements as any nightclub stripper. Perhaps more artful than most, because she meant it.

"Mike," she whispered. "I've been waiting so long."

"I'm sorry. I'd have come running."

"I don't mean tonight, Mike. I mean all my life."

She was close to me now. I could feel the heat from her body—the faint scent she wore began to drug my senses. There was a sick throbbing behind my eyes.

She raised her hands to my coat lapels. I looked from them into her eyes. They were limpid and wet, but suddenly I saw only ugliness. She was part of the nightmare still. She was lovely and might be as untouched as she claimed. Perhaps I was seeing something no other man ever had. But I saw it against the backdrop of Climonte, bleeding out his life on the floor of his dingy store; Tom Flynn, Clemmons and Hogan dying unavenged; the Greek unconscious in a hospital and Jerry in the morgue; Doc dying slowly of sickness in others—and I knew I couldn't add to the blackness and deceit around me. No matter what sort of heel Morgan Carmichael had proven himself.

I took her wrists and disengaged her fingers from my lapels. "No," I said. "Get in the other room and get dressed."

"Why, Mike? You want me. You know you want me."

"Not like this." I walked away from her to the door of the bedroom, threw it open. "Come back again some time," I said, "when you've got less on."

At first she gave me a twisted half-smile, thinking I was joking. She looked down at her flushed, nude body.

"How much less could I have?"

I caught her icy hand in mine, held it up, pointed to the brilliant engagement ring Morgan Carmichael had given her.

"You're still wearing too much for me," I told her. "Now get dressed. Get out of here."

She began to cry, emptily, dressing automatically, leaving the bedroom door open. The hurt in the sound made her younger than her years. I didn't believe it.

She came out dressed at last and went to the door. She hesitated, with her hand on the knob, not crying any more. "I thought you were a man," she said. "You're not a man at all."

I did not look at her. "Be glad you found it out in time."

I heard the door close, and knew she was gone. The room was suddenly cold. After a while the phone began ringing. The sound was without warmth, curiously forlorn.

I let it ring. The hell with it. Who would I want to talk to now? And who would really want to talk to me?

20

Finally the ringing stopped. I glanced at my watch. It was almost three in the morning.

All I could think now was that I had to go to bed, because I had to get up tomorrow. I could not think of a positive reason why tomorrow mattered other than that it would come and I would have to live through it.

Still, I could not stand the idea of lying alone and awake in my bed and suddenly wished the phone would ring again. And it did.

I pounced on it before the sound of the first ring had died.

"Ballard," I said.

"Clyde Waylin. There's a little trouble. In fact, you're it. They want to talk to you in eight-seventeen at City Hall."

Any other time I would have told Waylin to go to hell. It was 3:00 A.M., and their little trouble would keep. But at the moment I was glad to hear even Waylin's voice.

I said, "I'll be right over."

I was still dressed. All I had to do was put out the lights, get out and into my car.

When I entered Room 817, its atmosphere was cozy with scheming and tobacco smoke. The same little group was present that had been here the other night when Doc Yerrgsted was forced to knuckle under and sign a false death certificate. But one man had been added—Fred Carmichael sat at the far end of the long table, wreathed in cigar smoke.

Commissioner Mitchell let me sit down before he began. His voice was sharp. It was clear that whatever patience these men had had was already expended deciding what they were going to do about me.

"The charges against you are serious, Mike. You know that, or none of us would be here at this time of the night. Frankly, we don't know what to do about you. We've got the public to consider."

"God help them," I said.

"Smart talk won't buy you anything here tonight, Ballard. Mr. Carmichael is here because I asked him to come. He charges that you engaged in violent assault and blackmail against his son."

I shrugged. "What the hell? I was off duty."

"Cut it out, Mike," Waylin said. "I've done all I can for you. As a matter of fact, this is only one charge. The other is that by not taking your assignments, by placing yourself armed, and without orders, in the establishment of Spyrous Papolous, you precipitated a double killing which might include a third victim before the night is out."

I stared at them. "That's real interesting, Commissioner. Would you mind explaining to me how I precipitated a twin killing?"

"We have proved, Mike, that Jerry Marlowe, the young Palmer girl and Frank Sencho were merely on a kick—out for thrills. There were serious implications in their behavior, but they were not professional criminals. Now young Marlowe, a fine young man from a wonderful family, a college football star, is dead—the owner of the Greek's bar is dying—Frank Sencho is dead—and the Palmer girl has been placed in a rest hospital, victim of a complete collapse."

"I'm bleeding," I said.

"You will be," Mayor Bibb spoke up, "before we're through with you. We won't tolerate flagrant disobedience of orders any more than we'll tolerate a police officer who engages in blackmail. The worst crime is unnecessary shooting."

"Is that all?" I said. "Are you through?"

"Dammit!" Waylin's voice was ugly, low. "Isn't that enough?"

"I don't know," I said. I turned in the chair, tried to see into Fred Carmichael's eyes through the cloud of cigar smoke encircling his head. "Mr. Carmichael, on this blackmail charge. Are you stopping payment on the check? Did your son tell you what would happen to him if you did stop payment?"

"That's enough insolence, Ballard." Mitchell's voice shook. He had never heard anybody take that tone to Carmichael.

"That's all right, Stewart." Fred Carmichael leaned forward, staring at me. His lips pursed around his cigar. He removed it, glanced at it. "No, Ballard, we didn't stop payment on that check. We wouldn't think of it. We want it endorsed, put through the bank. We want it that way."

My grin matched his. "I'm sure you do."

"It's not going to buy you anything, Ballard."

"I never expected it to. But I'm happy for your son that you decided to pay it. He's a good boy. I like him."

"You brutally assaulted him," Mitchell said in a slightly wild voice.

"I had to talk to him in a convincing way. That's all I did. Nobody else had ever shown him what could happen to a man who was irresponsible, destructive, grabbing. He knows now."

"Are you telling me my duties as a father?" Carmichael asked.

"No. I haven't got time. It's already too late. But if you and the rest of the boys here had wept the kind of tears over Tom Flynn that you're shedding over his no-good, hopped-up brother-in-law, you'd make more sense. The Palmer girl was under dope and—as you said—just out for kicks. The hell with it. And that Frank Sencho. That other member of the junior League. I used to arrest him regularly when he was part of the Luxtro mob. He was a pusher until he got hooked, and then he became just exactly what he was when he got killed—a hired gun. You'll find it in the records."

Not one of them batted an eye.

"You've twisted the truth in a fine fashion, Ballard," Mitchell said. "But it won't help you. I'm going to order you suspended and we'll bring charges, public charges, if you try to get reinstated—"

"Just a minute, Stewart." Carmichael's voice was soft. "I thought we'd agreed to give Ballard a chance to straighten up."

Mitchell's mouth flopped open. He resembled a pink guppy.

"Oh?" He looked ill, confused. "Oh, yes. That's right."

"As all of you men know—including Stewart—" Carmichael said, "I used my influence four years ago to keep this man on the force because I always felt that he could be a power for good. Maybe we've made a mistake as you pointed out, Bibb—maybe we haven't given Ballard the proper incentive in the past four years. After all, he was a lieutenant in charge of a bureau. For four years, he's been a detective without rank. Perhaps this has contributed to these recent lapses. As Waylin pointed out during our earlier discussion, Mike Ballard might be a fine cop tomorrow if he were promoted to lieutenant, and given some of his old responsibilities back."

"Sounds great, Fred," Bibb said.

"He's made trouble," Mitchell put it. "But perhaps you're right, Fred. How do you feel about that, Mike? Lieutenant Ballard. It'd wipe off a lot of the old scores—oh, not all of them, but a promotion would show the town we wanted you on the force despite what the morning papers will say."

"I didn't know there was a lieutenancy open," I said.

"There are always changes in the department, Mike," Fred Carmichael said. "I know that from the years I've served this town. And in return for a promotion you would have to swear only adherence to duty—that you obey your superiors. Discipline is all we ask of any of our men."

I didn't say anything.

Mitchell said, "It seems to me that Mr. Carmichael is suggesting a splendid opportunity to redeem yourself, Mike. I don't feel personally that you deserve it. I won't even say I go for it. But if these other gentlemen do, I'll bow to their counsel. That's what we mean by discipline—we all have to submit to it. I'll see you stripped of a job and facing criminal charges if you refuse."

I glanced at each of them. They weren't going to spell it out again. They didn't have to. I really did not have much choice unless I wanted all out. And I just was not ready.

I shrugged and they accepted that as binding and suddenly I was a detective lieutenant again.

Carmichael smiled. "I was sure we could settle this matter—if we just sat down and talked about it. If we just—" he stared straight at me "—understood each other."

Then he picked up the telephone receiver, dialed while he smiled in apology. "Pardon me, gentlemen. I hate to do this, but I want to make a little call." He waited a moment and then he said, "All right, Lucy. Put the coffee on. I'm coming right home."

That broke up the meeting.

I went out to my car and decided to leave it. Doc Yerrgsted's office windows were dark. He had found something in those two bourbon bottles, even if it was only sleep. Doc asked little for himself these days.

I felt a faint tinge of regret that he failed to invite me to drink one of those pints with him. Maybe he would feel better tomorrow—then I suddenly remembered that I was a lieutenant again, and I doubted that Doc would even speak to me after he found that out.

I felt lonely, but I shouldn't have. I had company. They stepped out of the shadows and walked along with me. They could not seem to get close enough to me, they were so friendly. They hated the thought I might get away from them. One of them even jabbed a gun snout hard into my kidney.

"Just don't do nothing foolish, Ballard," one of them said.

The gun bit into my flesh again. I glanced around the darkened parking area. There was only one light in the whole empty block of parking space. This was in a telephone booth near the rear wall of the building. Suddenly I knew what Fred Carmichael's phone call, just before the meeting in Room 817 had meant.

I glanced over my shoulder. "Which one of you boys is Lucy?"

The one with the gun laughed. "We both are," he said. "And the coffee's on. Let's go."

21

There was no coffee perking in this room where the two goons took me. But we had fun without refreshments. They took turns working me over. They were not really tough. They were new generation punks, kids who had been living high off the hog. They tired easily. But one of them would hold the gun with the safety off while the other one battered me.

Still between them, they were enough.

I lay on the floor, bleeding. When I stared up at them, they looked ten feet tall. I tried to push up, couldn't make it and decided the hell with it. I'd make them use that gun—as they probably would, anyway, in the end. I remembered Clemmons and Hogan and wondered why all the preliminaries.

Finally one of them caught me by my collar, pulled me up and slammed me into a straight-backed chair.

"One thing you got to give this boy, Getz. He's tough. He can take it." Rosson laughed and smashed his gun into my face. "Hell, he's really tough. He cleaned out the mob once, four years ago, all by himself."

"Yeah. I heard about that."

Rosson brought the gun around again in a sweeping blow. The room was spinning, and when the metal struck my face, I barely felt the pain. The air turned a brighter red, the ringing in my ears was louder, that was all. I had no clear touch with reality any more.

I was on the floor again, but I could still hear their voices. They were laughing and joking until a banging on the door silenced them. I heard the sound of a door being unlocked.

Fred Carmichael's voice was the next sound I recognized, incongruously, as if in a dream. But I knew this was no dream. "Is he unconscious?" Fred wanted to know. "I told you two I wanted to be able to talk to him."

The two goons caught me and hauled me back to the chair.

"He can hear you, boss. He can't talk much, maybe, but he can hear."

"He'd better—it's almost daybreak," Carmichael said. "I've got to get home. Keep that gun on him, Rosson."

"Boss, you got nothing to worry about."

Carmichael bent over me. "Can you hear me, Ballard?"

It took a long time for me to nod—messages kept getting scrambled inside my head—but I finally made it.

"Do you know now who is running this town, Ballard?" Carmichael asked.

I managed to speak past the blood leaking out of my mouth. "Hell, Carmichael—I've always known."

Carmichael's voice rasped, "Don't outsmart yourself, Ballard. I can use you if you fall in line, but I'm wasting no time on you if you don't. This beating is just insurance. You've still got your lieutenancy—but you'll be working for me."

I stared up at him through the faint film of blood across my eyes. "I wondered why you didn't finish me off, as you did Clemmons and Hogan."

He snorted. "Clemmons and Hogan weren't worth bothering about. But you know your way around. You could be of some value to me. But I don't waste time on bad investments, Ballard."

Even if I had been thinking clearly, I would not have anticipated his fist. It came up fast and there was more power in it than in everything his goons had been throwing at me. For a moment I thought my head had come off. I went off the chair and struck the floor, sprawling. I tried to move and could not. Carmichael kicked me in the mouth.

From the top of a mountain I heard his voice. "The pay isn't bad if you work for me, Ballard."

He turned and walked out. Rosson and Getz followed him. I heard the door close, and then heard only silence.

I was in Doc Yerrgsted's office when he got there. I had found the two pint whiskey bottles in his wastebasket—both empty. When he entered I was in his swivel chair, my face on his desk blotter.

I think I had passed out. I came awake when Doc shook me by the shoulder. I saw his eyes flinch as he looked at my face.

"By hell, boy," he said. "You've got to stop playing in that block."

"Can you fix me up?" I rubbed coagulated blood from my mouth.

"I gave up performing miracles years ago," Doc said. He was opening his medical kit. "The churches were complaining. But I can patch you up so you won't frighten intelligent people between here and your home—I can't guarantee the reactions of morons. In the meantime I can be arranging for your plane passage—"

"What are you talking about?"

He was working on me, moving quickly, with an old expertness that was part of him by now. "I had a phone call this morning, Mike. I don't even know who was calling. He said to tell you no hard feelings as long as you stay in line."

"I've got the message, Doc."

"Don't do it, Mike," Doc said, and I began to feel better. "Don't sell out— as I did."

"The hell with you, Doc." I tried to make a grin. "What makes you think I'd do things you do. If I could, I'd heal the sick and put you out of business. Just now I'm tired. So goddam tired."

"Sure you are. I'll fix you up and you get on home, get in bed. I'll buy your plane ticket, make all arrangements. Any particular place you'd like to go?"

"No, Doc," I said.

22

I walked out to my car. People stared. The way Doc had my face wrapped up, I looked like something they'd dug out of an Egyptian tomb. Only I knew better. There was more life in any two thousand-year-old mummy than I felt right then.

I drove home, and didn't let myself think. I undressed and fell across my bed. I slept all day. Off and on I dreamed of Naomi Hyers, Morgan's red-headed fiancee, and of taking a trip with her someplace. But I never found the place.

The phone worked overtime, waking me.

I sat up in the darkened room. For a long time I didn't know where I was. When I tried to move, the room spun. The luminous hands of the clock on my night table stood at seven. The darkness at the windows was deepening. I had slept all day.

I reached out for the phone and the room danced crazily. I closed my fist on the receiver, clinging to it somehow and pressed it hard against my ear.

"Mike."

"Yes?"

"Grace. Grace Gault, I hate to bother you. Ernie was due home two hours ago. You know Ernie. Always right here. I haven't heard from him all day. Something was troubling him when he left this morning. I don't like to be a fool, but I've got a terrible feeling—I'm afraid something has happened to him."

Her worry was contagious. I contracted it instantly. Whenever Ernie had to deviate from his normal time table, he always let Grace know. If he had failed to check in with Grace he was in trouble.

For her sake, I tried to make light of the fear we both felt. "What could happen to him? He was probably held up somewhere by the job. I'll check. I'll find him and cart him right home."

"Will you, Mike?"

"I said I would. Now stop worrying."

"I can't help it. Two men were here at five o'clock looking for him. I told them he might be at the station. But they said they'd looked there. They worried me. I can't help it."

I asked a few questions, got her description of the two men, and said, "Okay. So I'll find him for you. Will you stop worrying?"

I put my feet carefully on the floor, afraid it might not be there. When I stood up, I almost fell. But I knew I had to keep going. Whether Ernie was alive or dead, time was running out.

I made it to the living room, had two long slugs of bourbon. After the first screaming rage of pain through me, I felt better.

I sat at the phone and began making calls. I didn't ask for Ernie Gault. I said I wanted to find two guys named Getz and Rosson. I sat there in my underwear and shivered, but I found out what I wanted to know. When I got up and went back into the bedroom to get dressed, I could almost walk straight.

I parked on Halsey near Maistre's Bar, went up the stairs in the Brick-alter Building. It was old, dry, musty, and dark.

It seemed a long way to the third floor. The room number I had been given was 308. I paused outside the door. A single dim bulb provided the sole illumination for the narrow corridor. Distantly, I could hear street noises.

I took out my gun, pushed off the safety. For a moment I listened at the door. I could hear two men inside, talking, but not what they said. I put my shoulder against the rotted, wooden door. It gave.

Getz and Rosson were sitting at a table with beer and sandwiches. They came up, moving fast. When they saw me, they hesitated for the space of a breath.

I didn't. I shot Getz first because he was nearest me. I got him in the hip, and he went flopping back against the wall, raging with the agony of a shattered pelvis. All the fight went out of him.

I didn't wait to check him. I had to shoot Rosson in the shoulder because he was going for his gun. He kept trying for it. I shot him again, in the same shoulder, a little lower. He spun around knocking a chair over as he hit the floor.

I collected their guns as pure precaution. They didn't even care. Getz was yelling for a doctor and Rosson was insane with fear that I was going to kill him. I didn't bother telling him if I'd meant to kill him, I'd have done it with the first shot.

I told them to quit crying. I found a phone, called the department and ordered a wagon. Getz screamed, wanting an ambulance, but I told him he was lucky to get a wagon and not to push his luck.

Rosson was whimpering. "We was just doing our job."

"And I'm just doing mine," I said. "Now it's up to you. I can finish this— or you can stay alive for the wagon and somebody might even get you a doctor. Take your pick."

Rosson was shaking all over by now. "What do you want?"

"A cop named Ernie Gault," I said. "And I've got no time to waste. Where is he?"

I brought the gun up. They couldn't talk fast enough. The only trouble was they both tried to talk at the same time.

I knew where the abandoned quarry was. I drove out there, pushing my old car as fast as it would go. I hit the turnpike with my horn wailing, and cars pulled over.

I was doing ninety before I reached the cut-off, stepped on the brakes and slewed into the side road. It was shell-paved, but so narrow that in order to pass, cars had to go off on the shoulders on each side.

I drove with my gun across my lap and the two I had taken from Getz and Rosson on the seat beside me.

I felt better that way.

As I drove, I felt my insides twist with contempt for these hoods, all of them, including the sweet-smelling Fred Carmichael. Carmichael claimed to be something new in racketeering power, but using this quarry showed what kind of imagination these slime had. Luxtro had used this place when he had a body he wanted to dispose of.

I heard the car ahead of me even before I saw it. And when I saw it, I knew I'd struck pay dirt. The black sedan was racing toward me, hell-bent to get away.

I felt the sickness fill my insides. If they were trying to leave, Ernie might already be dead.

I didn't stop to think about it. I swung the Olds hard, and then backed it, parking it across the narrow strip of road. Nothing on wheels could get around it between the car and the thick trees on each side.

The car lights came racing toward me. At the last minute the driver slammed on his brakes, rolling right up against the Olds.

Three hoods came out of that sedan, guns drawn.

But I was on the far side of the Olds, in the darkness waiting for them. When they threw open the car door, the dome light flared, setting them up like animals in a shooting alley.

I took the driver first because he was nearest. I shot him as his feet struck the road. He dropped his gun and went sprawling forward on his face.

The second punk jerked his gun up to fire and I shot it out of his hand. I was already running around the Olds, going toward them as I fired.

The third goon yelled, voice high-pitched, "Don't shoot. I'm throwing it away."

I came around the front of the Olds and they were waiting for me.

"Where is he?" I said.

They didn't fool around. They looked at two things, the gun in my hand and the blood-stained bandages on my head. They had pushed him off the side of the pit, and they had no objections to showing me where.

"Okay," I said. "Let's go."

It was dark at the rim of the old pit. The silence out there seemed to rise from the bowels of the earth. The moon was up and the stars laid a gray mist over the quarry.

I marched them to the brink of the pit. "You're going down there to get him."

"He's there," one of them said. "He landed on a shelf. Right there. We heard your car and decided to get out of here."

They went over the side of the pit slowly. The boy I'd shot in the wrist tried to talk his way out of it because of the pain. But when I backhanded him across the face with the side of my gun, he changed his mind. In fact, he was the first one of them to reach the shelf where Ernie was sprawled.

"All right, bring him up," I said. "And you'd better start praying he's still alive. Because if he's dead, you two are joining him right here."

"We were only doing what we were told." This from the one who had not been shot. The other boy was already lifting Ernie, pushing his limp body up the incline of the pit toward me.

I laid the gun on the rock beside me, caught Ernie under the arms and pulled him up.

When I got him over the lip of the pit, I laid him out on the ground and picked up the gun.

The two hoods were starting to climb up. I faced them with the gun in my hand.

"Where do you two guys think you're going?"

They stopped, promising no trouble. They were under arrest. One of them even began to yell that he'd heard Ernie breathing when he lifted him.

"I hope you're right," I said. "Now, both of you. Turn around on that shelf. Jump."

They began begging, at first not really believing that I meant what I said. And that just shows you how stupid Carmichael's new-era goons were.

"You jump," I said. "Or I put bullets in you."

"Dammit, copper—have a heart—"

"Sure. I'm giving you a chance. It's a long way to the bottom of this pit, but no farther for you than for Ernie. You might break both legs—even so, somebody may find you, maybe in less than a week. But if I put bullets in you, it won't do you any good to be found."

They were mewling down there on that shelf, but when I put a bullet into the rock between them, they stopped that. They stared up at me, shaking all over and then they went over the side.

I only waited long enough to see that both of them jumped. Then I knelt down and lifted Ernie in my arms. I listened, but could hear no sound of his breathing and there was no time to check. I moved as fast as I could in the darkness along the narrow road to the place where I'd left the Olds.

23

I stopped just once after I hit the Turnpike. I skidded the Olds into the first parking area where I saw a lighted telephone booth. I made four calls and then ran back to the Olds, jumped in. I thought Ernie moved slightly on the seat. But it might have been the movement of the car. I was doing sixty when I hit the Turnpike again.

Again I parked outside City Hall. A light was burning in Doc Yerrgsted's office.

I got out of the car, lifted Ernie in my arms and carried him across the parking area and into the side entrance of the building. There was nobody around. It was almost eleven o'clock. I was conscious of nothing, not even Ernie's sprawled dead-weight in my arms. He was weightless. There was nothing in me except this knot of nerves in the pit of my stomach—or maybe it was much simpler than that. It may have been cold fear.

I went along the silent corridors, pressed the elevator button. I stood waiting, watching the floor indicator above the doors, but wanting to wheel around and watch both ways along that corridor at once. One thing I knew. I had put Getz and Rosson in cells. Carmichael knew that by now.

The elevator doors opened. I stepped inside and we moved upward with that terrible slowness that elevators have. I could barely feel us move.

Doc Yerrgsted opened the door of his office. I carried Ernie along the corridor, wondering what Doc would have done if some of Carmichael's goons had stepped out into the dim hallway. Then I had the answer. Nothing mattered to Doc.

He had an examination table waiting and I placed Ernie on it. I was careful his feet and arms didn't hang over the sides. What the hell difference did his comfort make now?

I slumped down in a chair and could feel the shaking start, like waves radiating out from that cold knot in my stomach. I clenched my teeth. Any second the shakes would have me trembling all over.

Doc didn't speak for a long time. I sat, trying to keep that convulsive shivering under control, watching him work over Ernie.

"How is he, Doc? Is he dead?"

He glanced over his shoulder. "You didn't find out before you brought him here?"

"I didn't waste the time, Doc. I knew I had to get him here. The punks pushed him over the side of the pit. But they chickened out when they heard my car on the quarry turn-off.... Is he alive, Doc?"

"He has a pulse. He's still breathing. However the bullet is lodged in the left bronchus of the trachea—"

"Come on, Doc." My hands were shaking now.

"You should have taken him to the hospital. The left lung may be punctured."

"I couldn't take him to the hospital, Doc. You know that."

"Why not?"

"If we're going to save his life, there's only one way we can do it. You know that. Here. On the quiet. In this office."

"This man may die at any second. No one but an excellent surgeon could hope to—why, the tissue-thin lung alveoli may already be damaged and the least incision—"

"Doc. You got to do it."

"Don't be a fool. Why—I wouldn't have attempted a thing like this twenty-five years ago when I was your age. You must be insane to think—"

I looked up at him and the shaking was in my arms now. "I'm not insane. It doesn't matter, does it? He's gone anyway, isn't he? Isn't that what you once told me? One way is as good as another—when you're going to die, anyway."

"My God, boy. I—I'd need assistance, an expert surgery nurse—"

"You're gonna get help, Doc. It's on its way. Now stop talking and get ready."

He sagged against the examination table, his back to Ernie. "I bought you a plane ticket. You can't do anything for this man. Nobody can—"

"You're going to try. You talked big to me about what I could do in this town."

"I was a fool to tell you that. If I help Ernie, will you get on that plane?'

I shook my head. "I guess not, Doc. I found out something tonight. I found out how far I could be pushed. I'm pushing back."

My teeth were chattering. I had to stop talking. For a moment the room spun. I thought I was going to fall off the chair.

Doc moved toward me.

"Get away from me." My voice was savage. "You do anything, you do it for that guy on the table."

Doc paused. I don't know what he was going to say, but his door opened, and Lupe Valdez hurried in. She was wearing her white nurse's smock, her cape, cap and white crepe-soled shoes and looking like an olive-tinted angel.

"Here's your help, Doc. Now stop stalling. This girl has got more love and purpose than any nurse you ever saw. What you want done, she'll do."

Doc stood staring at his hands. They were trembling almost as badly as mine.

Lupe barely glanced at the man on Doc's examination table. She came to me, her eyes wide. "Mike. What's the matter? You look terrible."

I had to bite off the words to keep my teeth from chattering. "I ain't your patient, honey." Then, glancing past her, I saw the man in the doorway. I fought the gun from my holster, but Lupe caught my arm, pressing her soft, soothing hand against my face.

"Mike. Stop. Morgan wanted to come."

I stared at young Carmichael. He was standing stoop-shouldered, face pale, just inside the door. "What are you doing here?"

"I thought maybe I could help, Mr. Ballard. I was with Lupe when you called."

"Won't leave her alone, huh?"

Morgan tried to smile. "No, sir. I've got some sense—maybe you battered it into my head that day. I knew if I didn't have Lupe, I'd never have anything as long as I lived. I got rid of Naomi and I came back tonight—to stay, if Lupe will let me."

My knees felt weak. I had to lean against the chair. "Sure," I said. "Besides, she's got seventy-five grand."

For the first time Morgan laughed. "That's right," he said. "She's rich. I want to marry her for her money."

But we were just talking, young Carmichael and I. Lupe and Doc were already at work on Ernie.

There was no need for me to hang around. I was never a hand at moonlight and roses—with or without the fiddle. And before my night's work was done, I would be out of these people's picture.

I brushed past Morgan and went out the door.

24

The moon was lost behind the blackest bank of night clouds ever heaped in one pile, and its light silvered only the ragged edges. I drove slowly. I parked a block away from Fred Carmichael's big house in Flamingo Estates and got out, leaving the keys in the ignition. If things failed to work out as I intended, anybody with a license and who could drive could have the Olds.

As I marched along the wide walks, I could hear my own footsteps as I put each foot down carefully. Lights were blazing in the Carmichael mansion. I think they were on even in the cellar. Maybe, suddenly, Fred Carmichael was afraid of the dark.

I crossed the darkened lawn slowly, guided by shafts of yellow light flooding out through tall windows. Beside the pool deck I paused, remembering for no good reason the afternoon I'd walked up on Tom Flynn's pool and Naomi. I remembered with a sudden pointlessness that she was free. From here on she would be wearing less, as I had suggested that night in my apartment.

I drew a deep breath, thinking about her, the way she would look from now on. Was she waiting in my apartment with bourbon and ice and soft music tonight—while I was out here keeping a different, grimmer kind of date?

I circled the house. There was a man on guard outside, and I could see two other goons through the first-floor window.

The punk outside was easy. He was leaning against a tall pillar on the front veranda, smoking a cigarette. The way I laid the side of my gun behind his ear was so according to the detective's manual that I got a faint sense of lift out of it. Personally I might be a hell of a character. But one thing I knew was my job. He was not even bruised.

I caught him under the arms as he sagged. Then I dropped him.

A front door entrance was not indicated for what I had in mind. I went around to the side of the house, found an unoccupied room. Holding my folded handkerchief against the pane, I used the gun butt again and cracked a small opening in the glass. This time there was the small clatter of falling glass. I stood in the shadow and waited, counting slowly. Nothing happened.

I reached through the jagged break, unlocked the window. The place must be bugged with burglar alarms—none of which, I knew, registered to police headquarters. But an alarm of any forcible entry was given to Carmichael's own people—probably the goons I had seen through the window.

I shoved the window up, went through it, landing on the floor on my knees. Waves of pain rolled upward through me and I wasted a moment shaking my head, trying to clear it, at the same time getting out my gun. As I came up on my knees, the door was thrown open and the two goons came through it.

I had two things in my favor. One, I had been expecting them; two, I looked like a man from Mars who'd gotten caught in his own umbilical cord—my battered head had begun bleeding again, and the bandages Doc had wrapped around it were blood-stained and had jarred loose.

They stopped long enough to stare, open-mouthed, at the apparition I made, the bloodied gauze hanging loose around my swollen, purple face. It was the last mistake they ever made. I shot twice before either one of them recovered enough to fire the guns in their hands.

I came up off my knees as I fired and was running across the room before either one of them had hit the floor. One of them sagged against the wall beside the door, and I gave him a shove that toppled him over.

"Oscar! What the hell's the matter?"

I paused in the foyer.

Carmichael's voice came from the closed door at my left. I crossed the foyer, put my hand on the knob, thrust the door open.

I stood staring into a richly appointed, book-lined study.

Carmichael was standing behind his huge, polished desk, set well into the room. His face was twisted with contempt. "What do you want?" He let his gaze move over my battered face, the bloodied bandages. "Want some more, Ballard?" He pressed buttons on his desk top. "I thought you had learned your lesson."

"I did. I'm here to teach you yours."

We both waited, Carmichael with his finger on the buzzer. Nothing happened. He pressed it again. Something flickered in his eyes.

I stepped into the room, kicked the thick panel-oak door shut with my heel. I backed up against it, locked it. Then I leaned there because my knees were so weak they barely supported me.

"They're not coming, Carmichael," I said. "Nobody's coming to do your dirty work for you. Not any more."

He stared at me a moment, then that scarred brow tilted slightly and he smiled. "What's the beef, Ballard? I got tough with you because you pushed me. I had to do it. You've still got your job and I like your guts. Play along with me and I'll make you rich."

I shook my head. "I'm sick of playing along. I've played along until nothing's worth living for. Not money, women, friends or booze. I hope you feel the same way I do, Carmichael, because I got the word for you. This is it."

When he moved his hand away from those buzzers and brought it up, he had a forty-five in it. I don't know where he got it. My eyes were almost swollen shut. My reflexes were almost gone. Maybe his hand was always quicker than the eye—maybe that was how he made it to where he was. He was a big boy, all right, a tough man. And I was all that stood in his way.

He moved around the desk now, briskly, to take charge. He held the gun ready. "Don't be a jackass, Ballard, I'll kill you without thinking about it."

"Even if you pull the trigger first," I said evenly. "I'm still going to get you and I don't miss. Do you ever miss, Carmichael?"

"Get some sense, man. You know what a forty-five does to you? It'll tear you open. You'll spill all out—"

"It's not my rug."

He fired without telegraphing his movement in the least. The slug drove me back against the door as if somebody had nailed my hide there.

I remember thinking as the Police Positive began bucking in my hand that Fred Carmichael was tougher than any man I had ever met, and smarter, and faster—that I had to squeeze the trigger coldly, smoothly, the right way, the way you did when you were on the range and not shooting at a man at all. I kept pressing it seven times, not thinking about Fred at all, but thinking about Tom Flynn, the Greek, Ernie, young Hogan and Ed Clemmons—and even Jerry Marlowe.

When the gun was empty, I realized I was face down on the deep carpeting and firing into the floor.

I raised my head slightly and saw Fred Carmichael slumped on the floor, his back against the desk. I knew he was dead, because his big forty-five was on the floor beside his leg and he made no try for it. Then I put my head down and shut my eyes. From some far distance I heard the wailing scream of an ambulance and I knew Doc Yerrgsted had ordered it sent out here because he had guessed that anywhere I went tonight an ambulance would be needed, and he had never been so right.

Doc used that airplane ticket to take himself a vacation and he came back swearing he would never touch booze again. This I learned much later, after they operated on my thick skull. The Greek survived, and so did Ernie. He is a great pal of Lupe's and acts kind of like a grandfather to her kid—when he has time off from his duties as police commissioner, that is.

As for Naomi, I found out she was as good as she looked. We expect a baby of our own pretty soon.

THE END

HARRY WHITTINGTON

BY BILL CRIDER

Obsessed characters wracked by their passions—lust, greed, the desire for revenge—travel through the night-world of cheap bars, back-alley dives, and backwoods swamps: crooked cops and honorable ones, bent private eyes and those who live by a strict moral code, the dishonest and the noble, the seeking and the lost. Harry Whittington has written about them all, and many more, in a career that has covered parts of five decades. Under his own name and as Whit Harrison, Hallam Whitney, Harry White, Kell Holland, Clay Stuart, Harriet Kathryn Myers, and Ashley Carter, to name just a few, Whittington has been almost the prototypical paperback writer, always delivering a solid story and breakneck pacing for the reader's money. He has written, in addition to his mystery and suspense novels, Westerns, historical romances, backwoods romances, "mainstream" fiction, love stories, and nearly anything else that can be read, with the exception of science fiction and fantasy. He has written for such now-forgotten paperback houses as Handi-Books, Uni, Phantom, Carnival, Venus, Original Novels, and Graphic, as well as for such famous houses as Fawcett Gold Medal, Avon, Pyramid, and Ace.

Whittington was particularly suited to the emerging paperback market of the early 1950s because of his ability to produce saleable fiction at a rapid pace. After the sale of his first softcover original, *Slay Ride for a Lady,* to James Quinn's Handi-Books in 1950, he wrote and sold twenty-five paperback originals in the next three years. Whittington tells about these years in an interview with Michael S. Barson in Billy Lee's *Paperback Quarterly* (Volume 4, Number 2), explaining that "Gold Medal was the prestige paperback line" and that they also paid the best advance ($2500), while allowing writers to keep all foreign and movie rights. Gold Medal, after buying *Fires That Destroy* in 1951, naturally got to see most of Whittington's books before other publishers, and as Ashley Carter he continues to write for Gold Medal today, thirty-six years later, continuing the popular Blackoaks series. Other publishers in the early 1950s did not pay as well as Gold Medal, and Whittington recalls receiving a $750 advance for each of his Handi-Books novels, while Ace paid him $1000 each for *Drawn to Evil* (1952) and *So Dead My Love!* (1953). He had a unique arrangement with Mauri Latzen, whose firm owned Carnival, Venus, Phantom, and Original Novels. He could submit a three-page outline at any time and receive a check for $375. After sending in the completed novel, he received another $375, and each reprinting brought an additional $375. Graphic, like Ace, paid a $1000 advance.

Considering the size of the advances, a writer had to produce a large number of books if he intended to make a living at his typewriter, particularly if, like Whittington, he had a growing family to support. In a 1978 address to the Florida Suncoast Writers' Conference (portions of which are reprinted in *Paperback Quarterly,* Volume 2, Number 2), Whittington says that he "chose consciously to write swiftly and with spontaneity" and that he "sold as fast as [he] could write." He was trying to make a living, and he did not have time to spend six months waiting for the prestigious hardback houses to make a decision about his work. He needed to sell, and he needed the quick decisions of the paperback market, despite its lack of prestige. After all, hardcover snob appeal is not everything, and when reviewers did begin to notice paperback originals, Whittington received excellent notices. Anthony Boucher, surely one of the shrewdest critics the field of mystery and suspense has ever known, was one of the first to devote regular space to paperback authors, and in his "Criminals at Large" column in *The New York Times Book Review* he called Whittington "one of the most versatile and satisfactory creators" of the paperback original. In a review of *You'll Die Next!* (Ace, 1954), Boucher wrote that Whittington was capable of "the best sheer storytelling since the greatest days of the pre-sex detective pulps."

Such comments were the result of Whittington's ability to produce books that combined fast action, clever plotting, and three-dimensional characters in a rapidly-paced story. In his article "The Paperback Original," published in *The Mystery Writer's Handbook* (ed. Herbert Brean, Harper, 1956), Whittington writes, "it's as true in paperbacks as in trade editions—maybe even truer—that you must tell a vital, hard-hitting story; you've got to keep it moving and give it that old emotional pull." This was a lesson that Whittington had learned well, but there is more. The writer must also "Care. Make the characters come alive; get so involved in those people you're writing about that you yourself want to race right along beside them and see that they come out all right." All Whittington's best work involves characters the reader cares about, in situations which at first seem simple. The characters have goals that seem easily obtainable, but unexpected complications arise. Things suddenly get worse, and then worse still. Finally, when the character seems doomed or hopelessly trapped, when it appears that things could not possibly get any worse, they do. A good example of this technique is found in Whittington's first paperback, *Slay Ride for a Lady* (Handi-Books, 1950). Narrator, Dan Henderson, an ex-cop framed for murder, is released from prison to find the wife of a criminal/political bigshot. He finds the woman almost at once, but then she is killed. Henderson is framed again, beaten to a pulp by vicious cops, and betrayed by a girl he trusts. He survives, even prevails, but there is no false happy ending such as some writers might provide. It just wouldn't work in a story this hard-boiled, and though Whittington does believe in a happy ending most of the time, he avoids it here. In addition to refusing to provide the expected upbeat conclusion, Whittington throws in another unique touch. The murdered woman has a baby for whom Henderson feels a sense of responsibility. There is a memorable episode in which Henderson, chasing a murderer, blood pouring down his arm from a knife wound in his shoulder, pauses to feed the baby its milk from a bottle. Has any other hard-boiled hero ever done the same?

The device of the man framed for murder was one to which Whittington returned often and effectively, especially in two of his novels for Graphic, *Call Me Killer* (1951) and *Mourn the Hangman* (1952). The former combines the murder frame with amnesia as Sam Gowan, soft-boiled nebbish who is a far cry from Dan Henderson, wakes up in the office of a prominent businessman who has very recently been shot in the face. Sam is holding a gun and certainly appears to be a likely suspect in the murder. His situation is further complicated by the fact that he has been missing from home for some months and, as the reader eventually learns, has constructed for himself an alternate identity as "David Mye" while suffering from a loss of memory. Add to this a brutal cop named Barney Manton, who is determined to crack the case and pin the murder on Sam, no matter how illegally he has to proceed, and the result is a typical fast-paced Whittington story. In *Mourn the Hangman*, Steve Blake, a private eye working on a case involving a government supplier who is cheating on his contracts, is framed for the murder of his wife. He is pursued by the police, hunted by the bad guys, betrayed by his partner, and put through more twists and turns of plot than would seem possible. Like Sam Gowan, he hardly has time even to eat or sleep as he tries to set things right.

Gowan and Blake are typical Whittington protagonists, but he was anything but formula bound, as a look at another of his Graphic novels, *Mur-*

der is My Mistress (1951), demonstrates. The title is entirely misleading—there is no murder in the novel. That fact alone is enough to make the book different from the typical mystery paperback. And, murder is no one's mistress. In fact, the book's main character is a woman, and the story is one of psychological suspense as it follows the life of Julia Clarkson, whose past catches up with her. Now a middle-class housewife, Julia had twenty years earlier been the companion of a criminal, Paul Renner. She informed on him to escape the life she was living, but now she learns that he has been released from prison and begins to fear for her life. He torments her with a series of "accidents," and her life and marriage deteriorate rapidly.

Another female protagonist, though a very different one, is Bernice Harper, the mousy secretary of *Fires That Destroy* (Gold Medal, 1951). Bernice kills and robs her employer, a wealthy blind man, and gets away with it. Well, almost. Whittington's killers never *quite* get away with murder, though they often come close. The punishments that Whittington sets up for them are always interesting and always grow out of their characters. The punishments are also always wonderfully ironic, as in the case of Bernice and especially in the case of the lawyer in the excellent *Web of Murder* (Gold Medal, 1958), one of Whittington's best and most cleverly-plotted novels. The lawyer and his secretary, with whom he is having an affair, decide to kill the lawyer's wife. They succeed, but they are confronted with a cop much like Barney Manton from *Call Me Killer* (though this time the cop is an honest one). He is convinced that the pair are guilty of murder, but can he prove it? It would not be fair to tell, but it is not revealing too much to say that things—lots of little things—do begin to go wrong with the lawyer's beautifully planned "perfect" murder, leading to one plot surprise after another. Though each twist is carefully prepared for, each works to perfection, right up to the powerhouse conclusion.

A similar story, but one which does not work quite as well, is *The Humming Box* (Ace, 1956). The female protagonist, Liz Palmer, discovers a unique murder method and uses it to rid herself of the husband she no longer cares for, and of course to get his money. While not as strong a story as *Web of Murder,* this novel nevertheless has its moments, as Liz succeeds with murder only to be preyed on by a very slimy private detective before she meets her ironic fate.

Lethal women, though they figure prominently in Whittington's work, are not always the protagonists. Often they are secondary to the men who fall—and fall hard—for them. In *Satan's Widow* (Phantom, 1951), tough cop Barney Hodges falls for the widow of "Satan," a terrible but powerful man who, when alive, delighted in ruining people's lives. When Satan is poisoned, Hodges is certain the wife is guilty, though there are plenty of other suspects. He is so powerfully attracted to her, however, that he is determined to see that she is not arrested, no matter who he has to frame for the crime. Her guilt or innocence becomes irrelevant to him. There is a definite James M. Cain influence on this novel, and the sex scenes are fairly steamy stuff for a 1951 mass market book. In *The Mystery Writer's Handbook,* Whittington says that *Satan's Widow* is a revised version of a serial, *Body in the Bedroom,* that he wrote for the King Features Syndicate. He sold the novel against his agent's and editor's better judgment, but it was reprinted in five foreign countries and earned its author a lot of money, "although everybody says it stinks." Whittington evidently liked the novel well enough to use a *very* similar plot in a much stronger book, *Drawn to Evil* (Ace, 1952), in which the tough cop, once more drawn irresistibly to the prime suspect—the dead man's wife—goes so far as to conceal evidence and frame another, less likely, suspect for the crime. How tough is this cop? Listen:

I let him make his play. Before he got his knife out, I had a wad of shirt front in my fist. I jerked him off balance. When he spread his legs to steady himself, I drove my knee into his groin. Hard.

I released him without even looking at him again. I heard something clatter on the floor. It must have been his long-bladed slap-knife. He wasn't going to need it for a while. Not while he writhed.

Despite the similarity of this novel to *Satan's Widow,* they are two distinct stories, with completely different ways of working out the various plot threads. Overall, *Drawn to Evil* is the more successful and satisfactory book, and it has a bang-up ending that can stand with the best of Whittington's work.

Another novel with a dangerously attractive woman is *A Night for Screaming* (Ace, 1960), which also brings in a framed man on the run. Mitch Walker is a former cop innocent of the murder of which he is accused, though naturally he can't prove it. He is pursued by his brutal former partner, Fred Palmer, and winds up on a wheat farm in Kansas. (How many suspense novels set on wheat farms can you name? Leave it to Harry Whittington to come up with a setting like this and to make it seem absolutely real.) The farm is owned by Mr. Barton M. Cassel and looks like a good place to hide from the law, except that the work is brutal, the pay is low, and when Mr. Cassel's wife, Eve, takes a liking to you, well, sixteen hours in the sun at manual labor might be easier. There are plenty of twists in the story, and the suspense, a Whittington hallmark, never lets up.

The man-on-the-run theme also figures prominently in *You'll Die Next!* (Ace, 1954), in which Henry Wilson, an ordinary guy married to a woman whose past he knows little about, is viciously beaten, receives a threatening letter, loses his job, is involved in a hit-and-run accident (as the victim), and is accused both of beating his wife and shooting a cop—all in the first fifty pages. In the *New York Times Book Review,* Anthony Boucher wrote, *"You'll Die Next!* is a very short novel, which is just as well. I couldn't have held my breath any longer in this vigorous tale whose plot is too dexterously twisted even to mention in a review." High praise indeed, especially coming from Boucher, but certainly justified in the case of one of Whittington's cleverest stories.

Whittington also dealt effectively with the theme of "one man against municipal corruption." A prime example is found in *Violent Night* (under the name Whit Harrison, Phantom, 1951). Coast Town is a hotbed of teen prostitutes, dope dealers, and gambling dens. O'Brian, an honest cop with an invalid wife, has to deal with his mistress' leaving him, suspension from the police force, a hired killer imported into town to murder him, and a dead teenage girl found beside the road with three poker chips in her shoe. No one but Whittington could deal successfully with so many plot threads in such a short (128 pages) book, while compressing all the events into the period of a single fast-moving night. He succeeds almost as well in *So Dead My Love!* (Ace, 1953). Jim Talbot, a New York private eye, is called home to Duval, Florida, by the man who got his conviction overturned and got him out of one of Florida's toughest prisons some years before. The man is now married to Talbot's former sweetheart, the very woman who got him into prison in the first place. It's Talbot's job to locate a missing man, and in doing so he must deal with a fat, nasty sheriff who likes things just as they are and his psychopathic deputy. The small-town southern setting adds spice to the plot.

In fact, Whittington is particularly good at depicting the small towns and rural areas of 1950s Florida, and readers should not overlook certain of his books simply because their titles do not suggest mysteries. For example, *Backwoods Tramp* (Gold Medal, 1959) might seem from its title and cover to be a sort of "cracker romance" along the lines of *Backwoods Shack* or *Backwoods Hussy* (both of which first appeared under the Hallam Whitney name), but it is instead a powerful suspense story. It does feature an archetypal southern poor-white woman as a love interest, but it is really the story of Jake Richards, who is searching the swamp country for Marve Pooser, the man who engineered the robbery that cost Jake his job, his girl, and his reputation. Pooser is a psychopath any reader can hate, and Richards is a believable protagonist, no hero but a man who learns quite a bit about himself and his motives. By the end of the novel, Richards is able to face what he has become in his search for Pooser and to avoid becoming something worse.

A man who faces what he has become and doesn't even seem to care is the crooked cop Mike Ballard in *Brute in Brass* (Gold Medal, 1956). Ballard is at first a completely contemptible man, callous, indifferent to others, concerned only with himself and what he can get, no matter how he gets it. He always looks for the angle, the way to turn any situation to his own advantage. Little by little, Whittington reveals the reasons for Ballard's attitudes and surprises the reader by eventually eliciting sympathy for the man. Despite the book's strengths as a character study, however, it moves at the typical jet-like pace of any Whittington novel, a neat trick but one that Whittington pulled off with regularity.

Two more books that should not escape anyone's notice are *Married to Murder* (Phantom, 1951) and *Body and Passion* (as Whit Harrison, Original Novels, 1952). The former is the story of yet another cop framed for murder, one of Whittington's seemingly infinite and original variations on a single plot idea. The cop, Palmer, agrees to undergo plastic surgery and pose as the son-in-law of a wealthy New York woman in order to travel to Florida and help the woman's daughter, who is in some unspecified kind of trouble. Before he quite knows what is happening, he has had his appearance altered and finds himself sitting in the front seat of a car with a dead body in his lap, a body the old woman has been keeping in her freezer and whose dead face bears a striking and unsettling resemblance to the face Palmer now sees when he looks into the mirror. To top it off, when he gets to Florida, Palmer finds the daughter being kept as a virtual prisoner in her own house, held there in a drug-induced haze by none other than Palmer's larcenous and treacherous ex-wife.

Palmer's identity crisis, however, can't hold a candle to the problems of the protagonist of *Body and Passion*. He doesn't know who he is, and neither does anyone else. Two men, one a gangster and one an ambitious assistant district attorney, are trapped in a terrible fire at the gangster's hideaway cabin. Only one man survives, and he is so badly burned that there is no way to recognize him or even to take his fingerprints. (On the book's cover he is depicted as what cover-art critic Art Scott has called "the mummy in the tuxedo.") The D.A.'s parents want him to be their precious son, the mob wants to kill him, and the girl who loved the gangster wants him to marry her. But he simply can't remember his identity, despite living for a week both as D.A. and as gangster. And if that isn't enough, it turns out that a third man, a newspaper reporter who was spying on both the other men, has also disappeared on the night of the fire. The protagonist, X as he is called throughout most of the story, does recover his memory, but Whittington manages to keep the reader guessing most of the way through this unusual suspense novel.

Because he has written over one hundred paperback novels, Whittington did not manage to come up with a winner every single time, which is not surprising considering the amount of work. After all, even Sandy Koufax lost a few ball games. Two books that don't quite live up to the author's usual high standards are *One Got Away* (Ace, 1955) and *Hot as*

Fire—Cold as Ice (Belmont, 1962). In *One Got Away,* a man named Gosucki steals plans worth one million dollars from the government. Dan Campbell, who was assigned to watch Gosucki, tries to redeem himself by catching the thief, and in doing so travels from Chicago to Carolina to Indianapolis to Hawaii, while being pursued by his own agency. The chase elements and the race against time don't quite click in this one. *Hot as Fire* fails for different reasons, as a deepfreeze salesman tries to foil kidnappers who are keeping a dead body in a freezer he has sold them. It's a thin plot, a far cry from the incident-packed twists and turns of Whittington's best work.

According to Mike Barson's introduction to the interview for *Paperback Quarterly,* Whittington "retired from the paperback field in disgust" from 1969 to 1975, "convinced he was demeaning himself" after writing a series of movie and television show "novelizations," Westerns, and nurse novels for little pay and even less prestige. One of these novels was, however, one of Whittington's biggest successes with readers if not in a financial sense. Whittington, who also did many of the lead novels for *The Man from U.N.C.L.E.* magazine, wrote *The Doomsday Affair (The Man from U.N.C.L.E. #2)* for Ace Books. The book proved to be extremely popular with fans of the television series and drew more mail than any of Whittington's previous works. The book apparently sold well, but the sale did not particularly benefit the author, series books of this sort usually being on a work-for-hire basis and paying a flat fee instead of a royalty.

In 1975, Whittington began his comeback in the paperback field. As Ashley Carter, he took over Gold Medal's Falconhurst and Blackoaks series of slave/plantation historical novels and once more found himself a best-selling writer. Since that time he has written other historical works (*Panama,* Gold Medal, 1978), mainstream novels (*Rampage,* Gold Medal, 1978), and Westerns (six novels in Jove's Longarm series). Most of these books, though longer by far than the lean, mean novels Whittington wrote in the 1950s, nevertheless retain most of the virtues of the earlier works—clever plotting, fast pacing, and expert storytelling.

In spite of his well-deserved successes in the past twelve years, it is for his earlier work that readers of mystery and suspense fiction will remember Harry Whittington. He has said that his favorite writers at that time were Frederick C. Davis, Day Keene, and Fredric Brown, and that if there was any influence on his work it was James M. Cain. Readers might also note the influence of Cornell Woolrich, and Whittington encouraged would-be paperback writers to read Fitzgerald, Faulkner, Hemingway, Dostoyevski, O'Hara, and Wouk in his article in *The Mystery Writer's Handbook.* He also mentioned Brown, Woolrich, Chandler, and Roy Huggins. Some of these writers are revered today, some forgotten; some are still in print, others not. For far too long Whittington's has been the latter case, his best works available only to those willing to spend long hours in dusty used-book stores, searching through stacks of crumbling paperbacks in the hopes, in the hopes....

Of the great paperback writers of the 1950s, Jim Thompson eventually attracted a cult following. John D. MacDonald went on to take his place on the hardcover best-seller lists. Harry Whittington, on the other hand, saw his best work fall into neglect. Let us hope that posterity will rediscover his books and recognize him as what he is: one of the true masters of paperback fiction.

Other Stark House books you may enjoy...

Clifton Adams Death's Sweet Song /
Whom Gods Destroy $19.95
Benjamin Appel Brain Guy / Plunder $19.95
Benjamin Appel Sweet Money Girl /
Life and Death of a Tough Guy $21.95
Malcolm Braly Shake Him Till He Rattles /
It's Cold Out There $19.95
Gil Brewer Wild to Possess / A Taste for Sin $19.95
Gil Brewer A Devil for O'Shaugnessy /
The Three-Way Split $14.95
Gil Brewer Nude on Thin Ice /
Memory of Passion $19.95
W. R. Burnett It's Always Four O'Clock /
Iron Man $19.95
W. R. Burnett Little Men, Big World /
Vanity Row $19.95
Catherine Butzen Thief of Midnight $15.95
James Hadley Chase Come Easy—Go Easy /
In a Vain Shadow $19.95
Andrew Coburn Spouses & Other Crimes $15.95
Jada M. Davis One for Hell $19.95
Jada M. Davis Midnight Road $19.95
Bruce Elliott One is a Lonely Number /
Elliott Chaze Black Wings Has My Angel $19.95
Don Elliott/Robert Silverberg
Gang Girl / Sex Bum $19.95
Don Elliott/Robert Silverberg
Lust Queen / Lust Victim $19.95
Feldman & Gartenberg (ed)
The Beat Generation & the Angry Young Men $19.95
A. S. Fleischman Look Behind You, Lady /
The Venetian Blonde $19.95
A. S. Fleischman Danger in Paradise /
Malay Woman $19.95
A. S. Fleischman The Sun Worshippers /
Yellowleg $19.95
Ed Gorman The Autumn Dead /
The Night Remembers $19.95
Arnold Hano So I'm a Heel / Flint /
The Big Out $23.95
Orrie Hitt The Cheaters / Dial "M" for Man $19.95
Elisabeth Sanxay Holding Lady Killer /
Miasma $19.95
Elisabeth Sanxay Holding The Death Wish /
Net of Cobwebs $19.95
Elisabeth Sanxay Holding Strange Crime in Bermuda /
Too Many Bottles $19.95
Elisabeth Sanxay Holding The Old Battle-Ax /
Dark Power $19.95
Elisabeth Sanxay Holding The Unfinished Crime /
The Girl Who Had to Die $19.95
Elisabeth Sanxay Holding Speak of the Devil /
The Obstinate Murderer $19.95
Russell James Underground / Collected Stories $14.95
Day Keene Framed in Guilt / My Flesh is Sweet $19.95
Day Keene Dead Dolls Don't Talk / Hunt the Killer /
Too Hot to Hold $23.95

Mercedes Lambert Dogtown / Soultown $14.95
Dan J. Marlowe/Fletcher Flora/Charles Runyon
Trio of Gold Medals $15.95
Dan J. Marlowe The Name of the Game is Death /
One Endless Hour $19.95
Stephen Marlowe Violence is My Business /
Turn Left for Murder $19.95
McCarthy & Gorman (ed) Invasion of the
Body Snatchers: A Tribute $19.95
Wade Miller The Killer / Devil on Two Sticks $19.95
Wade Miller Kitten With a Whip /
Kiss Her Goodbye $19.95
Rick Ollerman Turnabout / Shallow Secrets $19.95
Vin Packer Something in the Shadows /
Intimate Victims $19.95
Vin Packer The Damnation of Adam Blessing /
Alone at Night $19.95
Vin Packer Whisper His Sin /
The Evil Friendship $19.95
Richard Powell A Shot in the Dark /
Shell Game $14.95
Bill Pronzini Snowbound / Games $14.95
Peter Rabe The Box / Journey Into Terror $19.95
Peter Rabe Murder Me for Nickels /
Benny Muscles In $19.95
Peter Rabe Blood on the Desert /
A House in Naples $19.95
Peter Rabe My Lovely Executioner /
Agreement to Kill $19.95
Peter Rabe Anatomy of a Killer /
A Shroud for Jesso $14.95
Peter Rabe The Silent Wall /
The Return of Marvin Palaver $19.95
Peter Rabe Kill the Boss Good-By /
Mission for Vengeance $19.95
Peter Rabe Dig My Grave Deep / The Out is Death /
It's My Funeral $21.95
Brian Ritt Paperback Confidential:
Crime Writers $19.95
Sax Rohmer Bat Wing / Fire-Tongue $19.95
Douglas Sanderson Pure Sweet Hell /
Catch a Fallen Starlet $19.95
Douglas Sanderson The Deadly Dames /
A Dum-Dum for the President $19.95
Charlie Stella Johnny Porno $15.95
Charlie Stella Rough Riders $15.95
John Trinian North Beach Girl /
Scandal on the Sand $19.95
Harry Whittington A Night for Screaming /
Any Woman He Wanted $19.95
Harry Whittington To Find Cora /
Like Mink Like Murder / Body and Passion $23.95
Harry Whittington Rapture Alley / Winter Girl /
Strictly for the Boys $23.95
Charles Williams Nothing in Her Way /
River Girl $19.95

Stark House Press, 1315 H Street, Eureka, CA 95501
707-498-3135   www.StarkHousePress.com

Retail customers: freight-free, payment accepted by check or paypal via website. Wholesale: 40%, freight-free on
10 mixed copies or more, returns accepted. All books available direct from publisher or Baker & Taylor Books.